THE
DETECTIVE'S
SONS

WALTER P. SIGNORELLI

ISBN: 979-8-89031-892-3 (sc)
ISBN: 979-8-89031-893-0 (hc)
ISBN: 979-8-89031-894-7 (e)

THE EWINGS
PUBLISHING

One Galleria Blvd., Suite 1900, Metairie, LA 70001
(504) 702-6708

CHAPTER ONE

Dennis Carbonaro had just moved out of his parents' house in Canarsie, Brooklyn, and into an apartment with his older brother, Ray, in Ridgewood, Queens. They shared a two-bedroom apartment on the second floor of a private home. Dennis had the smaller room on the left side of the hallway; Ray had the larger room at the end. It was a nice setup, and they liked the fact that they had a private entrance from the driveway on the side of the house.

The move had caused an argument in the family. Their father, Dominic Carbonaro, a New York City first-grade detective, had objected because Ray was always in some kind of trouble and had been arrested four times.

"Ray could be a bad influence on Dennis," Dominic told his wife, Marie. "One son in trouble with the law is enough."

Marie took the other side, saying, "Dennis is younger, but he's the mature one. He's more likely to keep Ray out of trouble better than either of us."

Dominic could see that Marie was for the move because she liked the idea that her sons would live together rather than on their own or with strangers.

"I hope you're right," Dominic had said when he reluctantly agreed.

Ray was twenty-three, five-feet-ten, and muscular. An avid body-builder, he worked out regularly with weights, and looked like a prize-fighter, which helped him in his job as a bar bouncer at the "Kit Kat Gentlemen's Club" in Bayside, Queens.

Dennis was eighteen. He looked similar to Ray, but thinner, and a little over six feet tall.

At first, he was enthusiastic about moving in with Ray, but after a month, he was having second thoughts. Ray kept late hours, and when he came home from the Kit Kat club, he was inconsiderate about making noise. Dennis had learned that living with Ray wasn't exactly conducive to getting a good night's sleep.

Something was always going on with Ray. About nine o'clock, on a hot Wednesday night in August, Dennis was watching a baseball game on television when Ray unexpectedly came home. Obviously, in a hurry, he left his red Chevrolet Camaro running in the driveway behind Dennis' car, a silver Honda. The whole neighborhood could hear the Camaro, which had a dual exhaust, and sounded like it had holes in the mufflers.

Ray ran up the stairs, rushed into his room at the end of the hallway, and rushed out again without saying when or whether he would be back.

From the window above the driveway, Dennis saw Ray jump into the Camaro and speed backward out of the driveway.

Dennis went back to the baseball game, then at eleven o'clock, turned the TV off and went to bed. He was starting a new job at United Parcel Service and had to be up early. But Ray wasn't home, and Dennis figured it would be another one of those nights when he would be awakened from a sound sleep.

After midnight, he heard a car pull up in front of the house. It didn't sound like Ray's Camaro, so he went to the window to see who it was. It was an unmarked police car at the curb and three detectives getting out. His heart sank as he thought they could come to notify him that his father had been injured, shot, or worse. He watched them enter the side entrance, and when he heard them on the second-floor landing, he opened the apartment door, but was surprised when they suddenly pushed the door into his face, and rushed into the apartment shouting "Police, don't move." In unison, the detectives grabbed him, threw him to the floor, held him face down, and twisted his arms behind his back to handcuff him.

Dennis instinctively resisted, but the three men held him down and twisted his arms harder.

"What's this about?" Dennis shouted.

"Just shut up," one detective said.

Another detective pushed his knee into Dennis' back, and after a brief struggle, they handcuffed him.

"Where's the gun?" a detective yelled at him.

"I don't know what you talking about," Dennis said.

They searched him. He had nothing on him. Then they pulled him up by his arms and sat him on a kitchen chair. The handcuffs were hurting his wrists.

The tallest detective towered over him; the two other detectives—one thin, one wide and heavy—stood on either side.

"I'm Detective McConnell," the tall detective said. "This is Detective Cruz, and this is Detective Matthews. If you cooperate with us, it'll go easier on you. We want to know where the gun is, and who was with you?"

"Cooperate about what? Who was with me when? I don't know what you're talking about," Dennis said. "And you know my father works in Manhattan South Homicide,"

"We know who your father is, and you should be ashamed for disgracing him."

Dennis was puzzled, then asked, "Is my father alright?"

"Your father's alright. Unfortunately, he's got a bum like you for a son."

Hearing that, Dennis realized what was going on. He was relieved because this wasn't about him. It was about Ray. Everyone in the Detective Division knew that his father had a son who had gotten into trouble. Ray must have done something, and they were mistaking him for Ray. Dennis wanted to say that right out, but was reluctant. He didn't want to say or do anything that could be bad for Ray.

"Can't you tell me what this is about?" he asked.

"You'll find out at the precinct.

"Can I call my father?"

"At the precinct."

"Am I under arrest?"

No one answered, and the detectives began searching the apartment.

"You can't search without a warrant," Dennis said, surprising himself at how forcefully he said it.

They ignored him and continued searching the living room and kitchen.

"You have no right to search without a warrant," Dennis said.

"Okay, wise guy," the tall detective said, "We have to make sure there are no guns or evidence here."

"Not without a warrant, or until I talk to my father, you can't," Dennis said.

"Watch us," Detective McConnell said.

Dennis decided he had to head them off. He didn't know if Ray had anything in his room that he shouldn't have. "You know, you're making a mistake. I'm not who you think I am."

"Really? Who are you?" Detective McConnell said.

"I'm not Ray," Dennis said.

"Don't give me that BS. We know you live here."

"Ray lives here. I'm his brother, Dennis. I only moved in a few weeks ago. If you let me get my wallet, I'll show you my ID."

The three detectives stared at him. Detective Matthews, the heavier man, took a folder out of his jacket pocket and held a mugshot of Ray next to Dennis' face. They looked alike, and there was no doubt they were brothers. They both had brown eyes and brown hair, though Ray's was a little lighter and longer.

"They look the same to me," Matthews said.

Detective Cruz, the thinner man, took the photo and turned it over. "How tall are you?"

"Six-foot," Dennis said.

"How much do you weigh?"

"One-ninety."

Cruz pointed to the pedigree of information on the back of the photo. "This says five-feet-ten, and two hundred and ten pounds."

They pulled Dennis up from the chair, and stood him back-to-back with Matthews, who was also six-feet.

"They're about the same," Cruz said. "Unless Ray grew two inches since his last arrest, and lost twenty pounds, it's not him."

The detectives conferred, whispering to each other. Then Cruz uncuffed Dennis, saying, "I guess we owe you an apology."

Dennis was relieved that he had been uncuffed, but McConnell said, "Sit down. I have a few questions."

Dennis sat.

"Where were you today?"

Dennis began to answer, then stopped himself. His father had taught him enough about police work. He knew to be careful about saying anything. They hadn't given him *Miranda* warnings, so he wasn't sure what his status was. He said, "Before I answer questions, I want to talk to my father."

"You don't need to talk to your father," McConnell said. "It's just a few simple questions. Like where's Ray, and when's the last time you saw him?"

Dennis's surprise and fear were wearing off. He stood up. "If I'm under arrest, I'm not answering any questions, and if I'm not, I'm going to ask you to leave."

McConnell's face turned red. He didn't like being challenged. "I've got a good mind to lock you up for resisting arrest."

"I didn't resist arrest. You threw me on the floor."

"You wouldn't let us handcuff you."

Cruz moved between them. "It was a misunderstanding. Let's let it go," he said, more to McConnell than to Dennis.

McConnell scowled. "Alright, but when you see Ray, tell him to call us. Here's my card."

The detectives left, but as they opened the door, the sound of a cars' dual-exhaust engine revved in the driveway.

Detective Matthews went to the window. "It's the red Camaro."

Dennis had an urge to run down the stairs to tell Ray to drive away, but there was nothing he could do. McConnell blocked his way, and Cruz held his arm, and said, "don't do anything stupid."

Minutes later, they heard Ray coming up the stairs. When he came into the apartment, the detectives showed their badges and surrounded him.

"Are you Ray Carbonaro?"

"What do you want to know for?" Ray answered.

"Let's not play games," McConnell said.

"Okay. I am. So what?"

"That's your Camaro in the driveway?"

"Yeah."

"Did you drive it today?"

"Why do you want to know?"

"It's an easy question."

Dennis figured the arrest must have had something to do with Ray's car. He stepped next to Ray. "He doesn't have to answer questions."

"What are you, his lawyer?"

"I've learned a few things from my father."

"Well, let's teach you something else," McConnell said as he pushed past Dennis and said to Ray, "You're under arrest. Put your hands behind your back."

Ray did as he was told. The detectives handcuffed him, frisked him, and walked him out of the house to the squad car, with Cruz reciting the *Miranda* warnings as they walked.

Dennis walked behind them. "What's the charge?" he asked.

The detectives didn't answer.

"Where are you taking him?"

"94th Precinct in Brooklyn."

Dennis shouted to Ray, "Don't say anything. I'll call dad."

As he watched the detectives shove Ray into the back seat of the squad car, he had a sinking feeling in his stomach.

When they drove away, he called his father, but there was no answer at home or on his cell phone. He decided to go to the house, but when he went downstairs, a police tow truck was blocking his Honda in the driveway and was hooking up Ray's car.

He asked the tow-truck operator why he was taking the car.

"Your Dominic Carbonaro's son?"

"Yes, I am."

"I know him a long time, a good man," the operator said. "The car was used in a robbery."

Dennis' heart sank. He had thought it was a vehicle offense, or maybe something with drugs, but not robbery.

"A robbery? When?"

"Yesterday afternoon, I think."

"Where?"

"In Greenpoint. A bad one. Somebody got shot."

Dennis felt a wave of heat coursing through his body. If Ray was involved, he thought, it would devastate his father and mother.

The tow-truck driver hoisted the car onto the flatbed and drove it away.

CHAPTER TWO

Dennis drove to his parents' house. It was a two-story brick home with a statue of the Madonna in the front garden. He went up the bricked staircase, rang the doorbell, and knocked hard on the door. No one answered. Assuming his parents were sleeping, he used his cell phone to call their number. Just as it rang, his father opened the door. He had his .38 Smith and Wesson revolver in his hand, pointed at the floor.

"What's the matter?" Dominic said.

"Ray's been arrested," Dennis said.

Dominic remained expressionless. He motioned Dennis into the living room.

"What for?"

"I think it's for robbery. They towed his car away."

"Where?" Dominic asked."

"They came to the apartment."

"Who?

"Detective McConnell, Cruz, and a third guy. They said they were taking him to the 94th Precinct."

Dominic shook his head. "If it's not one thing, it's another with that kid." He walked toward the phone. "I'll call the nine-four to see what it's about."

"Dad, the tow-truck driver said there was a shooting."

Dominic staggered and almost fell. Dennis knew he had recently been diagnosed with extremely high-blood pressure, and he helped him to the sofa. "You should sit down. I'll get you some water."

Dominic couldn't catch his breath. For Dennis, seeing his father almost collapse was a shock. His father had always been described as strong as a bull. His strength was built from years of working with his own father, laying cement. That was before he became a cop. Now, as he sat on the sofa, sweating, and trying to catch his breath, he looked old.

"I'll call a doctor," Dennis said.

"No. I'll be alright."

As he said that, Marie, in slippers and a pink bathrobe, came down the stairs. "What's the matter?" she said, near panic in her voice.

She felt her husband forehead. "What happened?"

"Ray got arrested," Dennis said.

Without saying anything, Marie got a wet towel and began wiping Dominic's face, neck, and arms. "Get some aspirins in the bathroom," she said. Dennis ran upstairs, came back with the aspirins, and got a glass of water for his father.

After a while, Dominic felt better. He asked Dennis to bring him the phone and dialed the Detective Bureau night-watch desk. Detective Larry Smithers answered.

"Hello, Larry. This is Dominic Carbonaro. Can you tell me if there's been a robbery and shooting in the nine-four in the last few days?"

Dominic waited for Larry to check the records and then listened as Larry gave him the details of a robbery that occurred at approximately three o'clock, Wednesday afternoon. Three males wearing masks entered a BMW car dealership in Greenpoint, Brooklyn, displayed guns, and robbed everyone, taking their wallets and watches, including a $10,000 Rolex. They forced the manager to open the safe and took more than $30,000.

"The perpetrators were probably male blacks in their twenties, although their faces were covered." Larry said. "They fired a shot to scare the manager, but it hit someone. There was a getaway car, a red Camaro. I believe they're chasing that down now."

"Any arrests?"

"Not that I've heard."

"What's the condition of the guy who was shot?"

"He's in Brookdale Hospital. Shot in the neck, in critical condition."

Standing close to the phone, Dennis heard the conversation. He was relieved that the suspects were three male blacks, but he worried about the getaway car, a red Camaro. They towed Ray's red Camaro away; there must be a connection.

"What are we going to do, Dad?" Dennis asked.

"There's not much I can do," Dominic said. "Going to the 94th Precinct would be a waste of time. Once headquarters finds out that Ray's my son, they'll send word down to everyone to keep their distance from me."

Stating the obvious, Dennis said, "We're gonna need a good lawyer. Do you know any?"

"I know plenty. I've dealt with the best."

Dominic had dealt with the best criminal lawyers in the city, mainly because he had been a successful investigator. The combination of his physical presence and his calm, courteous manner had served him well. He could get witnesses to cooperate where others couldn't, and he had gotten more voluntary confessions from suspects than most other detectives in the city.

Homicide investigations often involved a dozen or more detectives working on a single case. In the cases that Dominic had worked on, when it came time for trial, the district's attorneys often chose him as the main police witness because he made a favorable impression on the jury. He didn't get rattled by cross examination, and he stuck to the facts. If an answer favored the defense, he gave it objectively and fairly without trying to color it for the prosecution. Both prosecutors and defense attorneys appreciated that, and he was on good terms with most of them.

It was too early to call most lawyers, but Dominic knew the first hours of an arrest could be critical to the outcome of a case, so he called an ex-cop, Dan Carter, who had become a lawyer and did work for the Detectives' Endowment Association.

Dominic explained the situation and asked Carter to call the 94th precinct and tell them he represented Ray and that they should not question him without his lawyer present. Carter agreed and said that he'd call right away, and within a half hour, he called back to tell him that he had done what he'd asked.

"Thanks, Dan, I appreciate it."

"Do you want me to represent him?" Carter asked.

Dominic liked Carter, but he needed the best to represent his son. "It sounds like my son is facing twenty-five years," he said. "I'm thinking of Murray Klein."

"Good choice. If I can do anything, let me know."

"Now that you mention it, he'll be arraigned in Brooklyn Criminal on Schermerhorn Street. If I can't get in touch with Klein, maybe you represent Ray at the arraignment. I'm going to call over there to find out what time he'll be brought before the judge."

During the night, they had booked Ray at the 94th precinct in Greenpoint, transported to Central Booking on Tillary Street, and moved to the holding cells in the basement of the Criminal Court Building on Schermerhorn Street in Downtown Brooklyn. They charged him with attempted murder, assault, robbery, unlawful use of a firearm, and conspiracy. They didn't accuse him of committing the actual robbery and doing the shooting, but of acting as an accomplice to those who had. When people enter a conspiracy with others to commit a crime, whatever injuries are caused by any of the conspirators during the crime can be charged against them all.

At 8:00 a.m., Thursday morning, Dominic left a message on Murray Klein's answering machine. It amazed him that within ten minutes Klein called back. After a preliminary discussion, Klein said that he would represent Ray. The fee was $200 per hour and a $15,000 retainer. If the case went to trial, another $15,000 retainer would have to be paid beforehand.

"Okay," Dominic said. "Can you get to Schermerhorn Street for the arraignment?"

"I can't, but I'll send one of my staff attorneys," Klein said. "I'm going to call the precinct and tell them not to question him."

"Oh. I already did that. I had a friend of mine, an ex-cop, call and tell them," Dominic said.

"That was good, but I'll have to call. If that lawyer doesn't really represent him, it's no good. It has to be the retained or assigned attorney. But that's okay. It didn't hurt. I'll call now. In the meantime, see what else you can find out."

Dominic began calling friends and contacts to find out what he could about Ray's arrest.

At 11:00 a.m., Dominic and Dennis entered the courthouse. Dominic could avoid the metal detectors by showing his badge, but Dennis had to empty his pockets to go through. They went to Arraignment Part 1A and waited for Ray's case to be called. Court officers and other police officers recognized Dominic, but none approached him.

Dominic went up to one of the court officers. "How ya' doin'?" he said while showing his badge. "Can you tell me whether an attorney signed in to represent my son, Ray Carbonaro?"

The court officer checked the attorney's sign-in sheet.

"Not yet."

They sat and watched as the cases were called. Some defendants were seated in the courtroom. When called, they went up to the bench on their own; other defendants were brought out in hand cuffs from the holding cells.

When the court took a lunch recess, Dominic and Dennis went to the men's room. As they were washing their hands, Dominic remembered something. "This is where I first met Murray Klein," he said."

"Really."

"Yes. Really. I'll tell you about it someday."

They left the building and went to a luncheonette on Fulton Street. After their food was served, Dennis asked, "So, how did you meet Murray Klein in the men's room?"

It did not surprise Dominic that Dennis would ask him. Over the years, he had told his sons many stories about the job. Dennis always showed more interest than Ray did.

Dominic had hoped that Ray would follow in his footsteps and become a cop, and he convinced him to take the test. Ray passed, but his record prevented from getting hired.

Dennis also had taken and passed the test, but Dominic wanted more for him. He knew Dennis was exceptionally bright and had great potential. He knew this because Dennis was a phenomenal chess player who could think three and four moves ahead. He beat almost everyone in the neighborhood, and his father once took him to his police precinct where there were several avid chess players. Dennis beat them all except one, and that was a draw.

Dominic bought him chess books, but he didn't read them. He was like a musician who plays by ear but won't read the music. He had an independent, non-conformist streak that would sometimes frustrate Dominic.

Dennis read crime novels. He liked to find flaws in the plots and point them out to his father. Dominic said that Dennis knew more about law and police work than some cops he knew.

He thought Dennis should go to college, maybe become an F.B.I. agent, a lawyer, or anything else he wanted, but Dennis wasn't interested in college. He wanted to go to work right away, make some money, get a nice car, then go to college later.

Dominic didn't want to force the issue. He decided not to demand but to persuade, and he hoped that after Dennis worked awhile, he would change his mind.

After they finished eating and were having a second cup of coffee, Dennis said, "You still didn't tell me about how you met Klein."

Dominic paused for a moment, thinking whether he should tell him.

"At the risk of making you too cynical about lawyers," Dominic said. "I'll tell you, but you can't tell anyone else."

"Okay. I'll try."

Dominic smiled, knowing that most secrets are rarely kept.

He began, "When I was a young cop, I arrested this drug dealer. The defendant was one of those characters that in those days wore flashy clothes and gold jewelry and drove around in expensive cars. This guy had a thick gold chain and a medallion around his neck that must have weighed two or three pounds.

"I arrested him by chance when I went into a bar looking for a robbery suspect who I thought might have gone in there. As I entered through the side door, I stumbled on this guy passing out glassine envelopes of heroin. I grabbed him and he starts struggling, trying to throw the drugs away, but I handcuffed him and recovered some drugs from the floor and some from his pockets."

"Did you have to take your gun out?"

"I don't think so. But, in court, the issue was whether I had probable cause to arrest and search him."

"I see," Dennis said. "If you didn't have probable cause, they would suppress the evidence, the drugs."

"That's right. So, there had to be a hearing. But it kept getting postponed. Murray Klein was the defendant's lawyer. On the first three court dates, the judge asked the assistant district attorney and Klein whether they were going to proceed with the hearing that day. Klein would say, 'No, your honor. My witness, Mr. Green, hasn't arrived yet.' And the judge would postpone the case."

"Mr. Green meant Klein hadn't been paid?" Dennis said.

"Right. Then the fourth time we were supposed to have a hearing, I was in the men's room, the same men's room where we were today. Klein and the defendant came in, and they're arguing. I ducked into a stall, and I hear Klein say to him, 'I don't work for nothing. You've got to pay up.' Then the drug dealer says, 'I don't have it. A thousand is too much.'

"Klein tells him he'll have to get it somewhere, and the defendant says, 'Where?'

"Then Klein says, 'What about that a gold chain around your neck? That looks like at least a thousand bucks.'

"The defendant then says, 'No way. I need that.'

"Klein says, 'What for?'

"The defendant says, 'For business purposes. It shows people who I am.'

"Klein is about five-feet-six in boots. The defendant is over six feet and looks like he'd cut your throat for a nickel. Murray, looking this guy straight in the face, tells him, 'Take it off. I'll hold it as collateral.'

"The defendant says, 'I ain't givin' you nothing.'

"Klein tells him, 'You're making a big mistake,' and walks out.

"Inside the courtroom, when the case was called, the judge asked the lawyers whether they were ready for the hearing. And Klein says, 'Yes, your honor. Defendant is ready.'

"With that, the hearing began and the D.A. called me to the stand. In the weeks leading up to the hearing, I had prepared for what I thought would be a tough cross-examination. The D.A. conducted his direct examination. I answered the questions, then waited for Klein's cross examination. I assumed it would take an hour. Klein shuffled some papers, then stood and said, 'Officer, when you arrested the defendant in the bar, were the lights on?' I said, 'Yes, the lights were on.' Then Klein said, 'No further questions,' and sat down."

"That's all he asked?"

"That's all," and the judge immediately ruled that the people had established probable cause. He raised the defendant's bail to $10,000 and ordered the court officers to take him into custody. The defendant sat there wondering what had just happened. That was my introduction to Murray Klein."

"Can he do that?" Dennis asked.

"He did it."

"Never mind the court," Dennis said. "What about getting shot by the defendant? Wasn't he afraid of that?'

"Some of these lawyers are the toughest son of bitches you'll ever meet. They may not fight with guns and knives, but they know how to use the law to fight, and they stick together."

"I don't understand why you would hire a lawyer like that. He doesn't seem too ethical."

"That was a long time ago. Murray Klein is tough and smart, and that's what we need. I think of him like the Israelis, surrounded by enemies, but never backing down."

When the lunch break was over and court resumed, Jeff Rosen, the lawyer from Klein's office, arrived, signed in, and told the court officer that he was ready.

"Next case, Raymond Carbonaro," the officer announced, and another officer escorted Ray out from the holding cells.

Handcuffed behind his back, Ray stood at the defendants' table. He kept turning around to look at his father, shaking his head as though to say that he had done nothing wrong. The court officer told him to look front.

Rosen acknowledged the receipt of the charges and waived their formal reading. The assistant district attorney asked for $500,000 bail. Rosen asked for the defendant to be released in his own recognizance because he was a high school graduate, had roots in the community, was employed, not a flight risk, and, importantly, the case against was him weak and likely to be dismissed.

The assistant district attorney responded, saying that these were serious charges. A person had been shot and was hospitalized in critical condition. There was a strong case against the defendant, who had a criminal history and had been picked out by a victim in a photo array and in a lineup. Also, his car had been seen at the scene of the crime, a car dealership.

The judge said that he'd heard enough and set bail at $500,000 cash or bond.

Rosen asked for 180.80 hearing for next week on Thursday. The purpose of a 180.80 hearing was to determine whether there was sufficient non-hearsay evidence to hold the defendant for trial. If not, the defendant would have to be released in his own recognizance without having to post bail, unless, in the meantime, a grand jury indicted the defendant. In that case, the defendant could be required to post bail.

The judge scheduled the hearing, and a court officer took Ray back to the cells.

CHAPTER THREE

Dominic, Dennis, and Rosen left the court and took the subway three stops to Klein's office near Broadway and Chambers in lower Manhattan. The office was on the tenth floor of an older building that had seen better days, but Klein's office had been newly renovated.

The receptionist led them into a room with a large conference table surrounded by twelve brown leather chairs. Shelves of law books covered the two windowless walls. Through the soundproof windows on the opposite walls, one could see southeast to City Hall, the Federal District Courthouse, the Brooklyn Bridge, and north to the Empire State Building.

Dennis walked around the room and was impressed. Dominic whispered to him, "If you put your mind to it, you could have an office like this someday."

Klein entered, wearing a white shirt, a blue tie, and gold cufflinks. He asked everyone to sit down and took a seat at the head of the table. "Nice to see you Dominic, unfortunately."

"Yeah, unfortunately."

"We've been on a lot of cases together, but this time we're on the same side," Klein said.

"Let's hope it's the winning side."

Klein asked Rosen, "How did it go in court?"

"Sorry, I couldn't get a lower bail," Rosen said. "Maybe if the customer who was shot recovers, we can make a new bail application."

"It was a customer, not an employee?" Klein asked.

"Yes. Apparently, the shooter fired a warning shot to scare the manager, and the bullet ricocheted off something and hit the customer."

"Lucky guy," Klein said facetiously. "Let me see the affidavit and the supporting depositions."

Klein read the documents. Apparently assuming that Dominic had gathered some information, he asked him, "It looks like he wasn't inside the car dealership during the robbery, so how did they get an identification of your son?"

Dominic had spoken by phone with several detectives who gave him bits of information, and he had pieced them together. "The person they're claiming is my son, Ray, wasn't in the car dealership when the robbery took place. But the manager said that he suspected someone who had come in twice during the previous week. He was about twenty-five with long, light brown or dirty blond hair almost to his shoulders, and didn't look like he could afford a car. The guy pretended to be interested in buying a car and even began filling out a credit application. When the manager tried to look over the papers, the guy took them back and left. That made the manager suspicious that the guy was casing the place."

"They must have more evidence than that," Klein said.

"The dealership has security cameras outside to watch for vandalism to the cars," Dominic said. "The cameras picked up a Camaro with my son's plate number driving past and stopping three times over three days."

"Maybe he likes to look at cars," Klein said. "So far, I don't see how they think they have a case. Did they catch any of the other perps?"

"Let's not jump to Ray being one of the "perps," Dominic said.

"You're right, I stand corrected," Klein said.

"I think the mix-up might have been in the identification with the photo array," Dominic said. "Because they ran Ray's plate number, and got a photo from one of his prior arrests, which they used to show the manager, and the manager identified him as the guy casing the dealership. Once the manager picked out Ray's photo, a lineup was held, and he picked him out again."

"The question is always," Klein said, "Was the witness identifying the photo that was shown to him, or was he identifying the person who he saw during the actual incident? We're going to have to look closely at the procedures they followed. What color hair does your son have?"

"Light brown," Dominic said.

"Long or short."

"Short," Dennis said before his father could answer. "Over his ears, but not long."

"What was his hair like in the photo that they used in the photo array?" Klein asked.

"I don't remember," Dominic said. "Dennis, do you know?"

"I'm not sure," Dennis said. "I think his hair was long when he was first arrested on the cocaine charge, but it might have been shorter when he was arrested the second time for the assault in the bar."

"So, we don't know which photo they used," Klein said. "We'll have to get a copy. That could be important. And what were his prior arrests?"

"Twice for marihuana, once for possession of cocaine, another time for assault with a beer bottle during a bar fight," Dominic said. "And you should also know he was involved in a bad car accident. For the drug arrests, he paid fines. For the assault in the bar, he pled guilty to disorderly conduct. He got fifteen days and a fine."

"No robberies or guns."

"None."

"Okay, that's not too bad," Klein said.

They continued talking about the case until Dominic asked Klein, whom he recommended as a bail bondsman. Klein then asked Dennis and Rosen to leave the room for a minute. When they left, he used the intercom to ask a secretary to bring in the retainer forms for Dominic to sign. "We have to work out the retainer agreement."

Dominic signed the forms, then wrote a check for $5000 with today's date and another check for $10,000 backdated to next Monday. "I'll have to move money from my savings account to my checking account. I'll do it tomorrow."

"That's fine," Klein said as he took the checks. "Now, regarding the bail, think about it. I've seen people get burned too many times."

"What do you mean?"

"What I mean is that a $500,000 bond is going to cost you a $50,000 fee and you'll have put up the deed to your house as collateral."

"I can borrow the money."

"What if your son panics and flees? Are you prepared to lose the $50,000 and your house?"

Dominic didn't answer, but slumped back in his chair. "I don't think he would skip out on us."

"You never know. People facing a long prison sentence do strange things. My advice is to let him stay in jail, at least, till we find out what we're facing. At the 180.80 procedure hearing, we may get a break and maybe get the bail reduced, so it won't cost you so much."

"What if we can't?"

"Then you get your detective association to contact corrections and get him placed in protective custody as the son of a cop, separated from the general prison population. It won't be that bad."

Dominic didn't respond, thinking that it was easy for Klein to say that it wouldn't be that bad.

While Klein and Dominic continued talking, Dennis waited outside in the main office. He read the newspaper stories posted around the office walls about large verdicts that the Klein law firm had won, some for several million dollars. One was about a defendant who served ten years in prison before they found he was really innocent. The defendant was released from prison and sued the state for wrongful conviction because the detectives hadn't followed proper procedures during the investigation.

Dennis read an article where another defendant served eight years until it was found out that the police had withheld exculpatory information from the defense and the court.

There were at least five more newspaper articles like that. As he read them, he thought of the newspaper articles he had read about his father. The difference was that the articles about his father were for good police work, arresting criminals; Klein's articles were about bad police work and getting criminals off.

He heard Klein over the intercom asking the secretary to send Dennis and Rosen into the conference room. He went in, and Klein asked Dennis to sit next to him. "Tell me exactly what happened when they came to arrest your brother."

"Well, first, they arrested me."

That startled Dominic. "You didn't tell me that."

"Yeah. With everything going on, I forgot about that. They thought I was Ray. When they figured it out, they let me go. But just as they were leaving, Ray showed up, and they arrested him."

"Did they actually arrest you? Physically?" Klein asked.

"They sure did. They pushed the door open, threw me on the floor, and handcuffed me."

"Did you get hurt?"

"They twisted my arms pretty good. And that bastard McConnell said he was going to lock me up for resisting arrest. I didn't have a chance to resist arrest."

"We'll set up an appointment for you to see our doctor," Klein said. "But start from the beginning. When did you first see the police?"

Dennis told him everything he could remember and recounted, word for word, what they had said. He told him how he demanded to see a warrant, and how he told Ray not to answer questions.

Klein wrote everything down on a yellow legal pad. "You did very well," he said. "I think either you're a natural born lawyer or your father taught you well."

"I thought they couldn't come in without a warrant," Dennis said.

"They're not supposed to," Klein said. "If they enter without a warrant, any evidence they find can't be used in court. But that doesn't matter here because they didn't take any evidence."

"But they took Ray's car," Dennis said.

Jeff Rosen answered, "A car, they can take without a warrant as long as they have probable cause."

"Does anyone else drive Ray's car?" Klein asked.

"I do sometimes," said Dennis. "It depends on whose car is last in the driveway."

Dominic said, "I've used it when my car is in the shop."

Klein continued asking questions and taking notes. After thirty minutes, he stood up,

"Anything else?"

"Yes," Dominic said. "I'm surprised they didn't have an arrest warrant for Ray and a search warrant for the apartment. A sharp detective looking for evidence wouldn't have gone in without a warrant."

"Well, I've learned over the years," Klein said, "that all detectives are not as sharp as you."

"I won't argue with that," Dominic said. "And just so you know, Detective McConnell has a hell of a reputation. He's famous for bragging that he'd lock up his mother if he had probable cause."

"Sounds like a scary guy."

"That's an understatement. He did a tour in Iraq and saw a lot of combat. Supposedly he rescued a trapped unit, and fought his way out of an ambush, but not before a half-dozen of his buddies were killed or badly wounded."

"After going through all that, I guess being a cop is easy," Klein said.

"You would think so," Dominic said, "but they say he acts like he's still over there."

"Maybe he's got Post-Traumatic-Stress-Disorder."

"Maybe."

Klein shook hands with Dominic. "I think we've got plenty to work with here. I don't see a strong case against us, even if McConnell thinks so. But what we have to worry about is this. If Ray was in on the robbery, either as a getaway driver or casing the joint, and they bag one of the others who flips on him, then we've got problems. But we'll deal with it when the time comes. Right now, I feel good about our chances."

He shook hands with Dennis. "It was a pleasure to meet you, young man. Start thinking about law school. In fact, wait here." He took a book off the shelves, *Criminal Law for Beginners*. "I've always found this clear and concise. Sometimes, when I have a difficult legal issue, I go back to this simple book."

"I don't want to take your book if you need it," Dennis said.

"I've got more. Keep it, it's yours."

"Thank you very much. It was nice to meet you."

Dominic and Dennis took the subway to Brooklyn to get the car from the parking lot by the courthouse, then drove to the Ridgewood apartment. On the way, Dennis said, "Klein's got some operation there. I'm glad you picked him. Did you see the newspaper articles about all the big cases he won?"

"I've seen them before. It's all designed to impress potential clients."

"It impressed me."

At the apartment, they took the side entrance to go upstairs. Dominic wanted to look around to make sure there wasn't anything that could be incriminating, just in case the police came back. "They didn't come with a search warrant, but they could still do it," he said.

"Why didn't they?" Dennis asked.

"I don't know. They may have tried, and the judge turned them down because the case was so weak. But they could try again. Are there any drugs or anything here?"

"I don't think so," Dennis said.

"Well, let's look. You don't want them coming in and finding something of Ray's while you're here. You might get arrested."

They looked through all the dresser drawers and the closets. They found nothing.

When they finished looking, Dominic asked, "What've you got to eat?"

"There's some leftover McDonald's from Wednesday night."

"No thanks. Your mother will have something for me. Do you want to come back to the house?"

"No. I'm just going to crash here."

"Okay."

"But, Dad, when are we going to visit Ray?"

"We'll have to make an appointment. They don't want everyone coming at once. They couldn't handle that. The appointments are alphabetical. Ray's day is Monday, so we'll go then."

The Dominic hugged his son before leaving to go home.

After his father left, Dennis began reading the law book Klein had given him. He found it extremely interesting and read for hours. It gave him a lot of ideas that he could relate to Ray's case, and he kept thinking of Klein's million-dollar verdicts. It occurred to him it might be to Klein's benefit for Ray to stay in jail for a long time before getting exonerated so that Klein could sue for millions. But he dismissed that idea—who would do such a rotten thing?

CHAPTER FOUR

When Dominic got home, there was a phone message from his immediate boss, Lieutenant Bill Duffy. Although Duffy was technically his superior, they worked closely together as though they were on equal levels. First-grade detectives made the same salary as a lieutenant. In fact, they did better because on promotion they went directly to top pay for the rank while the lieutenants took three years to reach top pay. Lieutenants got promoted to their rank by civil service exams, while detectives were promoted for their investigative work, starting with detective third-grade, then second-grade, and then first-grade, which was a prestigious rank, with only about a hundred first-graders throughout the city, compared to about a thousand lieutenants.

A downside was that the detective designation could be easily rescinded, whereas lieutenants had civil service protection against a demotion.

When he was a young patrolman, Dominic was promoted to detective and transferred into the Detective Bureau because of an outstanding arrest he made. He was walking his footpost on Fulton Street in Bedford-Stuyvesant, Brooklyn. It was a freezing-cold night, and he was wearing his heavy winter uniform overcoat and gloves. A pedestrian ran up to him, pointing to a liquor store and said, "Something's going on in there."

Dominic peeked through the store window and saw a middle-aged black woman standing unnaturally stiff behind the cash register. He immediately pulled off his gloves and opened his overcoat so he could get at his gun.

Cautiously, he went in.

The woman looked frightened.

"Is everything okay?" he said.

She didn't answer.

As he moved closer to her, a man suddenly jumped up from under the counter and put a knife to the woman's throat.

The man looked crazed, and screamed, "Drop your gun or I'll cut her throat from ear to ear."

"Take it easy," Dominic said. "Don't do anything stupid."

"No. You don't do anything stupid," the man shouted back. "Drop your gun and move out of the way. I'm leaving, and she's coming with me."

"Take it easy," Dominic said again. "Don't make this any worse than it is."

"Move out of my way, and drop your gun," the man said again as he continued to press the blade of the knife against her throat.

Dominic thought he should back out of the store and call for help, but the man pressed the blade harder against her neck. "If you don't get out of the way, I'll cut her throat right here and now," he threatened.

Dominic thought about rushing the man and shooting him in the head before he could cut the woman, but again tried to calm him instead.

"Why don't we do this the easy way—you drop the knife and I'll put my gun away? Then we can talk."

"No way, you go first," the man said as he ushered the woman around the counter and toward the front door, still pressing the knife against her throat.

Dominic knew he couldn't shoot because he might hit the woman, but he couldn't leave her. Then, as the man and woman edged past him, Dominic grabbed a long-necked quart-bottle of whisky from a shelf and smashed it into the man's head, knocking him to the floor.

The woman ran out the front door while Dominic pointed his revolver at the man's head and said, "Drop the knife or you're dead."

The man dropped the knife, and Dominic kicked it away. Then he made the man lay face down on the floor, and handcuffed him.

When the police commissioner learned about the arrest, he was delighted because there had been a rash of police shootings recently for which the department had been criticized. He had his press office get as much publicity for the arrest as possible as an example of good police work.

The commissioner promoted Dominic to Detective Third Grade and transferred him to the Detective Bureau. Four years later, Dominic was promoted to Detective Second Grade, and four years after that, Detective First Grade, one of the youngest in the Department.

Dominic called Lieutenant Duffy back. "What's up, Bill?"

"First and foremost, I'm sorry to hear about your son," Duffy said. "It's tough to be a parent these days. But let me tell you why I called. The chief called me personally, and he wants me to tell you that you can't interfere in the investigation. And he's holding me responsible if you do."

"You mean I can't defend my son," Dominic said.

"As a private citizen, you can defend him all you want. But you can't use your position as a detective to work against the Department or gain inside information. We're investigating the case, and the DA is investigating the case. You can't work against us."

"I'm not working against anybody. Isn't an investigation supposed to find the truth, whether it leads to guilt or innocence?"

"Absolutely, but the investigator has to remain objective and impartial. You're the father, you're biased, you've got to stay away from the case and let it take its own course."

"I have a defense attorney, and I'm going to get information that way."

"You've got to build a wall between your defense attorney and the department. You can't be passing on confidential information to him."

Dominic didn't respond.

"Did you hear me?" Duffy said.

"I heard you."

"A word to the wise. If they find that you're compromising the investigation, they'll throw you out of the Bureau and send you to the auto pound."

Dominic hung up before he said something he shouldn't.

On Monday, Dominic and Dennis went to the Department of Correction Detention Center on Atlantic Avenue, two blocks from Brooklyn Criminal Court. The building was seven-stories with a glass exterior, which seemed odd for a jail. But the cells were not on the exterior walls; the inmates didn't have an outside view.

Considering his conversation with Lieutenant Duffy, Dominic signed into the visitor log as a civilian rather than as a detective.

They were ushered into another room, where they emptied their pockets. Dominic had left his gun in the car.

A guard said 'okay,' and slid open the metal-bar gate that led to a long hallway.

As they entered the hallway, the guard slammed the gate behind them. Dennis jumped in the air. His father laughed.

"I don't like that sound," Dennis whispered.

"Then stay out of trouble," his father said.

At the end of the passageway, a guard opened another gate, and they entered a large room where about a hundred visitors were waiting for inmates to be brought out. Dennis looked around and saw only poor, miserable-looking people. He thought they looked like war-zone refugees, not sure of what was going to happen to them next.

The inmates were brought in five at a time, and were seated at tables across from their visitors. Some visitors began crying right away, others began whispering as though plotting ways to get the inmate's release.

As the noise level kept rising, Dominic realized this would not be conducive for a conversation. He knew that down the hall were glass-enclosed cubicles that attorneys used when interviewing their clients, so he approached one of the older correction officers. Keeping his badge cupped in his hand, he showed it to the officer. "How're you doing?" he said. "I'm Detective Carbonaro. I work in Manhattan South Homicide."

"What can I do for you?" the officer said.

"I've been here many times over the years, but now I'm visiting my son in an unofficial capacity. Is it possible to use one of the attorney/client cubicles? I need to talk to him and find out what the hell happened."

"It's okay with me, but I have to ask my supervisor. Wait here."

"Thanks."

"The officer left, returned, and led Dominic and Dennis to a cubicle down the hall. After twenty minutes, Ray, dressed in an orange prison suit, was brought to the cubicle and sat across the table from them.

"I have to watch you through the glass," the officer said. "No physical contact. You have thirty minutes."

"Okay. Thanks," Dominic said.

The officer closed the door and watched through the glass.

In the cubicle, the father and his two sons sat for a minute saying nothing. The cubicle was sound proof from the outside noise, and the quiet seemed strange. Gone were the noises of the clanking of metal doors, the guards shouting instructions, and the crying of the visiting mothers and wives. It was a relief. Dennis felt for the moment that the whirlwind of events had slowed, and he could think more clearly about what had happened.

It surprised him to see tears in Ray's eyes, and more surprised to see tears in his father's eyes. They had enacted this scene before. After each of Ray's arrests, the disappointment had been palpable and oppressive. It was one thing for a son to get arrested and for a father to be disappointed, but when the father was a prestigious detective who, for so many years, had prided himself on fighting crime, drugs, and criminals, it was worse. Dominic saw Ray's arrests and his continual use of drugs as a betrayal of everything he stood for as a law enforcement officer. It was like his son joined the enemy; it was like treason.

Dominic would stand by his son even though the disappointment this time was much more serious than at any of the other times.

Ray broke the silence. "Dad, I didn't do it. And that's the truth."

This had a profound effect on Dominic, and he held his right hand across his mouth to keep anyone from seeing his jaw quivering. But he recovered quickly, took a deep breath, and cleared his throat. "That's good to know, so let's get down to business. Where were you last Wednesday about three o'clock?"

"I've been trying to remember everywhere I've been," Ray said. "Either Tuesday or Wednesday, I'm pretty sure it was Wednesday. I visited my girlfriend, Kathy Reynolds, at her apartment on McGuinness Boulevard in Greenpoint, but she had to leave for her job about three o'clock. She works as a waitress and barmaid at McCoy's bar and grill on Bell Boulevard in Bayside. I said I'd drive her, but she said she'd drive herself so she wouldn't have to worry about getting home."

"So, she left at three. Where did you go after that?"

"There's a couple of clubs in Greenpoint that hire bouncers on weekends. I went there asking if there was any work. They said they'd call me."

"Then what did you do?"

"I drove around some factories in Greenpoint looking to see if there were any job openings. I thought I might get a job in the daytime. But the places didn't look like much, so I went to McCoy's, where Kathy worked. I figured I could get a hamburger and she could be my waitress. We did that sometimes for fun. But when I got there, she was the barmaid, and her rule, or the house rule, was that I couldn't sit at the bar when she was on duty because her boss would figure that she was giving me free drinks, and she'd be talking to me instead of the customers. So, I left and drove around. Stopped for a couple of beers in a bar in Ridgewood, then went home. Dennis was already asleep."

"That's good," Dominic said. "We'll have to talk to Kathy, so she can verify it, and we'll need the names of the people at the other stops you made."

"Okay. But I don't know anybody's real name."

"Just make a list of where you stopped. Then how about Wednesday? Where were you?"

"I saw Kathy before she went to work. I worked out at Fitness Club on Metropolitan Avenue in Jackson Heights for a couple of hours, then stopped for a burger and a few beers, and went home. When I came in the door, the cops were waiting."

Dominic looked at Dennis. "Can you think of anything else?"

Dennis shrugged his shoulders.

"Alright," Dominic said, staring at Ray, "Do you hang out with any black guys?"

"No," Ray said, "Other than buying some weed from them once in a while."

Although Dominic was enraged by that answer, he refrained from saying anything about the "weed," and asked, "Could any of them have been involved in the robbery?"

"I don't think so."

"What's their names?"

"The only one I know is called Buster."

The correction officer knocked on the glass and pointed to his watch. He didn't protest when the family hugged.

"Thank you, very much. We appreciate it," Dominic said to the officer as they left.

Driving from the jail to McCoy's bar and grill, Dominic said, "Ray's account of his movements seemed plausible."

"Yes," Dennis said, although he had some doubts. He debated whether he should voice them to his father. He was troubled that even if his father could prove an alibi for Ray on Wednesday at the time of the robbery, Ray was not being charged with being there. The heart of the case against him was the manager's identification of him as being the suspect who came into the dealership the week before. Dennis decided not to say anything to his father. Why burst a bubble prematurely?

McCoy's had a polished mahogany bar over forty-feet long. It had comfortable cushioned-back stools at the bar, and tables and booths in the restaurant area. Usually, two bartenders worked the busy hours.

Brendan, one bartender, had been in America for forty years but still spoke with a brogue. Ray's girlfriend, Kathy Reynolds, was the other bartender.

She was twenty-one, about five feet six, with hazel eyes and brunette hair tied back. She was a bodybuilder and could be described as 'ripped.'

Dominic and Dennis ordered two beers. Kathy said to Dennis, "I'll have to see your ID."

"Okay, give me a coke," Dennis said.

Dominic laughed. "I'm his father. I can give him a beer."

"But my boss would have my head. You know how strict the cops are on bartenders."

"Yes. I do," Dominic said.

"You guys look familiar," Kathy said as she poured Dennis a coke.

"We've met," Dennis said. "I'm Ray's brother."

"Oh. I can't believe I didn't recognize you. But out of context...I only saw you once."

"Right. And this is Ray's father."

Kathy's voice became tense. "Is anything the matter? I haven't heard from Ray. Is he alright?"

"Unfortunately, he's not. He got arrested," Dominic said. "He's in jail."

"No. What for?"

"We're not sure of everything yet. It's pretty serious, but we don't think he did it. So, I'd like to ask you a few questions about when you've seen him over the last few days."

"Sure. You're a detective, aren't you?" Kathy said.

Dominic knew that he would have to walk a fine line between acting like an official police investigator and a private citizen. "Yes, but I'm not here as a detective. I'm here as his father."

"Okay. I hope I can remember. My days kind of run together, and sometimes I don't know one from the other."

"I know what you mean. When did you see him last?"

"About a week ago. I think it may have been Tuesday. He came to my place during the day, but I had to leave for work at three o'clock. Then he came here for a hamburger. I served him at a table. The boss made sure I charged him full price; although I did sneak him an extra beer."

"Did you see him after that?"

"No."

"Could it have been Wednesday instead of Tuesday?"

"Maybe, but that's the best I can remember. In this business, the days run together."

"Right."

Dennis wanted to press her on the discrepancy between Tuesday and Wednesday as the day Ray came to the restaurant. He said something, but his father made a motion indicated that he shouldn't.

"Thank you very much, Kathy," Dominic said. "We should stay in touch. I'll write my number down. And Dennis' too. Can I have your phone number?"

"Of course."

"And if you don't mind, I'll give your number to Ray's attorney. It's the Murray Klein law firm. They'll call you, I'm sure."

"One question. Can I visit Ray in the jail?"

"Yes. Make an appointment. I'll write the number down for you."

"Thank you. I hope Ray gets out."

"We hope so, too," Dennis said.

"What do we owe you for the drinks?" Dominic said.

"No charge."

But Dominic left money on the bar. As a cop, restaurants and bars that knew him rarely charged him, but he always left enough money to cover what the check would have been. This way, no one could ever accuse him of anything.

Dominic called Murray Klein, told him about the potential alibi information, and gave him Kathy Reynolds' phone number.

"It sounds like you did some real good work," Klein said. "Maybe we should pay you as our defense investigator."

"No, thanks."

"Okay. I'll send Jeff Rosen to take a statement from her," Klein said, "then we'll send an alibi notice to the DA."

"Let me know if there's anything else I can do."

"I'll see you Thursday at the 180.80 hearing."

CHAPTER FIVE

Dominic and Dennis arrived early for the 180.80 hearing on the fourth-floor hearing courtroom. The courtroom was closed, so they waited on a bench in the hallway. They hoped that after the hearing, Ray's bail would be reduced, or, better yet, that the case would be dismissed for lack of evidence.

After half an hour, Dominic grew impatient because Murray Klein hadn't arrived. Then, just as he stood up to call him, Klein came out of the elevator.

"Sorry I'm late," Klein said. "I was on the phone with the district attorney."

"Any news," Dominic said.

"Let's go in the men's room. I need to wash my hands."

As they walked into the men's room, Dominic and Dennis looked at each other, both realizing that this was the same men's room where Dominic had heard Klein demanding his drug-dealer client's gold chain as payment.

"There's bad news and more bad news," Klein said as he washed his hands.

"What?"

"The customer died. His name was Larry Coates, thirty-years-old."

"Damn it!" Dominic said. "So, what happens now?"

"They'll raise the charges to felony murder," Klein said, "and I'm sure they'll ask to increase the bail."

"What's the other bad news?" Dominic asked.

"Today's hearing will be adjourned because the case is going to the grand jury as we speak. So, there'll be an indictment by this afternoon, maybe even this morning, and they'll transfer the case to the Brooklyn Supreme Court, where Ray will have to be arraigned again. We'll ask for a lower bail, but don't count on it."

They walked back to the courtroom. It still wasn't open yet, so again, they sat on the bench to wait.

Dennis asked Klein, "What's the difference between felony murder and regular murder?"

Klein looked at his watch as though he didn't have time for questions, but answered, "For murder you need an intent to kill the person; for felony murder, you don't. Felony murder applies when the defendant, or an accomplice, commits certain violent felonies, such as robbery, burglary, or rape, and someone gets killed, even by accident. No intent is needed. The sentence is the same as for regular murder, twenty-five to life."

After another minute, Dennis asked, "Is there any defense?"

"You're thinking like a lawyer already," Klein said. "There is an affirmative defense. If the defendant can prove he didn't pull the trigger, wasn't armed, and didn't know any of his accomplices were armed, the felony murder charge could be dropped."

"Ray should be able to do that. He wasn't even there," Dennis said.

"Stop assuming that he was in on it, or knew anything about it," Dominic snapped at Dennis.

"You're right," Klein said. "The problem with the affirmative defense is that you admit you were involved. And that proves most of the case against you."

When the courtroom opened, two court officers, the judge's clerk, and the court stenographer were at their places. Five minutes later, Judge Harrison took the bench.

Ray's case was called. They brought him out of the cells in handcuffs and stood him at the defense table. Not knowing of the latest developments, he looked optimistic, even flashed a smile.

The district attorney began by telling the judge that the victim in this case had died, and that a grand jury had just indicted the defendant.

When Ray heard that, he began shaking.

Judge Harrison said, "This matter will be adjourned and transferred to Brooklyn Supreme Court, Criminal Division, for a new arraignment on Monday morning. I believe Judge Brown will be sitting. The district attorney will keep the court and all the parties informed. Bail is continued at $500,000."

Ray lost control and tried to shrug the officers off his arms. He didn't want to go back to the cells. "When do I get out of here?" he shouted. "When do I get to say anything?"

The court officers grabbed him and tried to move him back to the cells, but he was stronger than both of them and wouldn't move.

Dominic yelled to Ray, "Cooperate, don't resist! Stay calm. Just walk with them. The sooner you do, the sooner you get out of here."

Ray stopped resisting and went with the officers.

Later that afternoon, the district attorney notified Klein that there was a new witness. Someone came forward who saw a male white with long dirty-blond hair driving away from the car dealership in a red Camaro at the time of the robbery. The witness didn't get a plate number and couldn't identify Ray's photograph, but his general description of the driver fit Ray and could be used as circumstantial evidence against him.

Klein called Dominic and told him about the new witness.

On Monday at the Brooklyn Supreme Court on Adams Street near Borough Hall, Ray was arraigned on the indictment. The Honorable Clement J. Brown presided.

The judge was a big man who had played football in college. He had gained weight since then, but still looked athletic and formidable. He was known as a no-nonsense judge who would move the case along quickly, sometimes too quickly.

"Good morning, Mr. Klein," the judge said. "I'm always glad when you appear before me. We understand each other."

"Yes, your honor. It's always nice to appear before you," Klein said and gave a slight bow of his head.

"Okay. Bring the defendant out," the judge instructed.

Dominic and Dennis were in the first row of the spectator's section and watched closely as the court officers brought Ray out. He didn't flash any smiles, but looked straight ahead.

The judge moved quickly through the arraignment preliminaries, and looking at Klein, said, "Now, we'll read the charges."

"We waive the reading, your honor," Klein said. "I have a copy."

"Good. Now, in the lower court, you requested a *Wade* hearing?"

"Yes, your honor."

"Okay, let's get the *Wade* hearing out of the way," he said. "Two weeks from today. I trust you'll be ready."

"We'll be ready," Klein said. "Can you hear me regarding bail?"

"You can make a record, Mr. Klein. Go ahead, but these are serious charges. I'm not inclined to change the bail."

Klein enumerated the usual reasons that the bail should be reduced, but the judge quickly responded, "It remains at $500,000."

That afternoon, Klein held a meeting at his office to prepare for the *Wade* hearing. The district attorney had turned over discovery materials to the defense, including photographs of the photo arrays and the physical lineups. The photos were spread out on the conference table.

Of the three witnesses who remembered the person who allegedly "cased" the dealership during the week before the robbery, only the manager made an identification. The others said they couldn't because they weren't a hundred percent sure.

Klein said that the judge's remark about getting the *Wade* hearing out of the way was a bad sign. "He's not supposed to just 'get it out of the way.' He's supposed to look carefully and make sure the defendant's rights were protected."

Klein held up Ray's two prior arrest photographs. "Our best argument," he said, "is that they used this photo from the cocaine arrest when he had long hair, instead of the photo from the later assault arrest when he had shorter hair, like he has now. We can argue that it was unfair and suggestive. The other people in the photos didn't have such long hair, so Ray's photo with long hair stood out, and it wasn't his most current photo."

"I guess you'll have to prove that during the week before the robbery he had short hair and that he didn't cut it since then," Dominic said.

"Could you testify to that?" Klein said.

"I would, but I don't think I saw him that week."

"I did," Dennis said. "I didn't pay too much attention, but I'm pretty sure his hair was short."

"If you testify, you have to be more definite than that," Klein said. "Otherwise, it hurts more than it helps. How about Ray's mother?"

"I don't think she saw him that week either," Dominic said. "And I'd like to spare her the ordeal. She has some health problems."

"His girlfriend, Kathy Reynolds, saw him," Dennis said.

"Good," Klein said. "Will she testify?"

"I'm sure she will."

"Now let's turn to the lineup," Klein said. "They have a problem here because the other people they used in the lineup as fillers had varying lengths of hair. Ray's hair was the shortest. So, they put hats on everybody to hide the fact that Ray's hair was short. They made the ones with long hair shove it up under their hats, so they all looked like they had short hair."

"That doesn't sound fair," Dennis said.

"It's normal procedure," Dominic said, "because sometimes it's difficult to get fillers with the same characteristics as the suspect."

"But usually, it's done to hide something that would make the suspect stand out and would incriminate him," Klein said. "Here, they were hiding something that could've helped to exonerate him."

"That's going to be an interesting argument," Dominic said.

"You're right. See what else you can find out," Klein said.

Before they left the office, Dominic called Kathy Reynolds and left a message for her. He left Dennis' phone number as a callback and told

Dennis, "I've got to go to work for a four to twelve shift, and I don't want to be talking to her while I'm on duty. Call her later and see what she says. If it's helpful, make an appointment with her to come into Klein's office to look at the photos of Ray's hair."

Later that evening, Kathy Reynolds called Dennis back.

"I'm glad you called," she said. "I wanted to talk to you and your father about something."

"What is it?"

"You know, I've always been told never to talk on the phone about anything serious."

"Okay, where should we meet?"

"How about McCoy's parking lot?"

"I'll be there in twenty minutes."

In the parking lot at McCoy's, Dennis saw Kathy leaning up against her white Nissan Rogue. She was wearing a pink tank top and a short skirt. He pulled his car up beside her and reached to open the passenger door. She got in. The passenger seat was too far forward, so he reached under it to lift the lever to allow her to push the seat back. He couldn't help but look at her legs.

He drove to the back of the lot and parked.

"How's Ray," Kathy said.

"It's rough on him, that's for sure," Dennis said.

"I feel so sorry for him. And I'm worried that I said the wrong thing to your father and then the lawyer, Mr. Rosen."

"What do you mean?"

"Mr. Rosen came to the restaurant yesterday and asked the same questions your father did. He wanted me to say I was with Ray on Wednesday when I think it was Tuesday. Now I'm worried that I got the days mixed up. I don't want to ruin it for Ray by saying the wrong day."

"The police haven't contacted you, have they?"

"No. Do you think they will?"

"They might, especially if the lawyer puts you down as an alibi witness."

"I'll be glad to be an alibi witness. But I've got to get the days straight. Is it Tuesday or Wednesday?"

Dennis wanted to tell her it was Wednesday, but he knew that wasn't the way to do a proper investigation. His father had told him you can't put words in a witness's mouth.

"I can't tell you what to say," Dennis said. "You should do your best to remember. But frankly, I don't think it's that important. The main accusation against Ray is that he was in the car dealership the week before pretending that he was in the market to buy a new car. Do you know anything about that?"

"No. Why would he do that? He's got no money."

"You're right. But let me ask you something else," Dennis said. "Did you see him the week before?"

"Twice. What days, I'm not sure."

"How about Ray's hair? It's short now. Was it short during the last few weeks?"

"You're his brother, you should know."

"I paid little attention. Has it always been the same?"

"It's been short for a while. He used to keep it long, but that was a while back."

"You're sure."

"Yes. Sometimes I cut his hair for him to save going to the barber."

"That could be very helpful."

"Good. Glad to help. Want to go inside for a drink?"

"Sure."

Kathy and Dennis sat in the middle of the bar. Brendan served her a white wine and poured him a beer without asking for proof of age.

When Brendan moved away, Kathy asked, "So, what do you think Ray's chances are?"

"I don't know. There's going to be what they call a *Wade* hearing about the photo and lineup identifications. They'll probably ask you to testify about the length of Ray's hair."

"That's okay."

"But the lawyer is not too happy with the judge."

"Rosen?"

'No. Murray Klein. He's Rosen's boss. My father says that he's a great lawyer."

"Let's hope so. Do you want another beer?"

"No. I've got to work in the morning."

"Where do you work?"

"United Parcel Service."

"That's good."

"If you don't mind my asking," Dennis said, "how did you come to work here as a barmaid?"

"It's simple," she said. "I lived upstate near Saratoga. My father died when I was in high school, and my mother remarried. They moved to Long Island, and I didn't want to go with them, so I moved to the big city. But the rents were so high in Manhattan that I found a place in Greenpoint. I heard about this job. It's not too far, so I applied, figuring it was temporary."

"Did you have any experience as a barmaid?" he asked.

"No, but they hired me anyway."

"Of course they did. Who wouldn't hire a beautiful girl like you?"

Kathy smiled and brushed her hair back with her right hand. "That's true."

They finished their drinks and walked to Kathy's car. She hugged him and kissed him on the cheek.

"Let me know when you need me," she said.

The next afternoon, after working all day at UPS, Dennis went to Klein's office to meet his father, who was there reading police reports, witness statements, and transcripts that the district attorney had turned over to the defense.

Klein greeted Dennis, "Here comes our future star lawyer."

"How are you, sir?" Dennis said.

"I'm enjoying watching your father working his brains out on all this paperwork. We should pay him as our top investigator."

"That would be nice, but the Department would frown on it," Dominic said.

"In that case, why don't I hire your son here as an intern? He's seems interested in the law. He could be a great help. What do you think?"

"Fine by me," Dominic said. "What do you say, Dennis?"

"That would be great," Dennis said, "but I'm working at UPS as a truck helper."

"I'm sure you can get a leave of absence. Give them notice, leave on good terms, and you can go back. You know, truck helpers are fungible."

"What does that mean?" Dennis asked.

"Fungible means that something that's similar can replace something else. Meaning if I sold you a bundle of wheat but the wheat got lost, I could replace it with another bundle of wheat. It doesn't have to be the same one. And the same goes for people. For example, in the police department, if a cop doesn't show up for duty, another cop can replace him because we view cops as all the same. It's only when people develop advanced skills, like a tech-specialist, or a super lawyer, or a top-notch detective like your father, that they're no longer considered fungible."

"That's interesting," Dennis said. "Most people assume they're irreplaceable, but, in fact, most all of us are fungible."

"You've got it. And whether you're fungible or not, I'll pay you the same salary you're getting at UPS."

"Thank you. Can I let you know tomorrow? I have to go in to UPS."

"Of course."

"Maybe they'll give me a better offer," Dennis joked.

"You definitely have the makings of a good lawyer," Klein laughed. "If they do, we'll have to negotiate."

They laughed.

The next day, UPS gave Dennis a leave of absence, and he began working at Klein's office

On the day of the *Wade* hearing, Kathy Reynolds met Dennis and his father at Brooklyn Supreme Court.

Judge Brown took the bench. Ray was brought out from the holding cells and seated next to Klein at the defense table. He wasn't in handcuffs. A court officer stood behind him.

The assistant district attorney, Bill Walsh, called Detective McConnell to the stand as his first witness.

McConnell testified that on Tuesday, August 22nd, he had been called to the scene of the robbery and shooting at the car dealership. He wasn't able to talk to the shooting victim because he had been taken away in an ambulance, but he interviewed the manager and learned that three men wearing masks and carrying guns had robbed the place and the customers, getting away with cash and jewelry.

He also learned that a week before, a suspect had been in the dealership, apparently casing the place.

He testified he got the closed-circuit-TV videos from the outside security cameras. The videos captured a dozen cars that he considered suspicious. He checked the plate numbers of those cars through the motor vehicle bureau to determine who owned them. Then he cross-checked the names of the owners against the criminal-records database and found six who had criminal histories and photographs on file. Of the six, three fit the general description of the suspect who had scouted out the place the week before.

McConnell testified that on Wednesday, August 23rd, the arrest photographs of these three were each placed in separate photo arrays to be shown to the witnesses. The manager made a positive identification of the defendant, and then, at a physical lineup, the manager identified the defendant again. Based on that, he arrested Ray Carbonaro.

McConnell testified about how the photographs were shown to the witnesses, how it was all routine, and how he followed standard procedures.

ADA Walsh had no further questions for him.

"Any cross?" Judge Brown asked Klein.

"Yes, your honor," Klein said.

Klein shuffled some papers, then began a line of questioning that neither Dominic nor Dennis had expected.

"You know the defendant's father, Detective Dominic Carbonaro. Is that correct?"

"Yes."

"In fact, you were both promoted you to third-grade detective on the same day."

"I don't know when he was promoted," McConnell answered.

"You know when you were promoted, correct?"

"Yes."

"And that was twelve years ago, in December, right before Christmas, right?"

"Yes."

"Since then, you haven't been promoted, have you?"

"No."

"You haven't been promoted to second-grade detective, correct?"

"No."

You haven't been promoted to first-grade detective, correct?"

"That's right."

"But you know that since then Detective Carbonaro has been promoted twice, and is now a first-grade detective, correct?"

"I believe so."

"Over the years, you came in contact with Detective Carbonaro many times. Is that true?"

"Yes."

"You've had your differences with him. Have you not?"

"Only like with anyone else."

The judge interrupted, "Where is this going, Mr. Klein?"

"May we approach the bench," Klein said.

"No," the judge said. "Just where is this going?"

"Motivation and bias, your honor."

"All right, I'll give you a little rope, but we don't want to go down a rabbit hole."

Klein turned to McConnell.

"You were the lead detective in this case?"

"Yes."

"And you directed Detective Cruz to compose a six-person photo array for each of the three suspects you had selected.

"Yes."

"Each photo array had one photo of a suspect and five filler photos?"

"Yes."

"And the first photo array you showed to the witness included the photo of Ray Carbonaro?"

"Yes."

"And the manager picked out his photograph as the person who allegedly had been in the dealership the week before the robbery, correct?"

"Yes."

"After he made the identification, did you show him any other photo arrays?"

"No."

"Did you show him a photo array that included a photograph of the defendant with short hair?"

"No."

"You had identified three suspects from the car plate numbers. Is that correct?"

"Yes."

"Do you know the names of the other suspects from the plate numbers?"

"Not offhand."

"Shouldn't you have shown the photos of the other suspects to the witnesses?"

"There was no need because we had an identification," McConnell said.

"How is it that Mr. Carbonaro's photo was in the first array shown to the witnesses?"

"If I remember right, we went in alphabetical order, and his initial C was first."

"We have the names of the other people on the list of suspects from the plate numbers, and I'll point out to you that another suspect was named Anderson."

"Okay."

"So, your alphabetical list recollection doesn't hold up, right?"

"I don't really remember why Carbonaro was in the first batch."

"Could it be that it was because you recognized the name, and you focused on him because you had a personal bias against first-grade detective Dominic Carbonaro, his father?"

Judge Brown slapped his hand on his desk. "Enough. Move on."

"Yes, your honor," Klein said, as he retrieved two photographs from his case folder.

"Correct me if I'm wrong," Klein said to McConnell, "the usual practice when gathering photographs from the criminal records photo gallery is to input a description of the unidentified suspect into the computer database, and then the computer selects photographs of persons who matchup to the description. Is that right?"

"Yes."

"But you didn't do that here. You had Detective Cruz input names into the computer, whether they matched up with the description. Is that right?"

"Yes."

"And he retrieved two photographs of Ray Carbonaro, correct?"

"Yes."

Klein asked the judge, "May I approach the witness to show him the photos, defense exhibits 1A and 1B?"

"Yes."

Klein handed the two photos to McConnell. "Are these the photos that were retrieved?"

"Yes."

"One is from an earlier arrest, where my client had relatively long hair. Is that right?

"Yes."

"The other photo is from an arrest for two years later, and his hair is much shorter. Is that right?"

"It's shorter. I wouldn't say 'much shorter.'"

"But clearly shorter?"

"Yes"

"And you placed only the earlier photo into the array that you showed to the witnesses, right?"

"Yes."

"You didn't show the later, more recent photo to them, right?"

"That's right," McConnell said. "There was no need. We had a positive identification. I didn't want to confuse the witnesses."

"Didn't you confuse him by showing him an older photo when my client had long hair, instead of the more recent photo, closer in time to this robbery, when he had shorter hair?"

"I don't think so."

"You didn't show him a photo array that included a photo of the defendant with short hair?"

"No."

"And you didn't bother to show the manager the other photo arrays, the ones that included the other suspects who had criminal records."

"There was no need. I had a positive ID."

"And you didn't show the other photo arrays to the other witnesses, is that right?"

"That's right."

"If you had, maybe they would have recognized someone else from the other arrays."

"That's speculation."

"It's speculation because you didn't do it."

The district attorney stood and objected. "This is argumentative."

"Objection sustained," Judge Brown said.

Klein continued. "You stopped showing the other photos to the other witnesses because you were satisfied that you had a case against my client, the son of Detective Carbonaro, a competitor of yours in the police department.

Walsh stood. "Objection."

Judge Brown said, "Approach the bench."

Klein and Walsh stood before the judge.

"Mr. Klein, I sustained the objection. I think you're going beyond the purpose of this hearing. You can raise these biases or motivation issues at trial, but here we only need to determine whether the procedures were unduly suggestive to a degree that rises to a violation of the constitution or not. What's in the detective's mind doesn't matter at this stage as long as the standard procedures for identifications were followed. And, so far, it looks as though they were."

"I respectfully disagree, your honor," Klein said.

"That's your right. Do you have anything else?"

"Yes. I have a witness who can testify to the length of my client's hair at the time of the robbery and the week before the robbery."

"Alright, that shouldn't take too long," the judge said.

Klein called Kathy Reynolds to the stand. She testified she was Ray's girlfriend and was familiar with his hairstyle because she actually cut his hair from time to time.

"Please look at the defendant," Klein said. "Over the past few months, was his hair as short as it is now?"

"Shorter," she answered.

ADA Walsh didn't cross examine her.

"Anything else," Judge Brown said.

"Yes," Klein said. "Regarding the physical lineup…"

Judge Brown interrupted. "Again, that's beyond what's necessary for this hearing. The photo array identification is good enough for probable cause to arrest."

"Respectfully, your honor, the photo ID must be confirmed by an identification at the physical lineup," Klein said. "And we contend the improper photo-array of procedures tainted the lineup."

"I have seen no improper procedures, so your argument doesn't hold," the judge said.

"With all due respect, your honor we need to address the lineup, to see whether it was suggestive."

Judge Brown stared at Klein as though he was going to throw him out of the courtroom, but after a pause, while apparently thinking that he didn't want his ruling to be appealed, he said, "Alright, Mr. Klein. If you insist."

"I do."

"DA Walsh, do you have a witness?" the judge said.

"Yes. Recall Detective McConnell."

McConnell testified to how the physical lineup was put together, how fillers who looked like the defendant were assembled, except for differences in hair length and style. He testified that all the fillers wore baseball caps so that their hair was covered, no one would stand out, and the identification would be based mainly on facial characteristics, not hair. He testified that the dealership manager picked out Mr. Carbonaro.

On cross-examination, Klein asked McConnell, "You put hats on my client and all fillers, is that correct?"

"Yes."

"You did that because my client's hair differed from the others?"

"Yes."

"It was shorter?"

"Yes."

"The description of the suspect was of someone with relatively long hair, correct?"

"Yes."

"So, my client's short hair would contravene the description given by the witnesses about the suspect?"

"We don't know what his hair was like when he was casing the dealership," McConnell said.

"Objection, your honor," Klein said. "Move that the answer be stricken."

"Sustained," the judge said. "Strike the answer from the record. Rephrase the question."

"Without speculating about what the suspect was supposedly doing or thinking, my client's short hair is inconsistent with the description that was given by the witnesses about the suspect. Correct?"

"Yes."

Klein argued the police shouldn't have put baseball caps on the participants because that prevented the witness from seeing that the defendant had short hair, not the long hair of the suspect who had been in the dealership.

ADA Walsh countered that the baseball caps were used in order to prevent the defendant from standing out from the others, which would have been unduly suggestive. He argued that this was standard police practice and no reason to suppress the lineup identification.

Judge Brown said, "Let me see the picture of the lineup again." He looked at it and dropped it on his desk. "It looks okay to me. The hearing is over. I'll give you a written decision by the end of the week."

At the defense table, Ray shook his head. He looked at Dominic and Dennis and turned his palms up as though to say, "I can't win."

After court, Klein, Dominic, Dennis, and Kathy Reynolds went to a nearby restaurant. The four sat at a table that Klein had chosen in the back of the dining room so that they could talk without being overheard.

To Kathy Reynolds, he said, "Thank you so much for your testimony. It was excellent."

"Thanks," Kathy said, "but I don't think it's going to matter with that judge. He seemed totally against Ray."

"That's just his manner. I'm hopeful he'll rule the right way."

"I hope you're right," she said, "because I feel so sorry for Ray. He must feel that he doesn't have a chance."

Dominic said to Klein, "You did a great job, counsellor, despite the judge. You had McConnell's number all the way. And I agree with you, that bastard singled out Ray because of me."

Dennis asked, "Why should he be so bent out of shape because you got promoted and he didn't?"

Klein answered before Dominic could, "It's in their nature. Detectives get promoted by merit. It's highly competitive and becomes personal. Like all competitive people, and I'm thinking of lawyers like me, you view your competitors as adversaries, and when you lose a competition, jealously can rear its ugly head."

Klein's observation quieted the table until the server came to take their orders.

"What happens next?" Dennis asked.

"The judge's ruling is important," Klein said. "If we lose, we won't get a good offer from the DA. If we win, the DA's case will be weakened, and we might get a decent offer."

"What kind of offer?" Dominic asked.

"The case is too wide open to guess," Klein said. "As I've said before, if they ever catch the actual robbers, that will complicate things. The DA may offer Ray a deal to testify against them, or, worse, he may offer one of them a deal to testify against Ray."

"That assumes Ray was involved at all," Dennis said.

Klein nodded in agreement. "You sound like your father."

Although Dennis was terribly worried about his brother, in an odd way, he was enjoying his involvement in the case, working about twelve hours a day at the law firm for the same salary he had been getting at UPS for eight. But he didn't care. He loved it.

Although most of his duties were mundane, like filing, copying, taking folders to the storage room, retrieving them, and running errands, he made it interesting by reading some of the case folders, especially those on the cases in the newspaper articles posted on the office walls. He made copies of the important parts and wrote summaries in a notebook that he kept for himself. His priority was reading everything he could that related to Ray's case, and every chance he got, he asked Klein or Rosen legal questions about it.

Kathy called to ask if she could go with him to visit Ray at the jail. She didn't want to go alone. Dennis asked his father, who said that it wouldn't be a good idea.

"Why not?"

"Because he's miserable enough," Dominic said. "If he sees you and her together, he'll start thinking that you're stealing his girlfriend."

"I'm his brother. I'd never do that."

"Sure, you wouldn't, but Ray needs to believe that he still has a girlfriend waiting on the outside. I wouldn't do anything to undermine that or make him more miserable than he is."

CHAPTER SIX

J udge Brown's rejected Klein's *Wade* motion to prevent the use of the photo and lineup identifications, writing that they were done properly and there was nothing unduly suggestive about them. The identifications would be admissible at the trial.

Klein, Dominic, and Dennis visited Ray in the jail to tell him the bad news. Ray was disappointed, and Klein tried to give him some hope, telling him that there were several appealable errors in the judge's ruling. Jeff Rosen, an excellent appellate lawyer, would write the appeal.

"But it probably won't be decided until after the trial," Klein said.

"How come?" Ray asked.

"The Appellate judges will wait to see what happens. If you get acquitted, they won't have to address it. If you're convicted, they'll have to."

"That doesn't seem right. Those bogus identification shouldn't be allowed in the trial. McConnell probably pointed me out to the manager."

"You might be right," Dennis said.

"At the trial, I should sit with the spectators," Ray said, "and we'll see if the manager can pick me out."

"It's been done," Klein said, "but Judge Brown would never allow it."

"This judge won't do anything to give me a break," Ray said. "I'll bet if I was a different color, he would."

"Don't go there," Dominic said to Ray. "What's important is that your attorney did a great job, and, as I understand it, he can raise the identification issues again in front of the jury, and you only need a reasonable doubt to get an acquittal, so keep your chin up."

"There's more than reasonable doubt," Ray said. "This is all bullshit."

As the discussion continued, Dennis was watching Ray, and thinking that he had changed. When he was first arrested, he was shocked and afraid; now he was angry and combative.

If Ray had been involved in the robbery, Dennis thought, he wouldn't have been so shocked by his arrest. He would have expected it, but he had seemed completely taken by surprise. And it wasn't an act. Dennis knew his brother's expressions and mannerisms. He believed what he saw was genuine. If Ray was guilty, he couldn't be so sure of himself and wouldn't be so combative. Any doubts Dennis may have had about Ray's innocence were gone.

When working at Klein's office, Dennis spent most of his time in the storage room filing documents and marking boxes. No one bothered him when he was in there, and he had plenty of time to look through trial records that interested him. He read the transcripts of cases in which Klein had won large verdicts for wrongful arrest.

He found one for which Klein got a million-dollar verdict against the city police on behalf of an X-Crips' gang member. The gang member had spent nine years in prison for attempted murder for shooting someone, but then was exonerated. It was not a DNA exoneration but a case in which a tape recording surfaced of a second X-Crips' gang member admitting to the shooting. Based on the new evidence, a motion for a new trial was granted.

At the new trial, the second gang member was called to the witness stand, but he took the Fifth Amendment. Since he wouldn't testify, the defense could play the tape recording of him admitting that he was the one who did the shooting. Evidently, this was enough to raise a reasonable doubt, and the jury acquitted the first X-Crips' gang member.

Klein sued the city for wrongful arrest and imprisonment, and won the million-dollar verdict.

Dennis read the case folder again, trying to understand what had happened. He asked Jeffrey Rosen if he knew about the case. He did.

"Why didn't they prosecute the second gang member since he admitted the shooting?" Dennis asked.

"Because the five-year statute of limitations had passed. They couldn't."

"So, you mean to tell me," Dennis said, "that after the statute of limitations is over, someone can confess to the crime and get away with it."

"Yes. But for some crimes, the statute is longer," Rosen said. "Murder has no time limit."

"How long for attempted murder?"

"Five years."

"That's all. That seems baffling."

Dennis couldn't get the X-Crips case out of his mind and went to Klein's office to ask him about it. Klein was seated in his high-backed leather chair behind his Cherrywood desk. Through the window behind him, Dennis could see the midtown skyscrapers.

"Sorry to bother you, but can I ask you a question?" Dennis asked.

"Of course, sit down."

At that moment, Assistant District Attorney Bill Walsh called. As Klein picked up the phone, Dennis began to leave, but Klein signaled for him to stay, and put the phone on speaker.

Dennis was surprised that Klein would let him hear the conversation. ADA Walsh was conveying a plea bargain for Ray. It was a two-part offer. Part one, if Ray pled guilty to robbery first degree and manslaughter first degree, he would get ten to twelve years in prison, rather than the twenty-five to life he could get if they convicted him of murder or felony murder.

Part two of the offer was that if Ray would identify the perpetrators of the robbery and testify against them, he would get two years in prison, five years' probation, and would only have to plead guilty to robbery in the third degree.

"Let's start with the second part. That's a non-starter. He doesn't know who the perpetrators are because he wasn't involved."

"Maybe you don't think he was involved, but we do, and we can prove it," Walsh said. "You should give him a little time to think about it. Get him to tell you the truth. Two years is a blip. Why risk twenty-five to life, or even ten to twelve?"

"You can do a lot better than that," Klein said.

"Take it or leave it," Walsh said.

Klein hesitated as though he wanted to argue but simply said, "I have to convey the offer to my client, but I can't see him taking it. For the ten to twelve years, we can go to trial and, even if we lose, he probably won't get any more than that."

"With Judge Brown, he would."

"I'll get back to you," Klein said, and hung up.

Klein, Dominic, and Dennis went to visit Ray in prison to tell him about the offer.

He had been transferred from the Detention Center in Brooklyn to Riker's Island, the prison complex in the East River between the Bronx, Manhattan, and Queens. They had to drive to Queens to get to the causeway to the island.

They signed in at the visitors' center and had to an hour before Ray was brought from one of the other buildings.

When Ray arrived and saw his three visitors, he said, "This can't be good."

"It depends how you look at it," Klein said, and explained the district attorney's two offers. When he finished, Ray said, "No way. I'm not pleading guilty to something I didn't do."

"It's understandable that you feel that way. But you have to be practical," Klein said. "Whether you're guilty or not, you could be convicted and sentenced for a much longer time. By going to trial, you're gambling, gambling with a substantial part of your life. If you take the plea, with time off for good behavior, you could be out in six years."

Ray looked at his father, not with tears in his eyes as he had at the last visit, but with anger. "This is bullshit," he said. "I think the cops are framing me. What do you think, Dad?"

"I'm doing everything I can to find out what's going on," Dominic said.

They all fell silent. Dennis waited for someone to say something. When no one did, he asked, "What about the second part of the offer?"

Ray laughed. "That's a joke. How could I tell them who did it, when I don't know? Maybe I should make up three names, and frame them, instead of me."

"Don't laugh," Klein said. "It's been done."

"Did they get away with it?" Dennis said.

"Sometimes," Klein said.

"That reminds me," Dominic said, "don't talk to anyone in here. Jails are full of informers and snitches. They get a guy talking, or complaining, or bragging, and along the way he makes an admission, even a confession. Then the snitch makes a deal with the DA to get a reduced sentence and testifies against the guy. So don't talk to anybody."

"Don't worry. There's no one in here I want to talk to."

"And something else," Dominic said, "when you make a phone call, the calls are recorded, even a call to your lawyer. That's how a lot of wise guys get themselves jammed up."

"I didn't think they could listen to a conversation with your lawyer," Dennis said.

"In some cases, they can and they do," Klein said.

"I see."

"So, what's your decision?" Klein asked.

Ray looked at his father. "I'd rather go to trial and lose than go to jail because I admitted to something I didn't do. If they want to hang me, let them. But I will not give them the rope to do it."

As Ray was speaking, no one seemed to be breathing. Dennis thought his father looked proud of Ray's courage. And Dennis, too, felt proud, but also scared. His father had taught him a lot, and it scared him that Ray was being caught up in a system that chewed people up based on mistaken facts, mistaken identifications, false testimony, district attorneys playing hardball, and tyrannical judges.

He had thought of becoming a lawyer, like Klein had suggested, but he wondered whether it was a good choice to get involved in such a system.

His thoughts were interrupted when Ray spoke. "Mr. Klein, I have faith in you. My father said you're a great lawyer, so I'll take my chances at trial."

"I appreciate that," Klein said. "And I'll do the best I can for you."

That night, Kathy Reynolds left a phone message for Dennis. "I get off work at ten tonight. Can you meet me at McCoy's? I have something to tell you."

Wondering what it could be about, he changed his clothes and drove to McCoy's.

Kathy had finished her shift as a barmaid and was waiting for him. She wore a light green, flowered blouse that left her shoulders bare, and led him to a booth away from other customers.

"Have you seen Ray?" she asked.

"We saw him today."

"Oh. How was he?"

"He seemed okay under the circumstances. But I'm afraid they're really squeezing him. They offered him a plea bargain. If he pleads guilty, he'll get ten to twelve years."

"Oh, my God," Kathy blurted out. "That's terrible. I can't believe it. Ray's such a good guy. It's not fair. He didn't shoot anybody."

"There's another part of the offer. If he identifies the three guys who robbed the dealership and testifies against them, he'll only get two years in jail followed by five years' probation."

"But he doesn't know who they are."

"He's really between a rock and a hard place."

"I'm sick of this," Kathy said. "Can't sleep at night. You know I always cared for Ray, but I never realized how much until now. What did he say?"

"He won't take it. He said he'd rather go to trial."

"That's Ray."

A waitress came to their booth. "Can I get you guys anything?"

Kathy introduced them. "This is Belinda. This is Dennis, Ray's brother."

Belinda was pretty. She was Puerto Rican with black hair, dark eyes, and she wore the same styled bare-shoulder blouse as Kathy, only pink.

"Nice to meet you," Belinda said. "Sorry to hear about Ray. He's a great guy."

"Thanks."

"And you look just like him," Belinda said.

"Dennis is younger and better looking," Kathy said.

"Flattery will get you everywhere," Dennis said.

"What can I get you?" Belinda asked.

"A hamburger, medium rare, and a beer."

"Just like Ray."

When Belinda left, Dennis said, "I think you've got competition for Ray's heart."

"Yeah. When he gets out, they'll be girls lined up to date him. But I think Belinda may be more interested in you."

"That's not saying much. I'm not in prison."

Kathy laughed. "Belinda's a good skate, and a good friend."

Belinda brought over two beers and left them alone.

Dennis took a drink from the bottle. "On the phone, you said you had something to tell me."

"Yes. Detective McConnell was here. He asked about what hours I worked, and he asked whether Ray hung around with any black guys, and whether anybody sold marihuana in the bar."

"What'd you say?"

"I told him my hours were flexible. And I said that once in a while black guys come into the bar, usually with dates. They're regular guys, and nobody sells marihuana. The boss is always watching, and he'd throw them out in a minute."

"What else did he say?"

"He actually kind of threatened me. He said that people who make up alibis can go to jail for perjury."

"He must have heard about the alibi notice Klein sent to the DA. What did you say?"

"Nothing. I went to the other end of the bar and ignored him. Then the big dork moves down the bar and starts chatting me up like he wants a date. I ignored him until he left."

"He sounds like a real jerk, but a dangerous jerk. I think he was so embarrassed by Klein at the Wade hearing that's he's looking to get even somehow."

"He won't scare me," Kathy said. "If anyone asks me, I'll say Ray was with me every day, every minute. Even if I go to jail, it would be worth it to get Ray off."

"You two have a lot in common," Dennis said. "But don't go around saying that."

On Saturday, Dennis went to his parents' house as he often did. He let himself in and found his mother sitting on a chair under the crucifix affixed to the wall in the foyer. She had rosary beads in her hands, and he could see that she had been praying.

He kissed her, and she said for him to go into the kitchen. "I'll make you breakfast."

He had already eaten, but he said yes because he knew it pleased her.

His father came downstairs, and Dennis whispered to him he had to tell him something.

"Let's go in the backyard," Dominic said. "I don't want your mother listening to things that are going to upset her any more than she's already upset."

They went out the back door.

"McConnell went to McCoy's yesterday," Dennis said. "He tried to question Ray's girlfriend."

Dominic shook his head. "I guess McConnell's checking her out as an alibi witness, but I think he's on a personal crusade. The Department says I'm biased. Well, McConnell's biased, too."

Dennis related everything that Kathy had told him.

"She wants to know what days and times are important for her to know in order for her to say when she was with Ray," Dennis said.

"Dennis, listen to me," Dominic said. "Be careful, and don't be feeding her information."

"I didn't."

"Be sure you don't. You could get in a lot of trouble. There's a crime called suborning perjury. That's when someone encourages or assists someone to lie under oath."

"I don't think she's going to lie," Dennis said. "I just think she just wants to clarify what days are important so that she can try to remember the best she can. Remember, she told us that her days all run together."

"Listen. I've seen this a million times. Witnesses may have good intentions, but they mess things up. And when they get caught and face going to jail, they turn on everyone else."

"I'll be careful."

"And if the DA can prove that someone tried to tailor testimony, it would be worse for Ray. So, we'll do things by the numbers. Okay."

"Okay."

Dennis had breakfast with his mother, then drove to Klein's office. It was a weekend, and the traffic wasn't too bad. In the office, only a few lawyers were working overtime. Dennis wanted to look up a couple of legal cases that interested him, one in particular, a Supreme Court case, *Chambers v. Mississippi*. He was interested in that case because several of Klein's legal briefs had cited that case as a precedent that a defendant had the right to introduce evidence that someone had confessed to the crime for which the defendant was on trial.

In Klein's library, he found volume 99 of the Supreme Court Reports and turned to page 1038. *Chambers* was a 1973 decision regarding an incident in Woodville, Mississippi, that occurred in 1969 when a police officer was shot and killed.

Dennis read the case twice. It was a complex legal opinion that he had trouble understanding. He made notes and tried to put all the facts and the legal rulings in some order that he could follow. He heard his father say once that "bad facts make bad law." This case had confusing facts and confusing law.

It was about two Woodville, Mississippi police officers, James Forman and Sonny Liberty. They entered a bar and pool hall to execute an arrest warrant for a twenty-one-year-old man. The man resisted and when the officers attempted to handcuff him, a hostile crowd of about twenty-five men gathered and wrestled him free from the officers.

Officer Forman radioed for backup, and Officer Liberty retrieved his 12-gauge double-barrel shotgun from his patrol car.

Additional officers arrived, and when they tried to arrest the youth again, the crowd surrounded them. Someone in the crowd began shooting at the officers, and Officer Liberty was shot four times in the back. Before he fell, Liberty turned and fired his shotgun twice into an alleyway from where the shots appeared to have come. His first shot was wild, but the second shot struck Leon Chambers.

The officers who saw Chambers fall thought he was dead, and they made no effort to search him for the murder weapon. Instead, they placed Officer Liberty in a patrol car and rushed him to a hospital where he was pronounced dead on arrival.

In the meantime, friends of Chambers loaded him into a car and rushed him to the same hospital. He survived his wounds.

Chambers was arrested and charged with Officer Liberty's murder on the theory that Officer Liberty would have shot at the person who was shooting at him. In Mississippi, the murder of a police officer carried the death penalty. Chambers pled not guilty.

Dennis understood the first part of the case. The next part was more difficult, but it was what interested him. Chambers' defense team had heard about a man, Gable McDonald, who had been in the crowd when Officer Liberty was shot and who had told three of his friends that he was the one who shot the officer. The friends told a reverend, and the reverend notified the defense lawyers.

The defense lawyers interviewed McDonald, and he gave them a written, signed confession that he shot Officer Liberty.

They turned McDonald over to the local police, and, based on the confession, McDonald was arrested and jailed.

A month later, at a preliminary hearing, McDonald repudiated his confession, testifying that he only confessed because the reverend had promised him that if he confessed, he would not go to prison and would share in the proceeds of a lawsuit that Chambers would bring against the police for false arrest. The judge accepted McDonald's repudiation and released him from custody.

As Dennis read this part of the case, he was struck by the similarities to the cases in which Klein had won acquittals and then recovered large monetary awards.

He read that at the trial, a year after the shooting, Chambers testified, as he had at the preliminary hearing, that he did not shoot Officer Liberty.

The defense called McDonald, hoping that he would again admit that he was the real shooter, and thus exonerate Chambers. But McDonald took the Fifth Amendment.

Since the repudiated confession that McDonald had given to the lawyers was not admissible, the defense tried to introduce the oral confession/declaration against interests that he had made to his three friends before he spoke to the lawyers.

These would be hearsay statements, but, although hearsay statements were not admitted as evidence in trials, there were many exceptions, including dying declarations, confessions, admissions, and declarations against interests. McDonald's statements were declarations against interests because he was not the defendant. If he had been the defendant, his statements would have been called confessions.

The defense called the friends as witnesses, but the trial judge refused to allow their testimony.

Without hearing the evidence of McDonald's statements, the jury convicted Chambers, and he was sentenced to life in prison.

The case was appealed to the U.S. Supreme Court, and the Court made a monumental ruling that changed the law regarding the admissibility of hearsay statements in a trial.

The question for the Supreme Court was whether McDonald's initial statements to his three friends were admissible as exceptions to the hearsay rule and could exonerate Chambers. The Court ruled that the trial court should have admitted the statements into evidence, explaining:

Several exceptions have developed over the years to allow admission of hearsay statements made under circumstances that assure reliability and compensate for the absence of the oath and opportunity for cross-examination. Among the most prevalent of these exceptions is the one applicable to declarations against interest—an exception founded on the assumption that a person is unlikely to fabricate a statement against his own interest at the time it is made.

The Court overturned Chambers' conviction and ruled that the testimony of the three friends "was critical to Chambers' defense. In these circumstances, where constitutional rights directly affecting the ascertainment of guilt are implicated, the hearsay rule may not be applied mechanistically to defeat the ends of justice."

Reading this, Dennis realized the Court had made a ruling that favored defendants over prosecutors. Defendants could introduce certain types of third-party hearsay statements to exonerate a defendant, while prosecutors could not do the same to incriminate a defendant.

For days, he thought about the *Chambers'* case and the legal issues it raised. He studied the criminal law book Klein had given him and took a couple of other books from Klein's library to study at home. He wondered whether the *Chambers* case and the law on hearsay declarations-against-interest could be used in Ray's case.

CHAPTER SEVEN

Klein and the district attorney engaged in an ongoing negotiation about scheduling the trial. Klein wanted it as soon as possible, but the district attorney kept finding reasons to delay, suggesting that the trial could be held soon after the Christmas and New Year's holidays. Klein brought the issue to Judge Brown, who sided with the DA, and scheduled the trial for the fifteenth of January.

When Dennis visited Ray at Riker's Island to tell him, Ray put his head in his hands. "You mean, I'm going to be in here through Christmas and New Year's?"

"I'm sorry, but it looks that way," Dennis said. "But January is not that far off. Maybe that'll be the end."

"It'll be the end alright. I have no chance. They're out to get me, and even dad can't do anything about it."

"Yeah. He feels terrible," Dennis said. "The Department ordered him not to get involved. Even though I know he does what he can on the cue tee."

"Sometimes I think this is hurting him more than me," Ray said. "And Mom, she must be sick."

"How's it going for you in here?"

"It's like a nightmare," Ray said. "Not that I feel threatened or anything, but the boredom, the control, the nasty attitudes. I don't know how people survive it without killing themselves."

The Christmas holidays were difficult for the whole family. Ray's mother made Dominic go to mass with her every morning for a week.

Dennis called Kathy Reynolds to tell her about his last visit to Ray and how upset Ray was about being in jail over the holidays. She asked Dennis what he was doing for New Year's Eve. He said that he had no plans.

"Why don't you come to McCoy's? It's usually pretty good, and you could use some cheering up."

"Okay. Maybe I will."

They spent New Year's Eve together at McCoy's. Kathy was working as a server and helping at the bar. When she could, she sat and talked to him. There were three televisions over the bar, with three different stations showing the countdown to the ball-drop at Times Square. At midnight, people cheered and kissed one another. When Dennis and Kathy kissed, it was more than a holiday kiss. "I think I've grown close to you through all this," she said.

"I feel the same way," he said.

"When McCoy's closed, she asked him if he wanted to come to her place for a drink."

Dennis almost said yes, but thought better of it. He thought of what his father had said about stealing Ray's girlfriend.

"I'd love to," he said, "but I don't think I should."

"I understand," she said.

After New Year's, the upcoming trial grew larger on everyone's mind. Dennis spent most of his time at Klein's office reading legal cases and, when the lawyers weren't too busy, asking questions.

One afternoon, he passed Klein's office and saw that he didn't look busy, so he stood at the open door and asked. "Can I ask you a question?"

"Of course," Klein said. "Come in. Sit down."

"I was reading this case, *Chambers v. Mississippi*. Do you know it?" Dennis said.

"If I didn't, I wouldn't be much of a defense lawyer."

"I have some questions about it."

"Okay. Shoot."

"If the prosecutor had tried to introduce a statement from someone who wasn't in court, but who had told someone else that they saw Chambers fire the gun, would that statement have been admissible as evidence?"

"No, it's hearsay," Klein said. "You can't take evidence from someone who's not in court, not under oath, and not subject to cross-examination."

Dennis knew that, but he was playing a little dumb. He didn't want to tip his hand what he was thinking about. He asked, "Then why did the Supreme Court say that the defense should have been allowed to introduce the statements of that guy, McDonald?"

"Because the statements were exceptions to the hearsay rule," Klein said. "When people confess or make declarations against their interests, the courts allow the evidence to come in on the theory that no one would place themselves in jeopardy unless what they were saying was truthful."

"But how do you know it's truthful?" Dennis asked. "Couldn't someone just make something up?"

"You're right. That's a perennial problem. But the courts have certain criteria to make sure the statements have what they call 'an indicia of reliability.' Or a recognizable connection to the event. In *Chambers*, that McDonald guy didn't come from nowhere. He was in the crowd when the officer was shot."

"I see," Dennis said. "But this favors the defense."

"Right again, because the defendant has Sixth Amendment constitutional rights, the government doesn't. Courts can't infringe on it. They're reluctant to do anything to prevent an accused from putting on a defense."

Dennis was glad he had asked, because Klein confirmed his understanding of the case. "That explains a lot," he said. "Thanks."

"Anytime you have a question, just ask. Questions are often as helpful to me as they are to the person asking."

That afternoon, Dominic reported for duty at the Manhattan South Homicide squad, and found a department bulletin on his desk. It was about an arrest of four suspects in connection with an armed robbery of a beer distributorship in the Bronx. They were caught in the act because one employee pressed an alarm button and the police surrounded the building. The suspects gave up without a fight.

As soon as Dominic saw the names of the suspects—James Forrest, Willie Mumford, Shaquan Campbell, and Daryl "Buster" Johnson—he suspected that these were the same guys that had robbed the car dealership in Ray's case. Not only were the robberies similar, but the nickname "Buster" jumped out at him.

The week before when Dominic had been investigating Ray's case, he wanted to identify Buster, the drug dealer from whom Ray had said he bought marihuana. He conducted a computer check in the nickname database for "Buster." It was a common nickname, and there were about three hundred 'Busters' on the list, so he hadn't been able to do much, but now he had a full name. The match was too much of a coincidence and the Bronx and Queens robbery suspects were probably the same and Ray probably knew one suspect.

Not wanting to use a department phone, he went out to the street to use a pay phone to call Klein and tell him about the Bronx arrests, including about Buster.

"That's not good," Klein said. "See what else you can find out?"

Dominic called friends and contacts, but no one knew much about it other than what was in the bulletin. He suspected they had been told to stonewall him. Then, about midnight, as he was finishing up his paperwork, his desk phone rang. The caller didn't identify himself.

"This is a friend," the male voice said. "I think you should know that the crew that robbed the Bronx beer distributor is going to be arrested for the Queen's BMW dealership robbery."

"Okay, thanks for the info," Dominic said.

"Your problem is that one perp has flipped. He made a deal with the DA to squeal on all the others, including your son."

Hearing the words, "including your son," Dominic felt as though he had been kicked in the stomach. For a moment he couldn't think straight, and he felt dizzy like he had when he first heard that Ray had been arrested for the robbery.

Before he could ask questions, the caller hung up.

In the morning, he called Klein and told him, "One of the BMW perps is flipping."

Klein answered matter-of-factly, "We expected that. This is going to be a war, and we've got a lot of work to do. Can you find out which one is talking?"

"I'll see what I can do."

Klein knew how serious this was, and he moved into high-gear, immediately calling a meeting of the four staff lawyers he had working on the case. He told them to make the case their top priority. There would be follow-up meetings every day at five o'clock to go over developments and progress reports.

Leading up to the trial, Klein drove his staff hard. They prepared motions that might be needed before, during, and after the trial. They interviewed and re-interviewed witnesses who could be helpful or might testify at the trial. They wrote out possible questions and answers for each potential witness, and a computer technician composed digital slides for Klein to use at trial. Dennis attended most of the meetings and helped by running errands and making copies of records and photographs.

At one meeting, the lawyers discussed a speedy trial motion. They thought it was logical that the DA would try the Bronx case first, so that they could draw connections from the Bronx to be used in the Queens case.

"They have six months from the charges to start Ray's trial," Klein said. "Ray was charged in August, so they have until February. Let's hope they can't make it. If they can't, we'll have to be ready to move to get the case dismissed."

"Should we tell Ray?" Dennis asked. "It might give him some hope. I'm worried about him."

"No," Klein said. "False hope can make things worse."

Dominic kept trying to find out as much information as he could without signaling to headquarters that he was working at cross-purposes with the department. He told himself that he had to do it because blood was thicker than the job. He knew the district attorney's office delayed as long as possible before turning over information that could be helpful to the defense. Some information they wouldn't turn over until the trial started. So, he would get as much information as he could as soon as he could.

Dominic got the criminal records of the four robbery suspects and talked to some detectives who had arrested them in the past. He prepared a profile for each suspect.

Again, about midnight, the same unidentified caller phoned.

"The suspect cooperating with the DA is Daryl 'Buster' Johnson."

This was more bad news—the perp that was flipping was Ray's marihuana dealer, which would strengthen his identification of Ray.

"And get this," the caller said, "he's turned state evidence twice in the past. Both times he got suspended sentences instead of going to prison. And there may have been another one with the feds, but we couldn't find an official record of it."

"Thanks again for the info," Dominic said. "If I can ever repay you, let me know."

"You don't owe me anything," the caller said. "You don't know my name, but this is paying back for something you did for me a long time ago."

When Dominic got home, he lay awake trying to think who the caller could be. He thought it might be Detective Smithers with a disguised voice, but wasn't sure.

In the morning, when Dominic told Klein that Buster was a serial snitch, Klein said that he had struck gold.

At one of the attorney staff meetings, Klein announced, "I was right. The DA couldn't get their case ready to beat the speedy trial deadline. They moved to merge the trials and delay them, but it was denied. So, Ray will be tried alone. That's a relief, but we still have a difficult task ahead of us."

Klein asked Jeff Rosen to assess the case as it stood.

"To be frank," Rosen said, "Ray will probably be convicted, and he should reconsider the plea bargain they offered."

"What makes you say that?" one of the other attorneys, Jack Friedman, asked.

"Because the DA will rehearse this Buster character until he has his testimony memorized," Rosen said. "And accomplice testimony can be very convincing to a jury. Although they can't convict Ray on accomplice testimony without corroborating evidence, they have the corroborating evidence—the identification by the store manager."

"But that identification can be challenged because of the bad photo-array procedures," Friedman said.

"That argument didn't work with the judge, it won't work with the jury," Rosen said.

"Buster can be torn up on the witness stand," another attorney said, "not only for his rap-sheet that's a mile long, but also for the deals he's made in the past. He's a serial squealer. And you can tell the jury what deal he's getting to testify against Ray. That he'll say anything to stay out of jail."

"That's true," Rosen said, "but you have to counter it with something, something like good character evidence, which we don't have. Ray's record, and his so-called job as a bouncer in a strip club, is not the greatest endorsement."

The discussion went on for a while until Klein interrupted, saying, "You've all made good points, but the problem is that the plea bargain the DA offered may not be on the table anymore. They made the offer before they had Buster. Now their case is stronger. Before continuing with this discussion, I've got to see if the plea bargain is still available."

As the meeting ended, Dennis looked around at the lawyers. They didn't seem upset. They were joking with one another as though they had already forgotten that Ray was in jail. This made Dennis angry. Ray being stuck in jail was no skin off their teeth, he thought. They've given up on the case already.

To get away, Dennis went into the storage room, locked the door, then punched one of the file cartons to vent his frustration. He struck another carton with his elbow. He thought that all these lawyers talked a good game, but they have no answers. It seemed they just reacted to whatever the prosecution threw at them. And the DA's snitch would lie through his teeth to get out of jail. And $500,000 bail for Ray was ridiculous. Where was he going to run?

Dennis sat in the storage room and decided that he had to do something. He had a plan that he thought could work. It might be dangerous, but he didn't care. Ray had said he'd go down fighting rather than plead guilty, and Dennis decided he was going to fight right alongside of him.

CHAPTER EIGHT

The next Saturday, Dennis called Kathy Reynolds and asked her if she felt like going for a ride. She did, and they drove to Rockaway Beach in Queens and walked along the boardwalk. It was sunny and relatively warm for a January day, and they enjoyed the fresh air. After they walked for a while, Kathy asked, "How's the case going?"

"Not good," Dennis said. "One defendant flipped and will probably testify against Ray. And I'm afraid the lawyers are giving up. They'll try to get Ray to take a plea bargain."

"I can't believe this," she said. "If Ray was guilty, he'd be the one testifying against the actual robbers. Maybe against the one who fired the gun. But he hasn't, so I think he knows nothing. And he has no reason to protect these guys."

"You're right," he said. "And that's why we've got to do something about it."

"What do you mean?"

"It's getting too cold. Let's go somewhere warm, and I'll explain it and see what you think."

"Okay."

They went to a coffee shop a block from the boardwalk. Except for the owner behind the counter, no one else was in the shop, so they could talk freely at a small table. Dennis went to the counter, got two steaming hot chocolates, and brought them to the table.

"Hot chocolates are the best on a day like this, thanks," Kathy said. "So, tell me what you mean by doing something."

"I've done a lot of research and I've talked to the lawyers, even Mr. Klein," Dennis said. "And there's what you might call a giant loophole in the law that could be used in Ray's case."

"Really. You're sure?"

He leaned forward and spoke just above a whisper. "I'm certain. For example, if a defendant is on trial for a robbery, but someone else, let's call him John Smith, were to confess to the crime, confesses that he was the robber, that would raise a reasonable doubt about the defendant's guilt, and the jury would have to acquit him."

Kathy folded her arms. "Why would this John Smith confess to something he didn't do? He'd be putting himself in jail."

"Not necessarily," Dennis said. "He wouldn't have to testify in court; he would just tell a second person, and then that second person testifies in court that John Smith confessed to the crime. That's got to put a reasonable doubt in the minds of the jurors."

"I don't know too much about it," Kathy said, "but I don't think the court would let the second person testify to what Smith said."

"You're right. It's hearsay, but there are exceptions to the hearsay rule," Dennis said. "A confession is one of them, even when the confession is not to the cops, but just to another person. So, in Ray's case, if our John Smith confessed to someone that he was the one who cased the dealership and drove the getaway car, that would raise a reasonable doubt about Ray's guilt, and the jury would have to acquit him."

"I suppose so," Kathy said, "but what if they then charge John Smith with the crime?"

"It wouldn't be so easy," Dennis said. "All they'd have as evidence is the hearsay statement. Although it would be admissible as an exception because it was a confession, the law says that to convict someone based on a confession, they must have corroborating evidence that connects the person to the crime."

"Maybe they could come up with something," Kathy said.

"Not if we have someone who has an airtight alibi."

"That makes sense. What does Klein think about all this?" Kathy asked.

Dennis leaned back and sipped his hot chocolate.

"He doesn't know. I wouldn't tell him. But I don't think he'd care if someone came forward to talk about some other person confessing. He'd have to use it on behalf of his client."

Kathy looked away, thinking about the idea, then said, "Maybe. But I'm still not sure how it would work."

"Listen, let's say our imaginary John Smith confesses his part in the crime to you."

"To me!"

"Yes. Then you call the police tip hotline and tell them you know who did the robbery, and the cops would have to interview you. You tell them that "John Smith" confessed to you. Then the DA would have to inform Klein of this new, what they call exculpatory evidence, and Klein could call you to testify at Ray's trial that John Smith confessed to you."

"What if this John Smith denies it?"

"He could deny it, but it probably wouldn't matter. Klein will call him as a witness, and he'll either deny it or take the Fifth Amendment. What matters is that the jury hears about his confession from you."

"This is baffling. Who are you going to get to do this? Where are you going to find a John Smith?"

"How about me?"

Kathy laughed derisively. "You can't do it. You'd wind up going to jail yourself."

"You told me once that you'd say whatever was necessary to get Ray out of jail," Dennis said.

"That's true. I said that. But you've put me in a difficult position because now I don't want you to go to jail. I like you too much. And what I'm afraid of is that both of you will wind up in prison, and for a long time."

"I've thought this through," Dennis said, "and I really don't think so. As long as we keep our stories straight, I don't see how they could get me or you for perjury. All you're doing is repeating what I said to you."

"But what if they put you on the witness stand?"

"That's the kicker. I take the Fifth Amendment. So, if I don't testify, they can't charge me with perjury. All we need is for the jury to hear your testimony."

"The jury will not believe me. I'm Ray's girlfriend. I'm his alibi witness. They'd never believe me."

"Okay, that's a problem. I've been thinking about that part. Do you want another hot chocolate?"

"Okay."

Dennis brought two more hot chocolates to the table. "If we could show that you and Ray had broken up," he said, "that would take the girlfriend angle off the table."

Kathy went to the restroom. When she came back, she said, "I have an idea."

"What?"

She leaned forward and whispered, "What if I get Belinda to do it?"

Dennis smiled. "I thought of that, but didn't think I could convince her."

"We might do it together," Kathy said. "And we have to convince her she'll believe what she's saying is the truth."

"How do we manage that?"

"Let me think about it," Kathy said.

Dennis and Kathy drove back from Rockaway to her apartment in Greenpoint. She lived on the sixth floor. After she unlocked her apartment door, she took his hand and led him inside.

In the morning, Dennis woke up in her bed. She was already up and cooking breakfast.

"Do you want coffee?" she said.

Dennis laughed. "Where am I? How did I get here?"

"You know exactly how you got here," she laughed, and kissed him on the lips.

After a breakfast of bacon and eggs, Dennis lay on the couch with Kathy's head lying on his chest. Dennis thought how great this was, and how he could be happy here, but he was also feeling guilty. If this was anything, it was stealing Ray's girlfriend, exactly what his father had told him not to do.

"I guess we're not perfect people," Kathy said.

Dennis was taken aback. He felt she must have been reading his mind.

"I know I'm not perfect," he said, "but you're okay. You're not engaged to Ray or anything."

They spent the rest of the day together, went for a walk, dined in a local restaurant, and talked about Belinda. They made a plan about how to approach her and went over it several times. Kathy contributed more to the plan than he did.

"Do you think she'll do it?" Dennis asked.

"If anyone would, she would. I know her a long time, and she's a bigger risk-taker than most guys I know."

On Monday night, they put their plan into motion. It was Kathy's night off from McCoy's, but shortly before closing time, she went to the restaurant and sat in a booth. There were only a few customers left in the restaurant. Belinda was serving, and came over to take Kathy's order.

"You're out late," Belinda said." What can I get you?"

"Johnny Walker Black on the rocks," Kathy said.

"What's with you? You never drink whiskey."

"I need one tonight."

"Why, what's wrong?"

"Nothing."

Belinda came back with the drink. "Alright, what's wrong?" she said as she sat in the booth across from Kathy.

Kathy took a long drink of her whiskey.

Belinda stared at her. "I know something's wrong. Tell me. Is it Ray?"

Kathy looked away. It was hard for her to look Belinda in the eye. "You know Ray is innocent."

"Yes, I do."

"Do you know who did it?"

"No. Who?"

Kathy finished the rest of her drink. "Dennis did it," she said.

Belinda sat as though frozen in place. "No way, that's impossible," she blurted out.

"It's not impossible. He told me."

They stared at each other until Kathy looked away again.

"I don't believe it," Belinda said. "He wouldn't do that to his own brother."

"Well, he did. And he feels terrible about it. He wants to turn himself in. That's why he told me."

"Maybe he should."

"You're probably right, but I don't know what to say. He's supposed to meet me here in a few minutes."

"He's coming here?"

"Yes."

Belinda went to the bar and came back with two whiskeys, another one for Kathy, and one for herself. As she put the drinks down and slid into the booth, Dennis arrived, took off his jacket, and sat next to Kathy. Belinda stared accusingly at Dennis.

"I'm going to the ladies' room," Kathy said as she left the booth.

Dennis stared back at Belinda. "Kathy told you?" he said.

"Yes. How could you do it? How did you get mixed up in this mess?" Belinda said.

"It's a long story. Well, not too long. I owed these guys a lot of money," Dennis said. "So, they just wanted me to scout out the place. I did it, but then they moved the goal post and said that I had to drive the car."

"So, you really did it?"

"Yes."

Belinda was going to slap him, but pounded the table with her fist. "You need to turn yourself in," she said. "And why didn't you do it when they first arrested Ray?"

"I thought because Ray didn't do it, he'd get out right away."

"What you've done is horrible. And to your brother, no less. You've got to turn yourself in. Or, at least, tell Ray's lawyer."

"I've tried, but I couldn't bring myself to do it."

"Well, if you don't, I will. I can't sit here doing nothing while Ray wastes away in prison. It's not right."

"I can't argue with you," Dennis said as he gave her a slip of paper. "Here's the number for the police hotline. Call them."

"You can bet on it," she said, then got up and walked to the bar. She said something to the bartender, who announced, "It's closing time."

Dennis left the money on the table and went outside to the parking lot. Kathy came out of the restroom and said to Belinda, "Are you okay?"

"He told me he did it," Belinda said. "And I still can't believe anyone would do such a thing. If he doesn't turn himself in, I'll do it for him."

"Do what you think is right," Kathy said.

Kathy and Dennis drove in separate cars back to her apartment.

Dennis was pleased with how well their plan had worked. "I feel like it's going to work. Belinda will be a perfect witness."

"I feel rotten and dishonest," Kathy said, "manipulating Belinda like that."

"Well, it's done now. Let's see what happens. She may not even call."

They went to bed, but Dennis lay awake for hours, having second thoughts about what they had done.

CHAPTER NINE

On Tuesday, the consequences of their actions unfolded. Belinda called Kathy and told her she had called the tip hotline and told them she knew who had driven the getaway car. She said that "Right away Detective McConnell and two other detectives came to my apartment. They asked me the name of the person who did it. When I told them it was Dennis Carbonaro, McConnell almost jumped through the roof. The other detective, I believe his name was Cruz, said he didn't believe me. Then McConnell threatened me that if I was lying, he'd put me in jail."

"What did you say?"

"I told him I was just doing my civic duty, and it wasn't right that he put Ray in jail for something he didn't do."

"Wow. You're incredible," Dennis said.

Meanwhile, Dominic received three phone calls within a half hour from three different detectives, each telling him that someone was accusing Dennis of being one of the perpetrators instead of Ray. The detectives told him that a female, who gave her name as Belinda Ramos, told the hotline that Dennis confessed he committed the crime.

Dominic called Dennis' cell phone. He was still at Kathy's apartment.

"Where are you?" Dominic asked.

"I'm on my way to Klein's office," Dennis lied.

"Well, turn around and meet me at your place. I have to talk to you."

Dennis guessed that his father had found out what had happened. He quickly got dressed and drove to Ridgewood, feeling more nervous than he had ever felt in his life.

His father was there before him, sitting in his car outside the house. They went up the stairs to the second-floor apartment, and Dominic made Dennis sit on a kitchen chair while he stood over him and started asking questions, slowly and methodically.

"Who is Belinda Ramos?"

"She works in McCoy's with Kathy. They're good friends."

"Why did she call the hotline to say that you committed Ray's robbery?"

"Someone must have told her that."

"Who?"

Dennis took a breath and decided to get this over with instead of having his teeth pulled out one by one. I told her to do it to give Ray a chance to beat the charges."

"How is she going to do that?"

"Because I told this Belinda that I did it. And she'll tell the jury that a third person, me, confessed to the crime, and that will create enough reasonable doubt so that the jury will have to acquit Ray."

Dominic sat and put his elbow on the kitchen table with his right hand to his forehead, trying to absorb it all. "I can't believe you did this," he said. "You're putting your head in a noose. And for nothing. It'll never work."

"There's only one way to find out," Dennis said, his nervousness subsiding. "I've done a lot of research on this, and checked it out. There's a Supreme Court case that allows this kind of outside testimony. In fact, it requires that it be admitted into evidence."

"Remind me again," Dominic said. "What law school did you go to?"

"I can read a supreme court case.

Dominic looked up with a sardonic smile on his face. "You might find out that the local courts and local judges don't always read or follow the Supreme Court."

"Then we can appeal."

They sat without talking for a few minutes until Dominic asked, "How did you get this girl, Belinda, to call the hotline?"

"Well, that's the good part. She believes I told her the truth, and she's going to believe that she's telling the truth. She doesn't think she's lying."

Dominic nodded, as though he was understanding the plan. "This is quite a scam that you've cooked up. I just hope you don't wind up in prison. One son in prison is enough."

"Can they put two sons in prison for one crime?" Dennis asked, making a bad joke.

"They might," Dominic said. "Does Klein know about this?"

"No."

"We have to tell him."

Dominic phoned Klein's office to set up an appointment. The secretary said Klein would be available tomorrow, but Dominic insisted, "We need to do it today. It's urgent."

"Hold on," the secretary said. After a minute, she was back. "Can you be here by five?"

"Yes. We're on the way."

When Dominic and Dennis arrived, Klein was standing at his desk, obviously concerned. He knew Dominic wouldn't have said something was "urgent" unless it was.

"So, what's the emergency?" he asked and signaled for them to take seats in front of his desk.

Dominic explained what had happened. It took a few minutes and some stops and starts to outline the plan that Dennis had concocted to get Kathy's friend, Belinda Ramos, to call the tip hotline. "Belinda will testify to that," he said, "and if Dennis is called to the witness stand, he'll take the Fifth Amendment."

Klein sat quietly, absorbing all the information.

"Is that about, right?" Dominic asked his son.

"Yes. Exactly," Dennis said

Looking directly at Dennis, Klein said, "So, that's why you were so interested in the *Chambers* case. I thought you were up to something, but I couldn't have imagined that you'd go this far. You've heard the saying, 'What tangled web we weave when we first practice to deceive'? Haven't you?"

"Shakespeare, right?"

"That's what people think. But it's Sir Walter Scott."

"I didn't know that," Dennis said.

"Putting that aside," Klein said, "I have to give you credit for initiative, or creativity. From when I first met you, I thought you could be a great lawyer. But sometimes great lawyers are too creative."

"Should I take that as a compliment?" Dennis asked.

"Don't," Klein said as he swiveled his chair around and looked out the window, posing as though he were in deep thought. After a minute or two, he turned back to them and again looked at Dennis. "It is a compliment, but there's a problem. I have to fire you. The trial starts next week, and because you're a potential witness, you can't work on the case, or even work in the office. And I can't be a party to a fraud on the court."

Instead of acting as though he had been chastised, Dennis responded forcefully, as though he had been insulted. "You're not involved in any fraud on the court. As far as you know, I did it. And I'm saying I did it."

"But you didn't."

"How do you know?"

"So, you want to go to jail?"

"If I have to."

Klein leaned back in his chair and held his chin with his right hand. "I've got to think about this."

Dominic and Dennis waited until Klein finally said, "The best part of this is that if the DA doesn't tell me about this Belinda in discovery, I'll have an automatic appeal."

Dennis said something, but Dominic interrupted, "I'm pretty sure they'll tell you about the tip hotline. I had calls from three detectives who knew about it, so it's gotta be in the pipeline to the DA."

"We'll see," Klein said. "Sometimes they shoot themselves in the foot."

"That's for sure," Dominic said.

"And it would be something if Dennis' scheme winds up winning the case," Klein said. Then he turned to Dennis: "But, no matter what, you're stilled fired."

Driving back to Brooklyn, Dominic said, "Congratulations, you got yourself fired."

"Yeah. That hurt," Dennis said.

"I think you've bitten off more than you can chew. You're in the big leagues with these guys, and I hope to God that they never call you to testify. In fact, I hope Klein doesn't even call Belinda."

You're forgetting something, Dad."

"What?"

"Ray is still in jail, facing twenty-five years."

"I know. That's why I'm even listening to this insane scheme of yours."

"I've thought this through, every which way," Dennis said. "I don't think it's so insane."

"We'll find out soon enough. In the meantime, what are you going to do for a job?"

"I'll go back to UPS. I'm on a leave of absence and they told me I can come back anytime. So, I'll go back in three weeks. The trial should be over by then."

CHAPTER TEN

Ray's trial began on a Monday. As much as Judge Brown wanted to move the case along, the proceedings moved slowly. The lawyers had motions and arguments that they had to make and that the judge had to hear. It took all day.

On Tuesday, jury selection began with the judge and the lawyers asking the prospective jurors a series of questions about their knowledge of the case, their relationships with any of the parties or relatives of the parties, their personal history involving crimes and other trials, and their ability to be impartial. It took two and a half days. Ray sat at the defense table through it all. It was tedious for him, but he told his father that it was better than sitting in a cell not knowing what was going on. When the questioning was completed, the lawyers met with the judge in his chambers. Some prospective jurors were removed for cause and others by peremptory challenges.

By Thursday afternoon, jury selection was done. The survivors were six men and six women, four African Americans, two Hispanics, and six whites, and also two alternates in case one or two jurors could not continue.

Klein prided himself on picking good juries, but admitted, "You never know what they'll do. The slightest thing can turn them against you. Sometimes they go in directions you could never have imagined."

Dennis was disappointed that he hadn't been allowed to sit in the courtroom to watch the jury selection. Since he was listed as a potential witness, it barred him from the proceedings.

He waited across the hall in the attorney-witness room. To break the monotony, he took walks around the building, stopping in different courtrooms where trials or hearings were going on. He watched the proceedings to get an idea of what to expect when they called him to the witness stand.

Judge Brown told the jurors that the trial would start Monday, when they would hear the opening statements and witness testimony. He told them not to talk to anyone about the case, even other jurors, especially other jurors. "Conceivably, there could be media coverage of the trial," he said. "If you hear or see something about it, don't listen, don't read, don't watch. Your job is to decide based on the facts placed in evidence here, not what someone says in the media. With that said, have a nice weekend."

The weekend was crunch-time in Klein's office, with the staff in full gear preparing for the trial. The district attorney had turned over *Rosario* and *Brady's* discovery materials to the defense. *Rosario* materials are copies of all prior statements that potential witnesses gave to the police or the prosecution; *Brady* materials are any exculpatory materials that could be favorable to the defendant, such as leads about other suspects. For some time, prosecutors had been reluctant to turn over *Brady* material, but after several chastising court decisions, they now gave the defense everything, often throwing in as much irrelevant and meaningless material as they could in order to overwhelm the defense with paper work.

Included in the *Brady* material were dozens of hotline tips about the robbery; the tip of Belinda was among them. Klein was disappointed. He had been hoping that they wouldn't turn over Belinda's call, because that would have been an appealable issue.

On Saturday, Dennis couldn't just sit home and do nothing, so he drove to Klein's office to help. But Klein told him to go home. "I told you, you're on the witness list, so you can't be a part of the defense team."

"I guess that means you're going to call Belinda to testify," Dennis said.

"I haven't decided yet," Klein said.

"What about me?"

"Maybe. But if we do, I'll prep you as I would any other witness."

"Okay. See you Monday."

Dennis was glad that Klein was apparently going along with his plan, but he was also nervous about his testimony. He thought about whether he was doing the right thing. Even though he was doing it for his brother, who he believed was being railroaded by the cops and the DA, he worried that he might have made a big mistake. He felt it in the pit of his stomach. The way he was feeling, he didn't want to go home to an empty apartment, so he drove to McCoy's to see Kathy.

She was working behind the bar, and Belinda was waitressing.

He took a seat at the bar, but Kathy didn't acknowledge him or come over to wait for him. After a few minutes, she nodded toward the restrooms. He went down a hall into the back, where the restrooms were located. She followed him into the men's room and locked the door.

"You shouldn't come here until the trial is over," she whispered. "McConnell was here last night looking around, and I think there might be a couple of cops in the place now, watching."

"Okay," he said. "I'll call you later."

"Don't," she said. "They could tap the phone."

"You're getting paranoid."

"There's a sign on the back wall that says, 'Just because you're paranoid, it doesn't mean they're not out to get you.'"

Kathy didn't hug or kiss him and went back behind the bar. He left and drove home.

On Monday, the second week of the trial, Judge Brown didn't waste any time. The jury was seated; the defendant was brought out, and the Assistant District Attorney Bill Walsh began his opening statement. He read the charges against the defendant and described the crime. He told the jurors that they would hear witnesses who would identify the defendant as a participant in the crime.

"You're going to learn that three men wearing masks entered the car dealership, pointing guns at the employees and customers. They took wallets, money, and watches from them. The perpetrators also forced the manager to open a safe and turn over more than $30,000 in cash.

"Before they left, one perpetrator fired a 9mm, automatic pistol. The bullet ricocheted off a metal door and struck one customer, Larry Coates, in the neck. Mr. Coates subsequently died from his wound."

Walsh let that sink in, and the courtroom grew solemn.

Then, he continued, "Whether the perpetrator intended to shoot Mr. Coates or not does not matter. As the judge will instruct you, under the law, when a perpetrator, while committing a serious crime such as robbery, causes the death of a non-participant in the crime, the perpetrator is guilty of felony murder, a crime considered as serious as intentional murder.

"Under our law, all the accomplices to the robbery are also guilty of felony murder, whether they were present or not.

"The defendant on trial, Mr. Carbonaro, was not one of those three masked men inside the dealership at the time of the robbery, but the evidence will show that he was their accomplice. The evidence will show that the defendant's actions before and after the robbery prove that he was acting in concert with the masked perpetrators and was part of the conspiracy to commit the robbery.

"A witness, Mr. Ginelli, the dealership manager, will testify that, prior to the robbery, the defendant was in the dealership pretending to be shopping for a car, an expensive BMW. But, as you will see, the defendant had no capacity to buy such an expensive car. The People allege he was really there to case the dealership to prepare for the robbery, and that is one question you will have to decide.

"You're going to learn that after the robbery was completed, the defendant was seen picking up the perpetrators and driving the getaway car, a red Camaro, registered in his name.

"You're going to hear about the police response to the robbery, how their investigation led to the arrest of this defendant, how his photograph was identified by the witness, and how he was picked out of a lineup.

"That, ladies and gentlemen, is the evidence that will prove to you, beyond a reasonable doubt, that the defendant, Raymond J. Carbonaro, committed the crimes charged in this indictment.

"As jurors, there's going to be only one thing left for you do to, and that is to find him guilty."

When ADA Walsh finished, Judge Brown took a short recess before Klein would give his opening statement.

Klein didn't believe in long opening statements by the defense. He thought that if a lawyer promised too much during the opening statement but didn't produce the evidence to back it up, he would severely hurt his case. Actually, he would rather waive an opening statement entirely. There was no need to do it because the defendant had a right to remain silent and did not have to present any evidence. In some cases, Klein only gave an opening statement because the client was paying him a handsome fee, and expected his lawyer to work hard on his behalf.

Klein thought it wiser to wait to see what the prosecution presented before addressing it. He would save his best arguments for his closing statement, but he decided to give a short opening.

The jury returned from the recess, and Judge Brown said, "Proceed."

Klein stood before the jury box. "Thank you for being here," he began. "Your role as jurors is of the highest importance to our system of criminal justice and to the freedom of all of us."

He pointed to the inscriptions of the Declaration of Independence and the Bill of Rights displayed on the wall behind the judge's bench. "Your role is to fulfill the principles written in these documents, and your duty is to stand by these principles when deciding the fate of the young man who sits here accused of participating in a heinous crime."

Klein stood next to Ray and put his right hand on Ray's shoulder. "A crime he did not commit, and which he vehemently and categorically denies."

Klein moved back to the jury box and put his hands on the railing. "I ask you not to make up your minds until you hear all the evidence.

Sometimes jurors react to the first evidence they hear and make up their minds too early, rushing to judgment. Once they've made up their minds, they disregard or downplay subsequent evidence that contradicts their first impressions. I am asking you to wait until the last witness has spoken before even attempting to decide.

"You've heard the district attorney tell you what occurred inside the car dealership. Three men wearing masks entered with guns and robbed people and that Mr. Coates was shot and killed. But, you'll see, that Mr. Carbonaro was not there and was not involved. He was somewhere else at the time of the robbery.

"The witness, who has said that he saw the getaway driver, couldn't identify the defendant. And, just a thought for your consideration: the defendant's father is a New York City Police Department First-Grade Detective. His son, Ray, has a lot of familiarity with crime and police work. Would he use his own car, with his plate number, to commit this robbery?

"It's inconceivable to me."

Klein went back to the defense table and spoke from there. "As for the witnesses inside the dealership, they said that the suspect allegedly casing the dealership had long hair. The police then showed them an old photograph of Mr. Carbonaro when he had long hair. One witness picked him out from that and that's why Ray was placed in a lineup. But, at the time of the robbery, the defendant had short hair. And you'll learn that at the lineup the police put baseball caps on all the participants, covering up the fact that the defendant had short hair, not long hair, which would have allowed the witnesses to say, 'That's not him.'"

"Objection, speculation," ADA Walsh said.

"Overruled," Judge Brown said.

Klein walked back and forth before the jury box.

"Ladies and gentlemen, the person who committed this crime should be punished, but Ray Carbonaro is not that person.

"The prosecution is going to present a witness, one of the masked perpetrators, a person by the name of Daryl Buster Johnson, to testify against the defendant. But don't accept his testimony at face value until you hear about his record and his motivation. You'll learn that he makes a habit of testifying against others in order to avoid going to jail himself. Wait until you hear his answers to our hard and tough questions before making a judgment whether he is believable or not.

"So, I ask you to keep an open mind, use your common sense, watch whether or how the witnesses stretch or bend the truth, and make sure the prosecution meets its burden to prove their case beyond a reasonable doubt.

"In conclusion, always remember that Ray Carbonaro has the privilege of being innocent until proven guilty. A right we all have. He walked in here innocent, and once you've looked at the evidence, you'll find him not guilty, and he'll leave here innocent. Thank you."

After the opening statements, Judge Brown sent the jurors to lunch with the usual admonishment not to talk about the case. He intended to take testimony after lunch, but both the lawyers had arguments and complaints about each other's opening statements, which took an hour to settle, so the judge postponed the witness testimony until the next morning, and dismissed the jury for the day.

In conference with the lawyers, the judge asked, "Who's your first witness and how long will it take?"

ADA Walsh said he would call one of the dealership employees to establish the crime, then Detective McConnell, whose direct examination should take about two hours.

"How long for the detective's cross?" the judge asked Klein.

"It could go for several hours," Klein said.

"At this rate, we'll be here for a month," the judge said.

"Well, I'm hoping that after I cross-examine McConnell, the DA will drop the case."

"Good luck with that," Walsh said with a sarcastic laugh.

CHAPTER ELEVEN

On Tuesday, Dominic sat in the first spectators' row behind the defense table. Dennis couldn't be in the courtroom because he was a potential witness.

The first witness that ADA Walsh called was Jonny Fowler, one of the dealership employees. Fowler described how the masked robbers burst into the dealership, shouting, cursing and pointing guns at everyone. They took wallets, money, and a couple of watches. When they tried to take a customer's Rolex watch, the customer hesitated as if to resist. One of the robbers fired a shot to scare him, and the bullet must have ricocheted off something and struck the unfortunate Mr. Coates. The customer then gave up the watch.

Klein had only four questions on cross-examination.

"You couldn't see the faces of the three masked robbers. Is that right?"

"That's right."

"But you could tell their race?"

"Yes. I believe they were all Afro-American."

"When the robbery was occurring, you didn't see the defendant, Ray Carbonaro, in the dealership. Right?"

"That's right."

"And you don't have any reason to believe that he was in the dealership while the robbery was going on. Is that right?"

"Yes."

"No further questions."

Next, Detective McConnell took the witness stand and testified essentially to the same matters he had testified to at the preliminary hearing. He talked about responding to the crime scene, interviewing witnesses, calling the forensics unit, and recovering videos from the security cameras. He took a statement from the manager, Mr. Ginelli, who told him about a suspect who had been in the dealership the week before, apparently casing the place.

McConnell testified how, in an attempt to identify that suspect, he viewed the videos taken by the outside security cameras. For cars seen parked at or circling the dealership, he traced their plate numbers and identified the registered owners. Several of the owners fit the general description of the suspect, so he put their photos in a photo-array along with a photograph of the defendant. He showed the photo-array to the witnesses, and obtained a positive identification of the defendant. Then, he conducted a lineup in which the defendant was again identified as the suspect.

Klein's cross-examination went directly to the discrepancy between the length of Ray's hair at the time of his arrest and the length of his hair in the old photograph that the detectives displayed to the witnesses.

"The witnesses described the person they thought was casing the dealership as having long, dirty blond hair," Klein said. "Is that correct?"

"Yes. Not too long, but somewhat long," McConnell answered.

"Did some of them describe his hair as covering his ears and going down his neck?"

"Yes."

"When you arrested the defendant, you saw the length of his hair. Is that correct?"

"Yes."

"And would you agree his hair was shorter than the description the witnesses gave?"

"Yes. But we don't know how long his hair was the week before when he was in the dealership," McConnell said.

"Objection," Klein said. "Ask that the last part of the answer be stricken from the record. The witness is speculating."

"Sustained," the judge said. "Strike the words 'when he was in the dealership,' and the jury is to disregard those words."

Klein continued, "Did you do anything to find out how long his hair was that week?"

"What do you mean?"

"Did you interview family, friends, or acquaintances?"

ADA Walsh stood, "Objection, compound question."

"Let's see what his answer is," the judge said.

"Did you interview any of those people," Klein said.

"No."

"Detective, you had in your possession a photograph of the defendant with short hair. Is that right?"

"Yes."

"And the photo with short hair was more recent than the photo in which he had long hair. Correct?"

"Yes."

"But you didn't show the witnesses that photograph, the more recent photo with the shorter hair. Is that right?"

"Yes."

"And at the lineup, you had the participants, including the defendant, all wear hats to cover their hair. Correct?"

"Yes. But we did that so that no one would stand out."

"But the effect was that the witnesses couldn't see that the defendant's hair was much shorter than they had described. Is that correct?"

"Yes. But the point was that they were identifying his facial characteristics, not his hair."

"You just said that 'they' were identifying his facial characteristics. Who did you mean?"

"Mr. Ginelli, the store manager," McConnell said.

"Did anyone else, such as a customer, or another employee, positively identify him?"

"A few said that he fit the general description, but they couldn't be absolutely sure."

"So, none of these other witnesses identified his facial characteristics. Is that correct?"

"Yes. But the store manager did," McConnell said. "That was enough for an arrest."

"Correct me if I'm wrong, but your contention is that if one person makes a positive identification but several other witnesses say no, you still make an arrest. Is that what you're saying?"

"Yes. If the person making the identification is sure, it's enough for an arrest. It's up to the officer's discretion."

"Speaking of the officer's discretion, you know the defendant's father. Is that correct?"

McConnell shifted in his chair as though he was getting uncomfortable. "Yes," he said.

Klein then questioned him on the same issues raised at the preliminary hearing about competition, jealousy, and bias between detectives in the police department.

Judge Brown tried to cut it off and told the lawyers to approach the bench. "We don't want to go down this road," he said.

"At the hearing you cut off this line of questioning," Klein responded, "but you said we could do it at the trial."

The judge glared at Klein. "Alright, go ahead, but don't waste too much time."

"Yes. Your honor."

Klein questioned McConnell on his decision to focus on Ray, implying that he did it because over the years he had had disagreements with Dominic Carbonaro, Ray's father, a first-grade detective. Klein pointed out that McConnell was still only a third-grade detective and may have harbored some animosity, either conscious or unconscious, toward Dominic, and that animosity may have influenced his decision to arrest his son, Ray.

Judge Brown stood and boomed, "Enough."

Klein said "No further questions," satisfied that he had made the point to the jury, and relying on the old maxim that you can't un-ring a bell once it's been rung.

The judge announced, "Court is adjourned until tomorrow at nine o'clock sharp."

As Ray was taken out of the courtroom, he turned and gave a thumbs-up sign to his father.

At Klein's office, the secretary ordered sandwiches for everyone.

Dennis said, "Ray looked optimistic after the cross-examination of McConnell."

Dominic said to Klein, "You did a great job."

"That was the easy part," Klein said. "We knew what to expect. But tomorrow they bring on their star witness, and we don't know how it's going to go."

"He's a professional squealer," Rosen said.

Klein asked Dominic, "Have you come up with anything else on him?"

"I have friends checking with the feds. They don't generally give out anything, but I'm working on it."

"We need it by tomorrow. Let me know if anything is on the way."

"Okay."

Dominic had spent hours going through the files on Forest, Mumford, Campbell, and Buster Johnson, and the records of their known associates. He recognized the names of several people whom he had arrested or investigated in the past. One was an associate of Buster Johnson's who was known for sticking up illegal casinos and numbers spots. Those crimes are not generally reported to the police, and Dominic guessed that Buster may also have been involved in those robberies.

When Dominic left Klein's office, he drove to Washington Heights in Upper Manhattan to talk to his best source of information, Arturo Gonzalez, who was known as Arturo the Spaniard. Dominic had arrested him years ago when he had been assigned to the Vice Division and had raided an illegal gambling casino in a warehouse.

The night of the raid on the casino was unusual because, in addition to betting at roulette wheels, blackjack tables, or crap tables, the customers were betting on a world series baseball game that was being shown on a giant television screen. They bet on every inning, every batter, every pitch. Customers bet on whether the next pitch would be a strike or a ball. They would bet whether the batter would get a hit or an out, hit a fly or a grounder, strike out or walk, how many runs would be scored in each inning, or anything else they could think of that was worth a bet.

The raid had been conducted for maximum effect because it was World Series time, and there were more than a hundred customers in the casino and a lot of money was changing hands. It was expected that the boss, Arturo, would be there, too, because it was such a money-making night.

Before the raid, undercover police officers, pretending to be customers, infiltrated the casino and identified the casino workers, whether they were dealers, bankers, or managers. When the undercover officers gathered enough evidence, they signaled to their backup team, who raided the casino and shut down the gambling operation.

Not everyone was arrested, only the casino workers, but it took time to sort them out. Usually, there wasn't any trouble. The customers who may have thought they were going to be arrested were relieved when they found out they would be quickly released. And the workers knew that they'd only be getting a desk appearance ticket, meaning that they would be taken to the nearest police station, given a summons to appear in court at a later date, and released. The penalty was usually a fine, and most pled guilty.

While sorting out who was who, the police moved the customers to one side of the room. The workers, who were to be arrested, were seated on a row of chairs. They were frisked but not handcuffed. They knew the routine and wouldn't be handcuffed until they were taken to the police station. Arturo was sitting with the workers. He looked at Dominic, who seemed to be the senior detective in charge, and asked to speak with him privately.

"Sure. What can I do for you?" Dominic said.

"You know me, I'm always cooperative with the police. I know you're doing your job."

"That's right."

"But someone you have sitting here is not a worker."

"Which one?"

"That young man wearing the blue shirt. That's my son. He's eighteen."

"But he was identified as a banker. You know how it works."

"It must have been a mistake. He only came here because of the world series. He's a baseball fan. And he's a straight-A student, trying to get into West Point. If he gets arrested, it will destroy his chances."

Dominic thought for a moment. He had never heard that Arturo had a son working for him. It didn't make sense that such a bright kid would be involved in this, or that Arturo would allow it.

"But we have only six people, including yourself, as workers," Dominic said. "There must be more than that to deal with all these customers."

"I'll tell you who they are," Arturo said.

"Okay."

Arturo walked to the middle of the room and called across the room, "Fernando, Carlos, Raoul, Eric, come sit over here."

The four men did as they were told, left the customers, crossed the room, and sat with the workers.

Dominic pointed to Arturo's son in the blue shirt. "You're a customer, right."

"That's right," he said.

"Then go over and stand with the customers."

This is when Dominic and Arturo became friends.

Arturo did not become the typical informant for the police, but he knew what was going in the streets and the underworld. He didn't inform on other gambling operations, but if he knew who committed a particularly vicious crime, he'd be helpful to the police, and on several occasions had helped Dominic solve a case or locate a criminal.

Dominic told him that he appreciated his help, but it didn't mean that he wouldn't make an arrest in one of Arturo's places, or of Arturo himself, if he had to."

"Of course. I understand," Arturo said.

Since the night of that raid, Arturo had partly legitimized himself as a reputable businessman. He owned a dozen bodegas and had become the president of the Manhattan and Bronx Bodega Association, which brought him political connections. But he still had a foot in the underworld. The headquarters of the association was in the backroom of a storefront on St. Nicholas Avenue in Washington Heights.

Dominic had Arturo's phone number but wouldn't call him because it was possible that the call would be picked up on a wiretap by one law enforcement agency or another. Although Dominic was engaging in lawful police work, he didn't want it known who his source of information was. He would go to a bodega that Arturo owned and ask for him. Within an hour or so, Arturo would get in touch with him by calling from a pay phone, and name a time and place to meet.

So, Dominic drove to the Bodega Association where the counterman asked him what he wanted. The Bodega Association headquarters in the backroom was actually the headquarters for Arturo's gambling operations.

"Is Arturo around? Tell him Dominic Carbonaro would like to see him."

"Wait here," the man said, and went into the backroom.

After five minutes, the man came back and invited Dominic to follow him.

They walked through a large room where there were eight or nine men seated at tables playing cards or dominoes. On the side were three large paper shredding machines and three barrels filled with shredded paper. Dominic knew that these papers were number slips that the runners and bookies had written down to keep records of who won and who lost the daily lottery number.

The number was determined six days a week by the last three numbers of the total bets made at either the Aqueduct, Belmont, or Saratoga race track, whichever was operating. The bookies and runners had to turn the slips in to the headquarters bank before the end of the horse racing day.

The records had to be kept to resolve any disputes, but it was a crime to possess such records. As soon as possible, the records were shredded so that they couldn't be used as evidence for a charge of unlawful gambling. Dominic figured that the barrels filled with paper represented hundreds of thousands of bets, probably averaging five dollars each. That amounted to a lot of money, half of it profit, since the odds of picking the winning number were a thousand to one, but the payoff was five hundred dollars for a dollar bet. The cash for all these bets was not here. It was secreted somewhere else. Not getting robbed was the most critical part of the business.

The next room was Arturo's office. The counterman knocked, a buzzer sounded, and a young man wearing a hoodie opened the door. Dominic assumed he was a bodyguard and was probably armed. Arturo got up from behind his desk and shook Dominic's hand. He wore a blue-denim shirt and a brown leather sleeveless vest. "It's good to see you, my friend," he said. "What can I do for you?" Arturo always greeted him that way. It was what Dominic had said to him the first time they met.

"First, how's your son doing at West Point," Dominic asked.

"Great. One more year. And I always thank you for what you did for him."

"I'm glad. But now it's my turn. I don't know if you heard that my son was arrested in connection with the robbery of that BMW dealer in Queens."

"I did hear about it. I'm sorry."

"An informant is testifying against him tomorrow. He made a deal in exchange for his testimony. I was wondering if you knew anything about him that we could use. He was a stickup man and, in addition to businesses, robbed drug dealers, and numbers spots."

"What's his name?"

"Buster Johnson."

"Sit down, I may be able to help," Arturo said.

To the bodyguard, he said, "Go down the block to Cartwright's office and tell him to come here right away."

When the bodyguard left, Arturo said, "Harry Cartwright is my security guy. If anyone knows anything about stickups, he does."

While waiting, Dominic told Arturo about the case against his son.

Arturo listened and then said, "So, your son was not inside the car place. I'm surprised they didn't try to make a deal with him."

"Yeah. It makes you wonder. The detective who has the case is not a friend of mine, to say the least, and, I suspect, wasn't out to help my son."

"What's the detective's name?"

"McConnell."

Arturo nodded as though recognizing the name. "We had some dealings with him," he said. He began to say something else, but, at the moment, Cartwright knocked and came into the office. He was a large man, over six feet tall and packing about two hundred and fifty pounds of mostly muscle. He wore a three-quarter length black leather coat that he kept on. Dominic figured he had a gun underneath it.

"Yes, boss," he said to Arturo.

"Harry, this is my friend, Detective Carbonaro. He needs to know anything you know about Buster Johnson. You can talk freely."

Cartwright took a seat. "Buster, sure. He's a bald guy with the gold earring. Right?"

"Right," Dominic said. "He did stick ups, and is now testifying against everybody and anybody. What can you tell me?"

"A lot. He tried to shake down some of our number spots. I guess he didn't realize who owned them. So, he gave that up and started robbing regular businesses."

"Our business is a regular business," Arturo interrupted.

"Right, boss," Cartwright answered. "And Buster did a lot of other stuff—dealing coke, marijuana, steroids. One time he sold bad shit, and people got sick, one died. So, the feds went after him, and he got busted for a sale of five ounces of coke to a DEA agent. That's funny. Buster got busted. But it wasn't funny. He flipped, and didn't give anyone any slack. He named everybody, every dealer he knew, and I think he threw some people into the soup who didn't belong there. He gave so much information that the US Attorney declined to prosecute, and Buster never had to appear in court."

Dominic hadn't known about the DEA arrest, or non-arrest. "That's very helpful," he said.

"What's amazing is that even after he became an informant, he was still doing robberies," Cartwright said. "He must have thought he was untouchable. He could make some money, and then if he got caught, all he had to do was rat everybody out, and he'd still be out on the street."

"I'm surprised nobody put a bullet in his head," Dominic said.

"He came close a few times."

"Too bad," Dominic said.

"You're the police," Cartwright said, laughing, "You're not supposed to be routing for people to get whacked."

"It depends who the person is."

Cartwright laughed again. "So, if the person who gets whacked deserved it, the guy who killed him should get less time in the joint."

"Someone once said, sometimes it's hard to figure out whether a murderer deserves the electric chair or a medal," Dominic said.

"Isn't that the truth," Cartwright said.

They all laughed.

"Do you have any names, dates, locations of these robberies, and what happened in court?"

"Yes. I've got a lot written down. Anything that affects our business, I keep track of it all." He looked at Arturo, who nodded yes. "I'll make you a copy of the Buster stuff."

"That would be great."

"I'll be right back," Cartwright said, and he left the room to go to his office.

Arturo went over to a stainless-steel Expresso machine. "Would you like some Expresso?" he said.

Dominic didn't want any, it would probably keep him awake for two days, but he said yes. He had learned that when someone offers you something that they're culturally attached to, you should accept it.

Arturo drew two Expressos and put them on the desk, and he reached in a draw for bottle of Sambuca. "Want some?"

"Sure," Dominic said.

Arturo poured the Sambuca into the Expressos and they toasted to each other's health.

When Cartwright returned with photocopies of his notebook, Dominic looked through them, astonished at how detailed they were, with names, dates, locations, courts, even the lawyers involved.

"This is great," Dominic said. "I'm impressed. We could use you in the detective bureau."

"He makes more money here," Arturo said.

Dominic stood and shook Cartwright's hand. "Thanks so much, this will be very helpful."

Then he and Arturo shook hands.

"I'll be praying for your son," Arturo said.

"And I'll pray for yours," Dominic said.

Dominic drove South on East River Drive to his office on East 21st Street where he logged into the Department computer to see whether he could verify the information from Cartwright's notebook. He worked until four in the morning. He found records that matched almost everything, and printed them out. There was a redacted report regarding the DEA arrest of Buster.

Dominic went home, showered, and without any sleep, drove to the court. He met Klein just as he was arriving, and gave him a copy of the records. He was amazed how wide awake he was after being up all night. Maybe it was the Expresso coffee Arturo had given him.

CHAPTER TWELVE

A t 9 a.m. sharp, Judge Brown took the bench. He dispensed with some housekeeping details, then had the jury brought in. "Call your next witness," he said to ADA Walsh.

Walsh stood. "I call Daryl Johnson."

A court officer ushered Johnson in from the hallway. Johnson was over six feet tall, with a muscular body and a completely clean-shaven head. He raised his right hand and swore to tell the truth. He seemed confident and reached for a paper cup and the water pitcher on the witness stand. With steady hands, he poured a cup of water.

ADA Walsh began by bringing out that Johnson was a cooperating witness. The consensus among trial lawyers has been that it is better to bring out your witness' negative information up front rather than letting the other side bring it out later and act as though they had caught the witness covering up something.

"You're testifying here today under an agreement with the district attorney," Walsh said. "Is that right?"

"Yes."

"Part of the agreement is that you will testify completely and truthfully about your participation in the robbery of the car dealership."

"Yes."

"You're doing this in exchange for a promise of leniency and that if you are found to have been completely truthful, you will receive a sentence of one-year incarceration and three-year probation for your part in the robbery. Is that correct?"

"Yes."

"And if you are found not to have been completely truthful, the agreement will be void, and they could sentence you to the maximum punishment allowable by law. Correct?"

"Yes."

"Alright. Now tell us in your own words about your involvement in the robbery and who your accomplices were."

"Yes, sir.

Johnson, confidently and without an inkling of guilt, described how he and his friends, James Forest, Willie Mumford, and Shaquan Campbell, had been committing robberies. They robbed stores and business where there was cash not yet deposited in a bank. They usually worked with an inside man, an employee who knew where the cash was kept and when bank deposit runs were scheduled. They also robbed customers and employees of their wallets, and sometimes their watches and jewelry.

"We didn't have anyone on the inside in the BMW dealership," Johnson said, "but James Forrest knew this white guy who owed him a lot of money, about four thousand dollars for some illegal steroids James had sold him. The white guy got robbed of the steroids before he could resell them, so he didn't have the money to pay James Forrest.

"Instead of payment, James made him scout out the BMW dealership. If we made a good score, he'd forgive the money that the white guy owed him."

ADA Walsh interrupted, "And what was the name of this white guy?"

"I didn't know his whole name, but it's Ray Carbonaro."

"Look around the courtroom. Do you see him anywhere here?"

"Yes."

"Point him out, please."

"He's the guy sitting at the defense table next to the lawyer," Johnson said as he pointed to Ray.

"What's he wearing?"

"A blue shirt."

Judge Brown stood. "Let the record reflect that the witness has identified the defendant."

"Thank you, your honor," ADA Walsh said.

Walsh continued questioning Johnson, who explained that during the robbery "one customer balked at giving up his watch, a Rolex, so Shaquan fired a shot. He didn't mean to shoot him. He only wanted to scare him, and scare everybody, but somehow this other guy got hit."

Johnson explained that after the robbery, they drove away in the white guy's car into a parking garage where they split the money four ways. They didn't give any money to the white guy, but Forest told him the debt was gone, and, as a bonus, he gave him the Rolex watch that they'd taken from the customer.

ADA Walsh timed his examination so that it would end right before the one o'clock lunch recess. He did this so that Klein couldn't start cross-examining Johnson until after lunch. The jurors would be left through their lunch period with the prosecution's evidence fresh and unchallenged in their minds.

Klein used the lunch break to go over the records on Johnson that Dominic had given him, and when court resumed, he began cross-examining Johnson.

"Good afternoon. My name is Murray Klein, and I represent the defendant. I'm going to ask you some questions, and I want you to answer just yes or no, if you can. Is that okay?"

"Yes. Maybe."

Klein stood right in front of the witness. "You were not caught in the act of the BMW dealership robbery. Is that right?"

"Yes. That's right."

"But you were caught in the act of a different robbery at a taxi garage in the Bronx. Is that right?"

"Yes."

"And when the police questioned you, they gave you *Miranda* warnings. Is that right?"

"Yes."

"And you agreed to talk and tell them about the people who committed the Bronx taxi garage robbery. Right?"

"Right."

"You also told them about a second robbery, the robbery at the BMW dealership. Right?"

"Right."

"And you told them about the people who committed the BMW robbery. Right?"

"Right."

"And you made the deal with the police and the district attorney that in exchange for your testimony about these robberies, you would receive a relatively short sentence instead of what you could have received if convicted. Is that correct?"

"Yes."

Klein went back to the defense table and retrieved his notes.

"This is not new for you, is it?" he asked.

"What do you mean?"

"I mean committing robberies and then testifying against your accomplices in exchange for leniency by the courts."

"I guess so."

"You guess so. Isn't it a fact that regarding the BMW robbery you have agreed to testify against, as you described them, your 'friends,' Mr. Forest, Mr. Mumford, and Mr. Campbell?"

"Yes."

"Isn't it a fact that you have agreed to testify against your accomplices in the Bronx taxi garage robbery when that case comes to trial?"

"Yes."

"Let me ask you Mr. Johnson, how many other robberies have you committed in which you made deals with the police to testify against your 'friends'?"

"I don't recall."

"Can you give us a ballpark figure?"

"No."

"Was it more than five?"

"I don't recall."

"Less than five."

"I don't recall."

"More than ten."

"I don't recall."

"So, you can't recall any other incidents similar to the three we mentioned?"

"That's right."

While Klein continued the cross-examination, Dominic stood outside the courtroom door, looking through its small window. Suddenly, he realized he was not as wide awake as he thought he was. In the morning rush, he had forgotten to tell Klein about the poisoned drugs that Buster had sold.

He couldn't stand to make a mistake like that, and went into the courtroom, stood behind Klein, and cleared his throat.

Klein noticed him and asked the judge, "Your honor, can we take a short five-minute recess?"

ADA Walsh stood. "Objection," he said. 'You can't be in the middle of a cross."

Judge Brown frowned. "I think you've got that backwards. It's not your cross, it's his."

"Yes, your honor," Walsh said. "I apologize."

"Let's take fifteen minutes to give the jury a chance to use the restrooms," the judge said.

The courtroom emptied, and Klein and Dominic went to the attorney-witness room. Dennis was there.

"What have you got?" Klein asked.

"A redacted DEA report. The reason they went after Buster was because he had sold poisoned drugs, many people got sick, and someone died."

"Let me see it."

Klein read the document, made some notes on his yellow pad. "There's not much information here."

"But it gives you a legitimate basis to ask the questions," Dominic said.

"I'll give it a shot."

When court reconvened, Judge Brown told Daryl Johnson, "Remember, you're still under oath."

Klein began, "Mr. Johnson, you just testified that you don't recall any other robbery instances in which you testified against your accomplices. Is that right?"

"Yes, I don't recall."

"Isn't it true that this year in Queens, you sold three kilos of cocaine to an undercover federal agent of the Drug Enforcement Administration?"

Johnson's eyes widened. The question obviously took him aback. He said, "I don't recall."

"And isn't it true that they didn't officially arrest you because you agreed to cooperate with them and work as an informant?"

"I don't recall."

"And didn't you tell them about a push-in robbery in Jackson Heights, in which a drug dealer was robbed and killed?"

"I don't recall."

"And you were a lookout for that crime. Is that right?"

"I don't recall."

"And your accomplices were arrested for the crime while you weren't."

"I don't recall."

"And you testified against them in the grand jury. Isn't that so?"

"I can't remember."

Klein had used what he could from the official records he had. Now he tried to wing it based on the redacted DEA report.

"And Mr. Johnson, isn't it true that the DEA agents targeted you because you had sold drugs on the street that made many people very sick, and one person died?"

Johnson looked around the courtroom warily as though he were afraid of being attacked.

"I don't recall. I don't remember."

Judge Brown was scowling at the witness and said, "Mr. Johnson, answer."

"I don't recall," Johnson said.

Suddenly, the judge shouted so loud it seemed to shake the courtroom, "Is it you don't recall, or it didn't happen?"

The witness flinched, but didn't answer.

"If you say 'you don't recall,' it could have happened. Isn't that right Mr. Johnson?"

"I just don't recall."

'Well, you'd better recall," Judge Brown shouted even louder. "You're here to answer questions. You made a deal. Tell us everything, and truthfully. Not half-assed."

Johnson's eyes darted toward ADA Walsh asking for help. "I'm trying my best."

"Well, your best is not good enough. Did it happen or not?"

"I don't remember."

The judge slammed a folder on his desk. "I want an answer from you, Mr. Johnson. It's impossible to believe you wouldn't remember such consequential and memorable events. If you don't answer, I'm not only going to hold you in contempt, but I'm also going to tell the district attorney that you haven't been truthful, and your deal is going to go down the tubes."

This was unusual conduct for a trial judge. Judges weren't supposed to take over the role of the lawyers, although occasionally it had been done when there was a good cause. If the defendant was convicted because the judge acted improperly against the defendant's interests, the defendant would have grounds for an appeal. But if the defendant was acquitted because the judge acted improperly, the prosecutor couldn't appeal because an acquittal is final. The most the prosecutor could do was ask the appellate court to discipline the judge, which was not likely to happen.

The judge was now standing with his hands on the edge of the bench and leaning above the witness. "One more time, Mr. Johnson. Did you sell poisoned drugs on the street that harmed many people and killed one? Did it happen or not?"

Johnson looked far less confident than he had when the questioning began. His bald head was moist and gleaming from the lights.

No one in the courtroom was moving; their breathing seemed to have stopped as they waited for the answer.

Johnson hesitated, then said, "It may have. I'm not sure."

"It may have," the judge said, "well, that's progress."

Judge Brown sat down, leaned back in his chair. "Now, for the next question, were you involved in a drug robbery and shooting in Jackson Heights?"

"I don't really remember. I guess so."

"Don't guess. Were you involved or not?"

"I might have been."

The judge stood up again. "Stop playing games with me, Mr. Johnson. You informed on your accomplices in that robbery so that they wouldn't prosecute you for your drug sales. Isn't that so?"

"Yes."

"Alright, now we're getting somewhere. Mr. Klein will continue his cross-examination and you'll answer truthfully and completely. You understand?"

"Yes."

Klein was not sure he should continue cross-examining Johnson. The judge had all but destroyed him, and it might be better to just stop. But he couldn't resist, and from the defense table, he asked, "So earlier during your testimony when I asked you whether you had been involved in other robberies for which you made deals with the police to testify against your accomplices, and you said you couldn't recall, you were not being truthful. Is that right?"

"I couldn't recall."

"But it was not a truthful answer."

"It depends on what you mean by truthful." Johnson seemed to recover his confidence.

Klein decided to wrap it up.

"So, is it a fair statement that you have committed many crimes and have avoided much of your deserved prison time by testifying against your friends and accomplices? Yes or no."

"You might say that."

"Yes, or no?"

"Yes."

"And you're testifying against the defendant in this case, Ray Carbonaro, for the same reason. Correct?"

"Yes."

"And would it be fair to conclude that you'd testify against any accomplice, any friend, anyone, to stay out of jail?"

ADA Walsh objected. "Argumentative, speculative."

"Sustained," the judge said.

Klein was not deterred. "And it would be fair to conclude that in testifying against your accomplices and friends, you'd say anything necessary to please the prosecutors, anything to uphold your side of the deal, even if it weren't the truth?"

"Same objection."

"Sustained."

"No further questions," Klein said, satisfied that he had made the point to the jury.

CHAPTER THIRTEEN

B ack at Klein's office, Rosen told the other lawyers and the staff how the judge had torn apart the prosecution's star witness. The mood was jubilant. Dominic asked Klein whether the DA even had a case anymore.

"I wouldn't be so sure of that," Klein said. "They could have something up their sleeve. We'll find out tomorrow."

"The way the judge went after Buster, he showed he wasn't racially biased like Ray thought. He's an equal opportunity tyrant," Dennis said, getting a laugh from some.

"I've known the judge a long time," Klein said. "One thing's for sure--he hates drug dealers, white or black. And as soon as it was clear that Johnson was a drug dealer, Judge Brown's ire came out. I've heard him say many times that black drug dealers that were poisoning their own community--his community. He had seen too many members of his own family destroyed by drugs. Once, I saw him explode at a sentencing hearing when the defense lawyer said that selling drugs was a non-violent crime.

"The judge told him that he could show him a thousand pictures of dead people who died from drugs. 'They don't look like non-violent crimes to me,' he said. 'Poisoning is not a non-violent crime.' The defense lawyer didn't know what to say in response. The judge sentenced the drug dealer to the max."

Privately, Dominic asked Klein, "Since the case was going so well, is it still necessary to call Belinda as a witness. I was hoping that it wasn't, so that Dennis wouldn't have to be called."

"I understand your concern," Klein said. "We'll see what happens tomorrow before making up our mind."

At the Thursday court session, DA Walsh called Detective Martinez, who worked in the police department's videography section. Martinez played and described the videos that were taken outside the BMW dealership. He explained that there were three cameras that took timed videos, but none of them captured everything or every possible angle or every second.

The videos were from the week before the robbery, and showed a red Camaro passing the dealership several times and parking in the lot twice. None of these videos captured the driver through the closed windows of the car, but one of them captured a partial plate number of the Camaro. Four of the seven plate number digits could be discerned. They matched four numbers of Ray's car registration.

Detective Martinez showed the jurors a second video, which was from the day of the robbery. It captured a side view of what appeared to be the same red Camaro speeding up to the door of the dealership, and four masked men running out from the building, and getting into the car.

The car sped away. Because a dumpster in front of the dealership blocked the view, the cameras did not capture the plate number of the car.

On cross-examination, Klein asked a few perfunctory questions of the detective, choosing not to belabor the issue.

The next witness presented a new problem for the defense. Frankie Gonsalves was a young man who worked in a delicatessen near the dealership. On the day of the robbery, he was delivering an order of sandwiches to the dealership. As he approached the building, he saw the Camaro, with several men in it, pulling away from the dealership.

He sensed something was wrong and looked at the car and the occupants. He didn't get the plate number, but noticed that the hubcap of the right front passenger tire was missing. He went into the dealership to see what happened. When the police arrived, he told them what he had seen.

ADA Walsh's next witness was Detective Arroyo from the NYPD Property Section. He had photographs of Ray's Camaro that the police had towed away from his house. The photographs showed that the car was missing a right front hubcap.

After Detective Arroyo left the stand, the prosecution rested. It was good timing because the missing hubcap evidence was powerful and convincing, the kind of evidence that jurors could see as the last piece of the puzzle to justify a guilty verdict.

The jurors left the courtroom, and Klein, following the usual trial procedure, asked for the case to be dismissed because the prosecution had not proved a *prima facie* case.

Judge Brown denied the request.

The next morning, the defense would begin putting on its case.

At the evening strategy session at Klein's office, the mood was no longer jubilant. The lawyers and the staff poured over the security videos. Ray's Camaro was clearly seen outside the dealership three times during the week before the robbery, and also on the day of the robbery as the getaway car. Although the plate number of the getaway Camaro was not captured, the video could be used as circumstantial evidence against Ray.

After assessing the strength of the evidence, Klein decided that he would have to gamble and call Belinda and Dennis to testify.

Klein asked Dominic, "Can you have Kathy and Belinda at the courthouse tomorrow? I may call them to testify."

Dominic was disappointed but said, "Okay."

"I'll give you subpoenas for them if they need convincing," Klein said.

"If they need convincing, maybe you shouldn't call them," Dominic said, still hoping that Dennis could be kept out of it.

That evening, Dominic and Dennis drove to McCoy's. Dominic told Dennis to wait in the car.

"What for?" Dennis said.

"I want to keep this businesslike," Dominic said.

Inside, Kathy was bartending. Dominic told her about testifying the next day.

She said, "Great. What time?"

"Nine o'clock. I'll pick you up if you want."

"Not necessary. I'll be there."

"You know what you're going to say?"

"Yep. I've got it all mapped out in my head."

"Stick to the truth as best you can."

"It's going to be the truth," Kathy said.

Belinda walked past them, and Dominic nodded to her to meet him in the back near the restrooms.

She followed him.

"We need you to testify tomorrow," he said.

"Tomorrow."

"Yes."

"But I have to work, starting at three."

"We'll get it over first thing in the morning. I'll pick you up."

"Can't we do it another day?"

"No," Dominic said, taking the subpoena from his pocket and showing her the court salutation. You have to testify, otherwise the judge will hold you in contempt."

"What does that mean?"

"It means they'll put you in jail until you agree to testify. You're better off getting it over with. Give me your address again. We'll get to the court and be finished early."

"I don't know," Belinda said.

"You did say that you were going to help Ray. You can't back out now. If you do, you'll be killing Ray's chances, and he'll spend twenty-five years in prison."

"Okay. I guess I'll meet you at the court."

"No. It's better if I pick you up. This way, I'll get you in and out and back in time for work."

"But what am I going to say?"

"You know what to say. What Dennis told you."

"I'm not sure."

Dominic felt strange as he said, "We can't let Ray stay in jail for something Dennis may have done." Dominic knew Dennis didn't do it, but he had to pretend he did, accusing his own son felt like a betrayal. For a moment, he wanted to call the whole thing off, but Ray was in immediate danger. Dennis' danger was only potential.

Belinda interrupted his thoughts, "You're right, and I admire you for doing the right thing. So, I'll do it too."

"Good. I'll pick you up at eight-fifteen."

"Okay," Belinda said, and wrote down her address for him.

That night, Dominic couldn't sleep, which was unusual for him. Throughout his years in the police department, and as a detective seeing some terribly gruesome crime scenes, he had never had trouble sleeping. He had managed not to take the job home with him as so many of his colleagues did. However, this wasn't the job, this was the survival of his family. He worried for Ray, and also for Dennis. He went over how this had all happened. How each step led to another, and why there was no way to back out now.

He needed to be sharp tomorrow, and thought about taking a drink to help him sleep, but decided the alcohol would do more harm than lack of sleep.

Dennis couldn't sleep either. He worried about what would happen if things went wrong. Would he be responsible for Ray getting convicted, even though he was innocent? That was bad enough, but if he were found out, if he were accused of perjury or orchestrating false testimony, any chances of him becoming an FBI agent or a lawyer would be over. "Why the hell did I do this?" he said out loud,

At that moment, the phone rang. It was Kathy.

"I can't sleep," she said.

"Neither can I."

"Belinda called me. She's worried about getting in trouble."

'She doesn't have to worry. She only has to repeat what she heard me say."

"I think she suspects that we set her up for this."

Dennis remembered the many admonitions he had heard about talking on the phone, and made a self-serving statement if someone was recording the conversation. "I don't know why she would suspect that. We only told her the truth, and we don't want her to say anything unless it's truthful."

"Right," Kathy said.

"Don't worry," he said. "It'll all be over tomorrow, one way or the other. There's nothing more we can do now."

"I wish I was as confident as you," she said.

"I wish I was as confident as you think I am.

CHAPTER FOURTEEN

Dennis and Kathy arrived early. They were both anxious but hopeful. This was the day that the defense would get its turn. Klein and Rosen were waiting for them and they led Kathy to the attorney-witness room to go over her testimony. Dennis waited in the hallway. His father had not arrived yet, and he wondered whether he had picked up Belinda or had had a problem getting her to come. Without her, the plan would collapse.

When the courtroom opened, Klein and Rosen rushed across the hall. Klein asked Dennis whether his father had arrived yet. He said no.

"Let me know when he does," Klein said.

At 9:30am, the judge took the bench, the jury was brought in, and two court officers brought Ray out from the holding cells.

Dennis was watching through the door window and growing more anxious about Belinda not being there yet.

The jurors were seated, and the court officer called the case: "The People of the State of New York against Raymond J. Carbonaro."

As Judge Brown gave his standard greeting and instructions to the jurors, Dennis was relieved to see his father arrive with Belinda and lead her to a different attorney-witness room to keep her separated from Kathy.

Dennis entered the courtroom, signaled Klein, and gave him the thumbs up. At the same instant, the judge told Klein, "Call your first witness."

"I call Kathy Reynolds," Klein said.

She came into the courtroom and walked straight to the witness stand. She was dressed in a dark blue pants suit, white blouse, with her brown hair pinned-up neatly, and could have been mistaken for a young lawyer.

Looking her over, Judge Brown said only, "Swear her in."

Klein asked some preliminary questions about Kathy's relationship with Ray, about working out at the gym with him, about cutting his hair, and about what days and times she had spent with him around the time of the robbery.

At the defense table, Ray listened intently and nodded affirmatively at everything she said.

She testified that she had seen him several times during the week before the robbery, and also during the week that it occurred. She said that Ray usually came to her house about noon and left when she had to go to work at three. She worked at McCoy's bar and grill. Sometimes, he came there to see her, eat dinner, and have a beer.

Klein asked her about Ray's hair. She testified, as she had at the preliminary hearing, that it was short. She knew this because she cut his hair for him to save money.

Klein showed her the arrest photograph of Ray with long hair, and asked, "Is this how Ray's hair looked the week before the robbery?"

"No, his hair was much shorter."

"Is this how it looked around the day of the robbery, Tuesday, August, twenty-second."

"No. It was much shorter."

She was an excellent witness and made a good impression on the jury. Klein tried to keep her on the stand as long as possible with more questions, but Judge Brown cleared his throat, indicating that Klein was stretching it. Klein turned her over to ADA Walsh for cross-examination.

Walsh asked the standard questions about her bias in favor of Ray and about her interest in keeping him out of jail. He asked, "You'd say whatever you could to keep him out of jail, isn't that so?"

Klein objected. "This question had no basis and is argumentative."

Judge Brown overruled the objection, and allowed the question.

"No, I wouldn't," Kathy answered, "I'd only tell the truth."

ADA Walsh hadn't expected a different answer, but he had made his point to the jury about self-interest and bias, just as Klein had done when cross-examining the witness, Daryl "Buster" Johnson.

"Let me ask you, Ms. Reynolds," Walsh said, "during the week of September first to September seventh, do you remember when you were with the defendant?"

"I was probably with him, just as I explained before, every day between around noon until about three when I went to work," she answered.

"You just said 'probably,' is that right?"

"Yes."

"But you didn't say exactly," Walsh said.

"No, September 1st was awhile back."

"Well, if you can't remember the week of September First, how is it that you're so sure about the week from August fourteenth to the date of the robbery on August, twenty-second, which is even further in the past?"

"I'm not sure what you mean," she said.

"It's a simple question," ADA Walsh said, "if you're not sure of what you were doing in September, how can you be so sure of what you were doing in August.' He moved closer to her, posing while waiting for her answer.

Kathy looked away from him and turned to the judge to answer. "The reason is that on August twenty-third, Mr. Carbonaro, Ray's father, came to see me at McCoy's. He told me that Ray had been arrested, and asked me when I'd seen Ray. I remembered then because it was so recent, and I told him. When I went home, I wanted to be sure to remember, because it was obviously important, so I made notes. And I've looked at the notes a lot to make sure I could remember."

ADA Walsh had made the mistake of asking a question he didn't know the answer to, and getting blindsided by a devastating answer.

He was clearly taken off stride, but tried to recover. "So, you've memorized your testimony here today by constantly memorizing your notes."

"No. I just wanted to be sure of what happened."

Trying to look casual, Walsh asked, "Do you have these notes?"

"Yes. Right here," she said, taking them out of the inside pocket of her suit.

Klein stood, "Your honor, I'd ask the Court to examine the notes, and, if appropriate, admit them into evidence."

"I object," ADA Walsh said. "May we approach the bench?"

At the sidebar with the judge, out of the jury's hearing, Walsh told Judge Brown, "They're hearsay."

Klein argued that they could come in under the past recollection recorded exception.

"No," Judge Brown said. "Past recollection recorded can only come in when the witness can't remember. This witness remembers everything. So, the notes don't come in. Objection sustained."

"Thank you, your honor," Walsh said, "and, furthermore, I have to protest Mr. Klein's actions. I didn't know about these notes. If I had, I wouldn't have asked the question in the way I did. Mr. Klein should have told us about them. The jury should be instructed to disregard her answer, and I believe Mr. Klein's conduct calls for sanctions. The People's case has been unfairly undermined."

Judge Brown stared at Klein, "What do you say, counsellor?"

"Your honor, I give you my word, I didn't know she had these notes," Klein said. "My associate spoke with her, and she didn't mention it, and this morning before court, I interviewed her, and she didn't mention it. It was a surprise to me, just as it was a surprise to Mr. Walsh. Of course, my surprise was more pleasant than his."

Judge Brown actually laughed. "Alright, let's move on. Gentlemen, are we done here?"

Both attorneys agreed.

The judge dismissed Kathy from the witness stand. As she walked out of the courtroom confidently, Dominic was greatly impressed by her composure and self-assuredness. He thought that if Ray ever got out of this, the first thing he should do would be to ask her to marry him.

CHAPTER FIFTEEN

When court resumed, Klein called Belinda Cruz as his second defense witness. She wore a blue blouse and a skirt that matched. Ray was surprised when he saw her; he hadn't known that she would testify.

Belinda looked up at the judge nervously. Klein began his direct examination by trying to help her relax. He asked her how old she was, where she lived, who she lived with, where she went to school, and where she worked.

When she settled down, he said, "I'd like to draw you attention to the evening of Monday, January the Eighth, when you were working in McCoy's bar and had a conversation with your co-worker, Kathy Reynolds. Do you remember that night?"

"Yes. Very well."

"Can you tell us, in your own words, what the conversation was about?"

"It was about her boyfriend, Ray, who was in jail."

"And did she talk about Ray's brother, Dennis?"

"Yes"

"And what did she say?"

Walsh quickly stood. "Objection. Calls for hearsay."

"Objection sustained," the judge said.

"Alright," Klein said. "Can you tell the jury how Miss Reynolds appeared? What was her demeanor?"

"She was very upset. She'd been crying, and she ordered a whiskey, which I'd never seen her do before. So, I knew right away there was something wrong."

"And you sat with her while she drank the whiskey?"

"Yes."

"Did anything else happen?"

"Yes. Dennis Carbonaro came into the bar and sat with us."

"Then what happened?"

"When Kathy went to the ladies' room, Dennis told me…"

Walsh jumped up, "Objection, hearsay."

Klein asked to approach the bench. At sidebar, out of the hearing of the jury, he said, "Your honor, she's not going to testify to simple hearsay, but to a declaration against interest exception to hearsay. Dennis Carbonaro confessed to her that he did the crime."

"Really!" the judge said. "This is getting interesting."

The judge then excused the jury for a few minutes. When they departed, he said, "Why don't you have Mr. Carbonaro testify to that in person? He's available, isn't he?"

"He's present."

"Well, Mr. Klein, you know that to admit a declaration against interest, the original speaker must be unavailable, either dead, or injured, or out of state, etc."

"Yes. I know that, your honor, but he's invoking his Fifth Amendment right against self-incrimination. That makes him unavailable."

"Yes. That makes him unavailable," the judge agreed.

ADA Walsh said, "If he does take the Fifth, he has to do it in front of the jury."

"Mr. Klein can assert it on his behalf now," the judge said, "and then the jury will hear it after the Miss Cruz' testimony."

Klein thanked the judge, Walsh did not.

"Go ahead," the judge said.

Klein announced: "Mr. Dennis Carbonaro, my prospective witness, had informed me that if called in this case, he intends to invoke his Fifth Amendment rights."

"Duly noted, bring the jury back," Judge Brown said. "Let's hear what Miss Cruz has to say."

★ ★ ★ ★ ★

The jury was brought back, and Klein resumed the direct examination and didn't waste any time to ask Belinda what Dennis had told her.

"He told me that it was him, not his brother, who scouted the BMW place, and he was the one who drove the getaway car."

"What was your reaction?"

"I asked him again if he really did it, and he said yes."

"What happened then?"

"I told him that he should turn himself in so that his brother could get out of jail."

At the defense table, Ray looked astonished. They're trying to blame Dennis, he thought, this is crazy.

Klein continued, "To your knowledge, did Dennis turn himself in."

"No."

"As a result of this conversation, did you take any action?"

"Yes. The next day I called the police hotline and told them that I knew who committed the robbery."

"No further questions."

ADA Walsh suspected that her testimony was part of a ruse, but there wasn't much he could do to discredit her. He tried to get her to say that she was in love with Ray, and that's why she was trying to shift the blame to Dennis.

"That's ridiculous," she answered. "I like Dennis more than I like Ray, so why would I do this to him. I'm doing it because it's the right thing to do."

She was very convincing.

Walsh stumped her only once. He asked her where she got the number for the police hotline. She hesitated, first saying she didn't remember, then saying "I think I saw a sign somewhere, but maybe I looked it up. I don't remember."

This answer wasn't convincing. She was lying and Walsh sensed it. He tried to follow up, but she just kept answering, "I don't remember."

Klein sensed it too. He busied himself with some papers, trying not to look too concerned in front of the jury about her non-answers.

When her cross-examination ended, the judge told her to step down. As she left, although he wasn't exactly sure what was going on, Ray mouthed the words, "Thank you," to her.

While Belinda was testifying, Dennis waited in the attorney-witness room. He had a feeling of "the butterflies" in his stomach. He knew what he was going to say, but he worried that something would go wrong, and it occurred to him that the DA could grant him immunity. If they did, and he didn't testify, they could hold him in contempt. And if he did testify, what would he say? Would he have to pretend that he was involved in the robbery? Doing that would put him in jail. His father would be furious. Could he try the 'I don't recall' routine? He could be held in contempt for that, too. The uncertainties made him even more nervous. He hoped to God that they didn't give him immunity and that he could hide behind the Fifth Amendment.

When his name was called, he entered the courtroom, trying his best to look calm and confident. As he walked to the witness stand, he sensed that everyone in the courtroom looking at him. He glanced at the jurors, and saw either daggers or distain in their eyes. Obviously, they believed Belinda's testimony and that he was the criminal. Worse, to save his own skin, he let his brother go to jail for something his brother hadn't done. He couldn't blame them for hating him, but that was part of the plan.

When he was sworn in, Klein asked his name and address, then asked, "Do you know anything about the robbery of a BMW dealership in Greenpoint, Brooklyn that occurred on August twenty-second of last year."

Klein had instructed him to avoid saying anything in response, other than reciting the Fifth, not even a "No."

"I assert my Fifth Amendment right to decline to answer on the grounds that my answer might tend to incriminate me," Dennis said.

"Did you have a conversation with Belinda Cruz in McCoy's Bar in Bayside, Queens on January the eighth of this year?" Klein asked.

Again, Dennis said, "I assert my Fifth Amendment right to decline to answer on the grounds that my answer might tend to incriminate me."

Klein began to ask another question, but Judge Brown interrupted.

"Let's not waste time. Do you intend to answer any questions related to these proceedings?" he said.

Dennis, sticking to Klein's instructions, said, "I assert my Fifth Amendment right to decline to answer on the grounds that my answer might tend to incriminate me."

"Alright, you can step down," the judge said.

Glad it was over, Dennis headed for the door, but lingered before exiting, and heard Judge Brown say, "Call your next witness, Mr. Klein."

"We have no more witnesses at this time," Klein said. "The defense rests."

"The defendant does not wish to testify?" the judge asked.

"That's correct, your honor. I have conferred with him, and advised him of his right to testify, and he declines."

"Alright, I want to hear that from him. Mr. Carbonaro, stand up. You know you have the constitutional right to testify in your own defense. Yes?"

"Yes," Ray answered.

"You've discussed with your attorney thoroughly. Yes?"

"Yes."

"And you waive you right at this time. Yes."

"Yes."

"Let the record reflect the defendant has voluntarily waived his right to testify. Court is adjourned until nine o'clock tomorrow morning."

Dennis expected that since the testimony had gone as planned and so well in their favor, perhaps they'd go to a restaurant to talk about it. But he was disappointed by the others' lack of enthusiasm.

Klein said that he needed to go back to the office to work on Monday's summation.

Dominic said he would drive Belinda home, and left.

Kathy had already left the building, and Dennis called her cellphone. There was no answer.

Later that evening, he called Kathy again. He wanted to talk, but there was still no answer. He wondered whether something was wrong. He drove to McCoy's where Brendan told him that Kathy had taken the night off, and Belinda, too.

"I'll have a beer," Dennis said.

Brendan asked him how the trial was going.

"It's going as expected, but who knows. The lawyer says that juries are totally unpredictable."

"That's because they get bamboozled by the lawyers," Brendan said. "I had a lawyer back in the old country who could talk you into taking your eye out of your head, then tell you that you looked better without it."

It was funny, but Dennis didn't laugh.

Disappointed that he couldn't find Kathy, Dennis went straight to the Ridgewood apartment to go to bed, but couldn't sleep. The trial kept going around in his head. No matter how the trial turned out, trouble could be waiting for him? Could he be prosecuted for anything? What must his father be thinking?

He heard a knock at the door. His first reaction was fear. Maybe it was the police, either Detective McConnell or someone from the district attorney's office. He looked out the window to see whether there were any police cars. There were none. There was another knock, then he heard Kathy's voice through the door. "It's me."

He exhaled and opened the door.

"I couldn't sleep," she said.

"Neither could I," he said. "I'm glad you came. Maybe two can sleep better than one. Do you want something, a beer?"

"No, thanks.

Dennis took her hand and led her to the couch. "Do you want something to eat?"

"No," she said. "What do you think is going to happen tomorrow?"

"They'll be closing arguments."

"I know that, but what's the jury going to do?"

"The jury should find him not guilty," he said. "Your testimony, Belinda's testimony, the cops showing the wrong photograph, all that should be enough reasonable doubt for them to acquit."

"I hope so," she said.

"Me, too."

Kathy turned to look at him. "I need to ask you something."

"Yes."

"If Ray gets acquitted, what's going to happen?"

"He'll get released."

"I don't mean about that. I mean about us."

Dennis wasn't expecting this. He didn't know the right answer, and he didn't know what to say. His father had always told him, 'If you don't know, don't say anything.'

"I'm not sure."

"Really. You're not sure?" she said accusingly.

Now he understood where this was going. If Ray was acquitted, they'd have to decide whether she'd go back with Ray and take up where they left off, or whether they should tell Ray about their relationship and continue seeing each other.

Kathy sat silently staring at him, waiting.

He had to say something. "You know how I feel about you," he said. "My only problem is how terrible I feel about taking you from my brother. Taking you while he's in prison. I feel like I'm kicking him while he's down."

"I understand that. And I feel the same way. But we shouldn't throw away what we have."

He began to say "Yes, we have to stay together, I don't want to lose you, I …", but stopped himself. Instead, he said, "I agree. Let's sleep on it."

They went into his bed, too exhausted to make love, but slept wrapped in each other arms until morning. They spent the next two nights together.

CHAPTER SIXTEEN

On Monday, as the third week of the trial began, closing arguments were scheduled. Klein would go first, and Walsh second.

The courtroom was crowded with spectators, mostly regular trial watchers who had nothing to do with the case. Some lawyers came to see Klein's closing argument.

Dominic took a seat in the first spectator row. Dennis and Kathy sat three rows back. Across from them, a row was filled with family and friends of Mr. Coates, the customer who had been killed in the robbery.

When Klein began, he again pointed to the words from the Declaration of Independence and the Bill of Rights written on the wall above the judge's bench. "As I submitted to you in my opening statement," he said, "your role is to fulfill the principles written in those documents, and your duty is to stand by those principles when deciding the fate of the young man who sits here accused of participating in a serious crime.

"Nothing can be more important than to uphold these principles when one of our neighbors is misidentified and falsely accused of serious charges and forced to defend himself against the loss of his young adulthood.

"Ray Carbonaro is accused by people he does not know of being someplace where he wasn't and doing something that he didn't do. It is our duty to scrutinize these allegations and to see that justice is done. I thank you in advance for your dedication to that task."

Klein moved directly in front of the jury box.

"Simply put, this is a case of misidentification. It has been well known that eyewitness identifications are not necessarily reliable and are often mistaken. This can be due to anything from a suggestive identification procedure (whether intentional or not) to a witness's inaccurate perception of an event under stressful circumstances. Courts have confirmed that eyewitness misidentification is now the single greatest source of wrongful convictions in the United States, and responsible for more wrongful convictions than all other causes combined.

"The prosecutor, Mr. Walsh, promised in his opening statement that he would prove to you beyond a reasonable doubt that the defendant participated in a robbery and a conspiracy to commit robbery. The judge is going to tell you about reasonable doubt and what the People have to prove to meet that high standard. And it's a high standard because in our country we err on the side of caution when deciding guilt or innocence. I submit that the people did not meet their burden. Just pointing a finger at this innocent defendant does not make him guilty. It has to be proven.

"This is a serious and frightening case, because of the way Ray Carbonaro, who committed no crime, was arrested on the basis of faulty identification procedures. The police used an old photograph that did not accurately show what he looked like at the time of the crime. Ray had short hair, while the person who allegedly scouted the dealership prior to the robbery, had long hair. But the police showed the witnesses the photograph of Ray with long hair. And when the one witness identified that photo, the police, instead of pointing out the discrepancy, continued on with the flawed identification procedure."

Klein went back to the defense table to give the jurors a moment to absorb the important point he had made. It was the crux of his case.

"And remember," he continued, "Detective McConnell testified that only one witness identified the photo, and that the other four witnesses did not. That, in itself, is enough for you to find a reasonable doubt, acquit the defendant, and end this injustice.

"Despite those discrepancies, the police placed Ray in a lineup where there's always the question: Is the witness identifying the culprit they saw or are they identifying the photograph that was so improperly and dishonestly shown to them?"

ADA Walsh stood, "Objection, argumentative."

"Overruled," Judge Brown said. "This is argument. Continue."

Klein continued. "And, ladies and gentlemen of the jury, I submit to you that the lineup was improperly and dishonestly done. Detective McConnell, whom you heard testify, put hats on all the lineup participants, hiding the fact that the defendant had short hair, not long hair as depicted in the old, outdated photograph. The detective wouldn't allow Ray's short hair to be shown in the lineup. He hid the evidence that would have proven the defendant's innocence. Was this purposely done? Should it make us wonder why Detective McConnell would have done that? Was it a fair, unbiased investigation and arrest? These are questions you should ask.

"Based just on the improper identification procedures employed in this case, there's clearly a reasonable doubt that compels you to acquit the defendant. But there's more. You heard Ray's girlfriend Kathy Reynolds give alibi evidence that he was with her at times that would have made it impossible for him to be where the prosecutors say he was. You may say that her times were not exact, but whose times are exact when remembering just average days, such as those she was asked to remember. But her memory was better than most, because when she learned the importance of everything, she made notes to help her. Her testimony certainly raises a reasonable doubt.

"Furthermore, we have testimony that Ray's brother, Dennis Carbonaro, admitted that he was the one involved in the crime."

When Dennis heard his name, his ears burned and he felt the eyes of everyone, including the victim's family, staring at him.

"Dennis Carbonaro is not on trial here," Klein said, "so his guilt or innocence may be determined elsewhere, but the testimony of Ms. Ramos that he admitted committing the crime unequivocally raises a reasonable doubt about the case against the defendant on trial here today.

"Ladies and gentlemen, the primary error committed in this case was the improper identification procedures employed by the police. If it weren't for that, Ray Carbonaro would not be a defendant. Once he became the defendant, he became the target of every jailhouse informant trying to get himself out of prison. The prosecution produced such an informant, Daryl Buster Johnson. You heard his testimony. He admitted to being a career criminal who time and again, six times in all, had managed to get himself out of jail by testifying against someone else. Be skeptical of his testimony. He was under arrest for a different robbery, a robbery of a beer distributor in the Bronx, and he agreed to testify against his accomplices in that robbery, and he also threw in his accomplices in the BMW dealership robbery. His testimony against the defendant was valuable to the prosecution because the prosecution had no direct evidence against the defendant. So, to please the prosecutors, he agreed to testify against him, even if he had to make it up. Buster Johnson saw the opportunity to get out of jail free, and he took it.

"We're not saying that no one cased the dealership, but it wasn't the defendant. Buster Johnson said that it was Ray Carbonaro because that's what the prosecution wanted.

"I ask you to remember that there's a presumption of innocence that we all enjoy, and the prosecution has not overcome that presumption because there are so many things wrong with this case. First, Ray doesn't match the description of the suspect who supposedly was casing the car dealership, he has short hair, the suspect had long hair. Second, he wasn't there. He was with his girlfriend Kathy Reynolds. And, third, someone else has admitted to the crime, in effect, exonerating Ray.

"So, I ask you to correct this injustice before it goes any further, and send this young man home to his girl and his parents. Ray Carbonaro came here innocent. Let him stay that way. Thank you so much for your patience and attention."

Judge Brown said, "Ladies and gentlemen, take a ten-minute break. Don't talk about the case. When you return, we'll hear the People's summation."

Dennis thought that Klein had done a perfect job, except he made a mistake by wrapping up his summation so quickly. Dennis thought that he should have stretched it to the lunch break so that the prosecutor couldn't immediately counteract its impression on the jury.

When ADA Walsh began, he got the jury's attention right away.

He spoke from the lectern. "On that afternoon at the BMW car dealership, a heinous crime was committed. A trio of criminals with guns threatened and robbed a dozen people, took their property, and, worse, took the life of Larry Coates, who was only thirty-years old and the father of three children. That's why we are here today: To seek justice for Larry Coates and his family, and for the other victims of this crime, victims of this band of vicious and dangerous criminals.

"Now, before I review the evidence that was presented to you that proves the defendant's guilt beyond a reasonable doubt, I want to address some of the arguments that Mr. Klein raised during his closing statement."

Walsh retrieved a folder of papers from the DA's table, then spread them on the lectern.

"The defense argued that the identification of the defendant was not properly done. I submit to you that the police did everything according to standard and accepted investigation procedures. From the security camera videos, they identified vehicles with plate numbers that had been at the dealership. They obtained photographs of the owners of these vehicles, which included a photograph of the defendant. They didn't just show a single photo to the witnesses, but they put the photo in a photo-array with other photographs, and let the witness pick out the suspect. That's the fairest way to do it. They didn't suggest to any witness that this is the criminal, they left it up to the witnesses to choose.

"The defense argued that the police showed a photo in which the defendant had long hair, and somehow that made the identification invalid. But they didn't rely only on the photo identification, they put the defendant in a lineup with five other persons of similar descriptions, and the defendant was picked out on the basis of his facial characteristics, not the length of his hair, which, of course, could vary from time to time.

"The defense argued that the girlfriend's alibi testimony proved that the defendant could not have been at the dealership either the week before the robbery or during the robbery. Somehow, she remembered everything she and her boyfriend did during these times. Conveniently, she made notes of these times. I submit to you that if the time period was three months long, she would have told you about every lunch and dinner they had, and how many bites they took."

Several jurors laughed at this.

Walsh continued. "Please use your common sense. It's her boyfriend on trial; she has the motive to come in here and tailor her testimony to concoct an alibi for him; she could make things up out of thin air, and they're difficult to disprove.

"Speaking of thin air. A close friend of the girlfriend calls the police hotline to say that someone else did the robbery. The defendant's brother. For some reason, he supposedly admitted this to her. How convenient for the defense. Something else made out of thin air, and difficult to disprove. And how convenient that the brother takes the Fifth Amendment."

Walsh returned the folder he was using to the DA's table and retrieved another folder.

"Now, let's move away from the unsupported arguments of the defense and review the evidence that proves the defendant's guilt beyond a reasonable doubt," Walsh said. "Contrary to the thin-air arguments of the defense, we showed you concrete evidence. We showed you the video of the getaway car after the robbery, a car that matched the defendant's car, and which had three plate numbers that matched the defendant's plate. It would have been nice to have had the entire plate number, but the probabilities certainly point to the car being the defendant's car. Combine that with the fact of his visits to the dealership the week prior to the robbery supposedly to buy a BMW that he could hardly afford, and the manager's distinct sense that he was casing the business. And you heard the testimony of the accomplice, Buster Johnson, who told us that the defendant participated in the planning and shared in the proceeds. I submit to you, there is proof beyond a reasonable doubt that the defendant was a participant in this robbery.

"Ladies and gentlemen, this case has been proven to you beyond a reasonable doubt based on video evidence and credible testimony of police officers to confirm the defendant's identity. We're not saying he was inside when the actual robbery occurred and when Larry Coates was killed, but the defendant conspired to commit the robbery and was part of the planning.

"He was outside waiting to help his accomplices escape. He acted in concert with the others, was an accomplice, and, as such, is guilty of the robbery and the murder of Larry Coates. There's only one thing left for you to do. Do justice, and find the defendant guilty. Thank you."

Judge Brown stood. "Ladies and gentlemen, you must be tired. So, we'll take the rest of the afternoon off. I'll give you the charge tomorrow morning. Be here promptly at 9:30. If you're not here, we can't start. And remember, between now and tomorrow morning, you must not discuss the case among yourselves or with anyone else. I'll see you tomorrow morning."

As the judge and the jurors left, Ray remained slumped in his chair. His father approached him, and put his hand on his shoulder. "Keep your chin up, Ray," he said. "Mr. Klein did a great job."

Dennis also approached him. Ray looked blankly at him, as though not understanding who he was, as though he was a complete stranger.

"Are you okay?" Dennis asked.

Ray shook his head, signaling that he wasn't. A court officer put his hand under Ray's arm, encouraging him to get up, and walked him back to the holding cells.

As Ray was taken away, it hit Dennis that Ray might think that he was the one involved in the robbery, that he was the one who cased the dealership. No wonder he looked at me like that, he thought, like he didn't know me. We never told him what we were doing. We should have told him. Maybe I should tell him now. But, then again, maybe not. It might create more problems than it's worth. I'll see what happens.

As the courtroom emptied, Dominic, Dennis, and Kathy walked out together. When they were outside, Dennis asked his father, "Do you want to stop for something to eat?"

"No, I've got to get home to your mother," Dominic said. "But why don't you two come? I'm sure she's cooking dinner."

"Okay," Dennis said.

"Oh, I couldn't intrude on such short notice," Kathy said.

"She'll be glad for the company," Dominic said. "Come. We could all use a good meal."

"Okay. Thanks. I will."

At the house, Marie answered the door wearing an apron over her dress. "How did it go?" she asked.

"Fine, we go back tomorrow."

"How's Ray?"

"He's fine. This is Kathy, Ray's friend."

"Nice to meet you," Marie said. "I've heard good things about you. Come in, sit down, dinner's on."

Marie had a braciola simmering in meat sauce on the stove. The aroma filled not only the kitchen but the whole house.

Dominic sniffed, "Ah, my favorite dinner," he said as he kissed his wife.

"Thanks for having me," Kathy said. "Can I help you with anything?"

"That's okay, dear. It's almost ready. Sit down."

Marie served the food while Dominic poured Chianti for everyone.

Before eating, they all held hands as Marie said grace.

During dinner, no one talked about the trial. Both Dennis and Kathy did their best to start casual conversation. Kathy said that she had never had braciola before, that it was really delicious.

"Someday, I'll show you how to make it," Marie said, smiling at Kathy and Dennis together.

Dennis thought that his mother looked puzzled, and that she must have been wondering whether Kathy was Ray's or Dennis' girlfriend?

In a lull in the conversation, Marie asked, "What happens next?"

"Tomorrow the judge instructs the jurors," Dominic said, "then they start deliberating. It might take a few minutes or a few days."

"Could Ray get out tomorrow?" Marie asked.

"It's possible, but we can't count on it. Hope for the best, prepare for the worst."

"Well, if he does come home, we need to clean up his apartment. Clean sheets, laundry. He shouldn't come home to a mess. Knowing Dennis, though he's pretty good, I'm sure he's been too busy to clean up."

"I clean," Dennis said. "At least, sometimes."

Kathy laughed. She stood and said to Marie, "Thank you so much for the lovely dinner. It was delicious. I have to get home."

"I'll drive you," Dennis said.

Marie and Kathy hugged.

"Come anytime," Marie said.

"I will, thanks again."

CHAPTER SEVENTEEN

Promptly at nine a.m. on Tuesday, Judge Brown began giving his instructions on the law to the jury. It took almost an hour for him to cover all the pertinent legal principles that applied to the case. He emphasized some more than others because they were key to its outcome, adding his own understanding to the standard instructions. He covered the People's burden of proof, and emphasized that the defendant was not required to prove anything. The defendant could remain silent, and his silence could not be used against him.

Twice he went over the charge of felony murder, telling the jurors, "Under our law, a person is guilty of felony murder (murder in the 2nd degree) when, in the course of and in furtherance of the commission or attempted commission of a robbery, or in immediately flight therefrom, that person or another participant, causes the death of a person other than one of the participants."

He explained that there was no need to prove the death was caused intentionally. It could have been caused by recklessness, negligence, or by accident, and the death of a non-participant would be sufficient to charge felony murder.

He explained that a participant is an accomplice, and instructed the jury on the meaning of accomplice, first applying the term to Ray Carbonaro, the defendant, then to Daryl Johnson, the prosecution witness.

He explained that if they found that the People proved beyond a reasonable doubt that the defendant intentionally, solicited, requested, commanded, importuned, or aided another person to a commit the robbery, the defendant would be criminally liable for the crime.

Then he applied the term to Johnson. "In the present case, whether Daryl Buster Johnson was an accomplice was important, because it might determine the effect and weight of his testimony. Our law is especially concerned about the testimony of an accomplice who received, or expects to receive, a benefit in return for his or her testimony.

"Therefore, our law provides that a defendant may not be convicted for any crime on the testimony of an accomplice unless it is supported by corroborative evidence tending to connect the defendant with the commission of the crime.

"In other words, if you find that Mr. Johnson was an accomplice, and even if you find his testimony to be believable, you may not convict the defendant solely upon that testimony unless you also find that it was corroborated by other evidence."

He gave examples of corroborative evidence, such as physical evidence connecting a defendant to the crime scene, other witness testimony, or admissions by the defendant.

The judge concluded with an explanation of proof beyond a reasonable doubt, saying: "Proof beyond a reasonable doubt is proof that leaves you firmly convinced of the defendant's guilt. There are very few things in this world that we know with absolute certainty, and in criminal cases the law does not require proof that overcomes every possible doubt. If, based on your consideration of the evidence, you are firmly convinced that the defendant is guilty of the crime charged, you must find him guilty. If, on the other hand, you think there is a real possibility that he is not guilty, you must give him the benefit of the doubt and find him not guilty. But keep in mind, it's not just any doubt, it must be a reasonable doubt."

With the instructions completed, the judge gave the case to the jury. He told them that they would not be sequestered and could go home each day if they hadn't reached a verdict, but they would have to come back the next day. He told them again not to discuss the case with anyone or watch or listen to media reports about the case.

"Those are your instructions. If you have questions during your deliberations, you may send a note to me.

"Now follow the officer into the deliberation room," he said. "The officer will take your order for lunch. Order anything you like, as long as it's on the menu."

The jury deliberated for three hours into midafternoon, and sent a note to the judge that they hadn't reached a verdict but were having productive discussions. The judge asked whether they wished to continue deliberating today or go home and start again tomorrow. The jurors said that they would continue,

Dominic had gone home to stay with Marie, and Kathy had left to go to work. Dennis and Klein had stayed, and waited in the attorney-client room. "How long do you think the jury will be out?" Dennis asked.

"Could be quick or a week," Klein said, then asked Dennis, "What did you think of the judge's instructions?"

"To tell you the truth," Dennis said, "I have no idea what his definition of proof beyond a reasonable doubt was. It was too general, and could mean different things to different people."

"True, but it can't be too specific. It's really meant to give a legal aura to the commonsense decisions of twelve jurors. Verdicts often have as much to do with emotions or intuitions as they do with reason and logic, and if the jurors render a bad decision, the judge or an appellate judge can say the legal standard wasn't met because the case was not proved beyond a reasonable doubt."

The explanation didn't really help. Dennis switched subjects and asked about corroboration. "How much do you need? Does it have to be directly related to the crime or could it be about other matters related to the accomplice's testimony?"

"It has to be directly related. The accomplice can't testify that it was raining on the day of the crime and then the DA brings in a weather report saying that it was raining. That doesn't count. That's not the kind of corroboration you need."

"I see," Dennis said. "And about felony-murder. What if someone has a heart attack and dies while being robbed or burglarized? Is the criminal guilty of murder?"

"For most crimes, you have to prove causation," Klein said. "But for felony-murder, if the victim died during the crime, that would be deemed causation."

"I see."

"Now, it's my turn. Let me ask you a question," Klein said. "What if the victim dies a week later?"

That's a tough one," Dennis said. "I suppose if the heart attack started during the crime and it took a week for the victim to die, it would be murder. But if the heart attack happened later on its own, I would say no."

"Good answer," Klein said. "When this is over, I think I'm going to have to rehire you."

"That would be great, but I start working at UPS again on Monday," Dennis said.

"That's fine. When you're ready to come back, let me know."

"Thanks. One more question."

"Okay."

"I know all the accomplices are deemed as guilty as the one who shot the gun, but should the sentences be the same?"

"Sentencing has to take into account a defendant's record and the degree of his culpability. The ringleader might be the most culpable. So, it's possible for the shooter to get less time than the ringleader who planned the robbery. There was a case where the shooter who entered a store and shot someone to death got life, but the getaway driver who didn't go in, got the death penalty."

"That doesn't seem right. It doesn't seem like justice," Dennis said.

"Forget about justice," Klein said. "There's no such thing as justice. There's just chance and circumstances. People are controlled by their heredity and their environments, and they act accordingly."

"So, you're saying that they can't help what they do."

"By and large."

"With all due respect, I don't buy that."

"Then, maybe I won't rehire you," Klein said, jokingly.

Another hour passed and no verdict was forthcoming. The judge dismissed the jury for the day with the usual warnings, and told them to be back at 9a.m.

Dennis and Klein shook hands as they left the building.

Dennis drove to McCoy's. Kathy was behind the bar. She served him a hamburger and a beer, and when she wasn't busy, they whispered about the case.

"Ray must be worried sick," she said.

"I'm sure he is. I'm worried too. You know, I think I should have told him about Belinda and what we were doing. I'm worried that I may have hurt his case."

"Don't say that. It's done, and I don't see how it could have hurt. You were brave to try it, even if it doesn't work out."

"That's what I like about you. You stay positive."

"I try."

"Are you going to come to court tomorrow?"

"No. I wouldn't be able to stand it. Just call me as soon as something happens."

Brendan, the other bartender came on duty, and asked Dennis, "Did you see the local news?"

"No," Dennis said.

"They had a piece about your brother's case."

"Damn it. What was it about?"

"All they seemed to care about was that he was a cop's son involved in a robbery and a murder. I'd guess there'll be more in tomorrow's newspaper."

Dennis shook his head. "My father's going to go nuts. He hates newspapers."

Wednesday, the second day of deliberations, the lawyers had issues to discuss before the jury could begin again. A juror had complained that another juror had heard the news report on the television. And a second juror wanted to be excused because she found the deliberations too one sided.

143

The judge talked to the juror who had seen the television story. The juror said it was inadvertent and there was no information that would influence him either way. The judge told him that he could continue on the jury.

The judge also talked to the stressed juror. She said that some jurors were trying to intimidate others into voting that the defendant was guilty.

"That's part of the process," he said. "Listen to all sides and make your own judgments. If someone does threaten you, let me know. So go back and do your best. It's important. It's your civic duty."

In the hallway outside the courtroom, Dominic saw Arnie Friedman, the reporter from the local news station who had aired the report about the trial. Friedman was a longtime police reporter and Dominic had given him stories in the past.

Friedman approached Dominic. "I'm sorry to hear about your son."

"Don't be sorry yet," Dominic said. "And I don't appreciate you going on about the son of a cop angle and assuming that my son is guilty. He hasn't been convicted of anything."

"I'm just doing my job."

"Sure. The public's right to know, and all that. Bashing the police every chance you get has nothing to do with it. Right?"

"Cops make good stories."

"Especially when they do something wrong. You don't write too much when they do something right."

"Unfortunately, that's not news."

You could write about how my son is getting framed. Did you think of that?"

"Who's framing him?"

"When this is over, give me a call."

"I will."

Dominic walked away. He had purposefully planted a seed. He believed Detective McConnell had manipulated the case against Ray, and, in effect, was framing him. He'd like to prove it, if he could.

Although he had differences with Friedman, he knew he was a good reporter, and one who knows how to dig for a story and could be useful if pointed in the right direction.

Thursday wasn't much different than Wednesday, a lot of waiting in the attorney-witness room. Dominic played solitaire. Dennis tried to read a paperback book he had bought at the newsstand. Time dragged. Dennis thought that since it was going so slowly for him, how slow must it be going for Ray. What torture must it be?

A court officer came into the room. They thought that the verdict was in, but he only announced that the jury was going to lunch.

"Do you want to get something to eat, Dad?" Dennis asked.

"No. I can't eat. I'm just going for a walk. You get something."

"I can't eat either," Dennis said. "Can I come with you?"

"Of course," Dominic said as he kissed Dennis on the forehead. "What would I do without you?"

Dennis thought that his father hadn't kissed him in ten years. He must really be hurting, he thought, and he felt himself tearing up.

When they came back from their walk, the courtroom was busy. The jurors had sent out several questions to the judge, and he was discussing them with Klein and ADA Walsh.

"Is that a good sign or a bad sign?" Dennis asked.

"Who knows?" Dominic said. "They could be arguing over some minor legal issue, or over what charges they should find him guilty on. I think this is going to take a long time. On second thought, we should eat something. Here's some cash. Go to the deli down the street and get some sandwiches and sodas."

Dennis came back with the sandwiches, and as he was taking his first bite, a court officer opened the door and announced, "The verdict's in."

They left the sandwiches and rushed into the courtroom. Klein was already there. Spectators, including the family of the victim, were entering.

A court officer brought Ray out from the holding cell. The jury was seated, and Judge Brown announced, "This court is in session. Officer, go ahead."

The officer asked the jury whether they had reached a verdict on all four charges. The jury foreman said, "Yes."

The judge told Ray to stand. Klein stood with him.

The officer began, "On count number one, murder in the second degree, felony-murder, what is your verdict?"

Klein held Ray's arm, holding him so that he wouldn't overreact.

Dominic grabbed Dennis' hand.

The jury foreman unfolded a paper. He announced, "Not guilty."

There was a gasp from the victim's family.

Ray voiced a low, "Yes."

"On count number two, manslaughter second degree, what is your verdict?"

"Not guilty."

Cursing from the family members could be heard.

"On count number three, robbery in the first degree, what is your verdict?"

"Not guilty."

Spectators began talking amongst themselves.

"Quiet in the courtroom," Judge Brown bellowed, and waited for silence.

The court officer asked, "On count four, conspiracy to commit robbery, what is your verdict?"

The foreman unfolded another paper, "Not guilty."

ADA Walsh collapsed into his seat before Ray collapsed into his.

Judge Brown stood. He didn't look pleased. "Ladies and gentlemen of the jury, having rendered your verdict we wish to thank for your service. Jury duty is a difficult task, and you performed it in an exemplary manner.

"Ray Carbonaro, stand, please."

Ray stood.

"The jury having rendered its verdict, all the charges against are dismissed. You are free to go."

Ray and Klein banged their fists together.

Dominic and Dennis hugged.

Ray started to walk out of the courtroom, but the court officer held him. "You have to be released from Corrections."

"You're kidding," Ray said.

Klein said, "That's the procedure. It'll take only a few minutes. They have to give you your property back."

"I don't care about my property. I just want to leave."

"It can't be helped. You're still in custody until the jail gets the court order."

Ray was taken back to the cells. The others waited in the hallway for him to be released. When he appeared, they all hugged him and gave one another high-fives.

"This calls for a celebration," Klein said. "I'll make reservations at Forlini's for tomorrow night about six. It's a block behind the Manhattan Criminal Court. You know the place, Dom."

"Sure. See you then. I want to bring Ray home to his mother. It'll be a great surprise for her. Dennis, how about you?"

"I have to go to the apartment for something. I'll meet you at home."

In his car, Dennis called Kathy at McCoy's.

"Not guilty!"

"Oh my God. That's fantastic. Where's Ray?"

"He's going to his parents house."

"What's he doing after that?"

This was a pregnant question. What Ray did would be important to them. Would he contact Kathy? Ask to see her? Go to her apartment?

Dennis wondered what would Kathy do if Ray asked to see her.

"He'll probably be glad to sleep in his old bed at his mother's house, but he might go to our apartment in Ridgewood. That's why I'm going there to clean it up."

Kathy hesitated, then said, "I think I left a makeup kit there and some lipstick. There's no sense in letting him find it. It might be a shock, unless you said it was someone else's."

"I don't want to start making things up. I'll get rid of it."

"You could bring it here."

Dennis didn't answer that suggestion.

"Tomorrow night there's a party at Forlini's to celebrate the verdict. Do you know where that is?"

"No, but I'll find it."

"Okay. I'll see you tomorrow night. Forlini's. Six o'clock."

It was an unfinished conversation with questions still in the air, but they hung up.

CHAPTER EIGHTEEN

As Dennis was parking in his driveway, his landlord, Mr. Martucci, came out from the front entrance. He was a middle-aged man, wearing coveralls with the logo of an oil truck company over his breast pocket. "How are you?" he asked.

Dennis was sure that he knew about Ray's arrest and assumed he knew about the trial, though they had never spoken about it. As long as the rent was paid, Mr. Martucci apparently thought it was none of his business.

"We had good news today," Dennis said.

"Yes."

"My brother was found not guilty."

"Ah. That's good. It was a terrible thing, and he wasn't even there when it happened. I'm glad it turned out okay."

"Thank you, thank you for everything," Dennis said, meaning that he appreciated that the landlord had not given them a hard time.

"Your father and mother must be relieved."

"Yes. They are."

Dennis went upstairs to the apartment, found Kathy's makeup kit and lipstick, brought them downstairs, and put them in the trunk of his car.

Back upstairs, he began cleaning up, collecting empty beer and soda cans, and emptying the refrigerator of leftovers that had been there too long.

Ray's bed was a mess, and Dennis decided to change the sheets. There was a fresh sheet in the closet, and he stripped Ray's mattress.

The new sheet was tight, and he had to lift the mattress to get it over the corner. As he lifted it, he saw a tear on the underside of the mattress. He thought a broken bedspring or something might have torn it. Curious, he put his hand through the tear and felt a hard object in a cloth bag. He pulled the bag out, opened it, and was stunned to see a Rolex watch. There was no mistaking it. The rim and the wrist band were made of white gold and platinum. The clock face was black with luminous silver numbers and markings.

It took a moment for him to get over the shock and comprehend all that it meant. But it became clear. He shook his head, "I can't believe it. That stupid bastard. He was guilty all along, and he just lied to our faces."

Dennis tried to reconstruct what had happened, thinking that on the night Ray was arrested, he had come home earlier in a great hurry, ran into his bedroom, then ran out again. He must have had the watch, and hid it in the mattress. Then he went out, and when he came home again, he was immediately arrested and handcuffed. The cops never searched the bedroom. Dad had said that to search the apartment, they would have needed a search warrant. They could have gotten one, but they didn't.

He debated whether he should tell his father. As much as he was shocked and disappointed, it would be worse for his father, who would never forgive Ray for so bald-facedly lying to him and making everyone believe he was innocent.

Dennis couldn't figure out what to do. He could hear his father's voice, "When in doubt, do nothing." He could just remain quiet. Let things play out. Ray was out of jail, but Dennis didn't care anymore whether Ray was in or out. What he cared about was his mother and father. If they didn't know the truth, and believed Ray was not guilty, it would spare them the worst and give them some hope for Ray's future. But if he told his father what he knew, if he showed him the watch, it would be a devastating blow.

Besides the hurt for his family, Dennis remembered that a man was dead, an innocent man, minding his own business. He felt guilty himself, knowing that he was the one who concocted the scheme to get Ray off. Ray wasn't the shooter, but he was responsible nonetheless.

"He should be in prison," Dennis thought, "and I should be in prison with him. I made the crime worse. The dead man and his family can't even get justice." He remembered Klein saying that there was no such thing as justice. "Maybe he's right. There hasn't been any in this case for sure."

The apartment had grown dark, and he sat thinking of all that had occurred. He remembered that Klein had advised his father not to post the $500,000 bail. Klein's instinct had been right. If Ray was capable of this, he was capable of skipping out on the bail, and his father would have lost it.

He picked up the phone to call Kathy, but didn't call. He didn't know what to say, or whether he should say anything. If he told her, how would she take it? She was part of the scheme to get Ray off, and he had persuaded her to be in it. She might hate him more than she would hate Ray. He didn't want that. But if he didn't tell her, he'd never again be able to have an honest conversation with her. He didn't want that either.

As much as he tried, he couldn't figure a way out, couldn't figure how to get out of the box he had built for himself. A gnawing desperation was overwhelming him. He thought that this must be how people feel before committing suicide.

For a moment everything seemed surreal. What light there was reflected on the watch. He squinted to see it, and it looked for a moment like it was suspended in the air, floating around. "I've got to get rid of that damn watch," he said.

He took a hammer from under the sink, put the watch on the countertop, and began smashing it. The blows didn't break it. He hit it again and again, trying to separate the wrist band from the watch casing, but it seemed indestructible. The clock hands were still moving and the watch was still ticking. Then he swung the hammer with two hands from overhead. It finally broke and stopped ticking. But it was still identifiable, and he had to get rid of it.

He got some rocks from Mr. Martucci's garden, and put them in the bag with the watch.

At eleven-thirty, he went out. His father had told him that the best time to commit a crime is when the cops are changing shifts around midnight. Those getting off duty were not looking to get involved in anything if they could avoid it, and those coming on duty had to gas-up the cars and handle the 911 calls that were backed up from the prior shift.

He backed his car out of the driveway, and drove east on Myrtle Avenue to the Jackie Robinson Parkway. As he drove, his head was flooded with thoughts about what could happen. He wasn't paying close attention to his driving, then after about a mile, he saw a police car in his rearview mirror. Instantly, he felt his heart racing. He knew that if they stopped him, searched the car, and found the watch, they could charge him as an accomplice in the robbery and the murder. They could certainly charge him with possession of stolen property.

The Parkway had narrow lanes and sharp turns that were nerve-racking enough, now he was extra nervous, and drove as carefully as possible, making sure not to break any traffic rules, waiting to see whether the police would turn on their turret light or sound the siren for him to pull over. He wouldn't try to flee. He knew that was useless. He would just remain as calm as possible, and if they wanted to search the car, he wouldn't consent so that if they found the watch, the courts would suppress it because of the exclusionary rule.

But they didn't pull him over, and when he reached the Van Wyck Expressway, he was relieved that the police car didn't follow him onto it.

He took the Expressway north toward the Whitestone Bridge.

He drove over the bridge from Queens to the Bronx, and when he reached the Bronx side, he went through the cash lane to pay the toll. On the other side of the toll, he quickly made a U-turn to make sure no one was following him

He drove back towards Queens until he reached the midpoint of the bridge. Putting on his hazard lights, he stopped the car on the roadway. Taking the bag with the watch, he got out of the passenger side of the car, and climbed up onto the walkway.

Again, everything seemed surreal. It was like he was in a dream. Before him was a spectacular a view of the city—with the lights and skyscrapers of Manhattan shining between the boroughs of Queens and the Bronx. The wind was blowing in his face, and although it was almost midnight, there was plenty of traffic with cars hardly slowing down as they passed his Honda in the roadway. Some beeped their horns. Dennis' heart was pounding again. A car crash would be trouble.

The walkway fence was higher than he had remembered, and he wasn't sure he could throw the watch over it. He looked through the fence to make sure he was over water and not above the concrete foundation. Then, as though he were throwing a hand-grenade, he heaved the bag, with the watch and the rocks, as hard as he could to get over the fence, but it hit the top and fell back to the walkway. He retrieved it and, with a running start, heaved the bag up again. This time it went over, and through the fence, he saw it falling past him, but he couldn't see where it landed.

He got back into his car through the passenger side, and drove down the bridge, checking his rearview mirror.

"That's a relief," he said to himself. "But if someone finds it, and they connect it to me, then I'll know there is such a thing as justice."

CHAPTER NINETEEN

Forlini's was an old-style Italian restaurant located one block behind the Manhattan Criminal Court Building. Cops, detectives, DAs, defense attorneys, judges, and other court staff could exit the court building from the rear entrance, and walk across the Baxter Street Park to the restaurant on Mulberry Street. Although Forlini's was south of where the main section of Little Italy began, it was considered part of it.

Mulberry Street, with its Italian restaurants, cafes, pork stores, and bakeries, was the heart of Little Italy. The neighborhood was a vibrant tourist attraction. The Festival of San Gennaro every October was a major event that drew thousands to the area, and the neighborhood's reputation as a home-base of the mafia was a powerful draw of curious tourists.

Some restaurants even encouraged local side-walk men, who looked as though they could be cast as gangsters in the movies, to sit outside on stools or milkcrates, projecting the image of a mafia-controlled neighborhood. The "gangsters" got a free meal for their trouble.

Forlini's didn't have side-walk men, instead they had parking valets who kept the sidewalk and the street clear.

Inside, there was a long white-marble bar with well-stocked liquor shelves behind the bartenders. In the next room, there were salmon-colored booths, each with a colorful painting on the wall of an Italian scene—the usual gondolas, olive groves, marble statues, and the Tower of Pisa. Down the center of the room was a row of tables with white table-clothes. It was reserved for Klein's party.

The restaurant had been at the same location since the 1940s. Because of its proximity to the courthouse, police officers, lawyers, politicians, and others met there to discuss criminal cases, lawsuits, and the exchange of favors. Undoubtedly, many questionable deals and arrangements had been agreed to over pasta, veal, and wine.

Ironically, renowned former District Attorney Robert Morgan had patronized the restaurant regularly for decades. Known as a man of integrity and a staunch foe of corruption, he belonged to the elite and wealthy class of society who believed it was their duty to engage in public service. People from his circle would generally go to more upscale restaurants in midtown, but Mr. Morgan ate lunch at Forlini's twice a week. His secretary would call the restaurant to tell them when to expect him, and they would clear the same corner booth for him. It was known as Morgan's corner. Regulars said that even when he wasn't in the restaurant, the presence of his corner booth made people behave respectfully. The new district attorney didn't follow Morgan's practice.

When Dennis arrived at Forlini's, the bar was packed. He had to squeeze past people to get to where Klein and his guests were standing at the bar.

Ray saw Dennis, smiled, and opened his arms wide. "Here's my awesome brother now," he said.

"Your brother's going to be a great lawyer someday," Klein said.

"You can bet on that," Ray said.

Two lawyers passed by and congratulated Klein on winning the acquittal. Klein introduced Dennis to them, again saying that Dennis would be a great lawyer someday.

When a waiter told Klein that their tables were ready, the group moved to the next room and took their seats, with Klein at one end of the table, and Dominic at the other end. Behind Dominic was a mural of a blue and white Italianate fountain. Dennis couldn't help thinking that in this scene Dominic looked like the godfather.

Ray held a seat open for Kathy and asked, "Is Kathy coming?"

"She said she'd be here," Dennis said.

As they were ordering drinks, Kathy arrived and took the seat next to Ray. She acknowledged Dominic and asked whether his wife was coming.

"No." Dominic said. "She's going to make a big Sunday dinner to celebrate. You're invited."

"Thank you. I hope I can make it."

After the antipasto was served, Klein stood and made a speech. He was enjoying the moment, talking about how his client had adamantly and unequivocally proclaimed his innocence, how he refused to be bullied into a plea bargain, and how justice had ultimately triumphed.

Dennis wondered whether Klein believed what he was saying or was just mouthing platitudes. Maybe he had convinced himself that Ray was innocent? I could set him straight on that, he thought. Wouldn't it be something if I stood up and told everyone that I found the watch in Ray's mattress? Klein wouldn't be so pleased with himself, and Ray wouldn't think I was so awesome.

Dominic stood and made a short speech, thanking Klein and all the attorneys and staff who had worked so hard on the case. He began to say that it had been a pleasure working with them, but caught himself. Someone from the Department could be in the restaurant listening to him, and he wasn't supposed to be working for the defense. Instead, he said that he had been gratified to see such dedication and professionalism.

Dennis thought that his father might actually believe Ray was innocent.

After the main course, trays of Italian pastries were passed around, and some guests had cappuccino or expresso coffees. Then the party went to the bar for another drink. Ray ordered beers and offered one to Dennis.

"No. I was drinking wine. I'll stick with that."

Ray offered Klein a beer. "I have to go," Klein said. "All the best to you. Good luck."

As Klein began to walk away, Ray grabbed his arm. "What about my car? When do I get it back?"

Klein answered flatly. "We put in a request for the release. It'll take a few days."

"A few days, why?

Klein ignored Ray, turned to Dennis, and said, "When are you coming back to work for us?"

"Thanks. But not right away. On Monday, I start at UPS again. I promised them. So, can I call you in a couple of weeks?"

"Of course."

Klein turned back to Ray. "What about you, Ray."

"I'm gonna take it easy for a little bit," Ray said. "Then I'll find something"

"You could try UPS," Dennis said. "They're always hiring."

"I'll think about it."

Dennis looked at his father, and could see that he wasn't pleased.

"Well, you'd better think hard and fast," Dominic said. "I don't want you hanging out in those gyp-joints again. They're only trouble. You need to get a regular job."

Ray didn't answer, and after an awkward silence, he asked Kathy, "Ready to go?"

Dennis watched Kathy to see her response.

"I'm going straight home," she said. "I have to get up early in the morning. I'll see you Sunday at your mother's house."

Ray looked as though he had just been slapped in the face. This was his celebration, but it wasn't ending so well for him.

Hearing Kathy's answer, Dennis felt relieved. It was still an open question whom she would choose. She probably didn't know the answer herself.

Everyone said goodnight. Dominic drove Ray to the house in Canarsie to see his mother. Dennis drove to the Ridgewood apartment.

Dennis was glad that Ray didn't come to the apartment. He didn't want to deal with him tonight. He hadn't decided whether he was going to confront him about the watch, or wait for him to find that it was missing and ask what happened to it. Either way, it was going to be a difficult situation. As a kid, he had grown up idolizing his older brother, admiring his toughness and what he called his "cool" manner.

The admiration waned when Ray got into trouble with drugs and got arrested, but there was still a strong bond between them. He hoped that the trial, and the threat of going to prison, would change Ray, scare him straight, and get him to turn his life around.

He went to bed, but random, disjointed thoughts kept him awake. Thinking about the watch, he imagined a fisherman hooking it and turning it into the police. He second-guessed himself. Maybe I shouldn't have thrown it in the water. Maybe I should have buried it in the woods. But it could still be found, he thought. I should have smashed it up until it was unrecognizable, but there's no way of getting rid of it, no matter what you do.

He fell asleep for a short while, then woke up, and his thoughts began turning in his head again. Should he tell Kathy about the watch? He wanted her to pick him, not his brother, but if he told her that Ray was really guilty, it would be such a rotten thing to do to his own brother. On the other hand, she should know before committing herself. The fact is, Ray's a thief and a liar. It hurt to think that, but it was true.

On Saturday, Dennis stayed at the apartment, expecting Ray to show up. He wanted to be there if Ray came to look for the watch. He thought about what he would say to him, but Ray didn't come.

In the afternoon, Kathy called.

"How are you?" she said.

"I'm okay, how 'bout you?"

"Alright. But I have to tell you something."

"What?"

"Ray called me. He wants me to pick him up so we can go out tonight. He wants to go to McCoy's to show everyone he's out of jail."

"And?"

"I said yes. I don't know how I could've said no."

Dennis thought before he replied. "Going to McCoy's for old time's sake is okay."

There was a pause, then Kathy said, "He's thinking of new times."

Dennis resisted an impulse to tell Kathy about the watch. "Do whatever you think is right," he said. "Will I see you tomorrow at my mother's?"

"I'll be there."

Dennis thought that he'd have to wait for her to make up her mind. His father had once told him that although the man thinks he's chasing the woman, it's the woman who decides who will catch her."

At the Sunday dinner in Ray's honor, Dennis was surprised to see so many people there. His mother had invited her two sisters, Josephine and Carmela, and their husbands, Carmine and Antony; also, Dominic's sister, Marie, her husband, John, and their two daughters, Josephine and Donna, both in their twenties, both engaged to be married. The women were all busy, either helping Marie in the kitchen or setting the table.

Ray and Kathy weren't there yet. Dennis asked his father about them, and he said that they were on their way.

Dennis assumed that they must have spent the night at Kathy's. This isn't going to be a good day for me, he thought.

Ray and Kathy arrived just as the antipasto was being put on the table. "Here he is," someone shouted as Ray came in the door. People hugged him, patted him on the back, and introduced themselves to Kathy.

Ray and Kathy sat next to each other.

Assuming that he had lost Kathy, Dennis decided to go upstairs to the bathroom to get away for a moment. He stayed in the bathroom washing his hands until he heard his mother shouting, "Dennis, where are you? The foods on the table. We have to say Grace."

He went downstairs, and everyone sat quietly around the table holding hands as Marie made the sign of the cross and said, "In the name of the father, the son, and the holy ghost, thank you for this meal and for our family being here together, and for Ray being here with us. We ask your blessing. Amen."

Marie took one bite then got up to go into the kitchen to begin serving the lasagna. After that she would serve the fish, vegetables, and salad.

"It smells delicious," someone said.

"It always does. Marie's the best cook."

Dominic made a toast to Ray, wishing him a bright future. "And it's going to be a great year for us. My two nieces, Josephine and Donna, will be getting married, and who knows who else will be tying the knot," he said, looking at Ray and Kathy.

Dennis raised his glass, and looked across the table at Kathy. She looked away from him.

During the meal, Carmine, Dominic's brother-in-law, asked Ray how he was able stand being in prison for something he didn't do.

"It was hard," Ray said. "That's why I'm going to sue."

"Good," Carmine said, "on what grounds?"

Everyone at the table stopped talking and listened.

"Because they used a bad picture of me, an old picture from years ago. It looked like one of the robbers, but I don't look like that now."

"That's terrible," Donna, Dominic's niece, said.

As Dennis listened, he couldn't believe that Ray would even think of suing. What balls! To get away from the conversation, he went upstairs to his old bedroom and lay on the bed, thinking that Ray was convincing himself that he was innocent. Human beings do mental gymnastics to excuse or justify themselves, even when they're absolutely wrong.

He heard someone open the bedroom door. It was Kathy. "I wanted to see where you used to sleep when you were a little boy."

"This is the place," he said.

"It's nice, comfortable."

He looked at her, wondering what she was thinking.

"What's up?" he asked.

"I'm tired, and I have to work a double shift tomorrow. Goodnight." She kissed him on the cheek. "Call me."

Only minutes before Dennis had given up on Kathy, but now she said to call her. Apparently, she hadn't made her choice yet. He walked downstairs with her. Most of the guests were leaving, and he said his goodbyes to them.

Kathy said to Marie, "Thank you again for a wonderful meal. I enjoyed myself very much."

After Kathy left, only Dominic, Marie, Ray, and Dennis were left sitting at the dining room table.

"She's a lovely girl," Marie said.

"She sure is." Dominic said. "You're a lucky guy," he said to Ray. "But what's this talk about suing?"

"Why shouldn't I sue," Ray said. "It's not right what they did to me."

"Did Klein say you should sue?" Dominic asked.

"I made an appointment to see him on Wednesday."

Dennis thought that his was looking for trouble, for both of them. He stood up abruptly and gripped the edge of the table, surprising himself at how spontaneously he acted. "I think you're out of your mind," he said, and started to say that Ray was lucky he wasn't in jail, but then remembering his parents, stopped himself from saying anything more.

"What's the matter with you?" Ray said, as he stood up and glared at Dennis.

"Nothing's the matter with me," Dennis said, emphasizing "me," and pointing to himself.

Dominic looked quizzically at them, wondering what was the problem between his two sons.

"Take it easy, you two. Sit down!"

They sat down.

"I think Dennis is right," Dominic said. "The trial is over. Put it behind you. You think that if you sue, they're just going to hand over a pile of money to you. Don't count on it."

"Mr. Klein won a lot of cases for false arrest and false imprisonment," Ray said.

"He wouldn't even take your case," Dennis said.

"Why not?"

"There's not enough money involved," Dennis said. "Those newspaper cases that he puts up on the walls involved guys who spent years in prison, not a few months."

"That's right," Dominic said. "It costs a lot of money to sue, and he wouldn't even break even. Lawyers like Klein only sue when they have a sure thing."

"Then it's a rotten system."

Dennis laughed.

"What are you laughing at?" Ray said.

"Nothing," Dennis said. "I gotta go. I gotta get to work early."

He kissed his mother. "That was a great meal, mom. Love you."

Ray said, "I'll go with you"

"No. Why don't you stay here with mom," Dennis said as he left, in a hurry to get away.

CHAPTER TWENTY

The NYPD automobile pound was on twenty acres of landfill near the Belt Parkway in Brooklyn. As far the eye could see, there were cars parked in rows. They had been impounded for various reasons—forfeitures, accidents, stolen and recovered, or held for evidence. Many had been sitting there for years and by now would only be good for scrap metal.

The cars held as evidence couldn't be returned to the owner without a district attorney's release. After Ray's acquittal, Dominic had picked up the release, and they drove to the pound to pick up the car.

"I hope your car is still in one piece," Dominic said.

"Why shouldn't it be?" Ray said

"The place is notorious for thieves. They sneak in at night and take parts."

"What about the guards?"

"They can't see this whole place, even if they happened to be awake."

"That's real funny," Ray said.

At the security booth, Dominic showed his shield and the DA's release to one of the officers, who looked through a logbook and found the entry for Ray's car.

"I'm sorry, I can't release it to you," the officer said. "A new hold was put on it yesterday."

"But I have a release."

"That's dated last week. The new hold came after that and is in effect now."

"Who put on the hold?"

"Detective McConnell, Brooklyn North Robbery Squad."

"Was it from the DA, or the detective?"

"Not the DA. It says, 'For investigation.'"

"That son of bitch," Dominic thought. "He never gives up."

Dominic decided to go to the Brooklyn-North Robbery Squad at the 81st Precinct to talk to McConnell. They took the Belt Parkway to the Van Wyck Expressway to the Brooklyn-Queens Expressway and over the Kosciusko Bridge into Brooklyn. From the highpoint of the bridge, one could see the incredible panoramic view of Manhattan, but neither Dominic nor Ray looked. There was heavy traffic all the way and it took an hour and a half to get to Brooklyn. By the time they arrived, Dominic was doubly aggravated. He told Ray to wait in the car, while he went into the precinct.

He stopped at the station-house desk, showed his shield to the desk officer, and went up the stairs to the robbery squad office on the second floor. He walked through the gray swinging half-door that separated the visitor's area from the detectives' desks. The office walls were painted a drab green, and were covered with wanted posters and mugshots.

Detective-Sergeant Jim Meyers, whom Dominic knew and had worked with in the past, was at the front of the room. Dominic asked whether McConnell was on duty.

"He's in the back office," Meyers said.

Dominic passed the other detectives; the ones who knew him said hello.

McConnell was sitting with his feet up on his desk. "What can I do for you?" he asked.

"Why do you have a hold on my son's car? The DA released it."

"We need it as evidence for the trial of the other three perps."

"That has nothing to do with my son. He was acquitted. Not guilty. Remember?"

"Not guilty, doesn't mean innocent."

"What are you now, judge and jury. The law says he's innocent, no matter what you think. He needs his car back."

"He'll just have to wait till the trial is over," McConnell said, still sitting with his feet up. The soles of his shoes faced Dominic.

Dominic swept McConnell's feet off the desk, almost knocking him off his chair. "Get your feet out of my face, goddamn it," he shouted. "Is this how you treat people?"

McConnell got to his feet. "How'd you like a punch in the mouth?" he said, stepping forward, right up to Dominic's face.

"Try it, see what happens," Dominic said.

The other detectives didn't move to intercede, but Sergeant Meyers ran into the room and tried to squeeze himself between the two. Meyers was about five-feet-eight and thin. He had trouble keeping McConnell, who was tall, and Dominic, who was wide, separated. They had grabbed each other's wrists, and struggled with all their strength, trying to twist the other man's wrists.

"Come on, break it up," Meyers said, trying to pry their grips loose. He couldn't.

Finally, two of the other detectives helped him separate them.

"What's the problem between you two?" Meyers said.

"You know the story," Dominic said. "My son was found not guilty, the DA released his car, but this hotshot put a hold on it."

"We need the car for the trial of the other perps," McConnell said.

"First of all, my son is not a perp. He was found not guilty. Can you get that through your skull?"

"But we still need the car for the trial."

"That's bullshit. You have photos and videos. If the DA needed the car, he wouldn't have released it."

"That's enough," Sergeant Meyers said. "We'll have to check with the DA. Give me your phone number, and I'll call you when I get an answer."

Dominic left the precinct, and found Ray waiting outside of the car.

"How did it go?" Ray said.

"They're going to call the DA. You'd better drive. I've had enough traffic for one day."

On Tuesday, Sergeant Meyers called Dominic and told him that Assistant District Attorney Walsh wouldn't release the car. Meyers said that losing Ray's trial was not a plus for Walsh in the district attorney's office, and he was determined not to lose the case against the perpetrators of the dealership robbery.

Knowing that the trial could take months, Dominic rented a car for Ray. "This way, you'll have a car to look for a job," he said.

"Thanks, Dad. I appreciate your support and everything you've done for me."

"Okay, but please don't let me down. If you have questions about anything, or about getting a job, talk to me. If you can't find anything, I might be able to help. I have a friend who can give you a job, but it's not the best, and you should try on your own first."

On Wednesday morning, Ray went to his appointment at Klein's office to discuss suing the police for false arrest. He was surprised that Klein had already prepared the summons and complaint for the lawsuit. The documents were spread out on the conference room table. "Read them over. I'll be back and we'll discuss them before you sign."

Ray read the documents, but didn't fully understand them. It seemed repetitious to him. Klein returned and explained that they were suing the New York City Police Department, the City of New York, and Detectives McConnell, Cruz, and Matthews, for false arrest, malicious prosecution, false imprisonment, and violation of civil rights.

"Where do I sign?" Ray said.

"Before you sign, you need to know the risks involved."

"What risks?"

"First of all, if you lose, you could be charged with court costs."

"Could that happen?"

"Not likely, you have a legitimate case. But it's always a possibility."

"And when you bring a civil court lawsuit, you don't have the right to remain silent like you did in the criminal case. They're going to bring you in for a deposition, and you'll have to answer their questions under oath. If you don't answer, you can lose the case. And you could be subject to perjury."

"I'm not worried. I'm just going to tell the truth. I wasn't there."

"Okay, tell me again, where were you?"

"I was with Kathy Reynolds."

"Right, but if they can prove you weren't, you'll probably lose the lawsuit."

"I was with her, so how could they prove I wasn't?"

"You never know what can happen. You and Kathy are still on good terms, right?"

"Yes, we are."

"Good. We're suing in federal court because you have a better chance there and it'll be faster," Klein said.

"I don't want to jump ahead, but how much are we suing for, and how much can we expect to get?"

"We're suing for three million, plus one hundred and twenty-five thousand. It's right there in the last paragraph," Klein said pointing to the paragraph. "A million each on the unlawful arrest, malicious prosecution, civil rights violation, and a hundred and twenty-five thousand for the unlawful imprisonment."

"Wow," Ray said with a smile. "But how come only one hundred, twenty-five for the imprisonment, that was the worst part of it."

"The going rate for a month in prison is twenty-five thousand, and you were in for five months."

Ray laughed again. "That's a pretty good deal," he said. "I should have stayed in a few more months."

"Don't laugh," Klein said. "This is no joke, and we've got a long road ahead of us. You've got to be careful. Don't talk to anybody about the case. Watch what you say and watch what you do. And you'll have to go for therapy."

"Therapy, what for?"

"To prove damages. You've got to show that you were traumatized by the experience, and you've had lasting effects--bad dreams, fear of police. We'll make an appointment with Doctor Bedrossian."

"Is he a shrink?" Ray asked. "I don't want people to think I have mental problems."

"Temporary mental problems, just until the case is over."

"How much will it cost?"

"It doesn't cost you anything. If we settle or win a judgment, the cost will be deducted from your share."

"That's okay."

"But you have to cooperate with the doctor."

"What d'ya mean?"

"You may not realize the consequences of the trauma you suffered. He'll be able to explain it to you."

"I see."

"Good. Sign the complaint here by the red arrow, and sign this retainer agreement, which says that the law firm gets a third of any proceeds, and you get two-thirds of what's left after all expenses."

"What have I got to lose?" Ray said as he signed.

Dennis had worked overtime all week at UPS, and hadn't seen or talked to Ray or Kathy. About eight o'clock on Friday night, he arrived at the apartment. There was a car he didn't recognize in the driveway, a Chevy Malibu with rental plates. He parked behind it, went upstairs to the apartment, and heard noise coming from Ray's room. He saw rental car keys on the kitchen counter, grabbed the hammer from under the sink, and then crept quietly to the bedroom door. He opened the door slowly. Ray was sitting on the bed.

"You scared the hell out of me," Dennis said.

"Why? Who d'ya think it was?"

"Whose car is that in the driveway?"

"It's rented until I get my car back."

As the surprise wore off, Dennis noticed that the mattress was askew, and he figured that Ray had been looking for the Rolex.

"Were you looking for something?" he asked.

"Has anyone been in this room?" Ray asked.

"Yeah, me."

They stared hard at each other. Dennis didn't like the way Ray was looking at him. He looked like a different person, a person filled with anger and hate. Dennis was glad that he had the hammer in his hand.

Dennis had suspected that Ray was taking steroids for his bodybuilding, and they might be having an effect on him, making him more aggressive than he already was.

Ray stepped toward him. "What'd ya do with it?"

"With what?" Dennis answered.

"You know what." Ray raised his voice, "Where is it?"

"It's in the ocean."

"In the ocean?"

"Yeah. I threw it in the ocean."

"What the hell for?"

"Did you want the cops to come back and find it? You'd be on trial again and, most likely, so would I."

Ray looked accusingly at Dennis. "You didn't sell it, did you?"

"Of course not. I wanted to get rid of it as fast as possible."

"I can't believe this. How'd you throw it in the ocean?"

"I threw it off a bridge," Dennis said.

"Which bridge?"

"I'm not telling you. You'd be crazy enough to dive in and look for it."

Ray pushed past Dennis, and went into the kitchen. "I need a drink," he said, taking a can of beer from the refrigerator while Dennis put the hammer back under the sink.

They sat at the kitchen table without talking, looked at each other, and looked away. Finally, Ray spoke. "You know, you think you're so smart. You should know Klein's taking my case against the cops. He's filing the lawsuit for three million dollars."

Dennis was not surprised that Ray would sue, but was surprised that Klein would take the case. This is going to cause trouble, he thought.

"They always sue for millions," Dennis said. "That doesn't mean you get that, if you get anything. And, as a matter of fact, the only thing you're going to get is trouble."

In spite of Dennis' effort to remain calm and rational, anger overcame him. He slammed his hand on the table. "It's not as if you're innocent, remember."

"No. I am innocent. I was acquitted, remember," Ray answered.

"The Rolex says different," Dennis said.

That remark affected Ray. It brought him back to reality, to the truth. His bluster was gone, his head drooped, and he seemed uncharacteristically remorseful. "When did you find it?" he asked.

"The other night," Dennis said.

"Before or after the party at Forlini's?"

"Before."

"How come you didn't say anything?"

"I was still in shock, and hurt. I wanted to figure out what to do," Dennis said. He looked Ray in the eye. "What hurt more than anything was how you had made as all believe you didn't do it. You could have told me. I still would've done the same thing I did for you with Kathy and Belinda."

"I couldn't say it in front of Dad. It would've killed him," Ray said.

"That's for sure, but you still could've been honest with me."

"You're right," Ray said, then sat up straight and folded his arms. "Did you tell Dad about the watch?"

"No."

His short-lived moment of remorse over, Ray said, "So, you're not being entirely honest either."

"It's two different things," Dennis said.

"Okay, you're right. As usual, you're always right," Ray said.

He finished his beer then crushed the empty can in his hands, something that Dennis had seen him do many times, showing off in a bar or at a party.

Ray flexed his muscles, pulling his arms back, squaring his shoulders, and expanding his chest. Then he reached into the refrigerator, got another beer, and drank it down in three swallows.

"What's with you?" Dennis said.

"I'll tell you what's with me," Ray said, as she crushed the second beer can, this time with just one hand.

"I don't appreciate that while I was in prison, you tried to steal my girl."

Dennis hadn't expected this. He didn't have a quick answer. "That's not true," he said.

"I didn't try to steal her. It just happened, and it was more her doing than mine."

Ray kept glaring at Dennis, and Dennis kept talking. "We spent a lot of time together," he said, "making our plan about getting you out of jail. I went to McCoy's and we talked a lot, that's true, but that's as far as it went."

Ray reached into the refrigerator for a third beer. "I think it went farther than that," he said, looking directly at Dennis. "Kathy told me so."

Dennis didn't think Kathy would have told Ray that they had slept together. He thought that Ray was fishing, trying to trick him into a confession. He wouldn't be caught so easily. So, he went with his instinct, and called Ray's bluff. "That's not true," Dennis said emphatically. The brothers continued to stare at each other, reminding Dennis of what they used to do as kids to see who would blink first.

Ray picked up his beer and drank it in a few swallows. This time he didn't crush the can, but threw it across the kitchen into the garbage can.

"I'm going to McCoy's," he said. "I need to talk to Kathy and straighten this out, once and for all."

"I don't think you should drive," Dennis said.

"I feel fine."

"You had three beers. You may feel okay now, but they could hit you like a ton of bricks while you're driving."

"Don't tell me what to do, little brother."

"You don't want to get in an accident, or get arrested, or kill somebody." As soon as he said 'kill somebody,' he regretted it.

Ray glared at him. "I never killed anybody."

"I didn't say you did."

Ray stepped toward Dennis, and it seemed that he was going to take a swing at him, but, instead, he pushed him out of the way and grabbed the Malibu car keys from the counter. "I'm out of here," he said, as he left and slammed the door.

Dennis kicked himself for not stopping him. He should have hidden the car keys. Then he remembered that he had parked behind the rental car. He looked out the window and saw Ray trying to maneuver the Malibu around the Honda, but there wasn't enough room.

Good, he's stuck here, he thought. But Ray came running up the stairs and flung the door open. "You've got to move your car," he yelled.

"I'm not moving it," Dennis said.

"Well, I'll move it for you. Where are they keys?"

They both looked at Dennis' jacket laying on the couch, and both lunged for it at the same time. "Let go of my jacket. You can't take my keys," Dennis said as he tried to pull the jacket from Ray's hands. A sleeve ripped, and Ray tripped Dennis to the floor, put his foot on his chest, and yanked the jacket free.

Ray went through the pockets, got the keys, and left.

Dennis wasn't physically hurt, but it was a pivotal moment. He knew he would never feel the same way about his older brother again. Now he only saw Ray as a threat, both to him and to the family.

From the window, he watched Ray move the Honda, get in the Malibu, and drive away.

Dennis went downstairs and found the keys to the Honda still in the ignition. He thought of driving to McCoy's to talk to Kathy before Ray got there. Instead, he called her to warn her what to expect. There was no answer.

CHAPTER TWENTY-ONE

After Ray left the apartment in such an angry state, Dennis was worried, but he told himself that he had to get some sleep, and he lay on the couch to watch television so that the droning voices of some random documentary or an old movie would lull him to sleep. But it wasn't working, he was worrying about Kathy, and hoped that if Ray went to see her, she wouldn't let him in.

Besides worrying about Kathy, he had other worries. It was his lifelong habit to think about what problems could arise, and, depending on what they were, figuring out what would follow. He thought about Ray's lawsuit for false arrest and the can of worms it would open. First and foremost, Ray would have to answer questions. He couldn't claim the Fifth Amendment right to remain silent because he had been acquitted of the criminal charges, and to prosecute him again would be double jeopardy.

Ray would surely make mistakes under questioning, and any evidence uncovered could be used by the family of the deceased, Larry Coates, in a civil lawsuit for wrongful death.

In the civil lawsuit, the attorneys for the Coates family could easily prove that Ray participated in the robbery. They wouldn't have to prove it beyond a reasonable doubt, but only by a preponderance of the evidence, which is something more than fifty-percent of the evidence.

Ray would be found liable for the death and subject to a large judgment. Of course, he wouldn't have the money to pay it, but the judgment would hang over his head forever.

In any case, to either win or lose a criminal case or a lawsuit would cost a fortune in legal fees. His father would wind up paying the bills, and would probably have to sell his house. Dennis imagined how selling the house would affect his mother.

As the night wore on, he thought about his own situation. He would be drawn into Ray's case. The lawyers would question him as well as Kathy and Belinda, and incriminating facts would come out. The district attorney could charge them all with perjury or hindering prosecution for their fabricated testimony. Also, although he hadn't been involved in the robbery and murder, he might wind up being charged as a participant or an accessory after the fact.

Possibly making matters worse, if, by chance, the watch was found, it would connect him to the robbery. The cooperating witness would testify that the watch had been given to him, and the watch would corroborate that testimony, easily enough for a conviction.

All these possibilities increased his anxiety. He got up and paced back and forth. He thought it was only a matter of time before Ray did something crazy. Ray and steroids were a bad combination. He knew that some bar bouncers used steroids to bulk up, and it made them prone to violence. There'd been several cases of bouncers on steroids beating the hell out of people. Some had gotten arrested, and Ray was certainly a candidate. Something bad was sure to happen.

Besides all that, Dennis couldn't make up his mind to tell Kathy about the watch. She was under the impression that Ray had been falsely accused, and, in her mind, he had handled it bravely, refusing to be bullied into pleading guilty, which said something good about his character. What she didn't know was that. in fact, he was guilty, and had lied through his teeth.

If he told her, she might drop Ray and choose him instead. If that happened, Ray would never forgive him, and the family would be torn apart. And what if she stayed with Ray anyway?

Maybe that would be for the best, he thought. But it would be hard to take after the perfect days and nights they had shared together. He had hoped for many more.

It wasn't until about four o'clock in the morning he decided to definitely tell his father why the lawsuit should be dropped.

At noon, Dennis drove to his parents' house, ate lunch with them, then asked his father if they could talk privately. They went downstairs to the basement recreation room. There was a small home-made bar, an old brown leather couch, a pool table, a dart board, and Ray's high school trophies from football and wrestling. Photographs and sports posters covered the walls.

"Let's play a game of pool while we talk," Dominic said.

"Dad, this is important. Can we play after we talk?"

"Okay. So, what do you want to talk about?"

They sat at the bar.

"Ray filed a three-million-dollar lawsuit against the police," Dennis said. "Klein took the case."

Dennis could see that his father was surprised.

"He filed it already?"

"That's what Ray said."

"I knew he was thinking about it, but I didn't think he'd do it without telling me," Dominic said. "I guess Ray is over twenty-one. He can do what he wants."

"It's going to cause a lot of trouble," Dennis said. "With three million dollars on the line, the city's lawyers will fight tooth and nail. Ray and everyone else will have to answer questions. You've told me how these cases go, how people being questioned make admissions and mistakes. Not only Ray, but Kathy and Belinda will be grilled. And they'll call me to testify, and they could call you. You don't need trouble with the job. The Department will be watching the case."

"You're right about that. But Ray has the right to sue. He was the one wrongfully arrested and jailed."

Dennis was struck that his father still thought Ray was innocent. He was also struck that his father, a detective who over many years had been so skeptical of what people claimed, now so readily accepted Ray's claim of innocence.

"Are you sure of that, Dad?"

Dominic went over to the pool table and rolled a couple of balls around "I think Ray was dead wrong to be involved with the drug dealers, even associate with them for a minute, but that doesn't mean he was involved in the robbery. He was found not guilty, so let's just stick with that."

Dennis was picturing the Rolex, but didn't say anything about it. His objective was to prevent Ray's lawsuit, and he thought he could do it without revealing to his father that Ray had hidden the watch in the mattress.

"Dad, it doesn't matter if Ray was guilty or not, what matters is that he was acquitted because of what Kathy and I did. Kathy's testimony about my so-called declaration against interest, or confession, if you want to call it that, created the reasonable doubt that required the jury to acquit him. If Ray continues the lawsuit, it'll open up everything again, and our testimony will be challenged. In fact, my declaration against interest may not even be admissible in a civil trial. In a countersuit, Ray could easily be found liable for the robbery and murder. So, instead of Ray getting three million, he'll be held liable for a lot of money."

"Thankfully, he doesn't have a lot of money," Dominic said.

"Real funny."

"Let's play," Dominic said, and racked the pool balls on the table.

After fifteen minutes of shooting pool, Dominic put his pool cue down. "If what you tell me is true, I can't believe Klein would go ahead with this."

"Yeah, I was thinking the same thing," Dennis said. "I'm surprised he didn't talk Ray out of it. He knows what went on, what we did. I thought lawyers were supposed to present only evidence they believed to be true."

"Don't believe it. I've seen lawyers twist facts in whatever direction helps their case. They love to go around saying that all cops lie, but the lawyers are better liars. They're not above making up stories, and not above ignoring perjury when it suits them."

"Can't they get disbarred?"

"Very rarely. They're protected. The politicians and judges are all lawyers, and they make the rules. They say that lawyers have a duty to zealously represent their clients. Based on that, they excuse themselves for almost anything."

"Maybe I should think about going to law school, I could be good at that, he said in a way that seemed disparaging of himself."

"Maybe you should," Dominic agreed.

"Putting that aside, if I get into trouble because of the lawsuit, no law school would accept me. That's another reason you've got to get Ray to drop the case."

"I don't have the right to do that. He's the one who got arrested."

Dennis came close to blurting out that Ray had taken the watch, but he bit his tongue. Instead, he said, "Ray may not have been guilty, but just as you said, he was involved with the drug dealers. He caused his own problems, and I don't see why he deserves to get any money from anybody."

"So, you think he's guilty?" Dominic said.

Again, Dennis bit his tongue, and said, "I didn't say that. But what he's doing is only going to cause trouble for everybody. Klein's the only one who has nothing to lose. That's why he's going forward. He sees a big payday."

"That's what lawyers do. It's their business. When they have a client who gets acquitted, and they can blame the police, they jump on it like jackals."

"I thought you liked a lot of lawyers. I thought you liked Klein."

"I do. But that's the way the game is played."

"Dad, it seems to me that Klein is using Ray to get a payday, regardless of the consequences for us."

"You may be right. Let's call him and see what he says."

He got through to Klein and complained that he hadn't been consulted about the lawsuit.

"I understand," Klein said. "But Ray is my client. My obligation is to him."

"Of course, but there's more involved here. I'm here with my son, Dennis, and he's raised some serious questions, potential problems."

"Dennis has got a head on his shoulders."

"He does, and I tend to agree with him."

"I hate to cut you off, Dominic, but Ray is my client. I can't take input from you without his permission. I have a meeting scheduled with him on Monday afternoon at my office. If he agrees that you should be involved, we can all meet. Dennis also."

Dominic didn't like the way Klein was pushing him aside, and felt himself getting hot under the collar, but he only said, "Okay. What time?"

"Four o'clock."

Over the weekend, Dominic and Dennis tried to contact Ray, but there was no answer on his cell phone.

Dennis called Kathy's phones, but there were no answers there either.

He called McCoy's and spoke to Brendan, the bartender, who told him that Kathy had taken the night off. "She said she was sick," Brendan said.

"Is she going to work tomorrow night?"

"I think so."

Dennis thought that Kathy and Ray were probably together somewhere. He figured that their relationship was on again and that he was going to be the odd man out.

Sunday evening, he drove to McCoy's, but Brendan told him that Kathy had just called in sick again.

Dennis had a beer then drove to Kathy's apartment building. As he turned into her block, he saw a blue Malibu pulling out of a parking space. He didn't get too close but was sure it was Ray's rental car. He waited until the Malibu was off the block, then parked and went into Kathy's building. When someone came out of the front door, he got in, and took the elevator to the sixth floor.

He knocked at her apartment door but no one answered. He thought he heard movement, so he knocked harder.

Then, through the door, he heard Kathy say, "Go away. Leave me alone.

"It's me, Dennis."

"Go away."

"What's the matter? Is anything wrong?"

He knocked again, but she didn't answer.

With his cell phone, he called her number. Her answering machine picked up, and he said, "Kathy. It's Dennis. Are you alright? Please open the door." He could hear his voice through the door as his message played on her phone.

He kept knocking, and eventually Kathy opened the door. "I don't want to see anyone."

She was obviously upset. She didn't look like she had been crying, but looked angry.

"What's the matter? Can I come in?"

She left the door open and walked into her mini kitchen to get a glass of water.

He followed. "What happened?"

"Nothing happened."

"I saw Ray's car driving away. Did you have a fight?"

She didn't answer.

"Did you break up?"

"Break up! We're not together. He was here, and wouldn't leave. Yesterday and today. He just kept after me. Wouldn't stop."

Dennis noticed some swelling over her left eye. "Did he hit you?"

"You might say that." Kathy went into the leaving room and sat on the couch. "I'm so stupid," she said. "He kept pressuring me. Yesterday and today. I told him I didn't want to. But he wouldn't leave. I thought if I gave in, he would leave. I just lay there. That made him mad. He said he wanted it to be like it was. I said I didn't want to, that's when he got rough. He's strong as hell."

Kathy went into the bathroom and came out after five minutes.

"So, he raped you," Dennis said. "Is that what you're saying?"

"I don't know what to say. I don't know if you can call it rape. He just kept pushing."

"You told him you didn't want to do it?"

"Yes."

"Nowadays that's rape."

"Let's not talk about it."

"You struggled with him."

"I thought of hitting him with the lamp, but we've been together so much, it seemed crazy."

Dennis sat next to her on the couch and put his hand on hers. She moved her hand away. "Dennis, thanks for your concern, but I want to be alone."

"You shouldn't be alone now. Why don't we go out? Get something to eat."

"If he sees us together, he'll go crazy. He's very jealous. He asked me three times if we had slept together."

"And?"

"I told him no. We're just friends."

Dennis began to see the bigger picture. "Has this happened before?"

"Not as bad as today. But he wants what he wants when he wants it. That's what he told me."

"You should go to the police. And you should go to the hospital to get checked."

"I'm not doing that. We've slept together for so long; would anyone believe that it now suddenly turned into rape."

"You've got to do something, or he'll keep coming back."

"I'll put a bullet in his head first."

The way she said it, Dennis believed her.

"Do you want me to stay? I'll sleep on the couch."

"No. I've had enough of men for one day. Call me tomorrow."

"If he comes back," Dennis said, "call me."

When Dennis got home to Ridgewood, he wondered where Ray was, and hoped that he wasn't out somewhere getting drunk or high. He hoped that he wouldn't go back to Kathy's. If he did, and she called him, he'd go over there with the hammer from under the sink.

But no calls came, and at 7a.m., the alarm went off. He showered, shaved, got dressed into his UPS uniform, and left for work.

CHAPTER TWENTY-TWO

D ennis arrived ten minutes late for the scheduled meeting at Klein's office. His was wearing a blue denim jacket over his brown UPS work uniform. Dominic, and Ray were already in the conference room.

"Glad you could make it," Klein said. "How's it going?"

Dennis took off his jacket and sat next to his father across the table from Klein and Ray. "Things could be better, and this lawsuit doesn't help," he said.

"Okay, let's talk about it," Klein said. "But first let me set the ground rules. This meeting is covered by the attorney-client privilege, so, if later, we're asked about what was said, we'll be protected from having to answer. However, because there are so many of us, the privilege could be challenged, and we would have to answer questions about what was said. So, this is going to be a general strategy session. We shouldn't talk about specific factual events. Don't say anything you might regret later. You understand?"

Everyone nodded.

"Good."

Looking directly at Dennis, Klein said, "Your father just told me about your concerns, what's the main problem?"

Dennis didn't hesitate, "The main problem is that Ray's lawsuit is going to boomerang, and it'll turn into a criminal investigation of Kathy, Belinda, and me."

"It'll be my job to prevent that," Klein said.

"But you can't guarantee that," Dennis said. "As I understand it, we'll all be questioned at depositions before the trial. And the other side will be able to question us for hours, and go into all sorts of areas. They can go into our pasts, into our relationships, almost anything."

"That's more or less true, as long as the questions are aimed at getting relevant evidence," Klein said. "And you're right. Relevant evidence can be wide-ranging and personal. But I'll be sitting with you to keep the questioning in line, and I'll object to anything improper."

"I've read a few transcripts of depositions, and it didn't seem that having a lawyer sit next to the witnesses did any good."

"It depends who the lawyer is."

"And the questions went on for hours," Dennis said. "By the time it was over, the witnesses were rung out, and some of them were babbling, just agreeing to anything to get it over with."

Klein smiled. "I can't argue with that. Wearing the witness out is how we lead them into mistakes. So, we'll have some practice beforehand to make sure everyone will be ready."

Dennis wouldn't be dissuaded. "I'm not sure any of us can withstand a tough interrogation," he said. "And I'm worried. Kathy's so honest, she'll sink us all. And Belinda, she won't last ten minutes before they get her twisted in knots."

"Don't underestimate them. They both did very well testifying at the trial."

"True, but the other side is going to be loaded for bear, and they've got all day to cross-examine them. I don't think they'll hold up under tough questioning."

"What about me?" Ray said. "Do you think I'll cave in?"

"I don't know what to think about you," Dennis said in a disparaging tone. The tension between the two brothers was palpable.

"Are you two starting up again?" Dominic interrupted. "I don't know what your trouble is, but this meeting is to decide whether it's worth it to go forward. We have to weigh the risks versus the rewards."

"The risks are too great," Dennis said emphatically. "All that can happen is somebody gets indicted for false testimony or Ray gets sued for wrongful death, or both."

"So, that's it," Ray said. "You're worried about getting indicted. But don't I deserve to get some justice for what they did to me."

"If you got the justice you deserved, you wouldn't like it," Dennis said.

"And you might not like getting justice either," Ray said, raising his voice. "You're the one who concocted the phony testimony."

"I did it to save your ass," Dennis said.

"Who asked you to?" Ray said.

Dominic raised his hand, signaling his sons to stop. "Cut it out. We're not here to insult each other, we're here to make a decision."

"Keep in mind," Klein said, "Ray agreed for you two to participate, but ultimately the decision is his. He's the one with the complaint and the cause of action."

"That's right," Ray said. "I'm the one they threw in prison. I got a right to be compensated."

"Of course," Klein said, "and by going forward, we put pressure on the city to settle. I can't guarantee this, but in all probability, we'll get a settlement offer, at least enough to compensate him for the time he spent in jail.

"And if we don't settle, the city will make a motion for a summary judgment to dismiss the case, which will likely be denied, and the city will have to raise their offer."

"What's a summary judgment?" Ray asked.

"After the depositions," Klein said, "if there are no real factual issues left to be decided, the judge can decide the case himself, or, if there are, he can send the case for a jury trial. If he sends it for trial, the city, wanting to avoid a trial, usually raises their offer. It's cheaper for the city to settle than to gamble on a trial and a big jury verdict."

"It seems to me, we should keep pushing forward to get the best offer we can," Ray said. "What've I got to lose?"

"Maybe you don't have anything to lose, but we do," Dennis said. "And don't forget, you can still be sued."

"Let me worry about that."

"That's just like you, worrying about yourself." Dennis stood. "You want to score a big payday, but you're leaving the rest of us out to dry."

"The city gives away money all the time. So, if I can get a piece of it, why shouldn't I take it?"

"Because you don't deserve it, that's why," Dennis said.

There was a dead silence in the room. Ray knew what he meant, and Dominic and Klein began to realize that Dennis knew more than he had told them."

Ray jumped up, "I'd like to come around this table and knock your teeth down your throat."

Dennis got up, and took a stance, ready to defend himself.

Dominic stood and stretched his arms out to the side as though keeping them apart. "That's enough, you two."

To Dennis, he said,

"You keep implying that Ray's guilty. What's your proof?"

"You'd better sit down, Dad," Dennis said.

"I don't need to sit down. Let's have it."

Dennis took a deep breath, "Okay. About a week ago, I found a Rolex watch hidden in Ray's mattress."

Dominic took a moment to absorb what he had just heard.

"From the robbery?" he asked.

"Yes."

"How do you know?"

"Ray acknowledged it."

Ray blurted out, "You son of a bitch."

"Nice way to talk about your own mother," Dennis said.

"That's enough," Dominic said.

There was silence until Dominic said, "Where's the watch now?"

"I threw it off the Whitestone Bridge."

"What possessed you to do that?"

"I wanted to get rid of it. Get rid of the evidence."

"You told Ray that?"

"Yes. And he accused me of selling it."

"You should have minded your own business," Ray said.

Dominic came around the table closer to Ray. Suddenly, he slapped him across the face with the back of his hand. It was a lightning-fast move, and the force of the blow knocked Ray to the floor.

Ray instinctively started to get up, but looked up at his father, and stopped. He lay back on the floor, resting on his right elbow. He was obviously humiliated and frustrated. If anyone else had hit him like that, he'd be all over the guy, but this was his father.

The sound of the slap and the thud of Ray hitting the floor had stunned Klein, who stared at them open-mouthed for a minute, then said, "This is a law office, not a saloon." He tried to help Ray up by lending him a hand, but Ray was too heavy for him to pull up. Ray had to grab the table to get to his feet and onto a chair.

The secretary came to the door to find out what the commotion was. Klein told her, "Close the door."

No one spoke for several long minutes, until Dominic said, "Knowing what we know now, I have to agree with Dennis. The lawsuit shouldn't go forward."

"I'll take that under advisement," Klein said, "but remember, the final decision is Ray's."

"Try to talk some sense into him," Dominic said. "Let's go," he said to Dennis, and they left the office without Ray.

CHAPTER TWENTY-THREE

R ay moved out of his parents' house. His relationship with his father had been shattered. In the earlier instances when Ray had gotten in trouble, his father had never struck him. But, now, his father's backhand told him that he couldn't stay in the house any longer.

Ray packed his clothes, and drove to the Ridgewood apartment. He walked in on Dennis and told him that he was taking the apartment back.

"You mean you're moving back in," Dennis said.

"No. I'm taking the whole apartment. You're going to have to move out."

Because the lease was in Ray's name, Dennis couldn't stop him.

"But I just paid the rent for the month," Dennis said.

Ray took out a thick roll of bills, "I'll give you my half, but you have to be out by the end of the month."

He counted out and gave Dennis five hundred dollars. He was making good money at the strip club and the after-hours club.

Dennis noticed the money, and said, "They pay you pretty well."

"They do. And the girls throw me a percentage of their tips for making sure they don't get too hassled."

★ ★ ★ ★ ★

Dennis didn't move out of the apartment right away. During the month, he found that it wasn't such a bad living arrangement. He worked days, and Ray worked nights, so they were rarely in the apartment at the same time. Ray didn't get home from his job as a bouncer at the strip club until five or six in the morning, and sometimes he worked at an after-hours club as a doorman and wouldn't get home until seven or eight a.m. By that time, Dennis was either leaving for work or had already gone.

Despite the disagreements, they could keep the arrangement; however, one morning, as Ray came in from working all night and Dennis was leaving for UPS, Ray said, "You can stay another month if you need it to find another place, but that's as far as it goes. I'll put your stuff out on the street myself if I have to."

Later, Dennis called Kathy, and asked her if he could come over to see her. She immediately said, "No. I'll meet at McCoy's before I start my shift. About a quarter to three." He was surprised that she wouldn't let him come over.

When Dennis arrived at McCoy's parking lot, Kathy got into his car. They talked for a while then Dennis got to the question he wanted to ask.

"Ray moved back into my place, and I'll have to move out. How about I move in with you?"

She immediately said, "No."

"Why not? Are you still seeing Ray?"

"No."

"Then why not. If it doesn't work out, I'll move out. You'd just have to tell me."

"It's a nice idea, but I'm too worried about Ray. He's explosive. I'm afraid of what he might do. I told him I didn't want to see him anymore, but he still comes around. That's why I didn't want you to come to my place. Sometimes, he follows me. Thank goodness he works nights so he can't come around McCoy's too often."

"This is not healthy," Dennis said. "It sounds like he's getting crazy. You should get an order of protection."

"Maybe I should get a gun."

"Don't think like that. I'll talk to him, try to make him see how crazy he's acting."

"That's the last thing you should do," Kathy said. "You'd set him off. He already talks insanely about you. He told me that you betrayed him in front of your father and the lawyer. So, he's not about to listen to anything you say."

"You're probably right."

"So, tell me, what was it that you told your father and the lawyer that made Ray call you a turncoat?"

"That's what he called me?"

"Yes."

"I'm not going to tell you."

"Why not?"

"Because I feel terrible enough about what I said against my own brother, and I'm not going to spread it around any further."

"I guess it's none of my business," Kathy said.

"I wouldn't say that, but let's drop it for now."

"Alright, I have to go. I've got five minutes before my shift starts," she said, got out of the car, and began walking toward McCoy's front door. Then she turned around, came back to the car, and motioned for him to roll down the window. She leaned in and kissed him on the lips, then went back to McCoy's.

As she walked away, he watched her, and thought how easily that kiss had transformed his disappointment into desire.

At the Kit-Kat strip club where Ray worked as a bouncer, the girls danced on a platform behind the bar. They were not actually strippers; they were go-go dancers and pole-dancers, wearing skimpy outfits as close to nakedness as they could get without violating the indecency laws.

The Kit-Kat advertised itself as a Gentlemen's Club, an incongruous label, since the male patrons looked more like roughneck truck drivers, factory workers, and auto mechanics. Ray's job was to keep them in line without spoiling their good time, and, also, to make sure they bought drinks. A constant problem was with gawkers who tried to watch the girls without spending any money or by having one drink and staying for hours. When Ray spotted a gawker, he'd ask him if he wanted to buy a drink. If the gawker wouldn't, Ray would ask him to leave. If he refused, Ray would either convince him to go or throw him out.

Ray had been working at the club for almost a year, and had handled the job well. His boss, Aldo Manfredonia, liked Ray's work and had given him a raise. Only on two occasions had Ray hit someone. Both were drunks who swung at him. He blocked their punches and hit them in the solar plexus. They threw up as they were being thrown out.

Dealing with one unruly customer at a time was relatively easy. It was when a group of troublemakers came in that there could be real problems.

Ray was the only bouncer, but there were three bartenders who were supposed to come to his aid if needed. Once a group of seven young men came in and began shouting, cursing, and trying to touch the girls. Ray told them to quiet down or they'd have to leave. "Who's going to make us?" One of them said.

"You'll find out," Ray said, and signaled to the bartenders. They came around from behind the bar, holding bats, and stood behind Ray. Then Aldo came from a backroom; he had a Glock semi-automatic pistol in his waistband and made sure the young men saw it.

"What are you going to do," one of the young men said, "shoot us?"

"If I have to," Aldo said. "And don't think I won't. Use your head, young fella, you don't want to get in problem over this nonsense. It isn't worth it."

"Let's get out of here," another one said, "this place stinks." The group left.

Later that night, Ray asked Aldo about the gun. "The gun is licensed?"

"Of course," Aldo said.

"Would you have used it?"

"If I had to, but only as a last resort."

Aldo gave Ray an extra hundred collars. "Here, you did a good job tonight."

"Thanks."

"On Saturday nights, I want you to work in the after-hours club around the corner. My younger brother, Gino, runs it. Same pay. Okay."

"Okay."

The 444 club was around the corner from the Kit-Kat club. It was called the 444 club because those were the numbers on the front door, even though it wasn't the actual address. The heavy, wooden door had a sliding lookout slot that the doorman would open to peek through before allowing anyone to enter. Only members were allowed, which supposedly made it a social club rather than a commercial premises, and allowed it to operate without a liquor license. In fact, it was an illegal bar and casino with four blackjack tables in the back room.

Gino spent most of his time overseeing the blackjack tables. The blackjack dealers were young, attractive Asian women, and many of the customers who came to play blackjack were Asian.

Gino was thirty-five, about six feet tall, handsome with black hair and dark eyes. He always dressed in expensive, immaculate suits. His favorite was a pin-striped, gray, double-breasted. With it, he wore a gold watchchain connected from the suit's middle button to his pocket watch. Every so often he would take out the watch and flip open the cover to check the time. He took cash from the customers and gave them chips in exchange. When the customers wanted to cash-in their chips, they went to a side room where the moneyman sat inside a locked gate and made transactions through a slot.

At first, Ray thought Gino was overdressed and pretentious, but he soon noticed the deference the workers and the customers showed to Gino, and he came to see the value of his appearance. Some of the Asians even made little bows when they spoke with him.

Ray's job was to deal with any unruly customers and screen customers arriving at the front door. Customers who were members, or were with a member who vouched for them, were let in. Others were turned away. The most important part of the doorman's job was to make sure that no undercover cops got in. If they did, it would lead to a raid and the club being shut down.

Without the Ridgewood apartment, and without Kathy letting him move in with her, Dennis moved in with his parents. His father agreed on one condition: that he take some college night courses.

"But I wanted to wait until I saved enough money to go full time," Dennis said.

"That's fine, but if you keep putting it off, you'll never do it. Just take a couple of courses to get started."

"I'm not sure what I want to study yet," Dennis said.

"Worry about that later. Take whatever they give you, you might learn something."

So, Dennis registered for two courses at St. John's University, two nights a week. Because he didn't finish work until after seven, the first course he could take began at eight and the second began at nine-twenty, which made for a long day. His father said that it would keep him out of trouble.

After two months of attending classes, he was glad. He was taking English and history, and he felt that they were good preparations for his long-term goal of going to law school.

He called Kathy several times, but she didn't answer. She's driving me crazy, he thought, one day, she kisses me, then the next day, won't even answer my calls. He was both disappointed and concerned, maybe something was wrong, he thought. So, one night after school, he went to McCoy's about eleven o'clock. Kathy was bartending along with Brendan, and Dennis asked for a beer.

"Can we talk?" he asked her.

"I'm off at midnight, if you want to wait," she said.

"I'll wait."

"Why don't you have a burger while you do?"

"Okay."

"Take a booth, I'll bring it to you."

Dennis finished the burger, and at midnight, Kathy brought two beers to the booth and sat across from him. "What do you want to talk about?"

"I want to know why you won't take my calls."

She took out a hand-mirror, put some lipstick on, then, while not looking at him but in the mirror, said, "I haven't been home much. I've been staying at Belinda's a lot."

"How come?"

"Because Ray keeps coming around. He sits in his car on the block waiting for me to come out. I made the mistake of going out with him once. I wanted to tell him that it was over, but it only encouraged him."

"Has he been rough with you again?"

"No. But he can look very angry. Scary."

"Yes. I know."

"And I don't know what he wants with me," she said. "He's working in that stripper place; he can get all the girls he wants."

"Don't put yourself in that category," Dennis said.

"Thanks for saying that."

They both took slugs of beer.

"But I also called your cell phone, and you didn't answer."

"There was so much going on, I just didn't feel like talking."

"The reason I kept calling was because I wanted to tell that I'm talking some college courses at St. John's."

"That's good."

"And I had an idea that maybe we could take courses together."

Kathy was surprised by the offer. "That's a really nice idea," she said. "But when would I find the time."

"You could get two nights during the week off," he said.

"Maybe. I'll think about it," she said.

Suddenly, Kathy straightened up and looked past Dennis. "Damn it, he's here. He's coming in the front door."

From the frightened look on Kathy's face, Dennis knew who she was talking about.

Ray came straight over to their booth, keeping his right hand in his jacket pocket. Dennis noticed it, and held his beer bottle under the table, keeping it ready in case he had to use it.

"So here they are," Ray said, "the two lovebirds, my brother and my girlfriend."

"I'm not your girlfriend," Kathy said.

"You were till this bum stole you away when I wasn't looking," Ray stepped closer to them. Dennis stood up, and holding the beer bottle at shoulder level.

Ray took his hand out of the pocket, and opened his hand, showing that it was empty. "Did you think I was going to shoot you?"

"That's not funny," Dennis said.

"I don't need a gun, I can punch your lights out right now, beer bottle or no beer bottle." Ray took another step closer to Dennis, who stepped back and took a boxer's stance with the bottle in his right hand. He knew he couldn't beat Ray in a fight, but he was not going to back down in front of Kathy, and was determined to go down swinging if he had to.

At that point, Brendan, who had recognized trouble brewing, came around from the bar and got between them. "We don't want any trouble in here, fellas," he said.

Brendan ordered Dennis to put the bottle down. Dennis complied and sat back in the booth. Then Brendan put his arm around Ray, surreptitiously feeling his pocket to see if there was a weapon. "Come over to the bar with me for a minute, Ray, let us have a little talk."

Ray pushed Brendan's arm off. "Mind your own business."

"This is my business," Brendan said.

At that moment, Kathy stood. "Everybody, stop it! I'm not your girlfriend or your girlfriend," she said to Ray and Dennis in turn. "I'm leaving, and don't either one of you call me. I'm fed up with all this nonsense."

She took her purse from the booth and walked quickly out of the front door.

Ray started to walk after her, but Brendan grabbed his arm. "Be smart, this is not a good time," he said. "Why don't you and your brother sit down and talk it over? I'll bring you two beers on the house."

Ray pulled his arm away from Brendan, and ran after Kathy.

Dennis followed, and they saw Kathy's car speeding out of the parking lot. Ray ran to his car, and Dennis ran to his.

They followed her as Kathy made a right turn on red, then at the next intersection, went through a red light. She raced through the streets at almost 60mph into Greenpoint with Ray and Dennis keeping up with her in their cars.

Dennis thought it would be a miracle if they didn't crash or the cops didn't stop them. When Kathy reached her block on McGuinness Boulevard, she made a right turn, barely slowing down. She parked at the fire hydrant in front of her building and ran inside, getting through the building's outer front door, then, with her key, the inner door, before Ray could catch up to her. The inner door closed behind her, and Ray was locked out, stuck in the vestibule. Through the glass door, he could see Kathy getting on the elevator to go up to her apartment. He furiously rang the doorbells of other apartments to get someone to buzz him in, but no one responded. So, he gave up, and left the building. As he exited, Dennis was coming in. They stopped and faced each other.

"Why don't you leave her alone?" Dennis said. "You're acting crazy."

"Don't call me crazy," Ray said, as he pushed Dennis off the front step and into a bush, then he got into his car and drove off.

Dennis pushed himself up from the bush, and decided to wait around to make sure Ray didn't come back. He noticed Kathy's car was on the fire hydrant, and he realized that she would have to come outside to move it. So, he called her, and told her that she should move her car now while he was there.

"Okay, I'll be right down."

She moved her car to a legal parking spot while Dennis kept watch to see if Ray would come back. He walked with her into the building. "Did you mean what you said about me not calling you?" he asked.

"Right now, I don't know," she said. "I don't want to come between two brothers. It's not a good look for me." She opened the inner door, and held her hand up, signaling for him not to come in. The door closed and Dennis left.

CHAPTER TWENTY-FOUR

Staying at his parents' house, working full time, going to school two nights a week, and studying on the other nights, Dennis seemed to be living a calm and productive life. However, underneath the seemingly calm exterior, he was troubled about Ray's lawsuit and the upcoming depositions, and more so because Kathy wouldn't see him. He was sure it was because she didn't want to be responsible for splitting two brothers apart.

What she didn't know was that they had already split. Dennis hadn't told her about finding the watch. He grappled with the idea of telling her, thinking that if he did, she'd disown Ray. But he didn't like being called a "turncoat." He just couldn't do it.

At home one evening, he and his father went downstairs to play a game of pool. Dominic studied his son for a few minutes and asked why he seemed so depressed.

"I'm okay. Just busy, I guess," Dennis said

"Is your job alright?"

"It's fine."

"What about school?"

"School's great, a lot of fun. Thanks, for pushing me to go."

"Girl trouble?"

"No, everything is fine."

"Then what is it—Ray's lawsuit?"

"Yeah, it wakes me up every night."

"Sometimes a drink before going to bed solves that problem," Dominic said. "You want one?"

"No thanks, I'm alright."

On Monday, when Dennis came home after working all day and attending classes that night, he found a registered letter. It was a subpoena from the New York City Corporation Counsel's office for him to appear at a deposition in Ray's case against the police department. It was scheduled for the week after Ray's deposition.

Dennis was sitting at the kitchen table with the subpoena in front of him when his father came home after working a four-to-twelve tour.

"What's the matter?" Dominic said.

Dennis handed him the subpoena.

"Let's go downstairs," Dominic said. "Your mother might be awake. I don't want her listening."

In the basement, they sat on the bar stools.

"We expected this," Dominic said.

"Yes, we did," Dennis said. "And I warned Ray about it. I even warned Klein about it. This is nothing but trouble."

"Don't panic," Dominic said. "I've been deposed many times. You can get through it. Just give short answers, yes or no. If you can't remember, say so. And don't let them badger you into giving an answer. Just say, 'I don't recall,' and that's it."

Dennis knew that, but he had thought of all the things that could go wrong. "What if I do recall? What if they confront me with evidence? If I don't answer, they can hold me in contempt," he said. "And if I do answer, they can say my answers are false, and charge me with perjury."

"This is not a criminal case. It's a civil case. They don't usually do that," Dominic said. "When a witness gets caught lying in a civil lawsuit, it will affect the outcome of the case, but they don't put people in jail. They should, but they don't. The purpose of a deposition is to get all the facts and settle the case without going to trial."

"But they're going to try to tear me apart."

"Don't let them. Stick to your story, and you'll be alright. The city's lawyers usually just go through the motions. They're not killers like plaintiff lawyers. They're overwhelmed with cases, defending every kind of lawsuit imaginable, and when they finish one, they have to start another with only a couple of weeks to prepare. Plaintiff lawyers, on the other hand, can spend all the time in the world getting ready. They may have only one or two big cases, and they devote all their time to them. This is their chance to make a big pay day."

"So, you're saying the city lawyers are not that good?"

"I wouldn't say that, they're just overworked."

"Dad, this is more than just a civil case; behind it, there's the robbery case. And ADA Walsh, he was mad as hell at losing the case against Ray. He's going to take a pound of flesh from somebody, and it might be me. He'll get the transcripts from the deposition and use them against me."

"You'll do fine, and Klein can help you get ready."

"I don't think he can," Dennis said. "He represents Ray, not me. There could be a conflict of interest."

Dominic nodded and smiled. "You might be right. We'll have to get you another lawyer. And Klein was right—you should go to law school."

"I will, if I don't go to jail first. And if I do, I'm going to blame Klein more than Ray."

"Why?"

"Because Ray is just stupid, Klein is doing this for money."

"Ray's not stupid, he's just stubborn."

"Stubborn and muscle-bound," Dennis said. "I think the steroids he takes are messing up his brain. And Klein is just using him. To him, Ray is expendable. He once told me that people are fungible, and I think he sees his clients as fungible. He knows that Ray's guilty, yet he's going forward anyway. Remember when he accused me of committing a fraud on the court, now he's the one committing the fraud on the court."

"I don't know what we can do about it, now," Dominic said, "The wine is poured, now we have to drink it."

Dominic took down a bottle of Chivas Regal from the top shelf behind the bar. "I don't think I'll sleep tonight without a drink, want one?"

"Okay, I'll try it," Dennis said.

Dominic mixed the two whiskeys with soda water. "Don't worry, Dennis. We'll get through this."

"I hope you're right."

Later that same night, when Ray got home to the Ridgewood apartment from the Kit-Kat club, he found a subpoena slid under his door. It was from the district attorney for him to testify at the grand jury in connection with the dealership robbery case.

Even though he had known this was a possibility, he was stunned by the reality of it, and he was concerned that it was scheduled for the week after his deposition in his lawsuit.

It was late, but he called his father, who didn't hear the phone ringing. Dennis did and picked it up.

"Can I talk to Dad?" Ray said.

"He's asleep. It's four-thirty in the morning. What's wrong?"

"I need to talk to him."

"Can't it wait?"

"No. I got a subpoena to testify at the grand jury in the dealership robbery case."

"You're not in jail."

"No."

"In that case, Dad needs his sleep. I'll tell him in the morning," Dennis said, and hung up.

In the morning, Dennis told his father about Ray's subpoena, and Dominic made an appointment with Klein. Later, he and his sons drove to Manhattan. In the car, they hardly spoke. The last time they had met in Klein's office, Dominic had knocked Ray to the floor, and the prospects for this meeting weren't much better.

Klein's opened the meeting with a pronouncement: "I represent Ray in his lawsuit against the city, and I'm doing so on a contingency basis, so there's no charge until there's a settlement or a favorable judgment.

And regarding the grand jury subpoena, I should charge a fee, but, as a courtesy, I won't unless something develops. But it shouldn't. Ray can't be charged with the robbery because he's already been acquitted, and to prosecute him would be double jeopardy."

"So, I don't have to say anything," Ray said.

"It's not that simple," Klein said. "They want you to testify against the others, and as a grand jury witness, you'll receive immunity. They won't be able to use anything you say against you, but you'll have to answer the questions. And you'll have to be careful, and consistent, so that you don't get caught in a perjury trap."

"What if I refuse to answer questions?"

"They'll hold you in contempt and put you in jail."

Ray shook his head. "When the hell is this going to be over?"

"It all depends," Klein said.

Dennis reached across the table for a pitcher of water, and poured himself a glass. "What about my subpoena?"

"That's a different matter," Klein said. "I don't represent you. I'm willing to give you some guidance, but if it turns into something, you'll have to get your own lawyer. If you want me to recommend someone I will."

"Thanks," Dominic said. "I might take you up on that, but I want to check with someone first. I'll call you one way or the other."

"Okay, with that settled, I think we can adjourn the meeting."

Dominic called Dan Carter, the retired detective turned lawyer, who had represented Ray at the initial arraignment. Since then, Dominic had heard good things about Carter, and hired him to represent Dennis at the deposition. He wasn't disappointed. Carter gave the case his full attention, meeting with Dennis several times to go over the facts and to prepare for the deposition.

Dennis said to Carter, "Ray gives his deposition the week before. Will I know what his testimony was?"

"No. Not in advance, but during your deposition they may bring in his testimony and ask you about it," Carter said. "If they do, it's best to be noncommittal. If you didn't see him do something, or hear him say something, just say you don't know. Don't speculate on what he might have done or said. If they ask your opinion of something, or some possibility, say you don't know. If they ask you if you to remember something, and you don't remember it exactly, say you don't recall. Don't give them partial answers. Don't volunteer anything. Just answer 'yes' or 'no,' and don't embellish. If I object to a question, there might be a discussion between the lawyers. So don't answer until the discussion is over or I direct you to answer. If the lawyers can't resolve an issue, they can call the judge who'll give a ruling over the phone."

Meanwhile, Ray met twice with Klein to prepare for his deposition. Klein gave him the "don't volunteer anything" instructions, and Ray said that he understood.

He was supposed to have another meeting with Klein on the day before the deposition; however, he phoned Klein's office and left a message that he couldn't make it. He said that he'd meet Klein for the deposition at the Corporation Counsel's office on Church Street in Lower Manhattan.

Klein was furious and wanted to drop the case, but he had made a legal commitment and he had his reputation to protect. When he arrived at the Corporation Counsel, he asked the receptionist whether Ray Carbonaro had signed in. He hadn't.

He went to the designated conference room, a sparsely furnished, windowless room. Waiting was Dave Goldstein, the assistant corporation counsel, who would conduct the deposition for the city. They had known each other for many years. Goldstein was about forty, tall, thin, and looked like a runner. He was known as a lawyer difficult to deal with.

He and the court reporter were ready to begin, but after forty minutes, Ray hadn't arrived. "If he's not here in five minutes," Goldstein said, "I'll call the judge and get a default judgment to dismiss the lawsuit."

"That'll be a waste of time," Klein said. "I've been in this situation before, and the judge is not going to throw the case out so quickly."

Five more minutes passed, and Goldstein picked up the phone to call the judge. Just then, Ray arrived and Goldstein hung up.

Klein was still furious but said only, "We're ready."

The court reporter, who was a notary public, swore Ray in.

Goldstein began, "My name is David Goldstein and I represent the City of New York. I'm going to be asking you a number of questions today. If there is anything I ask that you do not understand, just let me know and I rephrase my question. Your answers need to be verbal so that the court reporter can take them down. Nods or "umms" are not acceptable. Okay?"

"Yes," Ray answered.

"If you want to take a break at any time, just let us know. We can stop for any reason. You don't even need to tell us the reason. But you can't stop while a question is pending. If I have asked a question, you must answer it before we take the break. Okay?"

"Okay."

"Before coming here today to testify, did you read or review anything to prepare for your testimony? Did you look at anything?"

"You mean today or anytime?" Ray asked.

Klein interrupted. "Just answer the question, yes or no."

"No," Ray said.

Goldstein continued asking questions about Ray's background, his medical history, where he went to school, where he had worked, where he worked now, where he had lived, who he had lived with, and who he lived with now. Ray became impatient with it. He wanted to get to the substance of the case, but Goldstein persisted, and the background questions went on for more than an hour.

Goldstein asked him how many times he had been arrested. Ray said he didn't remember, but Goldstein questioned him about each arrest, getting him to admit them. He focused on Ray's arrest for assaulting someone in a bar with a beer bottle.

"When you struck this man, you intended to injure him, isn't that true?" Goldstein asked.

"No. I was just defending myself. He wanted to hurt me," Ray said. "It was self-defense."

"You pled guilty in court. Correct?"

"Yes."

"You didn't claim self-defense in court. Correct?"

Ray answered, "I only pled guilty to get it over with, so I didn't have to keep going back."

Goldstein then asked questions about Ray's arrests and drug use—what kind of drugs, how often he took them, how much did he spend on them, where did he get the money to buy them."

"Have you taken steroids?" Goldstein asked.

"Whatever I took was for body-building."

"Did you have a prescription?"

"No."

"So, those steroids were illegal?"

"I guess so."

"Don't you know?"

"I'm not sure."

"Where did you buy them?"

"In gyms."

"You bought them from the gyms?"

"No, from guys in the gyms?"

"Can you give us their names?"

"No. I don't know their names. If you want to find out just go to any gym and ask around."

"Ray, just answer the question. Don't embellish," Klein said.

Goldstein open a folder containing two medical journals, and asked, "Have you experienced any side effects from taking steroids?"

"No. They just help build muscle," Ray said.

"How about psychological effects?"

"What do you mean?" Ray asked.

"It's been reported in scientific journals that steroids can make a person aggressive, even violent. Have you experienced those kinds of symptoms?"

"I need a break," Ray said.

"Answer the question, first, then we'll take a break."

"What was the question again?"

Goldstein had the court reporter read the question back.

"No. I haven't experienced those kinds of symptoms."

After the break, Goldstein asked about Ray's job at the Kit-Kat. He didn't ask about the job in the after-hours club because he didn't know about it and Ray hadn't mentioned it.

"So let me understand this," Goldstein said, "at this Gentlemen's Club, you're a bouncer."

"They don't call it that. I'm an employee who's there to help out and make sure everything goes okay," Ray answered.

"But you might have to throw customers out if that becomes necessary. Correct"

"I would assist, yes."

"How many times have you had to 'assist' in throwing someone out?"

Klein objected. "Don't answer that. It's irrelevant."

"It's not irrelevant," Goldstein said. "It goes to his propensity for violence, which is relevant to whether he would engage in a violent crime like the robbery that is the subject of this lawsuit. I'll ask it again. Will you let him answer?"

"You can answer but note my objection," Klein said.

Ray said, "I don't remember."

"Well, was it more than once?" Goldstein asked.

"I don't remember."

"More than twice."

Ray sat silently.

"You have to answer," Goldstein said. "More than twice?"

"I don't remember."

"More than five times?"

"I don't remember."

"More than ten times?"

"I don't remember."

Klein objected. "If you're going to keep badgering the witness, we'll have to call the judge," he said.

"I'm not badgering him," Goldstein said. "I'm just trying to get a straight answer."

"How much longer do you expect to go on?" Klein asked.

"Several hours," Goldstein said. "So, let's take a short break."

Ray bolted out of his chair and went to the men's room.

When the deposition resumed, Goldstein said, "Let's turn our attention to last August, the Monday that the BMW dealership was robbed. Do you remember that day?"

"No. I can't say that I do," Ray said.

"Do you remember being arrested last August in connection with the robbery of a BMW dealership?"

"Yes. That I remember."

Goldstein asked a series of questions about where Ray had been on the day of the robbery, and whether he had driven his red Camaro near the dealership.

To each question, Ray said, "I don't recall."

Goldstein asked whether he was the getaway driver for three people who had robbed the dealership."

Ray answered, "Absolutely not."

"In the days and weeks before the robbery," Goldstein asked, "or before you were arrested for the robbery, had you been inside the dealership looking to buy a car?"

"I don't recall."

"Had you been in the dealership for any reason?"

"I don't recall."

"Can you explain why you were identified as being in the dealership during the week before the robbery, or before you were arrested?"

"No, I can't"

"Can you explain why you were identified as picking up the three robbers and driving away in your car?"

"No, I can't."

"Can you explain why Mr. Johnson testified at your trial that you cased the dealership for the robbers?"

"No. I can't."

"Can you explain why Mr. Johnson testified that you drove them away from the dealership after the robbery?"

"No, I can't."

"Can you explain why Mr. Johnson testified under oath that you were given a Rolex watch, which was taken from one of the customers, as part of your payment for participating in the robbery?"

Ray hesitated before answering. What he was about to say would change everything. He took a deep breath, and speaking directly to the court reporter, said, "Because he must have had me mixed up with my brother."

"Your brother?" Goldstein said.

"Yes, my brother, Dennis."

Klein was stunned. "I object to this. The answer is unresponsive. It should be stricken from the record."

"You can't object to your own witness' answer. And it wasn't unresponsive. He answered the exact question," Goldstein said.

Before Klein could say anything, Goldstein asked, "What do you base your answer on?"

Now, without hesitating, Ray said, "At my trial, there was testimony that my brother admitted that he was the one who committed the robbery, not me. And there was testimony that he was given the Rolex watch, not me."

Klein stood up. "We need to take a break."

"No, we don't." Goldstein said. "You're interfering with my deposition."

"I have to confer with my client."

"He didn't say he wanted a break."

"Let's call the judge," Klein said.

They called the judge, and after listening to the argument, the judge ruled that if the witness had asked for a break, he could have it. But, there's no provision for a lawyer calling for a break if the witness doesn't want one. So, the questioning could continue.

Goldstein was quick to ask, "Did you give credence to that testimony, or, strike that, do you believe that testimony to be true?"

"Objection. Which testimony?" Klein said.

"Mr. Johnson's testimony about the watch," Goldstein said.

"Yes. I did," Ray said.

"And why?"

"Because I knew I didn't do it," Ray said.

"Anything else?"

"Yes." Ray hadn't planned to say what he said next, but he blurted out without thinking, "Because later I found the Rolex watch in Dennis' room."

"Say that again."

"I found the Rolex watch in Dennis' room."

Goldstein hadn't expected that answer and had trouble thinking of his next question, then asked, "Where is this watch now?"

"It's in the ocean," Ray said.

"How did it get in the ocean?"

"I threw it off the Whitestone Bridge."

For a moment, Klein didn't know what to say or do. Over his career, he had seen many witnesses blurt out unexpected testimony; he had seen many retract their earlier testimony; and he had seen many betray their friends and relatives; but he had never seen such a cynical ploy by one brother against another, a ploy that could send one brother to prison for a crime committed by the other. Ray had taken Dennis' story, reversed it, and adopted it as his own.

Klein stood, "This deposition needs to be adjourned. In light of all this new information, it's impossible to conduct it."

Surprisingly, Goldstein agreed, and they called the judge for his permission, which was granted.

Klein packed his papers into his briefcase, looked at Ray with disgust, and walked out of the room. He had never experienced a deposition as disastrous as this. He wanted to quit the case right then and there, but he wasn't in the habit of making rash decisions. After thinking it through, he realized that Ray's case was not compromised by the claim that Dennis was the one who committed the robbery. It would make it more complicated, it would certainly make it more distasteful, but the city would still settle, and, possibly, for more money than before.

CHAPTER TWENTY-FIVE

Returning to his office after Ray's deposition, Klein told his secretary that if any of the Carbonaro's called, "Say that I'm not in." Dominic and Dennis both called and were told that Klein was out of the office.

Dominic had called from his detective squad office while he was on duty for a four-to-twelve shift. Anxious to hear how the deposition had turned out, he called Ray three times without getting an answer, and called his wife Marie to see if Ray had gone home. He hadn't.

Dominic called Dennis, "Did you hear anything?"

"No," Dennis said. "I hope he didn't say anything stupid."

"There you go again, calling your brother stupid. He's stubborn but not stupid."

"Sorry, Dad. I guess the uncertainty of all this is getting to me."

"That's understandable. Ray's not home. Later, I'm going to take a ride over to the Kit-Kat club to see what's up."

At 1:30a.m., Dominic arrived at the Kit-Kat Club. A red-carpeted staircase with brass railings led to the club entrance. The entrance door was painted with the image of grinning Cheshire cat.

Dominic parked his car, and watched Ray escorting a drunk down the stairs. Ray told him, "Don't come back. That's my last warning."

Ray stood on the landing at the front door. The drunk didn't leave, and, holding the railing, began pulling himself up the stairs. When he reached the top step, Ray twisted his arm and, lifting him by the back of his belt, carried him down the stairs.

"You breaking my arm," the man shouted.

When they reached the sidewalk, Ray pushed him down the street and shoved into an alleyway.

From his car, Dominic watched. He hoped the man wouldn't try to come back again. Over the years, he had seen drunks stubbornly keep trying to reenter bars after they had been thrown out. They would come back four, five, six times.

This situation reminded Dominic of Ray as a little boy, about two or three years old, and how stubborn he was. He remembered Marie trying to get him to eat his vegetables. Ray had refused, and she had tried to spoon-feed him, but he wouldn't open his mouth. When he did, and she got some vegetables in, he'd spit them out. Dominic took over. He put Ray in his bedroom, and said that he couldn't come out until he ate something. Ray came out of the bedroom. Dominic put him back. Ray came out. Dominic put him back. This went on and on. Finally, Marie said to Dominic, "You're going to have to kill him. So, unless you want to do that, you'd better give up."

Dominic gave up. "Eventually, he'll get hungry," he said.

He laughed at that now, and thought that Ray was getting a taste of his own medicine from this drunk. He kept watching, and saw the drunk stagger out of the alleyway and walk in the other direction away from the club. "That's a relief," he thought.

He got out of his car, and went up the club stairs to talk to Ray. He had to move aside for a group of loud customers who were coming out of the club.

Ray was surprised to see him. "Hi, Dad. What brings you here?"

"What happened at the deposition today. I'm surprised you didn't call me."

Ray tried to say something, but couldn't think of the right words. He still hadn't absorbed what he had done, or why he had done it, and didn't know how to tell his father. He stammered, "I, I, it was okay."

Dominic stared at him. "Are you alright?"

"You know, I'm not sure."

At that moment, Aldo Manfredonia came out. "How's everything Ray? Did you get rid of that drunk?"

"Yeah. Aldo, this is my father."

"Oh, hello, sir. Nice to meet you. I've heard nothing but good things about you," Aldo said, putting out his hand.

Dominic shook his hand, but didn't say anything.

"I'll leave you two alone," Aldo said, and went inside.

"You told him who I am?" Dominic asked.

"He knows every cop on the force and heard of you before he hired me. That's probably one of the reasons I got hired."

"That, and you can throw people down the stairs. But, never mind that, how did the deposition go? What did they ask you?"

"Nothing that we didn't expect."

"And what did you say?"

Ray hesitated and told his father half the truth. "I told them I didn't do it, and that was what the trial found. I told them about the girls saying that Dennis admitted it. And I told them that Buster, the DA's informant, must have gotten me mixed up with my brother."

"But that might shift the blame to your brother," Dominic said.

Ray thought about telling him what he had said about finding the watch in Dennis' room, instead of the other way around, but he couldn't. He hoped that it would never come out. Maybe the City would just settle the case and the whole thing would go away. But he knew he was kidding himself. He knew that the lies were piling up and if they ever came out, it would be the last straw for both his father and his brother. Even his mother would disown him. *How did I get in this mess?* he thought. *I would have been better off just pleading guilty, going to jail, and getting it over with.*

Another group of customers, men and women, came out of the club. One of the men looked very drunk, and Ray helped him down the stairs.

"These stairs are the most dangerous thing about this place," Ray told his father.

"I'm sure there's more danger than that here," Dominic said. "I assume you're making good money, but I don't think it's worth it. You could get jammed up, arrested, or sued. You've seen what Klein does, right. It's no joke."

"You're probably right. I just want to build up a little nest egg, then I'll move on."

"How late are you staying here tonight?" Dominic asked.

"The place is almost empty now. So, I'll be leaving soon."

"Good. Be careful," Dominic said, and went to his car and drove away.

Ray didn't tell his father that when he left the Kit-Kat, he would be going to the 444 Club. His father would blow a gasket if he knew that. The Kit-Kat, although sleazy, was a legitimate business with licenses and insurance, while the 444 Club was an illegal operation, and could be busted for unlawful gambling and alcohol sales. His father would definitely disapprove.

Meanwhile, Dennis was waiting at home to hear how the deposition turned out. When he couldn't reach Ray, he drove to McCoy's on the chance that he would be there. He wasn't.

Kathy was bartending. She was dressed in a black vest, white blouse, and a red cowboy-string tie. To Dennis, she looked great.

"How are you?" he said.

"Fine, and you."

"I don't want to bother you, but did you hear from Ray today? Did you hear anything about his deposition?"

"No, and no."

Dennis felt like she was giving him the cold shoulder. "Okay, I'll see you around," he said, turning to leave.

"Dennis, wait," Kathy said. "You know we don't have to be so cold. We're still friends."

The warmth in her voice revived his feelings. "In that case, can I get a beer?"

"Sure."

As he drank, he watched her cleaning up behind the bar. Everything about her struck him as perfect.

She saw him watching her and came over to him. "It's closing time. Do you want to stop for one at an after-hours club I heard about? A lot of bar people go there."

"Where is it?"

"Not far. It's called the 444 Club."

"Okay. I guess I'll go straight to work from there."

They found parking spots and walked up to the 444 Club together. Neither one of them knew that Ray was working there as the doorman. Kathy knocked on the door, and Ray slid open the old speakeasy lookout slot. He saw them, but they couldn't tell it was him. He closed the slot. Five minutes passed, and Kathy knocked again. Then Dennis knocked harder.

"I'm sorry," Kathy said. "I thought they'd let us in."

"Maybe they think I'm a cop," Dennis said.

"Maybe we should leave," Kathy said. "We can go to a diner for breakfast."

Before Dennis could answer, the door flung open, and Ray stepped forward with his fist cocked behind his hip. "You've got some nerve coming here. Are you trying to taunt me, rub my nose in it?"

Afraid that Ray was going to throw a punch, Kathy shouted "Don't," and stepped in front of Dennis.

Ray didn't throw the punch, and looking passed her at Dennis, said, "I see you brought your girlfriend to protect you."

Kathy said, "I told you before. I'm not his girlfriend, and I'm not your girlfriend."

Hoping to avoid a confrontation, Dennis quickly came up with a reason for being there. "We came to find out what happened at the deposition. Can we come inside and talk?"

"Kathy can come in, but you can't," Ray said, taking another step closer to Dennis.

"Don't be ridiculous," Kathy said. "Are you afraid to tell us what happened?"

The question struck a nerve, and he reacted angrily. "I'm not afraid of anything," he said. "I stood my ground when they threatened me with years in prison. So, I don't think talking to you is gonna scare me."

"So then let's talk inside," Kathy said.

Ray relented. "Alright, come in if you want."

He told the backup doorman to watch the door, and took Kathy and Dennis inside.

The club was crowded with people standing around the square-shaped bar. Two bartenders were busy trying to keep up with the drink orders. A waitress took a tray of drinks to the blackjack and roulette tables in the backroom.

Around the bar, there were also a dozen small tables with yellow candles flickering on each one. At this time of night, candlelight was flattering. There was enough for light for people to sit and talk and enough darkness to provide some anonymity. The clandestine atmosphere with the illegal drinking and gambling attracted a wide variety of customers and characters. Some trying to revive the excitement of the city's speakeasy days.

Ray led Dennis and Kathy to a table in the corner. He waved his hand and a waitress came right over to take their order. Customers passing their table said hello to Ray, and Dennis could see that Ray enjoyed the attention.

After the drinks came, Dennis came right to the point, "So, what did they ask you?"

Ray answered the same equivocal way he had answered his father. "I told them I didn't do it. And their witness must have gotten us mixed up. I mentioned that you had admitted to being involved, though I still don't know why you did that. But, in the end, I have to give you credit, it helped get me acquitted. I guess I should be grateful for that."

"Anything else?"

"They asked a lot of nonsense questions."

"Did they ask about me?" Dennis asked.

"Not really." Ray didn't volunteer what he had said about the watch, or finding it in Dennis' room, or throwing it off the Whitestone bridge.

At that moment, the backup doorman came over and whispered to Ray. "We've got a problem. I think there's a cop at the door."

"In uniform?"

"No."

"Undercover or in a suit?" Ray asked.

"A suit," the doorman said.

"Go in the backroom and get Gino," Ray said to the doorman, and went to the front door.

Dennis followed him. He wanted to find out whether there was a way out in case the club was raided. As he followed Ray, he saw Gino go to the front door, and look through the lookout slot. "Damn it, it's that pain-in-the-ass detective again. I'll handle it," Gino said, and went outside.

After a few minutes, Gino came back in. He looked angry, and, not noticing Dennis, said to Ray, "This guy's a real bandit. Every time he sees that we're doing good business, he wants more or pumps me for information. Says he could close the place down if we're not cooperative. I told him that he can have the place. He can run it himself."

"What did he say to that?" Ray asked.

"He said he'd be back next week."

Dennis overheard most of this conversation, and it was clear to him that a detective was either shaking down the club or trying to get Gino to be a stool pigeon.

When Gino walked away, Dennis asked Ray, "Are we going to get raided?"

"No. Let's go back to the table," Ray said.

They sat down, and Kathy asked, "What's going on?"

Ray took a sip of his drink. "There's a cop giving us a hard time," Ray said.

"You're kidding," Kathy said.

"No, I'm not."

"We should get out of here."

Customers began getting up to leave, and Dennis said, "This would be a good time to get out of here. Is there a backway out?"

Ray said, "Yeah. Down in the basement, you can get out the window to a back alley, which goes to the next street behind."

"Maybe we should do that," Dennis said to Kathy.

Kathy stood, "I'm going out the front door. They can arrest me if they want."

Dennis followed Kathy out the front door, and down the street to their cars. He noticed an unmarked police squad car across the street with three men in it. He wasn't sure, but one of them might have been McConnell.

As Ray watched Dennis and Kathy leave, jealousy overcame him. He thought they're together, and I'm out. Some brother, he's such a smart-ass talker. I'm in jail, and he couldn't wait to move in on her.

His head and face felt hot, and he went into the men's room to splash some water on his face. Above the sink was a large wooden-framed mirror that hung askew on the wall, slanting outwards from the top. In the dim light, he looked at himself. The mirror made his head appear out of proportion, with a bulging forehead. His jaw, neck, and Adam's apple looked large and distorted. "Do I really look like that? That's a stranger, not me," he thought. "Maybe the steroids are changing me." He had heard of surreal experiences. This could be what they mean. It was like looking at himself through a prism.

He threw more cold water on his face, left the men's room, and went home.

Kathy drove to her apartment, and Dennis drove directly to his job at UPS, and, later that afternoon, he called Ray's cell phone.

"You should tell Dad about the detective shaking down the club," Dennis said.

"Why?"

"You need to tell him. If you get arrested there, he'll be furious, and it will not go over well in the Department. You know they gave him a lot of flak the last time you were arrested."

"Thanks for reminding me," Ray said sarcastically.

"Ray. You should tell him."

"I suppose if I don't, you will, like you told them all about the watch," Ray said.

There was a lot Dennis could say, but he only said, "I just think you should tell him. It's better that you do it, not me."

CHAPTER TWENTY-SIX

On Wednesday of that week, Dominic drove Dennis to the Corporation Counsel's office to give his deposition in the civil lawsuit of *Ray Carbonaro vs. the City of New York, the New York City Police Department, and Detectives McConnell, Cruz, and Matthews.* During the drive, Dennis wondered whether Ray had told his father about working at the 444 Club. He asked, "Did Ray tell you anything about his job?"

"I saw him one night at the Kit-Kat Club. Everything seemed alright. He said he's going home soon."

From that answer, Dennis guessed that Ray hadn't told Dominic about the 444 club.

Dominic dropped him off in front of the building, and Dennis met his attorney, Dan Carter, in the lobby.

"Are you ready?" Carter asked.

"As ready as I'll ever be," Dennis said.

Carter walked Dennis to the newspaper stand in the lobby, bought two chocolate bars, and handed one to Dennis. "We're going to need energy," he said.

They took the elevator to the conference room, where Dave Goldstein, the same City attorney who had deposed Ray, was waiting for them.

Carter and Goldstein exchanged pleasantries, and Dennis was sworn in by the stenographer. Goldstein gave Dennis the usual instructions about taking breaks and about objections. Regarding the right to invoke the Fifth Amendment, Goldstein put on the record that the judge had ruled that if the witness wanted to invoke it, he would have to do so question by question. "Is that agreed?" Goldstein asked.

Both Carter and Dennis said, "Yes."

Goldstein began the questions as he had in his deposition of Ray. He asked questions about background, family, education, employment, drug use. He asked Dennis whether he had ever been arrested or received a summons.

"Never," Dennis said.

Goldstein asked a series of questions about the BMW robbery: "Where were you on that day? Did you ever drive into the dealership parking lot? Had you ever been inside the dealership any time before the robbery?"

After each question, Dennis answered, "I assert my Fifth Amendment right to decline to answer on the grounds that my answer might tend to incriminate me."

Goldstein continued, "Did you tell Kathy Reynolds that you committed the robbery, not your brother?"

Dennis took the Fifth.

"Did you tell Belinda Ramos that it was you who committed the robbery, not your brother?"

Again, Dennis took the Fifth.

"Can you explain why they would have testified under oath that you told them that?"

"I take the Fifth."

Goldstein then took a folder from his briefcase, found the page that he wanted, and asked, "Did you read a transcript of your brother Ray's deposition testimony?"

"No."

"I represent to you, as an officer of the court, that he testified under oath in his deposition that he found a Rolex watch in your mattress, the Rolex watch that was taken in the BMW robbery, and that he threw it off the Whitestone Bridge. Do you have any knowledge about this Rolex watch?"

Dennis couldn't believe what he was hearing. He couldn't say anything, couldn't even think of the Fifth Amendment. Ray had reversed everything, turned everything upside down, putting the possession of the watch on him, instead of himself. Ray had provided false evidence implicating Dennis in the robbery. He might as well have stabbed him in the back.

Dennis sat mutely.

Goldstein pressed, "Can you explain why your brother would testify in that manner?"

Dennis still sat without answering.

"You have to answer the question," Goldstein insisted.

Carter was stunned, but he recovered, and objected. "It's a compound question. He doesn't have to answer."

"Then I'll break it down for him," Goldstein said. "Can you explain why your brother, Ray Carbonaro, testified under oath in his deposition that he found a Rolex watch in your mattress?"

"No, I can't," Dennis said.

Carter interjected, "Don't answer. Just take the Fifth."

"Can you explain why your brother, Ray Carbonaro, testified in his deposition that he threw the Rolex watch off the Whitestone Bridge?"

Dennis heard the question, but he couldn't respond. He was thinking, not about his testimony, but about what his brother had done to him. How he had destroyed their relationship, how he had destroyed their family.

"You have to answer," Goldstein said again.

"No, I can't," Dennis said.

"No, you can't answer, or no, you can't explain?" Goldstein asked.

"Objection," Carter said.,

"Let's call the judge," Goldstein said.

"Don't bother," Dennis said, "I take the Fifth," and he answered the remaining questions by taking the Fifth. He didn't care how the case turned out. It was Ray's lawsuit. Ray was the one trying to get rich. As far as Dennis was concerned, Ray could go to hell.

When the deposition was over, Dennis and Carter left the building together. "Your brother left you quite a surprise package," Carter said.

"Nothing my brother does should surprise anyone."

Dennis was already thinking about the possible ramifications of Ray's testimony.

"Could the DA use Ray's testimony in front of a grand jury to indict me for the robbery?"

"That's a good question," Carter said. "It seems weak to me, but the old saying goes that a district attorney can indict a ham sandwich if he wants to."

"I hope I'm not the ham sandwich," Dennis said.

Dennis went straight to his parents' house to tell his father what had happened. Any vestige of brotherly loyalty was gone. As far as he was concerned, Ray was "a bad actor," a term his father often used. However, when he got home, his mother told him that Dominic had been called into work to investigate a double homicide on the Lower East Side. It was an "all hands investigation," and he wouldn't be home until late, if at all.

She made supper for him, and he was glad to sit with her and talk about everyday matters, anything to forget about the depositions and his potential problems. She didn't know about the depositions, but she was perceptive and could see that he was upset about something.

"You look worn out. Is everything alright?" she asked.

"I'm fine. Just tired. Didn't sleep too well."

She persisted. "Have you talked to Ray lately."

"Not really."

She sat silently for a few minutes then said, "Am I wrong that you and Ray are having a problem over Kathy? I'm not sure which one of you is going to win her."

"That's a funny way of putting it. I'm not sure if anybody's gonna "win" her."

"Whatever happens, be a gentleman. Treat everybody like you would want them to treat you."

"Of course, Mom."

Dennis paced around the house. He was impatient to talk to his father, and at eight o'clock, he called his father's office. When a detective answered, he identified himself and asked, "Is my father there?"

"No. He's out on a case, a drive-by shooting, two DOAs."

"Is there some way I can get in touch with him?"

"He's probably at the Ninth Precinct, in the squad room there."

Dennis decided to drive to the Ninth. On the way, he took a detour to McCoy's to see Kathy. She seemed glad to see him, and they went into the same booth where they had convinced Belinda to report that Dennis admitted the robbery to her.

"How did it go?" Kathy asked.

Dennis collected his thoughts and tried to map out how he would explain everything to her. "You're not going to believe this, because it's hard to believe," he said.

"Okay, try me."

"First, remember when you wanted to know why Ray had called me a 'turncoat.'"

"Yes."

"Well, after Ray was acquitted, you remember that I went to the apartment to clean it up before he got home?"

"Yes."

"I even changed his sheets, and when I turned over his mattress, I found a cut in it."

"So?"

"A Rolex watch was hidden in the mattress."

Kathy stared at him as though not understanding.

"The Rolex that was taken in the car dealership robbery."

"No!"

"Yes. He did it. He was lying all along."

Kathy put her hand to her forehead, "But you didn't say anything."

"Right. He was my brother. I wouldn't turn him in. Maybe I should have. But all I could think of was to throw the watch off the Whitestone Bridge to get rid of the evidence."

"So, again, you tried to protect him."

"Right, but when he filed the lawsuit, I said that it was a mistake. It was going to get everyone in trouble, and that's when I told Klein and my father about the watch."

"That's why Ray called you a turncoat," Kathy said.

"Yeah."

Brendan, the bartender, came over to the booth to see whether they wanted anything. Kathy waved him away.

"But how can the lawsuit keep going forward? Both Klein and your father know about the watch," Kathy said.

"My father didn't think he was going to file the lawsuit," Dennis said. "But Klein's a crook like the rest of them. He filed the lawsuit without telling my father."

"This is a mess. You've got to do something."

"Wait. It gets crazier."

"I don't see how?"

"When Ray gave his deposition last week, he said that he found the watch in my mattress, instead of me finding it in his mattress."

"He what?"

"He testified that he was the one who found the watch, not me. And he said he threw it off the Whitestone Bridge.

"Did he?"

"Of course not. I threw it. He's lying through his teeth to win his lawsuit. I guess he figures since he's gone this far, he might as well go all the way."

"All the way to hell," Kathy said.

They both sat back as though physically exhausted.

"What are you going to do?" she asked.

"I'm going to go see my father now. He's in the middle of an investigation, but I've got to talk to him."

They embraced, and Dennis left, and drove to the Brooklyn-Queens Expressway to the Williamsburg Bridge, across the East River to the Lower Eastside of Manhattan.

The Ninth Precinct was on East 5th Street in the East Village. It was a notorious precinct that had policed waves of immigrants from the 1850s to the present. It had seen plenty of trouble, and had many stories to tell. It covered a high-crime area populated with the most extreme fringe elements of society. In stages, the precinct oversaw waves of hippie dropouts, unapologetic drug users, LSD proponents, free-love advocates, radical revolutionaries, and combinations of them all. The precinct building, like the face of a man who had seen everything, looked worn and tarnished. For decades it had needed a complete overhaul, but with the precinct's constant state of crisis, there was never time.

Dennis entered the building and stood in front of the high, mahogany station house desk. He waited for the lieutenant desk officer to acknowledge him, then asked to see his father. The lieutenant phoned up to the second-floor squad room.

A detective came downstairs to escort Dennis. "Hello, I'm Eric Radowski. So, you're Dominic's son. You look just like him. Your father said you can come up, but you'll have to wait awhile. He's in the middle of interrogating one of the shooters in that double homicide."

"That's okay, I can wait," Dennis said as they walked into the squad room, which was busy with detectives typing, talking on phones, or taking statements from witnesses. Five suspects were locked in the holding cell in the back corner of the room.

Radowski introduced Dennis to the other detectives. "This is Dominic's son."

One of the detectives, Jack Smith, greeted Dennis. "Wow. You got big. I remember you as a kid. Dominic used to bring you to our old command when playing chess was all the rage. I think I played you. Though I can't remember who won."

"I remember you," Dennis said. "You played a good game."

"Who won?"

"I don't want to say."

"That's very tactful. You *are* your father's son."

After a few minutes, the detectives went back to work. Radowski gave Dennis a chair at his desk, and pointed to the interview room. "Your father's in there with a suspect."

"How long do you think he'll be?" Dennis asked.

"Could be ten minutes. Could be all night. Do you want a soda?"

Radowski got a can of soda from a small refrigerator and gave it to Dennis.

When another detective opened the door and went into the interview room, Dennis saw the suspect on one side of a table and his father on the other. The suspect, who was about twenty years old with his hair in cornrows, was facing him. Dennis thought how calm and unconcerned the suspect looked. If I was being questioned in a homicide, he thought, I don't think I'd be so calm.

His father's back was to him and he noticed his father's empty holster on his hip. He knew that you wouldn't go into a room with a possible killer who could just grab your gun and start shooting.

Almost an hour passed until Dominic came out of the interview room.

"Sorry to keep you waiting, but this guy is a hard nut to crack" Dominic said.

"That's alright, Dad. I don't mind waiting."

"Okay. It shouldn't be too much longer. I guess you want to talk about your deposition.

"Yes."

"Alright, when I finish, we'll talk."

Another hour passed, and Dennis began to have second thoughts. Maybe he should have waited until tomorrow. Maybe he shouldn't have bothered his father in the middle of a big investigation. He had an urge to knock on the interview room door and tell his father that he was going to leave and he'd see him tomorrow. Then the door opened, and Dominic and the other detective came out. They looked pleased.

"Did he talk?" Radowski asked.

"It's the damnedest thing," Dominic said. "He seemed as tough as nails and would never talk. He wouldn't say anything, wouldn't even respond to the simplest questions. Then I asked if his mother was still alive, and he said 'yes.' I asked where she lived, whether she was religious, and what she would say if she knew about him shooting three people over a lousy drug deal. Suddenly, he began crying. To my surprise, he says, 'she'd be shocked that I would do such a thing. She'd disown me.'"

"That's an admission, maybe a confession," Radowski said. "It should seal the case."

"Right," Dominic said.

Dennis listened to the conversation, and for a moment he almost forgot why he was at the precinct. He wasn't sure that what the suspect had said amounted to an admission or a confession. The suspect could have meant only that if he did such a thing, his mother would disown him. He didn't actually say he did it.

But Dominic seemed convinced that it was an admission. Turning to the other detectives, he said, "Have you guys met my son?"

"Yes. We have," Detective Smith said, "We remember him from the chess games."

"That's right, I forgot about that," Dominic said, as he put his arm around Dennis. "I apologize, but I've got to get back to this guy while he's in a talkative mood."

"That's alright. I'll wait."

"Go up to the third floor," Dominic said. "There's a TV and a refrigerator. Take what you want. I'll call you when I'm done."

Dennis went upstairs to a large room that was a combination lounge/dormitory. There were couches, chairs, a table and bunk beds. He turned on the TV, and watched for about a half an hour. But he was too anxious to just sit there doing nothing, and decided that he had to talk to Ray. He had to ask him what he was going to say in the grand jury, whether he was going to repeat the same thing about the watch that he said in his deposition.

Unnoticed, he went down the stairs, left the precinct, and drove toward Ridgewood.

CHAPTER TWENTY-SEVEN

While Dennis had been at the Ninth Precinct, Ray had gone to McCoy's to see Kathy.

He approached Kathy with an uncharacteristic smile on his face. "Hi, honey," he said. She turned away and began to walk to the restroom. He grabbed her wrist. "What's the matter?"

She pulled her wrist away. "Get the hell away from me."

"Why? What's the matter?"

Everyone in the bar was watching them. She pointed at the booth in the corner.

They sat down.

"I'll tell you what's the matter," she said, her voiced lowered so that people couldn't hear, "you told them that you found the stolen watch in Dennis' mattress, when, in fact, it was in yours, and he found it, not you. How could you do such a thing? Do you want to send him to jail after all he did for you?"

"But you don't…," he began to say.

"I never want to see you again," she cut him off. "Don't ever call me."

She bolted out of the booth and went to the restroom.

Ray looked around and saw everyone staring at him. He saw Brendan behind the bar looking in his direction. It made him furious and gave him an urge to pick up the table and throw it, but he managed to control himself, got up, and left.

Leaving in this furious state of mind, Ray did what he often did when he was angry or upset; he went to the gym to work out with weights as a way to get rid of his pent-up anger. Before his workout, he took two anabolic steroids.

Meanwhile, Detectives McConnell, Cruz, and Matthews were at the district attorney's office meeting with ADA Walsh about the upcoming trial of the BMW robbery defendants, James Forest, Willie Mumford, and Shaquan Campbell. The informer, Buster Johnson, was not on trial because he had made a deal to testify against the others.

The meeting had been called because ADA Walsh had received information from the Department of Corrections about phone conversations between Forest, who was incarcerated at Riker' Island, and Campbell, who was out on bail. The Department of Corrections had the authority to eavesdrop on inmate phone conversations, and they provided transcripts of the conversations to the district attorney. Walsh had the transcripts displayed on an overhead computer screen so that they all could read them together.

The conversations were difficult to decipher because the speakers, knowing that their conversations could be overheard, used coded language. In the first conversation, Forest said to Campbell, "See if you can find my lost dog with the rat's tail and take him to the pound, and do it before the pound closes." Detective Cruz interpreted the words to mean that Forest wanted "the rat," Buster Johnson, killed. And he believed the words, "Do it before the pound closes," meant before he can testify.

In a second conversation, Campbell told Forest that "the rat must have run into the sewer," meaning into in the witness protection program.

"That's alright," Forest said. "The rodent will get crushed on the stand. But, what about the bull's son."

Cruz thought this was a reference to Ray Carbonaro, Dominic's son. Campbell didn't respond to Forest's question.

"I don't think they'd be crazy enough to take out a cop's son," Detective McConnell said. "It would backfire on them, and bring all of law enforcement down on them, including the feds."

"I agree, they'd be crazy to do it," ADA Walsh said, "and, frankly, I don't think Ray's testimony would be that damaging to them. He's told too many different stories. Though I'll have to use him anyway, for what it's worth."

When Walsh suggested that as a precaution the NYPD could provide protection for Ray until the trial, McConnell said, "We'd have to get permission from the Chief of Detectives, and we'd have to get Ray's permission, too.

At the end of the meeting, it was agreed that they would contact both Ray and Dominic to advise them of the threat.

Detective Cruz called Dominic at the Ninth precinct but was told that he was conducting an interrogation and couldn't be disturbed. Cruz said he'd call back later.

The detectives then drove to McCoy's, hoping to kill two birds with one stone—find Ray and have dinner.

As they entered the restaurant, Kathy saw them all but focused on McConnell. She told Brendan, "I'm going to take a break. Can you cover for me and serve them? I can't stand the way that big jerk looks at me."

"Sure, take a break," Brendan said.

The three detectives sat at the bar. Brendan greeted them cheerfully. "What'll it be fellas?"

"Has Ray Carbonaro been around," McConnell said.

"Haven't seen him," Brendan said. He took their orders for cheeseburgers and beers.

While the detectives were finishing their meal at McCoy's, Ray finished his workout at the gym and went home to Ridgewood. But the workout hadn't alleviated his anger. Kathy had humiliated him like he had never been humiliated in his life. Even being arrested hadn't been that bad. He kept thinking about what she had said to him and how so much had gone wrong. He had been acquitted in court, but it didn't seem to matter; the case loomed over everything. His life was a tangled mess, and he was unsure of how his testimony would go. He blamed Dennis for concocting his scheme and creating the situation that he was stuck in now. He couldn't figure any way out.

Dennis, unaware that Kathy had confronted Ray with his lies, arrived at the Ridgewood apartment.

Ray's car was parked at the end of the driveway, partially on the sidewalk. Dennis couldn't park behind it, so he kept driving until he found a parking spot a block away.

He walked back to the house, went up the stairs, and knocked on the door.

"Who's there?" Ray said through the door.

"Dennis."

"What do you want?"

"To talk."

Ray opened the door. He was wearing a tight-fitting, sleeveless workout shirt, and Dennis could see that he was pumped up.

"Were you working out?" Dennis asked.

Ray didn't answer, and didn't make way for Dennis to come in. He stood with his arms folded, staring malevolently at Dennis.

"Can we talk?" Dennis said.

Ray turned and took a few steps into the apartment. "Sure, we can talk. You like to talk."

Dennis followed him inside and began to say something, when Ray turned around fast and stood in front of him so that their faces were inches apart. "Did you like talking to Kathy about the watch? Did you enjoy telling her?"

"What?" Dennis said.

Ray suddenly punched Dennis in the face, knocking him to the kitchen floor.

"Are you crazy?" Dennis shouted.

"Don't call me crazy, you fuckin' rat," Ray said, and punched him again. The force of the blow knocked Dennis' head against a table leg. Dennis grabbed the table leg to try to pull himself up, but Ray kicked him in the head. Dennis saw Ray's enraged face and crazed eyes. The thought flashed in his mind that he was going kill him.

As Ray got ready to throw another punch, Dennis kicked upwards and got him in the groin. Ray backed up for a second, but that had only enraged him more. He came down with two fists, striking Dennis on a both sides of his head. Dennis blanked out for a second, then felt Ray choking him. This is it, he thought. He remembered a move his father had taught him. He twisted his body and crossed his right arm over Ray's wrists, breaking the chokehold.

Ray reacted by punching him in the face again, and Dennis rolled onto his stomach trying to protect himself. With a pushup motion, he tried to get up, but Ray was on his back choking him from behind. Dennis twisted around trying to get free. As he did, he reached under the sink and felt around for the hammer that he had put there the last time they had fought in the apartment.

With all the strength he had, Dennis thrust himself around and swung the hammer wildly at Ray. At the same time, Ray, with all his weight, was throwing a punch at Dennis. The hammer struck Ray in the left temple an instant before Ray's punch struck Dennis on the chin and knocked him unconscious.

The next thing Dennis knew, he was lying on the floor, looking up at the kitchen light. For a few seconds, he thought that he was in a hospital operating room. He didn't know how long he'd been lying there. Then, he turned his head to the side and saw Ray on the floor, facedown, three feet from him. Ray wasn't moving. The hammer was next to his head.

Dennis turned over and crawled closer to Ray. He couldn't see any breathing. He might be dead, he thought. He got closer and felt Ray's wrist for a pulse. He didn't feel anything, but still couldn't believe that Ray was dead, and hoped that he wasn't. He felt Ray's neck. Nothing. When he turned Ray over, he saw that Ray's eyes had rolled up in his head. Only the whites were showing.

Sitting on the floor, staring at the body, Dennis tried to collect his thoughts. "I have to call an ambulance," he said out loud. But he didn't, instead, he checked Ray again. He felt his wrist for a pulse, but still felt nothing. He leaned over and put his ear to Ray's chest. He didn't hear or feel a heartbeat. He put his hand over Ray's nose and mouth, and didn't feel any breath. What the hell am I gonna to do? They're going to think I came here to kill him. It was self-defense, but that doesn't mean that they're going to believe me.

Dennis looked at Ray again, not for signs of life, but shocked at the thought that his brother's life could have been taken in an instant. Fear, sadness, and revulsion ran through him. "I killed my own brother," he said, and stayed sitting on the floor, shaking his head, and muttering to himself, "What about mom? My God, how's she going to survive this? Her younger son killing her older son."

He thought about his father. How could he go back to the police department? Two sons charged with murder. I've destroyed everything he worked his whole life for. I can't face him, or mom. I'll never be able to face them. They'll have to sit in court and watch me get tried for murder. It was self-defense but that ADA Walsh will charge me with murder for sure. And Detective McConnell will help him. They blamed me for Ray getting acquitted, and now this is their chance to get even.

I don't know if I can prove it was self-defense, he thought, and went over what he knew about self-defense. He knew that a person in his own home doesn't have to retreat. So, Ray didn't have to retreat, but I did. And, you can't defend against physical force with deadly physical force. I had the hammer, he didn't. But he could have killed me with his hands. Everyone knows how strong he is. How strong he was. And the steroids made him crazy. Maybe I can use that as a self-defense argument.

"You're kidding yourself, Dennis," he said out loud, and thought, they'll say I went to the apartment to keep him from testifying in the grand jury against me. They'll bring up the watch, and they have all that deposition testimony they need to prove why I killed him. Juries like motives.

He pushed himself up and went into the bathroom to look in the mirror for injuries to his face and head. Nothing visible, nothing that he could use to prove self-defense. Bruises would probably show tomorrow, he thought, maybe I'll wait till then before I tell what happened. As he continued looking at himself, his mind raced. Why did I come here? Could I have really talked him out of testifying against me. Sometimes, I think I'm smarter than I am. Like our scheme to get Ray off. I outsmarted everybody, but look at the mess I'm in now. I don't want to face charges. I don't want to go to jail. They'll put an enormous bail on me, and I'll have to sit in prison waiting for months. And the trial will be a crap shoot. Maybe I can just walk out of here. No one knows I'm here. There's no physical evidence, because I lived here, and my fingerprints, DNA, or whatever are okay being here. They prove nothing. And I have an alibi. I was at the police station. What better alibi? If I get back there before they notice that I'm gone, I can say I was there all along.

With that, Dennis made a decision. "I'm taking my chances," he said to himself. "If it doesn't work, I'll be in the same boat I'm in now."

He looked at his brother's body again, and felt a cold shiver go across his back and shoulders. "I'm sorry, Ray. It didn't have to be like this. But I'm not taking the blame. You and your goddamn drugs, and your stupid, idiotic steroids. You punched me for no reason, you were going to kill me. What was I supposed to do?"

He looked around to see if he should move anything or take anything. Should he take the hammer, leave it on the floor, or put it back under the sink? It took him a few minutes to think it through. If I leave the hammer where it is, they'll know that's how he was killed. If I take it or put it back under the sink, they might think he died from some other cause.

Dennis looked at Ray again. There's wasn't any blood or marks that he could see. Maybe they'll think he died of a brain hemorrhage or a heart attack. He began to take the hammer to get rid of it, throw it away, maybe throw it off the Whitestone Bridge, but then had second thoughts. If I do that, I can never tell my side of the story and prove self-defense. He used a dish towel to wipe off any fingerprints or any traces of Ray's blood on the hammer, and put it back under the sink.

He turned out the lights, opened the door, and listened. He didn't hear anyone, and quietly went down the stairs. He walked past Ray's car in the driveway, turned right, and walked as normally as he could down the block toward his car.

As he walked, Dennis thought he saw a detective squad car coming towards him on the other side of the street. He had an urge to run but, instead, bent down as though to tie his shoelace, hiding behind a parked car. The squad car passed. Definitely detectives. He crouched between parked cars, watching to see where they'd go. They stopped in front of the house and went into the driveway.

When they were out of sight, Dennis ran to his car and drove away. His hands were shaking, his legs were shaking, and he felt sick to his stomach. When he turned the corner, he took a deep breath and tried to calm down. Right away he began thinking of what he was going to do next. He decided he'd go back to the Ninth Precinct and pretend that he was there all along.

CHAPTER TWENTY-EIGHT

Earlier that evening, when the detectives had finished eating dinner, McConnell suggested that they drive to Ray's place to tell him about the threat and ask if he wanted police protection.

Cruz drove, McConnell was in the passenger seat, and Matthews was in the backseat.

"Our visit is gonna shake him up," McConnell said. "Maybe he'll become more cooperative."

"I think he may be cooperating already," Cruz said. "That's why Walsh is calling him to the grand jury."

"I'm not sure he can cooperate," Matthews said. "If he testifies against the others, he'll have to incriminate himself."

"They'll give him immunity," Cruz said. "The only way he can get jammed up is if they get him for perjury."

"I wouldn't want to be in his shoes," Matthews said.

They turned onto Ray's block. While they looked for Ray's house on one side of the street, they didn't see Dennis walking away from there on the other side because he had ducked down. Near the end of the block, they saw Ray's car in the driveway. They parked behind it, and they went in the side entrance and up the stairs. They listened at the door, and didn't hear anything. Cruz bent down to check to see if any light was coming from under the door. There was none.

"Doesn't look like he's home," Cruz said.

McConnell signaled for Cruz to be quiet. He took out his cell phone, and gave hand signals that he was going downstairs to call Ray's phone and wanted Cruz to stay at the door and listen.

McConnell phoned, got no answer, and came back upstairs.

"I heard the phone ringing," Cruz said, "but no one picked up. He's probably not home."

"Then why is his car here?" McConnell said.

When they went outside and around house, Mr. Martucci, the landlord, saw them and opened a first-floor window. He leaned out, "Can I help you?"

"Police," Matthews said.

"You got a badge?" Martucci said. All three detectives showed their badges.

"We're looking for Ray Carbonaro," McConnell said. "Know if he's home?"

"That's his car," Martucci said. "He might be."

"But he didn't answer the door or his phone, we need to make sure he's okay," McConnell said. "Do you have a key to his apartment?"

"I do, but I couldn't let you in without his permission."

"We understand that," McConnell said. "But you're the landlord, so you have permission. Why don't you go in and check? We'll wait outside."

"You really think there's something wrong?" Martucci said.

"Yes. We do."

"Okay. I'll get the key."

Martucci came out with the key, and they followed him up the stairs. He unlocked the door and they pushed in behind him. Ray's body was on the floor.

"Oh, Madonna Mia," Martucci said. "What happened?"

McConnell bent over the body and felt Ray's neck. "He's dead. Let's not touch anything."

They called for an ambulance, crime scene, and the medical examiner.

As they waited, Martucci said, "What a shame. He was such a fine young man. I know he got in some trouble, but that was a mistake, wasn't it?"

"Yeah. It's a real shame," McConnell said sarcastically. "You'd better go downstairs, the fewer people in here, the better."

When Martucci left, McConnell, looking at the body, said, "I guess he got what he deserved."

"You're a tough man," Cruz said. "I think he just made a mistake and then things spun out of control."

"It wasn't just a mistake," McConnell said. "Somebody was killed."

"True, but he didn't pull the trigger," Cruz said. "He deserved prison, but not this."

The ambulance attendant checked Ray's body and pronounced him dead. The crime scene technicians photographed everything, and dusted for fingerprints. Later, the doctor from the medical examiner's office arrived, checked the body, and removed the shirt and pants to look for bullet or knife wounds. Then he looked closely at Ray's head. "We'll have to wait for the autopsy, but it looks like he was hit in the temple. That could do it."

"I don't see anything there," McConnell said.

"If you look closely, there's an indentation and a fracture. He must have been hit with something hard. A meningeal artery runs along the side of the head near the temples. The bone that protects the artery is thin and fragile. If the skull fractures from a strong blow, the broken bone can tear the artery, causing an epidural hematoma that can be fatal."

"That's really something," Cruz said. "Look at this guy. He's got muscles all over, yet a hit in the wrong spot does him in."

"Yep. We're all vulnerable," the doctor said. "An inch one way or the other can determine whether you live or die."

"That's scary," Cruz said.

"Alright, we'd better notify the district attorney's office that their star witness won't be showing up." McConnell said. "And someone's going to have to notify Dominic and the mother."

"I think we should get the captain to notify Dominic," Matthews said. "He'll want to tell his wife himself."

"That's going to be hard on them," Cruz said. He looked ashen. Being in the presence of death affected him more than the others. "I'll move our car out of the way," he said as he went downstairs.

While the crime scene was being processed, Dennis arrived at the Ninth Precinct. Still shaken, but holding himself together, he took a breath, went in, and stopped at the station house desk. The lieutenant, recognizing him from earlier, waved him to go upstairs to the second floor. Passing the detective squad room, he saw that it was busy. That was good, he thought, and went up to the lounge/dormitory on the third floor. He sat on one of the bunk beds, trying to calm himself for his return to the squad room. He went into the men's room and put cold water on his face. There was swelling, so he took an icetray from the refrigerator, and pressed it against his eye, lips, and cheek, where Ray had hit him. He had a bigger swelling on the side of his head, but it was covered by his hair.

After a few minutes, he went down to the second floor and walked into the squad room. Detective Radowski was typing a report.

"Is my father finished with the interrogation yet?" Dennis asked.

"Yes," Radowski said, pointing to the suspect being fingerprinted by another detective.

"He's being arrested?" Dennis asked.

"Yep. First-degree murder."

"That was fast," Dennis said, glad that it seemed his presence hadn't been missed. He might have established his alibi, though he still had to be wary of saying the wrong thing, or anything that could trip him up.

"Where's my father?" he asked.

"He's in the captain's office across the hall."

"Can I go see him?"

"No. You better wait here. He just got a call that sounded important."

Hearing that, Dennis' heart began beating faster, but he tried to appear calm.

"Was it about that case?" he asked, pointing to the suspect.

"Don't know," Radowski said.

Dennis took a seat close to the door, and nodded to each detective who passed him. A couple of them spoke to him.

Twenty minutes later, a detective came into the squad room asking, "Is Dennis Carbonaro here?"

"Right here," Dennis stood up.

"Your father wants to see you in the captain's office."

Dennis followed him across the hall, his heart pounding.

In the captain's office, his father was standing with Detective-Captain Bill Corcoran, several detectives, and a Chief, who was in full uniform, two gold stars on his shoulders.

Dominic put his arm around Dennis' shoulder. "We've got bad news," he said.

"What?"

"Your brother's dead."

Dennis wasn't sure how he should react. But he had thought about what to say, keeping in mind that, ultimately, if he was charged, he'd have to prove that he had acted in self-defense. So, he would be careful about saying anything that could compromise that; he shouldn't make any inconsistent statements that could be used to undermine his credibility later.

"How?" Dennis asked.

"We won't know for sure until the medical examiner determines the cause of death," Captain Corcoran said, "but it looks like he got hit in the head with something. Crime scene is processing the apartment now for evidence."

Dennis sat down, put his elbows on the desk, and put head into his hands, hoping that they wouldn't ask him any questions. After a minute, he looked up, "Dad, have you told mom, yet?"

"Not yet. I'm going home now. You should come," Dominic said.

"Of course."

Captain Corcoran told Dominic that there would be a meeting at the DA's office tomorrow at noon. "If you feel up to it, you could attend, even though Queens homicide has the investigation."

"I'll be there."

In separate cars, Dominic and Dennis drove home to tell Marie. When they arrived, they were surprised to learn that she had already been notified. A uniformed patrol sergeant from the local precinct had visited and notified her.

Marie had rosary beads in her hands. As she hugged Dennis, she said, "Thank God, I still have you."

Dennis hugged her tightly, trying to offset the weak feeling inside of him. What if she ever found out that it was me, he thought? Would he be able to explain that it was self-defense? Would it matter?

Marie released Dennis, and trying her best to hold herself together and hold back tears, said, "I'll call the funeral home. And the church. We could have the mass on Saturday."

The next day at noon, the district attorney's conference room was packed. Present were assistant district attorneys, detectives from Queens Homicide, Brooklyn North Robbery, Narcotics, Vice, and the Department of Corrections' investigations section. They had been brought together to form a task force for an all-out effort to solve Ray's murder. Because Ray was Dominic's son, it was going to be treated as though it were the murder of a police officer.

Everyone gave their condolences to Dominic.

Queens District Attorney Harold White arrived. He was very short and often the object of good-natured cop humor because he always stood on a box to reach microphones or see over podiums. Nevertheless, he was highly respected by the police because of his full support over the years.

Everyone stood. "Sit down, sit down," he said, then gave his full commitment to the investigation and promised his full support. "The murder of a police officer's family member affects us all deeply. We are an extended family, and we have to pull together to console and protect one another The case has our highest priority. I'll be watching your progress closely," he said, then left the room.

ADA Walsh began the meeting by having everyone introduce themselves. Then he gave an overview of the crime and what was known. He said, "I knew we should have put Ray under police protection right away."

Detective McConnell took offense and responded defensively. "We were on the way to do just that. These things take time," he said.

Captain Corcoran interceded, "That's old news. Where do we go from here?"

"Alright," ADA Walsh said, "let's start with the threats. Does Corrections have any more recorded conversations?"

Warden Henry Harmon, from Corrections, handed out transcripts of two new recorded conversations between Forest and Shaquan Campbell, including one in which Campbell said, "We saw his crib. 'LJ' was with us. No problem."

"Sounds like they cased the layout of the house beforehand," Corcoran said. "Do we know who 'LJ' is?

"No," Warden Harmon said.

Captain Corcoran asked McConnell, "Have the neighbors been canvassed?"

"Yes. And we might have caught a break," McConnell said. "This morning, before coming here, I stopped and talked to the landlord, Mr. Martucci. He told me that about a week ago, he saw three black guys in a gray Toyota SUV stop and look down his driveway. He saw them from his window. They drove off, but a little while later, they came back, driving very slowly and looking."

"Could he identify them?" someone asked.

"Maybe. One of them got out of the car for a second, but when he saw him in the window, he got back in and they drove away."

"Did he get a plate number?"

"No. But he was sure it was a Toyota 4Runner, which narrows it down some."

"That's something we can work with," Corcoran said. "Check the registrations of the suspects and any of their known associates. If that comes up dry, I want a list of every traffic ticket for Toyota 4Runners in Brooklyn and Queens. And I want every security camera in the area of the apartment checked."

"We're already doing that, boss," McConnell said.

"Good," Corcoran said. "Dominic, do you have any suggestions?"

"Several. First, you should know, Ray worked in the Kit-Kat club as a bouncer. We could put undercovers in there to fish around.

"Second, Ray got involved with drugs and, I think, steroids. So, the Narcotics Division should be involved.

"And, one more, how about placing an informant in the jail with Forest?"

Corcoran asked Walsh what he thought about those suggestions.

"Putting undercovers in the clubs is okay," Walsh said, "but we can't put an informant in the cells with any of them. They all have lawyers, so you can't use an informant to get around a defendant's lawyer."

"I understand that," Corcoran said. "That's no good because an informant would be our agent acting on our behalf. But, if someone in the jail comes forward on their own, that's okay. Isn't it?"

"Yes. That's okay," Walsh said.

"Alright. That's settled," Corcoran said. "Everyone's going to pitch in. My office will be open twenty-four-seven. I want copies of all progress reports forwarded twice a day. Anything urgent, call me anytime, day or night."

While Dominic was at the district attorney's office, Dennis bought three newspapers to see whether there were any stories about Ray. There was nothing about it in *The Times*, a brief story in *The Post* about a cop's son found dead in his Ridgewood, Queens apartment. *The Daily News* had a longer story that mentioned that Ray had been acquitted of the BMW dealership robbery and was going to testify against his alleged accomplices in the grand jury.

As Dennis was reading the newspapers, Kathy Reynolds called him.

"I just saw the newspapers," she said. "I can't believe it. I'm so sorry. It's terrible."

"Thank you, thanks for calling," he said.

"How did it happen?" she asked.

"They don't know yet," Dennis said. "My father went to a meeting at the DA's office. I'm sure they going to do everything they can to find out who did it."

"I hope they do," she said. "Who do they think did it?"

"Too early to tell."

"If you find out anything else, please call me."

"I will."

Dennis hung up although he had an impulse to tell Kathy that he was the one who did it, that he did it in self-defense. She knew Ray's temper and how aggressive he could be, especially on steroids, and she would believe it was self-defense. She could help him decide what to do. Should he turn himself in now, or wait to see if the cops make him a suspect? He knew his self-defense argument would be more credible if he came forward on his own now, rather than wait until the cops were closing in on him; but he didn't want to go through the ordeal of a trial like Ray had. He hoped that he could avoid the whole thing.

He thought about whether or not he should tell his father. It would be hard, and it wouldn't be right. He couldn't tell him unless he turned himself in. Otherwise, he'd be putting his father in a terrible position, either to turn his own son in or help him cover up the crime. Dennis decided not to tell him or anyone. He had rolled the dice when he left the apartment, and still had a chance to survive.

A wake for Ray was arranged for Friday and a mass on Saturday at Our Lady of Miracles Catholic Church on Flatlands Avenue in Canarsie, Brooklyn. The wake was crowded. The Carbonaro's had a large extended family, and relatives from three states came. Dominic was well known in the police department, and at least fifty off-duty police officers came to give their condolences. Ray's friends and acquaintances from the gyms that he and Kathy had worked out in also attended. The funeral parlor couldn't accommodate them all, people had to wait outside.

Dominic and Dennis stood by the open coffin and shook hands with people as they passed. Marie stayed seated with her close relatives.

Dennis was uneasy and anxious as he accepted the condolences, his mind shifting from present problems to future problems. He wondered whether anyone suspected him. He wondered what they would say when they found out. He had an impulse to walk out, get on a plane, and never come back. But, he couldn't. His mother looked old, and his father, though standing stoically at the coffin, had a defeated look on his face. Ray's trial and his catastrophic ending had taken so much out of him. He was no longer an impregnable rock, but vulnerable like everyone else.

Dennis avoided looking at Ray's body, but his mother told him that he needed to say a prayer. So, he knelt down in front of the coffin, not praying, but looking at what was once his brother. The body looked like a wax mannikin. He could see the left temple where he had struck him with the hammer, but it was covered in makeup, and no mark was visible. For a moment, a feeling of guilt came over him, but he shook it away. I did nothing wrong, he thought. Why should I be dead and not him? I should turn around right now and tell everyone what happened. Get it over with. Instead, he kept hoping that the whole thing would just go away.

At the mass, Kathy arrived at the same time that the black hearse with the coffin arrived from the funeral home. She was wearing her black, pin-striped suit, and as she walked down the aisle, everyone watched her. She sat next to Dennis and took his hand. Her touch was welcome, but he couldn't help thinking again whether he should tell her. He wondered what her reaction would be. Maybe he could convince her to move to California with him and put all this behind them. But it would never be behind them.

As the church organist began playing the funeral dirge, the pallbearers carried the coffin up the steps into the church, lifted it onto a gurney, rolled the gurney slowly down the aisle, walking beside it in perfect cadence with the dirge. They stopped in front of the altar, and the priest cast holy water and incense over the coffin.

The mass moved slowly. Dennis' mother signaled to him that he was supposed to be kneeling at one part of the mass. He knelt, and made the sign of the cross at the same time as everyone else. He watched the priest on the altar, and thought that before telling his father, he should go to a priest for advice and guidance. But, then, what good would that do? The priest would only tell him to turn himself in.

When the mass ended, the pallbearers loaded the coffin into the black limousine for the drive to Holy Cross Cemetery in Flatbush, Brooklyn. Dominic, Marie, Dennis, and Kathy rode in the second limousine, and two dozen cars followed them.

Dominic wasn't thinking of revenge as he watched his oldest son's remains lowered into the grave. He was remembering Ray as a child, and he was thinking of a special day when he had taken Ray and Dennis for a hike in the woods after a spring snowfall, and how beautiful it was, what fun they had, how great they all felt in the crisp, clean air, and what promise they had in front of them. But that was gone.

At the gravesite, when the coffin was lowered into the ground, Marie began to cry. Seeing his mother cry, tears filled Dennis' eyes. He thought that if he could only go back in time, he would have done so much differently. He would have stayed out of Ray's trial. He wouldn't have gone to Ray's place to confront him. He would have called for an ambulance right away and reported what happened. But, he didn't, and now that the funeral was over, his father would be pulling out all the stops to find the murderer. He assumed that if his father found out who the murderer was, he'd want to kill him rather than take him to court.

CHAPTER TWENTY-NINE

The task force investigating Ray's death was up and running immediately. A check of the suspects' and their associates' car registrations was negative; none of them owned a Toyota 4-Runner. The task force collected and reviewed security camera videos from the area and conducted a survey of traffic tickets. They found that an NYPD radio motor patrol car team in Queens had pulled over a 4-Runner the day before Ray's body was found, the same day of the last recorded prison conversation between Forest and Campbell, the conversation when Campbell said that they had seen the crib, meaning they had gone to Ray's house to check it out.

The patrol officers had stopped the Toyota 4-Runner for making a left turn from the right lane without signaling. It was a routine traffic stop, and the officers were unaware of the BMW dealership robbery or Ray's death.

Campbell was the driver. He had a license, but no registration. He said that he had borrowed the car from a friend because his own car was being repaired. The officers checked with the motor vehicle bureau, and learned that the car had not been reported stolen. They gave Campbell a ticket for no registration and for turning without signaling, and they made the passengers identify themselves. The first passenger was Willie Mumford who was scheduled to be tried for the BMW robbery with Forest and Campbell. The second passenger was Leon James, who hadn't been involved in the BMW robbery but had a long arrest record, including assaults with guns. The detectives speculated that he was the 'LJ' mentioned in the recorded conversation and that he was going to be the hitman.

Detective McConnell obtained photographs of the suspects to show Mr. Martucci to find out if he could identify any of them as the men who had been looking down his driveway. McConnell and Cruz went to Martucci's house.

"How are you, sir?" Cruz said.

"Still a little shaken," Martucci said.

"That's understandable."

"When will they take the crime-scene tape off the door so I can get into the apartment? I'm going to have to clean the place out and try to rent it."

"I'll call crime scene today, and let you know. They should be finished, but you never know."

McConnell went to the car and retrieved a folder containing photographs. "You told us about the men looking down your driveway," he said. "I have some photographs here that I'd like you to look at."

"You found them already?" Martucci asked.

"I can't say. I don't want to influence you."

McConnell placed the three photos of Willie Mumford, Shaquan Campbell, and Leon James on a dining room table. With each photo he placed five other photos, all of African-American males about the same age, for a total of eighteen photos, three of suspects and fifteen of fillers.

"If I pick one out, will I have to go to court?" Martucci asked.

"We'll cross that bridge when we come to it," McConnell said. "For now, you can just help us to be sure we're targeting the right guys. If we can get other evidence, or get one of them to confess, we wouldn't need you to testify."

"They usually squeal on each other, right?" Martucci said. "Like that guy who testified against Ray, although he was making it up."

"Exactly." McConnell said.

Martucci looked at the three groups of photos. Then he looked at the second group again, and pointed at the photo of Shaquan Campbell. "That's the one who got out of the car. The others stayed in the car, so

I couldn't tell you about them. I didn't see them well enough. But this one, I saw from my window. He looked right at me. That's him."

"You're positive," McConnell said.

"I'm sure."

McConnell called Captain Corcoran, told him about the identification, and scheduled a meeting for the next morning at the DA's office. Corcoran called Dominic and asked him to attend the meeting.

At the meeting, obviously remembering the photo-array problems at the BMW robbery trial, ADA Walsh questioned McConnell about how he conducted the photo identification. McConnell answered his questions curtly. Clearly, there were still bad feelings between them stemming from Ray's trial.

After reviewing the photographs that were used, Walsh said that he was satisfied that the identification had been conducted fairly and properly.

"And Mr. Martucci was positive?" he asked.

"Absolutely," McConnell said.

"The question now is whether we have enough to go to the grand jury for an indictment. The case is still only circumstantial," Walsh said.

"I think it's more than circumstantial," McConnell said. "We've got them talking about killing Ray and checking out the house. We've got their motive. They wanted to prevent his testimony. They showed up in the 4-Runner to case the house, and they went into the driveway where the side entrance to his apartment is. What other reason could they have for being there? They flee when Martucci sees them, which shows they weren't there for a picnic. The patrol officers stopped them in the area the day before the body was found, probably when the murder took place."

"It's all still circumstantial. There's no direct evidence," Walsh said.

"But Martucci is an eyewitness. That's direct evidence," McConnell said.

Captain Corcoran interjected, "It's direct evidence that they were in the driveway, but he didn't see them in the house or see him kill anybody."

"That's right," Walsh said. "And, so far, there's no physical evidence. Have the fingerprints come back yet?"

"Yes. Plenty," Corcoran said. "But none matching our suspects. They're all either Ray's or his brother's."

Walsh poured himself a coffee. "Help yourselves, if you like," he said to everyone.

No one took him up on the offer. The mood in the room was sullen.

Dominic cleared his throat. "I agree with the DA," he said. "We need more. I'm willing to put up a $20,000 reward for information that leads to a conviction."

"That should help," Captain Corcoran said. "We can advertise it on the tip hotline."

"And we shouldn't forget about the BMW robbery trial," Dominic said. "When is that going to happen? If you can convict one of them, he may flip on the others."

"I agree about the BMW case," Corcoran said. "In fact, we should go to the judge and get him to raise the bail on the two that are out."

"You're right, but it's a little late now. We should have done that right away," McConnell said, evidently paying back Walsh for his dig that he hadn't put Ray under police protection right away.

When Dominic came home from the DA's meeting, he told Dennis everything that had gone on. Dennis listened carefully, then went upstairs to his room and made notes of key points and questions that he had. As was his habit, he calculated what could happen next. His first take was that it was good for him that the police were focusing on the conspiracy between Forrest, Campbell and the others, and not on him, and he thought that the $20,000 reward would bring informers out of the woodwork, which would keep the detectives busy tracking down the bogus tips.

But the more he thought about it, the more worried he got. The detectives would soon find out that they were targeting the wrong guys. When the autopsy disclosed the cause of death, it would undermine the conspiracy theory. Surely, the conspirators would have shot Ray, not hit him with a hammer. There was no break in, and the detectives would realize that it had to be someone who Ray knew and let into the apartment. They would rethink their theory. Someone would suggest looking at the brother, and they would.

They'd question him, and he'd have to make a monumental decision, either to stick by his alibi or to come forward and tell them that he did it in self-defense? If he claimed self-defense, they'd ask why he hadn't said so sooner. He could answer by telling the truth—he didn't want his parents to know that he killed Ray, and he didn't want go through the ordeal of a trial. However, by not being forthright from the beginning, and being so calculating and deceptive, a jury would call him a congenital liar, and they would find him guilty because of it. He went over the options and decided that sticking to his alibi was probably the safest course.

The phone rang downstairs, and his mother called him. "It's the lawyer, Murray Klein."

"Where's Dad?" Dennis asked.

"He went out to the stores; he'll be right back."

Dennis took the call.

"I was so sorry to hear about your brother," Klein said. "I would have called sooner, but I was out of town and didn't find out until I got back."

"That's okay. Thanks for calling," Dennis said.

"That was a terrible thing. You know, in spite of everything, I liked your brother."

Dennis didn't respond.

"To be honest, I didn't like him as much as I liked you," Klein continued. "And my offer is still open for you to come back to work in my office."

"Thanks again for that. Right now, I'm pretty set, working at UPS and going to school at night."

"That's good, but keep it in mind for when you're ready. How are your mom and dad holding up?"

"They're doing as well as can be expected. My father's working on the case in a task force. That keeps him focused."

"Really?" Klein said. "That must feel strange for him, working on his own son's murder."

"It is strange, in more ways than one," Dennis said.

"What do you mean?"

"Nothing," Dennis said, realizing that he shouldn't have said that.

"Well, give your parents my regards," Klein said. "And there is another matter. I'd like to meet with your father about Ray's lawsuit. We have to substitute him as the administrator of Ray's estate, so that it can go forward."

"Why would it go forward, Ray's dead?" Dennis asked.

"It doesn't matter that he's dead. Ray suffered and he's entitled to compensation. And his estate is entitled to collect it. Think about it. A person's estate is responsible to pay their debts, so they need to collect what's owed them so they can pay off the debts."

"I see. That makes sense," Dennis said. "Your debts don't die with you."

"That's right, and neither do your accounts receivable."

"So, the lawsuits go on and on."

"Right. And another thing. If we can connect Ray's death to his wrongful arrest and incarceration, the lawsuit could be expanded."

Dennis didn't like that idea. He thought the lawsuit was the cause of Ray's death and his problems. Which were now his problems.

"I'll have my father call you about that. But before you go, can I ask you a question?"

"Of course."

"How's the case against the BMW perps going?"

"The trial is scheduled to start next month. I'm not representing any of the defendants. I understand that none of the defendants could afford a lawyer, so Judge Brown assigned a legal-aid lawyer to each one.

When Dominic returned from the stores, Dennis told him about Klein's call and about continuing the lawsuit in the name of the estate.

"I suppose that's a good quality in a lawyer, that he doesn't give up," Dominic said.

"He sees a payday," Dennis said.

"Well, he's put a lot of time in on the case, maybe he's just be trying to come out even."

"I don't like it. I wish the whole thing would go away," Dennis said, knowing that he had his own reasons for wanting it to go away.

"I think we need to hear him out," Dominic said. "I'll call him in the morning."

Two days later, Dominic and Dennis met with Klein at his office. The secretary and some of the other lawyers gave their condolences to them. Then in the conference room, Klein made a short speech about how difficult it was to hear of Ray's death. "As a lawyer, you always feel that maybe if you had done something different, the outcome would have been different."

Dennis couldn't agree more, but said nothing.

Klein went on to explain about having Dominic appointed as administrator of Ray's estate. The papers were already prepared, and he asked Dominic to read them over and sign them. Marie and Dennis would also have to sign forms.

"So, what's going to happen with the lawsuit?" Dennis asked.

"Once the court accepts Dominic as the administrator, it will proceed on schedule. But most everything is done. Your deposition is over, and you won't have to go through that again. The judge will make a ruling on the motions for summary judgment, and then I expect the city will offer a settlement."

"What if the judge rules against us?" Dennis asked.

"Then it's over."

"Okay," Dominic said. "We've gone this far; we might as well play it out."

As Dominic was reading the forms, his cell phone rang. He answered it, and Dennis saw a look of shock on his face, then a strange smile.

250

"What's the matter?" Dennis asked.

"You're going to like this," Dominic said to Klein. "Buster Johnson was just murdered, shot five times in front of the Pan Am Motor Inn on Queens Boulevard."

Klein also smiled.

"I knew you'd like it," Dominic said.

"This may sound hard-hearted," Klein said to Dennis, "but, for defense attorneys, it's always good when a prosecution snitch disappears, especially one like Buster."

"That's the difference between us," Dominic said. "I've got to go."

They had driven to Klein's in Dominic's unmarked squad car, and now he put the flashing police bubble light on the dashboard to drive to the 110th Precinct in Forest Hills, Queens, where the investigation was underway.

He drove up the East River Drive to the 59th Street Queensboro Bridge. Dennis was in the passenger seat. It was exciting to see the other cars move out of the way when Dominic sounded the siren.

At the Precinct, they went upstairs to the squad room. Dennis sat in a chair out of the way. Detective Radowski came over to him, "We meet again. I saw you at the Ninth Precinct and now the One-ten. You get around. Your father must bring you with him everywhere to keep you out of trouble."

"Yes. I guess so," Dennis said.

Dominic stood with Detective McConnell among the task force detectives and several other detectives while Captain Corcoran briefed them about what was known so far.

"Buster Johnson was due to testify in a couple of weeks about his part in the BMW car dealership robbery in which a customer was killed," Corcoran said. "We had information that there was a threat against his life to prevent him from testifying. He had been given a different ID and had been stashed in the Pan Am Motor Inn with plainclothes officers in the adjoining room for protection. But it seems he couldn't stay home and made a call to buy some marihuana. We figure that the marihuana dealer must have tipped off our suspects.

"Buster went outside and waited for the dealer in the bus-stop shelter. A car must have pulled up, and the rest is history. They shot him five times. One was a contact shot in the head. We don't have any witnesses."

"And they say marihuana is not dangerous," a detective said, getting a laugh.

Corcoran continued, "We're guessing that one of the shooters got out of the car to fire that last shot. A passerby found the body and called 911."

"Any shells recovered?" a detective asked.

"Just one, a 9mm automatic, the shooter most have picked up the other discharged shells. We'll know more when the bullets are removed from the body."

The Pan Am has security cameras, maybe they recorded something," a detective offered.

"We're in the process of getting the tapes," Corcoran said. "Now we have to canvas all the guests in the hotel because most of them will be gone by the morning. And then we'll canvas the buildings on either side and across Queens Boulevard."

"It's a long way across the Boulevard, nobody's going to see anything from there," McConnell said.

"Don't be so sure," Corcoran said. "Remember the Alice Crimmins case in the 1960s."

"In the 60s, I wasn't even a cop," someone said. Another said, "I wasn't even born."

"Well, you missed it," Corcoran said. "She killed her two children. She said they were asleep and someone must have kidnapped them during the night. But, a witness, Sadie something, from across the Boulevard, saw her walking with the two kids and taking them to a car, blowing up her kidnapping story. So, you never know. You may think you haven't been seen, but witnesses come out of nowhere to sink you."

As Dennis listened to the captain, his left hand began to shake. He shoved it into his pocket to hide it, and thought that if someone had seen him leaving the apartment after the fight with Ray, and had seen him duck down when the detectives passed, then run to his car, not only his alibi, but his self-defense story would also be destroyed. People would want to know, why he didn't run to the detectives and tell them what had just happened. Dennis felt his face flush, and hoped no one noticed. He was glad when his father said that he'd have to stay on duty and that he should take a cab home. "Tell your mother that I'll be home as soon as I can, but not to wait up for me."

Dennis didn't go straight home but stopped at McCoy's on the way. It had been a long day, and he wanted to tell Kathy about it all.

She had finished her shift tending bar, and sat with him in their usual booth. He told her everything that had happened, and it felt good to talk to someone who understood what he was going through. When he finished, he saw that she was on the verge of tears.

"I know this has been tough on you as well," he said. "How are you doing?

This was just what she needed. She had gone through a lot, too, and she talked about her mixed emotions, how devastating it was for her when Dennis told her about Ray's lies, yet how devastating it was when he was killed. "Sometimes I feel guilty myself," she said.

"For what?"

"For not being closer to him, for acting as though I approved of it when he acted like he was the toughest guy around," she said. "He was always trying to prove something. He had to be the strongest guy in the gym. He had to have the fastest car. I encouraged him, but I should have been showing him that there were other things in life."

As she talked, she was looking into the distance as though remembering past times. He was looking at her, and thought how fantastic she was, how he wanted to make her his and his only. But he was reluctant to be too forward. He still hadn't told her about killing Ray. If they resumed their relationship again in earnest, there'd come a time when he'd have to tell her. He'd have to tell her before he told anyone else, or the police, or his parents. If he told Kathy first, and she knowingly went into the relationship, that would be the best. But, if he told her afterwards, she'd feel betrayed. He knew he should tell her now, but he was afraid to risk it. She might break off with him.

Her right hand was on the table, and he put his hand next to hers, touching her pinky with his. A current, like an electric spark, ran between them. They both flinched for a second, then she took his hand, looked in his eyes, and said, "Your place or mine."

"Unless you want to sleep in the room next to my parents, I guess it's yours."

At that, they broke up laughing.

Brendan came over to the booth. "Ah, it's been a long time since I've seen you guys laughing like that," he said.

Dennis wasn't sure they'd ever laughed like that, but it was nice for Brendan to say.

CHAPTER THIRTY

The press reports about the shooting of Buster Johnson were not well received in the mayor's office or at police headquarters. The city was experiencing a crime spike that had adversely affected the tourist industry; headlines about assassinated witnesses wouldn't help the situation. Captain Corcoran was called to a meeting in the Chief of Detective's office, which was on the thirteen floor of police headquarters, a fourteen-story building in lower Manhattan that the rank and file nicknamed the "puzzle palace." Chief of Detectives Nick Nicoletti asked him to explain how Johnson could have been killed while supposedly under police protection. Corcoran explained that the officers guarding him were in the next room in the hotel and they had told him not to leave without telling them. Evidently, Johnson wanted to smoke some marihuana, so he snuck out. "Unless we tied him up or handcuffed him to the bed, there was no way to stop him."

Corcoran was asked why the officers didn't stay in the same room with him.

"Johnson was glad for the protection," Corcoran said. "It didn't seem necessary at the time."

Chief Nicoletti ended the meeting without assigning blame and without openly giving instructions, but later that day word was sent to Corcoran that the chief hadn't been pleased with how the case was going and wanted somebody arrested for something, and as soon as possible.

Corcoran arranged a meeting with ADA Walsh to discuss the situation. Dominic and McConnell attended.

Walsh annoyed at the pressure from above, asked, "So, who are we going to arrest?" "We don't have any witnesses, or physical evidence connecting anybody to the shooting. You can't speculate your way into an arrest."

"Let's get search warrants for their houses and cars," McConnell said. "Maybe we'll come up with the gun."

"I still need evidence to get search warrants," Walsh said.

Dominic suggested that they had more evidence about Ray's case than they did about Buster's murder. He asked whether the M.E.s report had been done yet.

Walsh said. "They classified it as a homicide, caused by a blow to the temple by a hard object."

"How about the toxicology?" Dominic asked

"Yes," Walsh said. "Ray had high amounts of anabolic steroids and cocaine in his system."

Dominic had expected the steroids, but was surprised and disappointed about the cocaine. How many times had Ray told him that he was clean?

McConnell suggested that they start with Ray's homicide case.

"I agree," Walsh said. "We could get an arrest warrant for Campbell because he was recorded on the jail conversation and was the one Martucci identified as being at the house, and we could get search warrants for Mumford and LJ."

The next morning at 5:00 a.m., detectives executed a search warrant at Mumford's apartment in Bedford-Stuyvesant, Brooklyn. They recovered a .45 caliber automatic pistol, which was not the weapon used to kill Buster Johnson. The detectives arrested Mumford for unlawful possession of the weapon. They also recovered several watches and gold chains that they planned to check out to see if they had been reported stolen.

At the same time, other detectives executed arrest and search warrants at Campbell's apartment in Bushwick, Brooklyn. When they knocked on the door and announced, "Police, we have a warrant, open the door," Campbell fled out a window and down the fire-escape. Other detectives were waiting for him at the bottom, and he was arrested. No weapons, stolen property, or other contraband were found in his apartment.

A search warrant at LJ's last known address proved fruitless. The apartment was empty and the detectives had no information about where LJ had gone.

Both Mumford and Campbell were booked at the 112th Precinct, placed in separate interrogation rooms and given Miranda warnings. Detective McConnell interrogated Mumford while Dominic interrogated Campbell.

The interrogations were recorded and transmitted to a side office where Captain Corcoran and other detectives could listen to them as they occurred, so that if one of the suspects said something to one interrogator that could be useful, the information could be passed on to the other interrogator.

In interrogation room number one, Mumford, in exchange for a lighter sentence, was willing to talk right away. He claimed that he was in the Toyota-4Runner with Campbell and Leon James (LJ). They were looking for Buster Johnson to threaten him and warn him not to testify in the BMW case. But, when they drove up to Buster at the bus stop, LJ suddenly began firing. He fired four or five shots, and Buster fell to the ground.

"LJ got out of the car and put another one in his head," Mumford said. "I didn't know he was going to do it."

"You knew LJ was packing, right?" McConnell said.

"Not until he took it out and I saw the gun," Mumford said.

"What kind of gun?"

"It was a Glock automatic."

"Before he started shooting, what did you guys say to Buster?"

"Nothing."

"But you said that you were looking for Buster to warn him. Wouldn't you have talked to him?"

"We intended to, but didn't have a chance. LJ surprised everybody by shooting without saying a word."

In room number two, Dominic questioned Campbell about driving around in the Toyota-4Runner with Mumford and LJ. Although Dominic was asking about Ray's murder in Ridgewood, Campbell was confused and thought Dominic was talking about the shooting of Buster at the bus stop, and he told the same story that Mumford had told. "We didn't know LJ was going to shoot him. We never got a chance to even ask him what was happening."

Dominic let him finish talking, then switched the subject to Ray's murder. "You stopped at the home of Ray Carbonaro to see what the place looked like, right?" Dominic asked.

"I don't remember that," Campbell said. "We were driving around all over looking for Buster. I wasn't driving, Willie Mumford was driving. He stopped at a few places. I wasn't paying attention to everything. I was tired, probably nodding out half the time."

"So, you were never at Ray Carbonaro's house?"

"Not that I remember."

"But we have you on video walking down his driveway," Dominic said. He didn't have video, but he said so because if Campbell thought he did, he might start talking and try to explain it.

"I told you, I don't remember," Campbell said. "We were driving around all day, we stopped at a lot of places."

"But you walked down the driveway. It was a private house, why would you do that?"

"I don't remember doing it, so I can't tell you why."

During a break, the detectives went into the office where Corcoran was listening to the interrogations.

"We're not getting anywhere with Campbell," Corcoran said. "Maybe he should play him his jail conversation with Forrest."

"I don't think so," Dominic said. "I don't believe in telling them everything we know. Let them spin their stories, then confront them later when it's too late for them to change."

"It looks like Mumford and Campbell got their story together somewhere along the way," Corcoran said. "We've to use the tapes now. We won't get another chance."

Back in room one, McConnell continued questioning Mumford. "You'd be willing to testify to everything you've told me?"

"If I get a deal. Yes."

"Okay. I'll run that by the DA. But we still have to talk about the other murder."

"What other murder?" Mumford asked.

"You know what other murder."

"I don't know what you're talking about."

"Listen, we know James Forrest ordered you guys to find Buster and kill him, right?"

"What do you mean?"

"We have the conversations."

"But we were just looking for him to scare him, I didn't know LJ was gonna shoot him."

"Okay, we can agree on that," McConnell said. "But Forrest also ordered you to kill Ray Carbonaro to stop him from testifying against you in the BMW case, right?"

Mumford didn't answer.

"And you drove to Ray's house in Ridgewood to case the place, right?" McConnell persisted.

"When?"

"You drove with Shaquan and LJ."

"When?"

"Remember you were stopped by the cops and they gave you a traffic ticket."

Mumford thought for a minute, then said, "Yeah."

"Well, that's the same day you drove to Ray's house."

"No. That was a different day," Mumford said, immediately realizing that his answer was a mistake.

"Okay, maybe it was a different day," McConnell said, "but you guys drove to the house, and Shaquan went down the driveway and into the house. Right?"

"If you say so."

"I know so. And when Shaquan came out, he told you that he had killed him?"

Mumford's eyes darted back and forth, as though deciding which way to go. The room was silent. Then he said, "I didn't go into the house."

"We're not saying you did, but you saw Shaquan go in," McConnell said.

"I'm not sure."

"You have to be sure. You made a deal to tell us what happened between LJ and Buster, but we also need you to tell us what happened here with Shaquan. You must've seen him go into the house. He was gone for a while, right."

"Yeah."

"That's what we need you to testify to," McConnell said. "If you do, the deal will be good for both cases. Assuming the DA goes along, of course. But I don't see why he wouldn't. You didn't kill anybody. I'm sure you'll get a good deal."

Mumford shifted around in his chair, "Okay. I could do that."

"Very good," McConnell said. "But just one more thing. When Shaquan came out of the house, he said 'it's done' or something like that."

"I don't remember."

"Try to remember."

"I'm not exactly sure what he said."

"But something like that, right?"

"Yeah."

On another break, the detectives met in the side office. "Good job," Captain Corcoran said to McConnell, who looked pleased with himself.

"Now get Mumford to sign a written statement," Corcoran said, "and we'll have enough to charge them for the Buster case."

"What about Ray's case?" Dominic asked.

"That's not so clear," Corcoran said. "Shaquan didn't admit anything about Ray's murder. Let's get Martucci in for a lineup to see if he can confirm the photo identification of Campbell."

"He's already on his way, and we're getting stand-ins ready," one of the detectives said.

"Whether he does or not," McConnell said, "if you charge it as a conspiracy, everyone in it can be held for everything that occurred, even if they didn't do it themselves. So, Mumford and Campbell didn't shoot Buster, but they're guilty, too. And they're all guilty of Ray's death because they conspired to do it."

"I agree," Corcoran said.

In the next hours, Mumford signed a written statement; Campbell refused. Then lineups were conducted: Mumford in one, Campbell in another.

Mr. Martucci viewed them both. He didn't recognize Mumford, but picked out Campbell. "He's the one I saw in my driveway."

Based on the accumulated evidence, Captain Corcoran called ADA Walsh and got the approval to charge Mumford, Campbell, Jones, and Forrest with the murders of both Buster Johnson and Ray Carbonaro.

The defendants were turned over to uniformed officers to be transported to Central Booking, held overnight, and then taken to court for arraignments in the morning.

"That was a good day's work. Let's go for a drink somewhere," Corcoran said.

"That sounds good," McConnell said. "How about McCoy's? They got the best burgers."

CHAPTER THIRTY-ONE

Dennis and Kathy spent all the time they could together. When she was working, he came to the bar. Sometimes he drank beer; sometimes coke. One night, he was there when his father, Captain Corcoran, McConnell, and Cruz came in. It was the night after they had finished the interrogations of Mumford and Campbell, and were given the go-ahead to make arrests for the murders of Buster and Ray.

They were in a celebratory mood and asked Dennis to sit with them.

It was the last place Dennis wanted to be, sitting with the police investigating Ray's death. But his father motioned for him to sit down, and he did.

"How's everything," Dennis said.

"Very good," the captain said. "We had a productive day. Let's order first, then I'll tell you all about it."

Kathy came from behind the bar. "Hello, Mr. Carbonaro."

"Hi, Kathy, nice to see you."

"The waitress will be here in a minute," she said. "Do you want to order drinks?"

They ordered beers, and she went to the bar to get them.

Noticing that McConnell looked at Kathy as she walked away and then looked at him, it crossed Dennis' mind that McConnell could be thinking that he and Kathy were going together and Dennis might have wanted Ray dead.

Detective Cruz was also looking at Kathy, and asked Dominic, "She must have been heartbroken when she heard that your son was murdered."

Dominic answered, "She was."

Dennis remained silent, struck by Cruz saying that Ray had been murdered. He wanted to ask how he came to that conclusion, but didn't dare. This was treacherous territory; the less he said the better.

When the waitress came, everyone ordered cheeseburgers. Then Kathy came back with the beers.

Captain Corcoran raised his glass. "Here's to solving the case. It's a special case for us. And I'm sure I speak for everyone here and for everyone in the Bureau how much we've admired Dominic's professionalism as he has dealt with such a personal tragedy."

Dominic raised his glass, acknowledging the remarks.

Dennis could not hold back. "You solved the case?" he asked.

"Yes," Corcoran explained for the benefit of Dennis. "It should be in the papers tomorrow. We got the perps of the BMW robbery who killed Buster Johnson and your brother. They killed them to stop them from testifying. We know that from a recorded jail house conversation where they said so. And, it so happened that the landlord of Ray's apartment saw three suspicious guys at the house in a Toyota-4Runner. We got lucky because uniformed patrol officers had stopped a 4-Runner in the area, gave a ticket to the driver, and identified the passengers. Two of them were perps from the dealership robbery, and they were on the jailhouse call."

Dennis was surprised that the captain would tell him so much. Everyone was looking at Dennis, waiting for his response. He realized that someone was going to be charged with Ray's murder when there hadn't been a murder. His face went pale. They kept staring at him. He had to say something.

"That was good police work," he said

"Good and lucky," Corcoran said. "We've arrested two of them. The third, we're still looking for him. And, the fourth, who's in jail, we'll charge when they're all indicted."

"That's great," Dennis said, without enthusiasm. "I have to go to the head."

When Dennis left, Dominic said, "He took his brother's death hard. He looked up to him, and Ray was so strong. It's hard for him to believe he's dead. It's hard for me to believe he's dead."

In the men's room, Dennis stared at himself in the mirror. This changes everything, he thought. The heats off me, but somebody is going to jail. Can I just stay out of it? Say nothing?

McConnell came in to use the men's room. Dennis didn't bother to use the urinal, and left to avoid any conversation.

Back at the table, Dennis forced himself to finish his cheeseburger although he didn't feel hungry. "I gotta go. Have to get up early for work. Congratulations on solving the case," he said, and left, glad to get away.

The newspapers carried the story of two arrests in connection with the murder of the witness, Buster Johnson, in front of the Pan Am Motor Inn, and the murder of Ray Carbonaro, in his Ridgewood apartment. The papers said more arrests were expected.

Chief of Detectives Nicoletti called Captain Corcoran and congratulated him. "And give Dominic my regards."

"I will, thanks, chief."

Dennis read the newspapers at work, and some other workers asked him about it. He said he didn't know anything more than was in the papers.

After work, he went to school, where some classmates asked him about it. He was surprised that they knew about his connection to it. He told them the same thing that he had told his coworkers.

During the next weeks, Dennis stuck to his routine of going to work, school two nights a week, and seeing Kathy whenever he could. He continued to hope that Ray's death would fade away, but it didn't. People being in jail for a crime that he knew they didn't commit weighed on his mind. On one hand, he hoped that they'd be quickly released, on the other, if they were released that might turn attention to him.

The newspaper stories continued to run, and his father gave him updates about how the investigation was going, and that the taskforce had arrested Leon James (LJ), in the Bronx, and found him in possession of the Glock automatic that was used to shoot Buster Johnson. The ballistics matched, and Dominic laughed when he told Dennis about it. "How stupid can you be not to throw away a murder weapon?"

"Maybe he thought he needed it for protection," Dennis said.

"Could be, but he could've sold it to some unsuspecting fool, and used the money to buy another gun," Dominic said.

LJ's arrest generated more news, and an assemblyman, Joseph Barronti, who was running to unseat Queens District Attorney White, began giving news conferences. He claimed that DA White should have provided better protection for Buster Johnson and Ray Carbonaro. He also claimed that White was soft on crime and that his prosecution record was underwhelming. He said that White relied too much on making sweetheart deals with informers and let too many defendants off with light sentences. Barronti wanted the death penalty to be revived and enforced. He pointed out that it was still on the books in New York State, but was not enforced by liberal district attorneys and judges. He said that the assassinations of these two witnesses, Johnson and Carbonaro, qualified for the death penalty. Barronti pointed out that the law was written so that a person who commits murder with certain aggravating factors, such as killing two or more people, or killing a police officer, or a judge, or witnesses to prevent them from testifying, was eligible for the death penalty.

There had been several cases throughout New York State where juries imposed the death penalty for murder with such aggravating factors, but Barronti said that the judges always found excuses not to impose it and, instead, imposed prison sentences.

While playing pool in their basement, Dennis asked his father what he thought about Barronti pushing for the death penalty. "My professors are all against it."

Dominic put his pool stick down and handed one to Dennis.

"I wasn't for the death penalty until I worked on the Wendy's case as a rookie detective in 2000."

"What was that?"

"These two lowlifes went to Wendy's at closing time. At gunpoint, they herded seven employees into the store freezer, bound and gagged them, then shot each in the head with a .38 caliber automatic pistol. Five of the victims died. Two survived with serious injuries. Within two days we arrested the bums without laying a hand on them. One was mentally challenged, so to speak, and probably was the follower. He pled guilty and got life. But the other one, John Taylor, who planned the whole thing, went to trial.

"It was clear that Taylor intended to kill the employees all along because he used to work at Wendy's, and the employees knew who he was. So, that's why he killed them. The jury convicted him and voted unanimously to give him the death penalty. But the courts threw it out."

"How come?"

"Well, as best I can understand the legal mumbo-jumbo, the courts didn't like the murder statute because the judge was required to instruct the jurors that if they didn't unanimously vote for the death penalty, then the judge would have to sentence the defendant to life in prison with a possibility of parole, meaning that the defendant could get out in twenty years or so. The Court of Appeals ruled that the judge's instructions pressured the jurors to vote for the death penalty, and that made the whole death penalty statute unconstitutional."

Dennis didn't say anything right away, then said, "Instead of making the whole thing unconstitutional, why didn't they just take out the part about telling the jurors about the possibility of parole?"

"That makes sense to me, and that's what District Attorney White argued. He tried hard, but he had no chance. Our judges don't have the stomach for the death penalty, so they'll find any excuse not to impose it."

"If it's the law, they should. It's their job," Dennis said.

"They should, but they don't. And Taylor and the other guy will be getting out of prison soon, while the five young people they killed never saw another day. I don't think any of the judges who threw out the death penalty had lost a son like I had."

Dennis shivered to think that Dominic would want the death penalty for whoever killed Ray.

CHAPTER THIRTY-TWO

District Attorney White held a news conference to announce the indictments of three defendants in connection with a conspiracy to eliminate witnesses in the upcoming BMW robbery/murder trial. The press room was crowded to capacity. White's press people had made sure that every possible news outlet had sent reporters to attend the announcement. He needed the good publicity because his opponent in the upcoming election for his office, Michael Borranti, was polling well, and had generated a dozen negative news stories about him.

With Captain Corcoran, Dominic, McConnell, and ADA Walsh standing behind him, DA White read the names of the indicted defendants—James Forrest, Shaquan Campbell, and Leon James—charging them with the murders of two witnesses, Buster Johnson and Ray Carbonaro, who both had been expected to testify in the BMW robbery-murder case. DA White explained that Forrest, from prison, had directed the others to commit the murders. "We have recorded conversations and other evidence establishing that fact, and there is also an unindicted coconspirator, William Mumford, who won't be charged or tried at this time."

White explained that because Buster Johnson and Ray Carbonaro had been assassinated, the BMW case against Forrest, Mumford, and Campbell would have to be postponed. The perpetrators of that robbery had worn masks, and without the witnesses' testimony, it would be difficult to prove the case. So, at this time, he was moving forward with the case of the conspiracy to murder the witnesses.

"I congratulate all the detectives who worked so diligently on this case. It was an especially troubling case for all of us because one of the victims, Ray Carbonaro, was the son of one of our own, First-Grade Detective Dominic Carbonaro. We give our condolences to him and his family."

That statement created a buzz in the room as the reporters sensed a juicy story. They started raising their hands to ask questions.

A reporter asked. "Are we correct to assume that the un-indicted co-conspirator is cooperating and will testify against the others?"

"That's a reasonable assumption," White said, "and our expectation."

A reporter asked, "Isn't it ironic, that you are using an informant to testify in a case in which your other informants were murdered?"

"We're not in the business of irony, we just follow the facts and prove cases as the evidence allows," White said. He handed the microphone to an assistant, and left the room, with reporters shouted questions after him. One reporter shouted the loudest, "Will you be able to protect this new informant better than you protected the others?"

The media gave the case major coverage day after day. Dennis followed the stories, and wanted to know more. He had questions about whether evidence from the BMW case could be used in the conspiracy-murder case. He asked his father questions, and did legal research on his own, learning that the general rule of law was that a prosecutor couldn't prove a case by showing other crimes committed earlier by the defendant. However, there was an exception, which allowed proof of the earlier crimes to prove the motive for the new crime. So, although the BMW robbery case had been postponed, ADA Walsh made it clear that he intended to introduce the facts of that case to show why Buster Johnson and Ray Carbonaro were murdered.

Dennis worried that he could be drawn into the case, either by the prosecution or the defense. He worried that a light bulb would go on in someone's head that he could be a suspect. He had access to the apartment; he had a motive, and his alibi could be broken. The words of Captain Corcoran, "You may think you haven't been seen, but witnesses come out of nowhere to sink you," were stuck in his head. It may not be an eyewitness that sinks me, he thought, but something totally unexpected.

During the week before the start of the conspiracy-murder trial, the detective task force worked overtime. They were in a full-court press to be prepared. Dominic received a subpoena from the DA to testify, which was expected, and Dennis received two subpoenas, which were not expected, one from the DA, and one from the defense. "What do they want from me?" he asked his father.

"Walsh will talk to you before he puts you on the witness stand, so you'll know what to expect," Dominic said. "As for the defense attorneys, you don't have to talk to them beforehand. I wouldn't. That might keep them from calling you. If they do get you on the stand, they'll probably use your testimony from the deposition. Just answer truthfully, the way you did, and don't volunteer anything."

On Friday, Kathy called Dennis and suggested that before the trial starts, they should go out for a nice dinner to relax.

"That's a great idea," he said.

Kathy picked an Italian restaurant on Arthur Avenue in the Morris Park section of the Bronx. Arthur Avenue had a row of Italian restaurants that had become even more popular than those in Little Italy. It was easy to get to them, and easier than driving into Lower Manhattan, and the food was as good or better than in Little Italy, and less expensive.

Kathy had called for reservations and asked for a special booth in the corner.

"How come you picked this place?" Dennis asked. "Have you been here before?"

"Not in a long time."

He wondered if she had been here with Ray, but didn't ask.

In the candlelight, Kathy looked more beautiful than ever, and Dennis ordered a bottle of wine. She made a toast: "To the future, better days, and putting this all behind us."

"*Salute.* I'll drink to that," he clinked his glass with hers.

Their meals were delicious, and they shared plates.

When they finished their meals, the waiter refilled their glasses, and asked whether they wanted to see a dessert menu.

Kathy, who usually avoided sweets, said, "I'll have a tiramisu."

"The same," Dennis said.

The waiter left, and Kathy took Dennis' hand. "Remember when you asked if you could move in with me?"

"I certainly do."

"Well, I've thought about it, and I've changed my mind. I want to make some changes in my life, and in yours, if you're willing."

"What kind of changes?"

"I'm going to quit my job at McCoy's, and get a regular job, something with a future. And I'll take you up on your offer to go to college at night with you."

"That's great. You can do my homework for me."

"I was thinking you'd do mine."

"We'll worry about that later. And what about me moving in?"

"Yes. I think it's a good idea. I make good money at McCoy's, but starting a new job will be a pay cut. We could share expenses."

"When?"

"Tonight, if you like."

"I like."

Dennis was excited about the idea, but remembered that he had moved in with his brother to share expenses. He hoped this would turn out better. "These are big changes you're making," he said.

"Yes. I am. We've got to think about where we're going to be five years from now."

Dennis sat back, folded his arms, and smiled broadly, "Are you asking me to marry you?"

"One step at a time, but if it works out, why not?"

"Why not, indeed?" Dennis said, then laughed. "But I'm supposed to ask you."

"Go ahead, ask me," she said.

He took her hand. "I love you very much. Will you...," he began, but remembering Ray, stopped himself in midsentence.

He let go of her hand. "It's going to be hard, but I have to tell you something first."

"What?"

At first, he couldn't get the words out. He stuttered, "When Ray, when Ray was, was killed, I went to the apartment…I was going to ask him if he was going to testify against me."

"Yeah"

"He was in a rotten mood, angry. He accused me of telling you about finding the watch in his mattress. Then he punched me in the face, and was choking me. He was strong as hell. I thought he was going to kill me. I was half under the sink. I grabbed a hammer and swung it. It hit him in the head."

"Oh, my God," Kathy said, staring in astonishment. "I can't believe this."

"He was going to kill me."

"That, I can believe."

"You had to see the look in his eyes."

"You hit him with a hammer?"

"Yes."

"How many times?"

"Just once. He punched me at the same time, and I was knocked out. When I came to. He was on the floor, not breathing, dead. I'll never forget it."

Kathy began to cry, tears running down her face. "This is too much. I don't think I can bear it." She took the table napkin and went to the bathroom.

I knew this would happen, Dennis thought, I don't blame her for walking out. Ray was her boyfriend. They were destined to get married. And I killed him, how could she stay with me.

Ten minutes passed and she hadn't returned. He wondered whether he had missed seeing her leave the restaurant. They had driven there in his car, but she could have gotten a cab to take her home.

He signaled to the waiter to bring the check, and as he was paying, Kathy came out of the bathroom, still drying her tears with the napkin.

"How are you?" he asked.

"It was my fault?" she said.

"Your fault, why?"

"I shouldn't have told Ray that you told me about the watch. And then, to make it worse, I told him I never wanted to see him again. That must have set him off, and that's why he attacked you."

Dennis shook his head. "It wasn't your fault. It was bad timing. After you broke off with him, I showed up at the apartment. I shouldn't have gone there. Things happen beyond our control, like they were meant to happen."

They sat in silence for a long time, then Kathy said, "All that matters is that you acted in self-defense."

"I hope you're right. What worries me is that the DA is gonna say I went there to stop him from testifying."

She held his hand. "This is bad but you'll get through it. We'll get through it together."

A feeling of relief came over him that she was not blaming him and was sticking with him.

"And we were talking about you moving in," she said, "tonight or tomorrow?"

"Whatever you think," he said.

"Tomorrow, would be better. We'll get a fresh start. But before we do, you have to promise me that you'll tell the police what happened. You can start by telling your father."

He leaned back. His relief turned to anxiety. "I don't know if I can do that."

"Why not? You only defended yourself. Everyone knows what Ray was like."

"They'll put me on trial," he said. "I don't want to go through that. And I don't want my mother and father to know."

"But there's more than just you involved," she said. "People are in jail, accused of a murder that wasn't a murder. And they're talking about reinstituting the death penalty."

"They can't use the death penalty retroactively," Dennis said. "It's what they call *ex post facto*."

"Alright, but someone is in jail for something they didn't do. Do you want that on your conscience?"

"I guess not."

"And I can't live with this hanging over our heads."

Dennis realized he had to make a decision now. And, if he wanted to keep Kathy, it had to be the right one. "Okay. I'll tell them, but you're going to stay with me through it all."

"Yes, because we love each other," she said.

He took a deep breath. "And I was in the middle of asking you something."

"Go ahead."

"Will you marry me?"

"I have to think about it," she laughed. "Okay, I've thought about it. Yes. I will."

They were the last couple in the restaurant, and as they were kissing across the table, the waiter came over. "Would you care for something else?"

"No thank you," Kathy said. "We're fine."

On Sunday, they went to his parents' house for dinner. When they sat down at the table, Kathy asked them how they were. "I can't imagine how terrible you feel."

Marie didn't answer.

Dominic put his glass down. "It feels like being stabbed in the heart and the knife is still there," he said.

No one spoke for a while, then Dennis said, "Okay, we have to move on. We have some good news to tell you."

"Yes," Marie asked.

Kathy had wanted Dennis to tell them about Ray before announcing their marriage, but he had convinced her that it would be better to start with the good news to soften the bad news.

He stood up, "Kathy and I are going to get married."

The mood instantly changed from solemnity to joy. In unison, Dominic and Marie said, "That's wonderful." Marie kissed them both, and Dominic retrieved his best bottle of wine from the basement.

They talked enthusiastically throughout the dinner. Marie asked Kathy whether she had told her parents. "Not yet," Kathy said. "We're going to drive out to Long Island to tell them in person."

When dinner was finished, Kathy helped Marie with the dishes, and Dominic took Dennis downstairs. "I don't see an engagement ring."

"I'll have to save up for it."

"No. You don't want to wait. I'll give you a check for it now as part of your wedding present."

"Dad, you're the best."

"No, son, you're the best."

They began playing pool, finished one game, and began another one. Dennis kept putting off what he knew he had to say. Then Kathy came down the stairs. She had a determined look on her face, and to Dennis, she said, "Did you tell your father?"

"Not yet."

"Tell me what?" Dominic said.

"Dad, let's sit down," Dennis said.

"Every time you ask me to sit down, there's a problem."

"And, Dad, this is a big one."

"Okay, what is it?"

It took Dennis a moment, but he said, "I'm the one who hit Ray in the head with the hammer."

In a calm sounding voice, Dominic said to Kathy, "Maybe you should go upstairs. It's better for Dennis and I to talk alone."

"Alright. And I'm so sorry, Mr. Carbonaro," she said as she turned to go upstairs.

"I think I will sit down," Dominic said, and collapsed on the old, leather couch.

Dennis walked back and forth in front of him, telling him everything that had happened, how he realized Ray was dead, and then decided to leave the apartment. When he finished, feeling as though he had tossed a weight off his shoulders, he sat on the couch next to his father. "I'm sorry about everything, Dad."

Dominic didn't say anything at first. He sat motionless, trying to absorb it all. Finally, he said, "I thought you were upstairs in the Ninth Precinct lounge."

"I was for a while," Dennis said, "but I wanted to talk to Ray about his testimony. I didn't know what was going to happen. And after it happened, I went back to the precinct. No one seemed to know that I had been gone. So, I kept my mouth shut."

"Come to think of it, when I told you that Ray had been killed, I was amazed at how calm you were. You didn't seem shocked. I remember thinking that you were like an old, grizzled detective who wasn't surprised by anything. You weren't shocked because you knew it already."

"I guess so."

"What time did it happen?"

"I'm not sure. I think between seven and eight."

"That's about when McConnell and the other detectives found the body."

"As I was leaving, I saw them driving down the block. They didn't see me."

"That was a close call. But you would have been better off flagging them down and telling them what happened."

"I know that now. But I've boxed myself into a corner."

"You sure have. If you had told them, you could have claimed self-defense."

"It was self-defense. And Kathy wants me to turn myself in."

"I don't like you saying 'you're turning yourself in' as if you were a criminal. Knowing you and knowing Ray, there's no doubt in my mind that he attacked you, and you had to defend yourself."

"That's the truth, but that doesn't mean the district attorney is going to believe me," Dennis said. "The sooner I turn myself in, the better."

"Stop saying that. And, in fact, maybe we should think about this. As of now, no one suspects you."

"But these other guys are on trial, and they didn't do it. It's not right. I have to say something."

"No, you don't. I'm not worried about them. They agreed to commit two murders, and they killed Buster. So, they're already murderers, and they went to Ray's house to kill him. That's attempted murder. If they get convicted of his murder, they deserve it."

"Whether they did it or not?" Dennis said.

"I've seen this dozens of times. Some bum goes to prison, and then later they say he was the wrong guy. He wasn't guilty, and everyone cries over him. But he committed a hundred other crimes that he didn't get caught for. These guys committed plenty of crimes."

Dennis didn't respond. He understood what his father was saying. He understood how jaded his father had become from years of being a homicide detective. Reluctantly, he challenged him, "You can't justify convicting someone because they committed other crimes."

Dominic went over to the pool table and rolled some balls around. "You're right, of course," he said. "I'm not thinking clearly. My instinct is to protect you. I've lost one son; I don't want to lose another."

"You're not going to lose me. Even if they charge me, I won't be convicted. The evidence is on my side. I hit him once with the hammer, in self-defense. If I went there to kill him, I would have hit him more than once or would have done something else. Would anyone believe that I would start a fight with Ray when he was built like a bull? He was a professional bouncer. It was a freak accident. I swung the hammer because he was choking me."

"You make a convincing argument, but there are always two sides to an argument. And I can see a strong case against yours. Before you jump into the fire, let's think about it. What's the harm in waiting to see what happens and waiting to see if they begin to suspect you?"

"That was my thinking. I was hoping that Forrest and his friends get convicted for shooting Buster, and the DA doesn't bother with Ray's case. Or, if they get charged with the murder, they get acquitted. But, there's more to it than that."

"What?"

"I have Kathy to think about. I really love her, and I want to marry her, and I want our marriage to be clear, untainted. I don't want her thinking that I didn't do what was right."

At that moment, Kathy came a few steps down the staircase. "The coffee and desserts are ready."

"Alright, we're coming up," Dominic said. "Let's sleep on this. Maybe we should talk to Murray Klein and see what he thinks."

As Dennis and Kathy were driving back to what was now their apartment, she said, "I hope you don't think I was snooping, but I was at the top of the stairs and heard you tell your father that you loved me, and you didn't want our marriage to be tainted, and you had to do what was right. That made me want to marry you more than ever."

Dennis laughed. "How do you know I wasn't just saying that for your benefit?"

"You were not," she said, and gave him a friendly punch in the arm. "I'm going to have to get used to your sense of humor."

"We're both going to need a sense of humor to get through this."

CHAPTER THIRTY-THREE

Murray Klein greeted Dominic and Dennis as they arrived at his office. He expressed his condolences again, and led them into the conference room.

"What do you want to discuss?" he asked.

Dominic hadn't told him over the phone what it was about, just that it was extremely serious and extremely confidential.

Dominic glanced at the two female staffers seated at the table. "Can we do this privately?"

"They work for me, and they're covered by the privilege," Klein said.

"I'd feel more comfortable with just us, until we make a formal arrangement."

"Alright, young ladies, if you don't mind," Klein said.

The two women left the room.

Klein sat back, waiting for Dominic to talk.

"This is covered by the privilege, right?" Dominic asked.

"Well, since you're being so careful, let's sign something first," he said, then pressed the intercom and asked the secretary to bring in two retainer forms.

The secretary brought in the forms, and Klein said, "We'll make these retainers for one dollar each with additional fees to be determined later. That should establish your attorney-client privileges."

They signed the forms.

"Okay. How can I help you?"

"I'll come right to the point. On the night my son, Ray, was killed, it wasn't the robbery gang. It was Dennis."

"Say that again."

"Dennis went to Ray's apartment to ask him about his testimony, and Ray attacked him. He punched him and was choking him, so Dennis defended himself by swinging a hammer. Hit him in the head, and Ray collapsed and died."

Klein, who had heard a lot in his career, was taken aback and didn't say a word.

Dominic continued, "It was self-defense. And Dennis wants to turn himself in. My question to you is, should he? And, if he should, what's the best way to do it?"

Klein looked around, obviously trying to formulate his thoughts. He stood, "The last time you came in here like this, Dennis had his wild scheme to get Ray out of jail. Now, I wonder."

"It's no wild scheme," Dennis said. "Like my father said, it was self-defense."

"Alright, let's talk about it," Klein said. "Start from the beginning."

Dennis repeated the same narrative that he had told his father, and as he remembered what happened that night, his emotions overcame him. When he finished, he covered his eyes with his hand.

Klein waited for him to look up, then asked, "Where did you get the hammer?"

"It was under the sink."

"Did you find it by accident, or did you know it was there?"

"I knew it was there. That's where we kept it. And I had gotten it from there not too long ago when I came home and I thought there was a burglar in the apartment. There wasn't. It turned out to be Ray in his room, so I put the hammer back."

"But you knew it was there, and you purposely retrieved it."

"Only after Ray attacked me. I wound up under the sink and found it by chance."

Klein continued asking Dennis questions. Why did he go to the apartment? Why didn't he report the fight right away? Why did he go back to the Ninth Precinct, and why didn't he tell anyone there what happened?

Klein asked more and more questions, repeating some of them to see if the answers would change. But Dennis' story stayed consistent.

Klein got up, walked around the table, and put his hand on Dennis' shoulder. "I'm sorry for all your trouble. It seems to be following you. And you've painted yourself into a corner."

"Everyone seems to agree on that," Dennis aid.

Dominic, who had remained quiet until Dennis finished, asked Klein, "Well, should he turn himself in or not?"

Klein said to Dennis, "You're under no legal obligation to turn yourself in."

"What about my moral obligations?"

"I deal in legalities, not moralities."

There was silence for several seconds until Dennis said, "Maybe you don't, but Kathy, my fiancée, deals in moralities."

"She knows?" Klein asked.

"Yes, and she blames herself."

"Why would she blame herself?"

"Because she broke up with Ray, and told him that I told her about the Rolex watch. That made him furious with me. I saw it in his eyes that he was going to kill me. I had no doubt about it."

Klein leaned back in his chair, "Remember what you just said, and how you said it. You may have to repeat it in front of a jury just that way."

"So, you think I should turn myself in."

"I didn't say that. But you have to be prepared for all possibilities."

"You think it's possible that they'd put me on trial."

"More than possible; it's probable."

"What will they charge me with?"

"It depends," Klein said. "If they believe you went there intending to kill him, they'll charge murder. If they think it was a spontaneous fight, and you hit him without intending to kill him, they'll charge manslaughter."

"What's the difference?" Dennis asked.

"The difference between fifteen to twenty-five for manslaughter and twenty-five to life for murder."

"No death penalty, right?" Dennis asked.

"That's up in the air right now," Klein said.

They all remained silent for a few moments, then Dominic stood, and gesturing with his hands to illustrate, said, "To me, it was a freak accident. Dennis swung the hammer blindly. If it hit Ray anywhere else—in the shoulder, in the neck, even the forehead—it wouldn't have been much more than a bruise. But it was a lucky hit, actually an unlucky hit."

"I agree. That's a good argument. But let's back up a bit," Klein said to Dennis, "Did I hear you say that Kathy was your fiancée? When did this happen?"

"This week."

"That's great, congratulations. She's a wonderful girl. You're a lucky guy."

"It remains to be seen how lucky I am."

"You've heard the saying, 'Luck is the residue of design,' so we've got to do some planning," Klein said as he turned to look out of the window.

Klein hadn't answered the main question, so Dennis again asked, "Should I turn myself in or not?"

"Let's wait awhile, and see what happens. In the meantime, don't tell anybody else. Keep a low profile, a very low profile."

Dennis had a mixed reaction to the advice. He had wanted something definite. This was just more waiting and uncertainty. "Isn't it better that I turn myself in sooner, rather than later?"

"Not necessarily. Time can solve a problem."

"And it can make it worse."

"You're right, but no one knows what comes next. That's what makes practicing law so interesting."

Dennis thought that Klein was practicing, but for him, this wasn't practice.

"Let's meet again in a few days," Klein said, "or sooner if something comes up."

That evening, Dennis told Kathy about the meeting with Klein.

"So, he thinks you should turn yourself in," she said.

"No. He said wait and see what happens, see if I get charged."

"What about the guys that are in jail for something they didn't do?"

"He said he deals in legality, not morality."

"Maybe he should," Kathy said. "Maybe, instead of calling lawyers, we should be calling priests."

"Yeah. Right."

"I'm beginning not to like Mr. Klein," she said, and went into the bedroom and closed the door.

At the Task Force office, Captain Corcoran told Dominic that he should work on the Buster Johnson case, but stay out of Ray's case. "We've got to have an objective investigation, and we don't want to create any appearances of impropriety."

Dominic agreed, but couldn't help watching and listening for any developments in Ray's case. He noticed McConnell talking with two detectives on the other side of the office, and when he walked towards them under the guise of going to the water cooler, they stopped talking.

A few minutes later, he received a phone call from Detective Cruz, who had been with McConnell when they found Ray's body. Cruz asked him to meet at a coffee shop. Dominic went there immediately, and found Cruz seated in a booth. "I didn't want to talk in the office," he said. "People could be listening."

"Listening to what?" Dominic asked.

Cruz waited until the waiter finished bringing their coffees, and said, "I hope I'm not doing the wrong thing, but I thought you should know that McConnell thinks Dennis had something to do with Ray's death."

Dominic tried not to show the alarm he was feeling. "What makes him think something as ridiculous as that?" he said.

"I heard him tell Matthews that he had a hunch."

"A hunch! He's off his rocker! He's still angry about being made a fool of at Ray's trial. I'm sure he thinks that it killed his chances for promotion. He's got an obsession."

"Yeah, and he's spending all his extra time investigation your son. I know he followed him a few times, and he asked me to help him. I told him you just can't open investigations on a hunch. He said that it was more than a hunch. He said Dennis had wanted to steal Ray's girlfriend, and that was the motivation. Or maybe they got in an argument, and it got out of control."

Although Dominic realized that McConnell's hunch was not too far from the truth, he said, "That's pure bullshit."

"That's what I said, and I told him that Dennis had an alibi. He was in the Ninth Precinct lounge."

"That's right. McConnell's way off base," Dominic said.

"He doesn't think so," Cruz said. "He came in on his day off to interview Lieutenant Jensen."

"Who's Lieutenant Jensen?"

"Bill Jensen. He was the desk officer at the Ninth Precinct on the night Ray was killed."

"So?"

"So, while we all assumed Dennis was upstairs in the lounge watching television, Jensen says he remembers Dennis coming into the precinct about nine o'clock. He remembers recognizing him from earlier in the night and giving him permission to go upstairs."

Dominic knew exactly what this meant, but feigned ignorance. "What does that mean?"

"It means that Dennis could have left the precinct and driven to the Ridgewood apartment to confront Ray," Cruz said. "It means that his supposed air-tight alibi doesn't hold up."

Police department regulations required a desk officer to make a log entry in the precinct blotter when allowing civilian visitors to go upstairs in the building. Dominic started to ask Cruz whether the lieutenant had made a log entry regarding Dennis coming back to the precinct, but asking the question would seem to be conceding that Dennis had left the precinct, so he decided not to ask and to find out for himself.

Dominic thanked Cruz for the information, then went to the Ninth Precinct, where he identified himself to the desk officer and said that he had to make a report on the interrogation he had conducted of the suspect in the double-murder shooting. He said that needed to confirm what times the suspect had been at the precinct.

"Who was on the desk?" Atkins asked.

"I believe it was Lieutenant Jensen," Dominic said.

"Alright, come around. There's the blotter, be my guest."

Dominic perused the blotter and was relieved to find that there weren't any log entries about Dennis entering or leaving the precinct.

From the 9th Precinct, he drove north on the East River Drive. He had the habit of taking long drives while he worked out a problem. He was worried that Cruz had adopted McConnell's suspicion of Dennis, and if McConnell could convince Cruz to suspect Dennis, he might be able to convince others.

When he reached the Harlem River Drive, he thought of Arturo Gonzalez, and remembered that when he had met with him to get information about Buster Johnson, Arturo had said something about McConnell. At the time, Dominic didn't inquire further because he didn't want to press Arturo, but now he decided that he had to.

At the Bodega Association Headquarters, Dominic asked the counterman whether Arturo was in. He wasn't, but the man said he'd make a call and went into the backroom.

Five minutes later, he came out and told Dominic to meet Arturo in the *El Malecon* restaurant two blocks away.

At the restaurant, Arturo greeted him, and they sat at a table in the back, away from the other tables. Arturo's bodyguard sat three tables away, facing the front door.

Dominic nodded toward the bodyguard, and said, "Expecting trouble."

"You never know," Arturo said as he poured a coffee for Dominic.

"I was so sorry to hear about your son," he said. "It struck home with me because I remember we agreed to pray for each other's sons."

"Thank you. And how's the army treating your guy?"

"Good, very good, I'm grateful to say," Arturo said. "He's waiting for a promotion. But, like all young people, he's impatient. Says if he doesn't get promoted, he may leave as soon as his five-year commitment is up."

"I'm sure he'll get promoted," Dominic said.

"Either way, it's all good. What'll you have?"

"The same thing I always have, *arroz con pollo*."

"Good, choice. You can't go wrong," Arturo said. "So, what did you want to see me about?"

"You know, in my job, I have to remember things. And I remember the time that I asked you about, Buster Johnson, you said something about Detective McConnell. Like you knew him, but not in a good way."

"So, what's the problem?"

"Since he can't go after my son, Ray, anymore, now he's going after my other son, Dennis."

"What for?"

"I can't go into that now, but he's obsessed with him. He still blames him for getting Ray off in that robbery case. And now I'm afraid he's going to frame Dennis for something."

"That's interesting," Arturo said. "We've been having our own problems with McConnell."

"Really. Like what?"

"You know that I have interests in the Kit-Kat club, and the 444 Club. And McConnell's a constant thorn in my side, always pressuring my employees, searching them, and threatening to lock them up."

"Lock them up for what?"

"Alcohol, gambling, or whatever he could think of. The Kit-Kat is legit, but some of my employees don't have green cards. And he comes around and threatens to get them deported."

"How much did you have to pay him?"

"It wasn't money he was after. He wanted information so he could make big arrests. He's a crusader, straight as an arrow. Wouldn't take a dime, but he wanted to see his name in the newspapers. I think he was obsessed with becoming a first-grade detective like you. It seemed stupid to me. You don't make that much money."

"No. I don't. And McConnell was crazy for doing what he did. Maybe he wasn't looking for money, but he could still get jammed up for extortion or coercion or some kind of federal charge."

286

The *arroz con pollo* came, and they talked as they ate. "I don't want to be personally involved," Arturo said, "but my people could provide some information. Aldo runs the clubs, and my man, Cartwright has records on everything."

"I remember his records. They were very helpful in getting Ray acquitted. I owe you big time for that."

"We're even," Arturo said. "And if you want to notify Internal Affairs about McConnell, I can have Aldo and Cartright provide the torpedoes to sink him."

Dominic thought that over, but he didn't want to encourage anyone to make something up.

"Let's hold off on that," he said. "Although, I don't like the guy, I can't call IAB on a cop who's not taking money, not stealing, who's doing his job. Maybe he's too aggressive, but I wouldn't drop a dime on him for that."

Arturo shook his head. "Even to help your son? I don't understand you. You've got, how they say, moral scruples."

"I don't know about that, but McConnell thinks he's doing what's right."

"Okay, if that's what you say."

After two demitasse coffees with Sambuca liquor, they shook hands and agreed to stay in touch. "If you change your mind," Arturo said, "or, more likely, if you're forced to change your mind, let me know."

CHAPTER THIRTY-FOUR

Kathy finished her shift at McCoy's, and as she was driving home, she noticed a car following her. It looked like an unmarked detective car with two men in the front seat.

To see if they were following her, she made a turn faster than she normally would. They followed. She made another fast turn, and they followed her again. After her third turn, she saw the police red bubble light on the dashboard of the car, and the passenger signaling her to pull over.

Assuming they were police, she pulled over, but left room to accelerate away if they weren't. They pulled behind her, and she watched through her mirrors, waiting for them to approach her car. They didn't exit their car right away, and she waited for what seemed a long time. Finally, the driver got out. It was McConnell.

He walked up to her window, and signaled for her to roll it down. She did.

"Hi, Kathy," he said, "How ya doing?"

"What are you stopping me for?" she asked. "Do you want to see my license and registration?"

"That won't be necessary," he said. "I just wanted to ask you a few questions."

Nervous and suspicious, Kathy said, "It's a little late. What do you want to ask me?"

He shined his flashlight into the backseat of her car. "I'll come right to the point," he said." I know your history with both Ray and

Dennis, and, by the way, give Dennis my condolences for the loss of his brother."

"You were going to come to the point," she said.

"Okay. On the night that Ray was killed, you were with Dennis at McCoy's, right?"

Kathy gripped the steering wheel tighter. "Is this the time and place for this?"

McConnell smiled. "I thought since we were both up late, we could cut to the chase, save time, and avoid having to bring you into the precinct to answer questions."

Kathy thought how much she despised him and wanted to give him a piece of her mind, but she was also a little afraid. She looked in her side mirror to see where the other detective was. He was at the rear passenger side of her car, shining a flashlight into it.

"I don't have time for this. I have to get home," she said.

"It won't take much time. It's a simple question," he said. "Were you with Dennis that night? Where were you, and from when to when?"

Kathy put her car in drive. "That's not a simple question, and unless you want to arrest me, I'm leaving."

"Suit yourself," McConnell.

"Bye," she said, and drove away.

It wasn't until she had driven two blocks away that her knees stopped shaking. She wasn't sure whether it was from fear, hatred, or anger.

When she got home, Dennis asked her, "How was your shift?"

She started to say that it was okay until on the way home she was pulled over by McConnell, but stopped herself. If she told him now, he wouldn't be able to sleep all night. Her mother had once told her that troubled times need sleep, and she would abide by that maxim. She'd tell him in the morning.

So, Dennis slept soundly all night, but Kathy didn't. She woke up every half hour, then fell asleep just before it was time for Dennis to get up. She almost missed him as he left to go to work, but she heard the door, and jumped out of bed and ran into the hallway. He hadn't gotten on the elevator yet. She called him back to the apartment, and told him about what had happened and the question McConnell had asked her.

"That son of a bitch," Dennis said. "What did you say?"

"I essentially told him to get lost and drove away."

"Good," he said, and kissed her. "I hate to go, but I gotta run. I'll call you later, go back to bed."

As Dennis drove to work, he used his cellphone to call his father, who was also driving to work, and told him about McConnell stopping Kathy.

Dominic listened and felt a knot tightening in his stomach. "That bastard," he said. "Sooner or later, we're gonna have it out."

"Dad, I don't want this to cause you to get in trouble," Dennis said. "Kathy's fine. She can handle herself."

It seemed odd to Dominic that his son was telling him not to get into trouble instead of the other way around.

When Dominic arrived at the task force office, Captain Corcoran, Lieutenant Brady, of the Queens Homicide Squad, and McConnell were assembled in the captain's office. Dominic and McConnell scowled at each other. "You look like crap," Dominic said to him. "I guess that's from being up all night, harassing young women."

McConnell looked surprised that Dominic knew about him stopping Kathy. "I wasn't harassing anyone. I was just asking a question."

"Hold on. What's this about?" Corcoran asked.

"About three this morning, this guy," Dominic said, pointing to McConnell, "pulls over Kathy Reynolds and starts interrogating her."

"In case you forgot," McConnell said, "that's my job. I'm investigating your son's murder."

"And you're doing this while you're off duty. And you're doing it alone, without a partner, following her from McCoy's. Maybe you have some other interest in her," Dominic said.

"I resent your implication," McConnell said. "I wanted to interview a key witness, and I knew what time she got off work."

"A key witness to what?" Dominic asked.

"Where your son Dennis was on the night of Ray's death, that's what."

"So, now you want to frame Dennis like you framed Ray."

"I didn't frame anybody."

"You tried with those old photographs you used for his identification," Dominic said.

Captain Corcoran stood up. "Dominic, before you say something you might regret, there's been a new development."

Dominic noticed a look of satisfaction on McConnell's face.

"What new development?"

"You remember when we collected all the security videos looking for the Toyota 4-Runner that Mr. Martucci saw at the house."

"Yeah."

"We stopped looking at the videos when we found that patrol officers had given the 4-Runner a ticket and identified the occupants," Corcoran said. "But Detective McConnell decided to look at them again. This time looking for your son's car."

McConnell interrupted him, "And lo and behold, look what we found—a video captured Dennis' silver-gray Honda leaving the block of Ray's apartment twenty minutes after Ray was killed."

Dominic was stunned by the news. This was evidence that could be used to prosecute Dennis. Although it wasn't conclusive evidence, when combined with Dennis' false alibi and his failure to report the death, it looked very bad. He thought it best to say nothing in response. He didn't want to show how upset he was, and how furious he was at McConnell for gloating that his son might go to prison.

There was an awkward silence until Corcoran spoke, "In light of the new evidence, we should call Dennis in for an interview. Dominic, maybe you could arrange that."

"I'll talk to him, but to advise him I need to know if the video got a plate number or captured the driver."

"It got a partial plate number," Corcoran said, "two letters that match his plate, but it didn't capture the driver."

McConnell looked disapprovingly at Corcoran for divulging that information.

"Thanks for that," Dominic said. "I'll talk to his lawyer. But, if he does agree to come in, I don't want McConnell involved. It should be somebody who does interrogations with a little more integrity."

"What kind of remark is that?" McConnell raised his voice. "I've done a hundred interrogations, and never had a complaint."

"Really, I read the transcript of your interrogation of Willie Mumford. You put words in his mouth and just about bribed him to squeal on the other guys."

"That's not true," McConnell said.

"Yeah, well go back and read it. You told him that to get the deal he had to say that Shaquan went into the house, then came out, and said, 'It's done.'"

McConnell didn't have an answer.

Corcoran asked, "Is that true?"

McConnell again didn't answer.

"The transcripts in the file," Dominic said.

"I'll read it," Corcoran said. "If that's what it says, it could be a problem for ADA Walsh. But that's another matter. Let me know if Dennis will come in for an interview."

"Who'll do the interviewing?" Dominic asked.

"We'll find somebody," Corcoran said, indicating that it wouldn't be McConnell.

Dominic met Dennis in front of the UPS terminal in Maspeth, Queens, and told him about the video that showed his Honda coming out of the block right after Ray's death. Dennis began talking rapidly. "I knew it," he said. "I knew it was going to happen. I knew it from when that Captain Corcoran said witnesses come out of nowhere to sink you. And I guess he was right. It wasn't a witness; it was a camera, but that's worse."

"Calm down," Dominic said. "It's not good, that's for sure, but it's not over, yet."

"It's over," Dennis said. "They're going to arrest me."

"Probably. But an arrest is not a conviction. We'll go see Klein."

"I know what he'll say," Dennis said. "He'll say take the Fifth."

"We're not there yet. You don't have to say anything. You don't have to go in for an interview. And if any detectives approach you, tell them to call your lawyer."

The next morning, they took off from work and went to see Murray Klein. As expected, Klein advised Dennis not to submit to a police interview. "If you had some explanation, then maybe you could sit down with them, but you don't. The fact is that you were there."

"Yes. I was there. And why don't I tell them that, and explain that it was self-defense?"

"The downside of that is that you would be admitting ninety-nine percent of the case against you. As of now they probably don't have enough evidence to charge you. But, if you tell them what happened, they'd have enough."

"Okay, but if I don't talk to the police, can't I go before the grand jury and tell them that it was self-defense?" Dennis asked.

"As far as we know, there's no grand jury sitting on your case yet," Klein said. "If you get arrested, then a grand jury will have to vote to indict or not. That's when you'll have a right to go before them. But I'd advise against it."

"Why not?"

"Although there's a chance they'll buy your self-defense argument, it's a crapshoot, and you'll give away too much."

Dennis understood his point.

"How soon will they arrest me?" he asked.

"Don't be so pessimistic. There's always the chance they won't. DAs don't want to take a case unless they're sure of a win."

Convinced by Klein, Dennis agreed not to submit to a police interview or request to go before the grand jury.

Dominic called Captain Corcoran to tell him that Dennis wouldn't come in for an interview.

That same day, District Attorney White's political advisers had a meeting to discuss a poll that had Congressman Borranti moving ahead of White in the upcoming election for Queens district attorney. They agreed that White needed to generate some good publicity, so they reviewed ongoing investigations that were ready or almost ready to be concluded with arrests. There were several big drug cases, a business fraud, a cold-case homicide, and Ray's case.

Ray's case was novel, and would generate the most publicity, so they recommended that an arrest be made as soon as possible.

District Attorney White called the Chief of Detectives, who called Captain Corcoran, who called Dominic at home.

"I've got bad news," Corcoran said. "We're going to arrest Dennis. Out of courtesy to you, he can surrender at the 112th Precinct tomorrow morning."

"Thanks for that," Dominic said. "I'll have him there."

When he hung up the phone, he collected his thoughts. He had a lot to do. He called Klein, who said that he would meet them in Queens Criminal Court. "I'll come about noon. He should be booked by then." Then he called Dennis and tried to make it sound like it wouldn't be so bad. "Alright, tomorrow we start to get this over with. We have to go to the 112th Precinct in the morning. They're going to arrest you. But it should go quickly. Klein will meet us at the court."

Dennis had thought about this day and how he'd react. He was determined to put up a brave front. "Should I meet you at the precinct or should I come to the house?"

"I'll pick you up," Dominic said, thinking that if Dennis didn't get out right away, his car would be stuck at the precinct.

"What time?"

"Eight o'clock. And just bring what you need. No rings or watches."

"How about a tooth brush?"

"That's not funny, but not a bad idea."

"Okay, dad. See you in the morning."

The next thing Dominic had to do was tell his wife that Dennis was going to be arrested for killing Ray. He had kept it from her by pretending that what had been going on, all the whispered conversations, were about Ray's lawsuit for false arrest. But when he told her, he got a surprising response.

"I knew it was going to happen," she said.

"How did you know?"

"I heard certain things, and put the pieces together."

"Why didn't you say anything?"

"I thought you didn't want me to know, so I didn't want to upset you.

Dominic was amazed at how stoic she was.

When Dennis told Kathy, he had a more difficult time. She cried, and said she couldn't take it anymore. "Once with Ray in prison was enough, now it's you. And this is worse. I told you that you should've told the truth right away."

He let her vent. There was nothing he could say or do to console her.

She went into the bathroom, slammed the door, and stayed in there for a while. He went to bed, hoping that he could sleep.

He couldn't sleep, and felt sick to his stomach, thinking about going to jail.

Then Kathy came into the bedroom. "I'm sorry," she said. "You must be feeling terrible. You must be scared."

Though he was scared, he didn't want to admit it. "Let just say I'm not happy about it. But I'll get through it."

"I told you before, we'll get through it together."

CHAPTER THIRTY-FIVE

In the detective squad room at the 112th Precinct, Captain Corcoran, Detective Cruz, and Detective Matthews were waiting for Dominic and Dennis.

McConnell wasn't present, and Dominic was grateful for that. Cruz told him that the captain had ordered McConnell to steer clear of the case. Cruz was now the lead detective and would make the arrest.

"I'm sorry," Cruz said to Dennis. "But I'm placing you under arrest for the murder of Ray Carbonaro. Empty your pockets on the desk."

As he complied, and as Cruz frisked him, Dennis felt like this wasn't real, like he was in a movie with everyone in the world watching as he played his part.

Cruz fingerprinted and photographed him, then gave him the *Miranda* warnings. "Will you answer some questions?"

"I'm going to remain silent," Dennis said. "And if you want to question me, I want my lawyer present."

"Okay, that's fine," Cruz said, "turn around and put your hands behind your back."

Dennis complied, and Cruz handcuffed him in order to take him to court.

The handcuffs weren't tight, but Dennis hated being in such a helpless position, unable to even break his fall if he fell while going down the stairs.

Riding in the back of the squad car, the handcuffs were uncomfortable. "How long do I have to keep the cuffs on?"

"Until we get to the holding cells at the court."

At the courthouse, they drove around to the back entrance. News photographers were waiting for them. Someone must have tipped them off. and they took photos of Dennis as he was brought into the building. "I guess you're going to be a celebrity in the morning," Cruz said.

"My friends are going to love it," Dennis said facetiously.

"Just so you know," Cruz said, "it wasn't us who tipped them off. I think it was the district attorney's office."

"More likely, it was McConnell." Dennis said.

"No comment," Cruz said.

As Dennis was walked to the back entrance, photographers ran ahead of him snapping pictures, and a reporter shouted questions at him.

Dennis ignored the reporter and entered the building. He was frisked again, and put in the holding cell, which was crowded with prisoners who apparently had been there all night.

He was grateful that it was only an hour until he was brought out to the courtroom for arraignment. Klein was there. After the charges were read, Klein argued for his release on bail. He told the judge that Dennis was employed full time, attended college at night, and was engaged to be married. He was not a flight risk.

"$50,000 bail, cash or bond," the judge said.

Klein had enlisted a bail-bondsman to post the bail. Dominic paid him a $2500 fee, and signed a lien on his house.

Dennis was released within an hour, and never felt so relieved. He hoped that while he was out on bail, no one would know about it, and he could get back to his regular life, job, and school. But his hopes were quickly dashed when the morning newspapers came out. One tabloid had a photo of him on the front page, and others had stories about the case. His supervisor from UPS called and suggested that he take a leave of absence until his problems were over. Dennis agreed, and then decided to drop out of his college night classes.

"What are you going to do for a living," his father asked.

"I'm not sure."

"A friend of mine has a moving van company, I can get you a job with him."

"Okay. If that's what I got to do, that's what I got to do."

The Queens County Grand Jury had to decide whether to indict Dennis. Klein received a letter from the district attorney advising him that the grand jury was meeting and that Dennis, as the defendant had a right to testify in his own behalf if he waived his immunity. Klein declined the invitation.

Grand juries consist of twenty-three citizens empaneled from a pre-selected registry to hear and examine evidence concerning the commission of crimes. Sixteen members must be present for a quorum. To issue an indictment, twelve members, after having heard all essential and critical evidence, must affirmatively vote that there was sufficient evidence to believe that a crime was committed and the accused person committed it.

The district attorney presents evidence, question witnesses, and carries out requests for additional evidence. Witnesses are given transactional immunity, meaning if they answer a question related to a crime, they receive immunity for that crime and cannot be prosecuted for it.

Defendant are not generally present, unless they request in writing to be present. If they make the request, they must waive their immunity, and can be prosecuted for the crime that they are questioned about.

If the defendant is present, his or her lawyer can be in the room to observe, and to advise the defendant, but should not take an active part in the proceedings. However, it hasn't been uncommon for defense attorneys to make comments to the grand jurors or whisper answers to the defendant. In such cases, conflicts often arise between the defense attorney and the district attorney, and the judge will be called on to intervene.

Klein told Dennis that the grand jury was meeting.

"When do we find out?" Dennis asked.

"It could be today, or it could be weeks. They may have other witnesses the DA wants to bring in."

This alarmed Dennis. "What other witnesses? It was just Ray and me in the apartment."

"There's nothing we can do now but wait," Klein said.

Waiting for the grand jury verdict was hell for Dennis. He couldn't think of much else. Although Kathy tried to get him to do some normal, everyday things, like go to a movie, or take a trip, he wouldn't. When he was with people, he saw them, talked to them, but was always thinking of what was going to happen, and when. At night, he thought about what prison would be like. Would being a cop's son make it difficult for him? Troubling him most was that Kathy again would be waiting for someone to get out of prison. Could he ask her to do that? Would he lose her, like Ray lost her? He wondered whether they should set a wedding date, or whether he should buy her an engagement ring. His father asked him about it, and he took Kathy shopping for an engagement ring. He wanted to buy one with all the money his father had given him, but Kathy said it was too much. "He gave it to you as a wedding present," she said. "We don't have to spend it all on a ring. We could use it for something else." They bought a ring for half the money that Dominic had given them.

For Dominic, also, waiting for the grand jury verdict was like hell. The troubles with his sons had taken a toll on him, and he had black circles under his eyes. Marie kept asking him to take some time off, take a trip, but he said he had to be around. Marie told both Dominic and Dennis not to worry, it was all in God's hands.

Dennis began working for the Santoro Moving Company. After three days of carrying furniture in and out of apartments and houses, he was exhausted. "This was real work," he said to Kathy, "It'll either get me in shape or kill me."

On the fourth day at Santoro's, he got a message to call Klein's office. Nervously, he called back, and Klein told him, "Bad news. They indicted you. I'm sorry."

Dennis couldn't respond at first, then recovered and asked, "What's the charge?"

"Four charges: murder, manslaughter, criminally negligent homicide, and first-degree assault."

Hearing the charges affected Dennis physically. He was glad he was talking on the phone and not in person; no one could see him shaking.

"How come four charges?"

"That's the way they do it."

"I guess I'll be seeing a lot of you," he said before hanging up.

Then he called his father, who said, "It's only an indictment. You've got a good defense. Don't lose hope."

Dennis was undecided whether to call Kathy or wait until he got home to tell her. If he called, it would give her some time to absorb the news on her own, but he decided that he should tell her in person.

Kathy had a nice dinner waiting for him: roast beef dinner with mashed potatoes, almond-string beans that he liked, and a bottle of white wine on ice.

"How did it go?" she asked.

"Not good. They indicted me."

Her head dropped, but then she looked up, and said, "I expected it. You know, hope for the best, expect the worst."

"I can't believe I might be going to prison."

"It's just the indictment," she said. "You still have a good chance at the trial. So, sit down. Let's enjoy our meal like it's our last"

"Let's hope it's not."

CHAPTER THIRTY-SIX

More than a month had passed since Dennis' arrest, and a month since Arturo Gonzalez had read the newspaper stories about Dennis being charged with the murder of his brother. Arturo remembered Dominic telling him that Detective McConnell was trying to frame Dennis for something, though he hadn't told him it was for fratricidal murder. The newspaper stories quoted McConnell, who seemed to be taking credit for solving the case. This incensed Arturo, who thought that if McConnell wanted to be in the newspapers so much, he'd give the papers something to write about. He had offered to provide Dominic with evidence of McConnell harassing and threatening his employees, but Dominic had declined. So, Arturo decided to do it on his own. "It will be good citizenship," he said to himself.

Arturo ordered Cartwright to call the police department Internal Affairs Bureau (IAB), and make a complaint about McConnell's conduct, particularly for violating his employees' civil rights and forcing them to submit to unlawful searches. Cartwright met with IAB investigators and provided records with dates, times, and places. Aldo gave a statement, and gave IAB cellphone photographs of McConnell coming and going to meetings. He even had a recording of an incriminating conversation.

It only took IAB a few weeks to complete their investigation, substantiate the allegations.

On a Monday, at the Task Force office, Dominic heard that McConnell had been transferred to Staten Island. No one in the office knew why, except Captain Corcoran, who denied knowing the reason.

Detective Radowski said, "It can't be good. McConnell lives in the Bronx. It's a long commute to Staten Island."

The secret wasn't kept long, and it was soon all over the department's grapevine that the F.B.I. was investigating McConnell for civil rights violations. Two weeks later, the F.B.I. arrested him, and he was suspended from duty.

When Dominic learned the details of the allegations, he knew it was Arturo's doing. Although, on one hand, he hated McConnell for going after his sons, on the other, he was nevertheless saddened to see an officer's career destroyed, not for corruption or bribery, but for being overzealous. Dominic felt that he shared some of the blame. If he hadn't mentioned McConnell to Arturo, it wouldn't have happened.

He thought McConnell's downfall had resulted from a series of coincidences, and by two separate and distinct chains of events intersecting in unpredictable ways. He thought the same about Ray's death, how it happened because of a series of coincidences. Who could have predicted it would happen that way? And the same for Dennis' story, which was the most convoluted. A bad decision that set into motion a chain of events that had a life of their own, all inexorably leading to Dennis swinging the hammer at his brother's head.

Detective McConnell was devastated and infuriated by his arrest. The F.B.I. agents who arrested him treated him badly, not as a law-enforcement colleague, but as a corrupt cop. McConnell blew his top, cursing at the agents. "While I was in Iraq fighting for my country, you were shuffling papers behind a desk."

At his arraignment in federal court, the Assistant United States Attorney characterized McConnell's conduct as a betrayal of the trust given to police officers and the worst kind of abuse of authority, especially because McConnell had targeted minority immigrant groups and violated their civil rights. "People immigrate to our country for a better life, to escape oppression," the AUSA said, "not to be threatened and terrorized by the police."

McConnell took a threatening step toward the AUSA, but the court officers restrained him.

The judge imposed $50,000 bail. Until he could post the bail, McConnell was held in the U.S. Federal Detention facility, which was directly across from the NYPD police headquarters at One Police Plaza in Lower Manhattan.

Being a defendant instead of an arresting officer had turned McConnell's world upside down. His job had been his life. His position of authority had given him his high self-esteem, but now that was plummeting. Making things more difficult, he had recently gone through a divorce, the result of him always being away from home working and neglecting his wife and kids.

When McConnell finally got out on bail, he tried to hire Klein as his defense attorney, but Klein declined because of possible conflicts of interest, and referred him to another attorney, John Kilkenny, who specialized in federal civil rights cases.

McConnell met Kilkenny at his law office, and immediately began ranting about what a frame up this was.

He told how he had only been trying to enforce the law. "These bodega owners are all fronts for unlawful gambling, lotteries, and drugs," he said. "They're well organized, and hire illegal aliens who can just go back to their own country if they get arrested. I've got a whole dossier on them. They pay off the politicians, and those bastards, to get the vote of the minorities, pressure district attorneys to target cops and throw them to the wolves whenever they can."

"Why do you think they targeted you?" Kilkenny asked.

"Did you ever hear of the Spaniard? His real name is Arturo Gonsalves. He runs the whole bodega organization. I was getting too close to him, and he must've called up the politicians that he has in his pocket to shut me up. He sent his flunkeys, Aldo and Gino, to make up these lies about me. Someone should put a bullet in their heads."

Kilkenny told McConnell that he would have to look into the case a little further before agreeing to take it.

After McConnell left, Kilkenny called Klein.

"Thanks for nothing," he said. "This guy's a psycho."

"In this business, you can't always choose your clients. Are you going to take the case?"

"If he can pay the fee, I will. But I want the money up front. He's a loose cannon. You don't know what he'll do next."

Meanwhile, with the indictment of Dennis for the murder of Ray, the district attorney had no choice but to dismiss the murder charges against Shaquan, Mumford, Forrest, and JL. Technically, they could have been charged with other crimes, such as conspiracy and attempted murder, but it would have been a weak case with someone else on trial for the actual murder. The four, however, were not in the clear yet. The district attorney would still prosecute them for the murder of Buster Johnson.

Dennis' case was transferred from criminal court to Queens Supreme Court, and Judge Stephen Bartlett was picked to preside over the trial. Judge Bartlett continued the $50,000 bail that had been set at the arraignment, allowing Dennis to go home.

Dennis and Dominic went to a meeting with Klein who told them that because Dennis was not in jail, the judge wasn't in a rush to start the trial like Judge Brown had been in Ray's case. Judge Bartlett set a schedule for preliminary motions and discovery that would not get the case to trial for at least three months. When Dennis heard this, he was exasperated. "Why don't I make a deal right now for a year or two, and get it over with?" he said.

"Unfortunately, they're not offering a year or two. They're offering a plea bargain to manslaughter, with a minimum of ten years."

Dennis realized how Ray must have felt when he was given a comparable offer, and he was determined to be as courageous as Ray had been. "I'm not pleading guilty to something that I'm not guilty of."

"You sound just like your brother," Klein said.

"He was right to fight it," Dennis said, "and he was acquitted."

"Not without a little help," Klein said, nodding toward Dennis with a knowing look. "Who's going to help you?"

"I'm just going to tell the truth as best I can, and it'll be in God's hands," Dennis said.

"That's a good attitude, but you can't leave it up to God. You'll have to be more involved than that. This is not a case where the defendant can remain silent. You're the star witness, and the only one who can tell your story. So, we'll be coaching you how to act. We'll be coaching you so much that you'll be ready to win an academy award."

To bolster Dennis' claim of self-defense, Klein also planned to present evidence of Ray's violent nature and his steroid use. He hired a medical expert to explain to the jury how steroids can make even peaceful people violent, and how they can make people with propensity for violence even more violent.

He would use Ray's participation in the BMW robbery to show his propensity for violence, and his earlier arrest for assaulting someone in a bar with a beer bottle.

Klein said to Dominic, "By the way, you might be interested to know that McConnell's lawyer says that he's making crazy threats. He's acting paranoid and thinks there's a conspiracy to get him. I would caution anyone to be wary of him. Be careful."

"Thanks, I will."

As Dennis' trial date neared, he had to give up working for the Santoro Moving Company. He said the work made him too exhausted to think straight, and he had to put all his energy into preparing for the trial. It was a tension filled time. He had up days and down days. On a down day, he told his father, "I should have testified at the grand jury. I could have convinced them that it was self-defense."

"Maybe, but it would have been too risky," Dominic said. "You'd have to give them all the information they would need to hang you. Your best bet is at the regular trial, where to convict you, they need proof beyond a reasonable doubt, which is a much higher standard."

"I know that, but there's no doubt that I was there. There's no doubt I hit him. They won't believe it was self-defense."

Hoping to lift Dennis' spirits, Dominic said, "At the trial, all you'll need is one juror to believe you, and you'll get, at least, a mistrial. So, stay optimistic."

"Okay, I'll try. How about a game of pool, Dad?"

"Alright, let's see what you can do."

CHAPTER THIRTY-SEVEN

While Dominic and Dennis were shooting pool in their basement. Arturo, Aldo, and Gino were leaving a meeting at the Bodega Association headquarters on St. Nicholas Avenue. As they began walking on the sidewalk, a black SUV, being driven on the wrong side of the street, pulled up next to them at the curb. The driver leaned out of his window and fired a barrage of shots from an Uzi submachine gun at them.

Arturo was the first to see the gunman. He dove to the sidewalk, saving his life, but was struck by a bullet in his right side.

Aldo pulled his pistol, took a combat stance, and fired several shots back at the gunman, but Aldo was struck three times, the bullets tearing into his neck and chest.

Gino ran to get back into the bodega headquarters, but was struck in the back twice.

The black SUV drove off, and within minutes the street was mobbed with people wanting to see what had happened.

The police arrived quickly, and transported Arturo and Gino to Columbia-Presbyterian Hospital three blocks away on Broadway. Aldo was dead, so they left his body lying on the street, covered with a plastic blanket.

Meanwhile, as Dominic and Dennis were finishing their third game of pool, the phone rang. It was Detective Larry Smithers from the

Detective Bureau, calling to notify Dominic that there had been a drive-by shooting in Upper Manhattan on St. Nicholas Avenue and 170th Street. One person was killed and two wounded. The deceased was identified as Aldo Manfredonia, and the two wounded as Gino Manfredonia and Arturo Gonsalves.

Many times, Dennis had seen his father take notifications about shootings and other crimes, always remaining calm and businesslike, but now he looked shocked and upset. He didn't say why.

Smithers said, "The Chief of Detectives wants the Task Force to run the investigation in coordination with Manhattan North Homicide and the 33rd Precinct detective squad. And Captain Corcoran picked six guys from the Task Force, including you."

Dominic turned to Dennis, "I've got to go to work, a drive-by shooting in Washington Heights."

"Can I tag along?" Dennis asked.

Dominic stared at him. They both remembered the last time Dennis was with him on a drive-by shooting.

"I guess not," Dennis said.

"I'll tell you all about it when I get home," Dominic said, and left the house.

Arriving at the crime scene, Dominic saw a half-dozen police cars blocking St. Nicholas Avenue and officers detouring traffic to side streets. Several unmarked detective squad cars, a crime-scene unit van, a morgue wagon, and an ambulance were parked in the block.

Lieutenant Bill Duffy was standing in the street, supervising the investigation. Detectives were canvassing the area for witnesses, but people in this neighborhood were notoriously reluctant to get involved in gang warfare, and, other than the information about the black SUV, no one came forward with any useful information.

The sidewalk in front of the bodega headquarters was cordoned off with yellow crime-scene tape, and detectives were taking photographs. They placed small cardboard index cards next to discharged spent shells on the ground to identify them in the photographs. With tape, they marked bullet holes in the bodega door and windows, and some bullet holes in parked cars and a building across the street. With a yellow marker, they circled blood stains from the victims. With chalk, they outlined Aldo's body on the sidewalk.

When the photographing was completed, the detectives recovered the spent shells from the sidewalk and dug bullets out of walls in the bodega and from parked cars.

Dominic watched as the body of Aldo was lifted into the morgue wagon. He asked Lieutenant Duffy whether the victims had said anything.

"That guy," Duffy said, pointing to the body, "didn't have a chance to say anything. The other two were taken to Columbia-Pres."

"What kind of shape are they in?" Dominic asked.

"Not too good," Duffy said. "One of them' s in bad shape and couldn't talk. The other one was okay but didn't want to talk. My guess, it's gang warfare."

When Captain Corcoran arrived, Lieutenant Duffy and Dominic told him what they knew so far. They walked around the crime scene and went into the bodega.

"There's not much for sale on these shelves," Corcoran observed.

"No. I think this place is just a front," Dominic said. "The backroom is supposed to be the headquarters for the Manhattan bodega association, but, more likely, it's a numbers bank or a bookmaking operation." Although he had been in the backroom and knew what was in there, his first instinct was not to tell the captain all he knew. If he did, it could lead to questions about his relationship with Arturo.

"Did anyone check the backroom," Corcoran asked the uniformed police officer who was guarding the premises.

"No, sir," the officer said, "the door's locked. We might need a warrant."

"Bullshit," Corcoran said. "This is an emergency. There could be someone in there bleeding to death."

"I tried the door," the officer said, "It's really solid and shut tight."

"We've got to go in," Corcoran said. "Call Emergency Service."

Two unformed emergency service officers arrived, and using a hydraulic tool that was called "the jaws of life," forced open the door.

Inside, no one was bleeding to death, but there were cartons of illegal gambling records that would have to be confiscated.

The crime scene unit sergeant, John Fuller came into the bodega and reported to the captain that they had recovered a .9mm Glock automatic pistol under Aldo Manfredonia's body and ten spent shell casings on the ground. They also recovered six spent bullets from parked cars and a building across the street. "So, there's four bullets unaccounted for. They either hit the shooter, his car, or other passing cars," Fuller said.

After most of the preliminary investigation was done or underway, Captain Corcoran said, "Let's take a break," and he led Lieutenant Duffy, Detective Cruz, and Dominic to Coogan's Bar and Grill on Broadway and 169th Street. They could eat and discuss the case at the same time.

Coogan's was a mainstay of the Washington Heights area. Its green exterior proclaimed its Irish heritage. Located a block from Columbia-Presbyterian Hospital, doctors and nurses lunched or dined there. The bar also was a hangout for cops and nurses, and local politicians frequented the restaurant. Coogan's had been in business for decades, first catering to the Irish immigrants to the area, then to other groups, African-Americans, Puerto Ricans, and Dominicans. There was no place in the city with a more diverse clientele. The bar sponsored events and sports activities for the youth of the neighborhood. Photographs on the walls depicted the restaurant's history and the personalities who had been customers.

Corcoran loved the place and seemed to know everyone. The four men sat at a table, and ordered beers, except Cruz who didn't drink.

"So, do we have any suspects?" Corcoran asked.

"There's always turf battles between these gangs," Duffy said. "Arturo Gonsalves, in addition to running his clubs and businesses, runs most of the numbers in the city, and someone might be trying to move in and take over his empire."

"If that's the case, why not whack him when he was alone?" Corcoran said. "Why shoot him when he's with other people? Maybe the other two guys were targets, too."

Dominic was thinking the same thing. Aldo and Gino had both made the accusations against McConnell that got him arrested for a charge that would likely send him to prison. But Dominic didn't want to be the one to say it, and was relieved when Cruz did.

"I hate to say it," Cruz said, "But you can't rule out McConnell as a suspect. After all, two of these guys just destroyed his career, and they both work for Arturo. So, McConnell, naturally, could believe that Arturo put them up to it and used his influence to get him arrested by the feds."

Dominic mentioned that McConnell's lawyer had said that McConnell was acting like a psycho and threatening people.

Lieutenant Duffy said, "He had a hard time in Iraq, saw his buddies get killed and badly wounded, and was angry as hell when the politicians pulled the troops out after all the blood they spilled, making it all for nothing."

"That's true," Cruz said. "I've worked with him, and he was always raving about crooked politicians, how they're all on the take, how they don't back up the cops, and how they'll take the word of some dirtbag from the street over a cop. He told me that there's always been collusion and money exchanged between gangsters, politicians and lawyers. The gangsters get off, the politicians get elected, and the lawyers get rich. He liked to say that they should all be hanged together."

"It sounds like he needs a psychiatrist," Corcoran said. "You're always reading about some disgruntled employee killing his co-workers over some grudge. This could be a similar situation."

"And this is more than a grudge," Duffy said, "his career has been destroyed."

"We'd better talk to him," Corcoran said.

"I'm not sure we can," Duffy said. "He's got a lawyer, so we might not be able to question him without his lawyer."

"We don't have to question him," Corcoran said. "But we can look at him, put him under surveillance, and check with people around him to see how he's acting."

"I'll go. I know where he lives," Cruz said. "An apartment building in Riverdale."

"I'll go with you in the morning," Dominic said. "For now, let's go to the hospital to talk to the victims."

"They wouldn't talk before," Duffy said.

"We can try," Dominic said.

At the hospital, both Arturo and Gino were in the intensive-care unit. The detectives assumed that if they asked for official permission to see them, it would be denied, so they would do it informally. They took the elevator to intensive care, identified themselves to a nurse, and asked her to let him see to the patients for a minute.

The nurse was cooperative but said that they couldn't see Gino because he was going into the operating room. A bullet had severed his spine. "I hope he'll be able to walk again, but right now he's paralyzed from the waist down."

"My God. The poor guy," Dominic said.

Cruz shook his head. "What a shame," he said. "He was such a good-looking guy, and dressed like a million bucks."

"He's still good-looking," the nurse said." Let's hope the surgeons can fix him up."

"How about the other one?" Dominic asked.

"You can talk to him, but just for a few minutes."

"I'll be quick, thanks."

Arturo was glad to see him, and clasped his hand. He was in a lot of pain because the bullet had broken a rib on his right side. Breathing was painful.

"I'm so sorry this happened to you," Dominic said.

"Me too," Arturo said in a whisper.

"Is there anything I can do for you," Dominic asked.

"I appreciate that, but I'll be okay."

"Alright. Let's get this out of the way," Dominic said. "Do you know who did this?"

"No."

"Did you see the shooter?"

"No. I saw the gun come out the window, and I dove on the ground."

"Can you tell me anything to help me catch whoever did it?"

"If I could, I would."

They talked for a few more minutes until the nurse came into the room.

"Okay, nurse, I'm leaving," Dominic said. "Thank you, and please take good care of my friend. He's a good man."

"Yes, he is," she said as she adjusted Arturo's pillow.

Dominic and Cruz drove to McConnell's apartment building in the Riverdale section of the Bronx. They identified themselves to the managing agent, Charlie Townsend, who gave them some basic information. McConnell had recently moved in, lived alone, and his rent was paid. He hadn't made any complaints or been the subject of any complaints.

"Does he have any friends of relatives in the building?" Dominic asked.

"Not that I know of. He's new. He keeps to himself."

Townsend didn't seem to know that McConnell was a detective, and they didn't tell him.

McConnell had a parking space in the building's basement garage, number 101. "Do you mind if we take a look?" Dominic asked.

"No problem," the agent said. "I'll show you."

They walked downstairs to the garage, but no car was parked in space 101.

"Do you track when cars enter and exit?" Cruz asked.

"No. The tenants have a touch pass to open the gate. The gate keeps a count of how many cars enter and exit, but it doesn't identify them."

"Would you know the make, model, and registration of his car?" Dominic asked.

"Yes. We need it for the touch pass."

They walked back to the management office, and Mr. Townsend told them it was black Chevrolet Blazer SUV and gave them the registration number, which matched the car that McConnell had on file with the Department, and the description of the car from which the shots were fired.

"Does someone on your staff check the garage every day?" Dominic asked.

"Yeah. The maintenance man is supposed to," Townsend said.

"Would it be possible for him to check spot 101 to see if a car parks there?"

"No problem. We'd be glad to. Anything to help the police."

"Well, thank you so much for your cooperation. Here's my card. If a car shows up, please call."

"I will."

"By the way, if you talk to Mr. McConnell, please don't mention that we were here."

"I certainly won't."

The task force investigators did not have much to go on. No one had gotten a good look at the shooter, so a composite sketch of the suspect couldn't be done. As for the car, all they knew was that it was a black SUV; they didn't have make, model, or even a partial plate number.

Detectives tried all the standard investigative techniques—collecting security camera videos, canvassing registered informants, making arrests and debriefing the defendants for information, and setting up a hotline for tips. Most of the tips that came in were nonsense or unusable.

Dominic thought that the investigation had too many cooks going in too many directions. He thought the first priority was to find McConnell and his car and check to see whether any of Aldo's unaccounted for bullets had struck it or him. Aldo had taken a combat stance and returned fire, so there was a good chance he hit the car, and a chance that a bullet or shattering glass had struck or grazed whoever was shooting from the car.

Detective Cruz agreed and suggested that a city-wide search for the vehicle be undertaken. He also suggested that "Wanted Cards" should be entered in the National Crime Information System (NCIS) requiring any officer who came into contact with either McConnell or the car to alert the Task Force immediately.

"We can't do that," Corcoran said. "There's no basis to justify calling him a suspect. And it might set up a confrontation with officers pulling McConnell out of his car. Someone could get shot."

"When they suspended him, they took his authorized guns," Cruz said.

"But he could still own guns privately. If he was involved in this shooting, he probably does," Corcoran said.

Since the city-wide search and the wanted card ideas were turned down, Dominic and Cruz agreed to take turns visiting McConnell's apartment building twice a day and checking on his parking spot. For three weeks, there was no sign of him or his car.

"He's clearly hiding his car," Dominic said. "Which leads me to believe it might have some bullet holes. Let's check all the collision shops."

They checked more than two dozen but did not locate the car. They subpoenaed McConnell's telephone records from the phone company. The records would show the phone numbers of incoming and outgoing calls. But when the records were picked up, there were no entries. "He's obviously keeping a low profile," Cruz said. "Either he's not talking to anyone, or he's using a burner phone."

Dominic and Cruz decided to attend McConnell's next appearance in federal court, which was scheduled for the upcoming Monday at the U.S. District Court in Foley Square in Lower Manhattan on the federal civil rights. They hoped to see what condition McConnell was in, or whether he had any marks on him. They also planned to follow him when he left court to find his car or find where he was staying.

"We're going to need a team of eight to ten guys to follow him from the court," Dominic told Captain Corcoran.

"Why so many?" Corcoran asked.

"When he leaves the court, he can go in so many different directions. He can take the subway, could have a car, or take a cab. We'll need guys on foot and in vehicles."

"There's no other way to locate him?"

"We've tried. This is our best bet."

"Okay," Corcoran said. "Lieutenant Duffy will coordinate and make the assignments."

The U.S. District Courthouse was similar in style and structure to the U.S. Supreme Court in Washington D.C. It was designed by the same architect in the same neoclassical style, and was the most imposing building in Foley Square, which also encompassed several other impressive buildings: City Hall, the Tweed Courthouse, Surrogates' Court, and the New York County Supreme Court. The square could remind one of the ancient Roman Forum.

Massive granite steps led up to the main entrance of the U.S. Courthouse, which was fronted by ten four-story high Corinthian columns supporting the portico that sheltered the entrance. Decorating the façade were friezes depicting symbols of justice and sculptured images of Plato, Aristotle, Demosthenes and Moses. Atop the six-story base building was a thirty-story tower that housed more courtrooms and government offices.

Detectives on the surveillance team were stationed at the entrances, and others were on the street. They all had Kel transmitter radios with earbuds to communicate.

Dominic and Cruz went inside to the first floor. The interior of the base building, with its gleaming marble floors and walls, twenty-five-feet ceilings, and huge wooden courtroom doors, was designed to overawe its visitors with the majesty of the law and the power of the federal government.

In the courtroom where McConnell was scheduled to appear, they took seats in the back. They didn't see McConnell, but saw his attorney, John Kilkenny, who was standing at the defense table. Kilkenny wore a gray suit with a perfectly pressed white shirt and a blue tie that matched his silver-gray hair. He looked prosperous and like the perfect lawyer.

The Assistant United States Attorney, Henry Silverman, was a smaller man and wore a brown suit.

When federal district court judge Jerome Hanson entered the courtroom, everyone rose. The bailiff announced that court was in session, and McConnell's case was called. The bailiff read the sections of the federal civil rights statutes under the United States Code that McConnell was charged with violating.

"Where's your client, Mr. Kilkenny?" the judge said.

"He hasn't arrived yet, your honor."

"Do you expect him?"

"I'm not sure."

Dominic laughed to himself. He had seen this many times—a lawyer placed in the uncomfortable position of representing a client who doesn't show up, and having to speak on the client's behalf without saying anything detrimental to his interests.

Federal judges, with their lifetime appointments, were generally less tolerant and less sympathetic than state court judges.

"Did you speak to your client this morning," the judge asked.

"No, your honor."

"You couldn't spare the time to call him."

As perfect as Kilkenny looked, he didn't sound confident.

"My office called, but I understand there was no answer."

"Did they leave a message?"

"I understand his message machine was full."

Dominic again laughed to himself, thinking that Kilkenny said "I understand" to avoid having to speak from personal knowledge, and to avoid lying to the court. If what he said turned out not to be true, he could always blame his staff.

"If he's not here in twenty minutes," Judge Hanson said, "I'm going to issue a warrant for his arrest."

Dominic whispered, "I can't believe he didn't show up."

"He must have flipped out," Cruz whispered. "Who would be crazy enough to blow off a federal court?"

Dominic left the courtroom, and in the hall, radioed to the surveillance team, "Has anyone seen the subject?"

The radioed answers were, "Negative, negative, and negative."

Back in the courtroom, Dominic told Cruz, "No one has seen him. Captain Corcoran's not going to be pleased with this waste of manhours."

"Look at the bright side," Cruz said. "If the judge issues a warrant, the feds will get him, and we'll know where he is."

"That may not be so easy. Although he may have gone psycho, he still knows all the tricks how to disappear. And I'm worried. He shot three people, who else might he shoot."

"He doesn't like you," Cruz said.

"Thanks for reminding me. But I'm more worried about my son and his girlfriend, Kathy. You remember McConnell followed her one night, like he was stalking her."

You may be right to worry. I worked with him quite a bit, and he's always obsessed with something or other."

In a half hour, the bailiff called the case again. McConnell hadn't appeared.

"Any news?" the judge asked Kilkenny.

"No, your honor. I request on behalf of my client, who as you know is a respected member of the New York City Police Department, for an adjournment for one week. And I'll do my best to get him here."

"As a member of the police department, he should know better," the judge said. "And I've got a good mind to double the bail."

"We would oppose that, your honor," Kilkenny said. "We're only asking for one week. If at that time…"

The judge cut him off. "What's the government's position."

The Assistant United States Attorney Silverman said, "May we approach the bench, your honor."

"Yes. Come up."

"We're not requesting a bail increase," Silverman said.

"Why not?" the judge said.

"Because, your honor, one of our key witnesses has been killed, and another witness is in the hospital in critical condition. They were both shot. And we have to reassess our case."

The judge stared at Silverman. "When were you going to tell me this?" he said.

"I intended to do so when the defendant showed up. But he didn't and I didn't get a chance."

"It seems to me that if witnesses are being shot, there's all the more reason to raise the bail," Judge Hanson said.

"Of course, your honor. But, to be fair, we have no evidence connecting the defendant to the shootings. The witnesses were known to engage in illegal activities, and there are many other people who possibly could have been involved."

"The judge turned around in his swivel chair, turned back, slammed his gavel, and said, "Bench warrant! The bail remains the same. Call the next case."

"As they walked out of the building, Cruz said, "What do we do next?"

"I don't know. I'm taking some time off," Dominic said. "My son's trial starts Wednesday."

"I didn't know it was so soon."

"You should team up with someone else for a while, but call me if anything develops."

"Okay. And good luck to your son."

CHAPTER THIRTY-EIGHT

On Wednesday, Dennis' trial began at the Queens Supreme Court in Kew Gardens. He walked into the courtroom with his father by his side. Marie would not attend; it would be too much for her.

Dennis had told Kathy that she didn't have to come, and that it was going to be a boring day of jury selection, but she insisted that she would stay with him throughout the trial.

Indeed, it was a tedious day. The judge assigned was Lisa Mandelbaum, a relatively young judge. It was her first murder trial, and she projected a severe and serious demeanor. Most male judge had taken to wearing a suit on the bench, but Judge Mandelbaum always were her black robes. Someone said she did that because she didn't want to be mistaken for a clerk.

Klein let Rosen handle the jury selection. Rosen was careful, methodical, and slow. Nevertheless, by the end of the day, ten men and two women were selected. The racial makeup was six whites, three blacks, and three Hispanics.

On Thursday, ADA Walsh gave his opening statement, telling the jury about Ray's robbery trial and Dennis' testimony in it. He talked about Ray's lawsuit for false arrest, and the deposition testimony of both Ray and Dennis. It was a confusing aspect of the case, and the jury looked bored, so he moved on to the love-triangle between Ray, Kathy, and Dennis, which he claimed was the motivation for Dennis to kill his brother. This got the jury's attention. Walsh insisted that Dennis purposely went to Ray's apartment to kill him, and this was borne out, he said, because Dennis had sneaked out of the 9th Precinct, drove to the apartment, struck Ray with a hammer, and left him lying dead on the living room floor, not even calling for an ambulance. He then returned to the 9th Precinct without telling anyone what had happened. "This was neither an accident, nor a spontaneous fight," Walsh said, "but a premeditated murder."

Listening to the accusations against him, Dennis clenched his fists and shook his head as though to say "no." Klein patted him on the shoulder trying to calm him.

When Klein's turn came, as he had done at Ray's trial, he gave only a brief opening statement, and turned the case over to ADA Walsh who began calling his witnesses.

Walsh wouldn't call Detective McConnell because of his arrest. His next choice was Detective Cruz, currently the lead investigator, but Cruz refused, saying that he was conflicted because of his close relationship with Dominic, and he couldn't testify against Dominic's son.

Lieutenant Duffy summoned Cruz into his office and told him that testifying was part of his job, and to refuse could subject him to discipline, possibly a transfer out of the Detective Bureau. Cruz nevertheless said that he wouldn't testify. The matter was dropped, and ADA Murphy used other detectives to present the case.

Walsh called Detective Matthews to the witness stand. Walsh tried to question him about Ray's robbery trial, and about Dennis manipulating Brenda Ramos to say that he had admitted to committing the robbery. However, Klein continuously objected that this testimony was irrelevant and, even if relevant, it was unduly prejudicial against the defendant.

Klein and Walsh approached the bench to argue their positions. Walsh said that the evidence was relevant and he was introducing it to show Dennis' motive for the murder. Klein argued that since the ADA had claimed that the motive was the love triangle, allowing evidence about the robbery case would confuse the jury.

Judge Mandelbaum overruled the relevancy objection. But she sustained the unduly prejudicial objection because Dennis' conduct in Ray's trial was criminal, and, although there were exceptions, the general rule was that a prosecutor can't prove the current case by showing that the defendant previously committed other crimes. The judge ruled that it would be too prejudicial against the defendant.

As Klein walked back to the defense table, a wry smile crossed his face. He seemed pleased to have won an argument that he shouldn't have, but he'd take it.

Matthews continued testifying, and described how, with McConnell and Cruz, he went to Ray's apartment and found the body and the hammer next to it. Then he described how the crime-scene unit detectives took photographs and processed the evidence.

As Dennis listened to Matthews describing the crime scene, he remembered the struggle with Ray, and he had a flashback to when he saw Ray's crazed eyes. Klein asked him whether he was okay.

"This is a little rough, but I'll be alright," Dennis said.

When Matthews finished his testimony, the court adjourned for lunch. Klein and Dennis went to attorney/client room. Dennis said I'm glad you were able to keep all that evidence about Ray's robbery trial out of the case.

"Well, we've got a win now, but that doesn't mean it won't come in later," Klein said.

"If it's prejudicial, why would it come in later?" Dennis asked.

"Because when you testify, if you testify," Klein said, "your credibility becomes the main issue, and the door will be opened for them to cross-examine you about everything. They'll bring out all your past false statements, and anything the reflects on your honesty or dishonesty. Ray's trial will give them plenty of ammunition."

Dennis had been sure that as soon as he told his story of what happened in the apartment, the jury would have to believe him and that would be the end of it. But he realized that if the prosecutor could prove that he was a liar, the jury would turn against him. He realized how critical his testimony would be. The rest of his life would depend on it.

When court resumed, Walsh called crime scene unit detective Bill Jackson, who, using a large, overhead computer screen, showed the photographs taken at the crime scene and pointed out the pertinent items of evidence.

Klein cross-examined Detective Jackson briefly. He finished by asking, "Detective, did the condition in the apartment indicate that there had been a fight?"

"Yes. Things were knocked over, and stuff from under the sink was out on the kitchen floor."

"No further questions," Klein said. Nothing Jackson had said had undermined Dennis' claim of self-defense.

Next, Walsh called Chandra Choudry, the Medical Examiner, who had performed the autopsy on the body. Dr. Choudry estimated the time of death as between six and seven p.m., and she described the cause of death as a fracture to Ray's skull. The fracture was caused by a hard, blunt object striking the temple area. The dimensions of the injury to the skull were consistent with head of the hammer that was found next to the body.

When Klein cross-examined the doctor, he didn't challenge her credentials or challenge her interpretation of the physical evidence, which many defense attorneys routinely would do. Although she was the prosecution's witness, Klein intended to use her testimony to the advantage of the defense, and hoped to make some favorable points.

Klein stood next to the jury box so that the doctor's answers would be directed at the jurors.

After preliminary questions, he asked, "Doctor, would you agree that the deceased was a powerfully-built and athletic young man?"

"Yes, he was" the doctor agreed.

"And your report indicates that he was two-hundred and twenty pounds and five foot ten inches tall?"

"Yes."

"There was only one injury to the deceased, correct?"

"That's right, a skull fracture at the temple."

"As far as you know, he was struck only once with the hammer?"

"There were no other external injuries."

"You've been conducting autopsies for many years, correct?"

"Yes."

"And part of your procedure involves examining the circumstances surrounding such an event as this?"

"Yes."

"Because the circumstances could shed light on whether the even was a homicide, a suicide, an accident, or a natural death, correct?"

"Yes, that's right."

"The police gave you background information on this case, correct?"

"Yes."

"And the police reports indicate that the deceased was a bouncer at a strip-club and also at an after-hours club, which would make it fair to assume that he was a pretty rough customer. Do you agree with that?"

"Yes. That's fair."

"In your opinion, based on your experience, if someone was planning to intentionally murder a person as powerful, rough, and athletic as the deceased, wouldn't it be likely that the person would bring a gun or a knife?"

"That's a possibility."

"Wouldn't it be more than a possibility, but, actually, a probability that someone who was going to confront this powerfully-built bouncer, and try to kill him, would bring a gun or a knife?"

"I can't speculate on that."

"Let me put it this way. If they didn't bring a gun or a knife, wouldn't that indicate that they did not have the premeditated intention to kill him?"

"That's a reasonable inference, but I don't know."

"And wouldn't it be more probable that the blow with the hammer would have been struck as a result of a spontaneous fight, not a pre-planned murder?"

"That's possible."

"Again, more than possible, and with some degree of probability. Can you agree with that?"

"I would agree that there is some degree of probability, but we don't know how much," the doctor said.

At this point ADA Walsh stood up, and objected. "This is all speculative," he said, obviously trying to keep his witness from giving too much help to the defense.

"Overruled, "Judge Mandelbaum said. "Continue."

"Thank you, your honor," Klein said.

Klein retrieved several crime-scene photographs and handed them to the witness.

"Doctor, you've seen these photographs?"

"Yes."

"And they show things in the apartment out of place, knocked over, strewn about on the kitchen floor."

"Yes."

"In your experience, combining that with the other facts in this case, would it be fair to conclude that there was a fight between the decedent and the defendant."

"Yes."

"In a fight between two young men like these, anything can happen. Would you agree?"

"Yes."

"And, as for premeditation, we would have to know who started the fight. Would you agree?"

"That would be helpful."

"If the decedent started the fight, you couldn't reasonably conclude that the defendant had gone to the apartment to kill him. Correct?"

"That would make it less likely."

Klein paused and nodded to the jury, hoping to emphasize the last answer. Then he retrieved a report from the defense table.

"Doctor, a toxicology examination was done on the victim?"

"Yes."

"I'll hand you the report. Please look it over. When you're done, let me know," Klein said.

"I know what's in it," the doctor said.

"Fine. Can you tell the jury?"

"Yes. The decedent had anabolic steroids and cocaine in his bloodstream."

"Doctor, is it true that anabolic steroids can make a person aggressive and violent?"

"There are studies that say that."

"And the combination of steroids and cocaine could make a person even more aggressive and violent. Is that correct?"

"I would say so."

"Thank you, doctor."

ADA Walsh tried to re-direct the doctor's testimony to counteract the points that Klein had gotten across to the jury, but without much success.

The prosecution rested, and court was adjourned until Friday, the next morning, when the defense would begin presenting its case.

Thursday's full day of testimony had left everyone exhausted. Nevertheless, Klein asked Dominic, Dennis, and Kathy to come to his office to prepare their defense. Kathy was going to testify, and he wanted to go over her testimony once more.

At the office, Dennis watched Klein, who seemed to be doing four or five things at once. He had Kathy talk about the night of Ray's death. Then, he asked her questions that ADA Walsh might ask her on cross-examination. While doing this, he took a phone call, made a phone call, and gave orders to his staff. Dennis wondered where he got all his energy.

Kathy was tired but gave clear answers. Klein tried to trip her up, but her answers remained consistent.

They discussed having Kathy testify about the times that Ray had forced himself upon her physically and sexually. It had pros and cons. Kathy was willing to testify about it, but Klein decided against it, because it would have established a motive for Dennis to kill Ray.

With Kathy's preparation done, Dennis asked Klein, "What time will I testify?"

"It might not be tomorrow. It depends how long the other witnesses take."

"Then I wouldn't testify until Monday?"

"Probably."

"I don't think I can stand waiting the whole weekend," Dennis said.

"You know, on second thought, maybe it would be best if you get on the stand tomorrow," Klein said. "At least, I can start your direct examination, and the jury will have that in their minds over the weekend before Walsh gets a chance to cross-examine you on Monday."

"I'd like to get it all over with tomorrow."

"Of course, you would, but we'll see," Klein said.

CHAPTER THIRTY-NINE

Klein's first witness on Friday was Doctor Raj Alawadi. He was called not as a fact witness but as an expert who would give his opinion on the effects of anabolic steroids and cocaine. To qualify him as an expert, Klein went over the doctor's background, his degrees, his experience, and his writings on the subject. After establishing his credentials, Klein asked the judge to qualify the doctor as an expert.

ADA Walsh, going through the motions, conducted a *voir dire* to challenge his qualifications, but the judge quickly certified the doctor as an expert and allowed him to testify as to his opinion.

He was an impressive witness who spoke clearly and emphatically as he explained scientific principles and how chemicals can affect a person's behavior and state of mind. Then Klein asked him about Ray's condition.

"Doctor," Klein asked, "In your opinion to a reasonable degree of professional certainty could the chemicals in the decedent's bloodstream have caused him to be overly aggressive and violent."

"Yes," the doctor said, and went on to explain the results of various medical studies that supported that proposition.

"And, doctor," Klein asked, "Is it correct that people with mesomorphic, or heavily-muscled, body types would be more prone to over-aggression and violence that people not built that way."

"Yes, numerous studies have shown that."

On cross-examination, ADA Walsh tried to undermine the doctor's testimony. He went on for a long time, but the more he tried, the better the doctor looked to the jury. Finally, Judge Mandelbaum said, "Mr. Walsh, it seems you covered everything."

"Yes, your honor," Walsh said. "No further questions."

"Any re-direct," the judge asked Klein.

"No, your honor," Klein said, fully satisfied with the doctor's testimony.

Next, Klein called Kathy to the witness stand. Keeping her direct testimony within limits, he was careful not to ask her about Ray's trial, Dennis' role in it, or her role. He kept her testimony confined to the night of Ray's death, how she had broken off their relationship, and how Ray angrily left her apartment.

Since Walsh would not be able cross-examine her outside the scope of her direct testimony, he shouldn't have been able ask her about Ray's trial, a subject not favorable to her or Dennis. Nevertheless, he tried.

"Ms. Reynolds," Walsh said, "isn't it true that you testified in Ray Carbonaro's robbery trial that the defendant, Dennis Carbonaro, told you that..."

Klein jumped to his feet before Walsh could finish his sentence. "Objection," he shouted. "This is outside the scope of the direct testimony."

"The objection is sustained," the judge said.

Walsh asked to approach the bench and argued to the judge that he had the right to prove the defendant's motive, and the jury needed to know the background of the case.

Klein countered that Walsh was mischaracterizing the testimony in Ray's case, because Kathy's testimony in that case had not been admitted into evidence because it was hearsay.

"We don't need to get into that," the judge said. "Move on, Mr. Walsh. It's outside the scope."

Walsh tried again. "Isn't true that you convinced Brenda Ramos to testify in Ray Carbonaro's robbery trial that..."

"Objection," Klein shouted again.

"Sustained," the judge said. "Move on."

Walsh slammed a manila folder on the prosecution's table. The judge stared menacingly at him.

"I apologize, your honor," Walsh said, then, moving closer to the witness chair, he asked, "Miss Reynolds, you're engaged to the defendant, are you not?"

"Yes. I am."

"And you love him?"

"Yes. I do."

"And hope to be married and spend your lives together, correct?"

"Yes."

"You don't want him to be convicted of this crime, isn't that true?"

"Yes."

"So, you'll say whatever's necessary to help avoid being found guilty?"

"I'm only going to say what I know to be true," Kathy said emphatically.

"And what made you transfer your feelings from Ray to the defendant?"

"A lot of things."

"Was it because Dennis told you that Ray was really guilty of the robbery case for which he had been acquitted?"

"No."

"Then what was it?"

Kathy sat up straighter in her chair. "The main reason was because he been physically abusing me, and forcing himself on me sexually. I tried to break off with him, but he kept coming around."

Those paying attention realized that Walsh had made the mistake of asking an open-ended question without knowing what the answer would be.

Dennis remembered that Walsh had made the same mistake the last time he cross-examined Kathy during Ray's trial.

As Kathy continued her answer, Walsh looked up to the ceiling as though asking for help from above.

"I had lost my feelings for him," Kathy said, "but he wouldn't accept that. He wanted things to stay the way they were, and he wouldn't take no for an answer."

Walsh moved closer to the witness stand.

"Did you report these incidents to the police?"

"No. I didn't."

Walsh hesitated. He didn't want to ask another open-ended question, but he couldn't avoid it, and asked, "And why not?"

Kathy looked down before answering. "We had been together so long," she said. "It wasn't like I hadn't slept with him before. I just wanted to end it. And I thought that if I was, let's say, unenthusiastic, he would get tired and break it off himself. But, he didn't. He would follow me, and push his way into my apartment."

As Dennis listened, he was sure that Klein was angry at Kathy for disregarding his advice not to bring up the abuse. Although it was helpful to show Ray's violent nature, she had given the prosecution an opportunity to prove Dennis' motive for killing Ray.

Walsh tried to press that point, trying to establish Dennis' motive. "So, you broke off with the decedent, Ray Carbonaro, and you began seeing the defendant, Dennis Carbonaro. Correct?"

"Yes."

"Let me ask you this. Did you tell Dennis about Ray abusing of you?"

Kathy wanted to say no, but wouldn't lie. "Yes, I did."

"And what was his reaction."

"He said I should report it."

"Did you?"

"No. He said I should report it as a rape, but I didn't want to go there."

"What happened after that?"

"He said I should get an order of protection."

"Did you get an order of protection?"

"No."

"He must have thought it was serious and dangerous enough to suggest to you to get an order of protection from the court?"

"I suppose."

Walsh moved back to the prosecution table, and skimmed over a folder. "One more question," he said. "Did Dennis ever have a physical confrontation with Ray, that you know of?"

"Not that I saw," she answered.

"Had you heard about physical confrontations between them?"

Klein immediately objected, "Calls for hearsay."

"Sustained," the judge ruled.

Walsh had no further questions, and Kathy was excused.

As she left the courtroom, Dennis exhaled with a sigh of relief. Although he realized her testimony could be used by Walsh to prove that he had a motive to kill Ray, he thought it was helpful that she brought out Ray's violent nature.

During the lunch recess in the attorney/client room. Dennis put his feet up on a chair, closed his eyes, and pretended to sleep. He wished that he could go into a closet by himself, but this was all he could do. It seemed to be his best defense against the outside world, and kept people from talking to him. The was quiet until the court officer entered and announced that court was resuming.

Dominic handed Dennis a cup of hot coffee. "Just stick to your story just the way you told us. And remember, you didn't do anything wrong. You had a right to protect yourself."

"Like mom says, 'It's in God's hands.'"

When court resumed, Dennis was ready to take the witness stand. However, Walsh had some legal points to discuss with the judge, and asked to approach the bench.

Judge Mandelbaum said, "Let's discuss them in my chambers," and the judge, Walsh, Klein, and the court stenographer left the courtroom and went into her chambers. Because of recent court rulings, Dennis was entitled to be present for any such discussions, and went in with them. Dominic tried to go in with them, but the lawyers said he couldn't.

The judge sat at her desk, with flags on either side, and diplomas and other testimonials on the wall behind her. The others sat in in front of her desk.

There was no small talk, and they got right down to business. Several issues were discussed about Dennis' prospective testimony and his prospective cross-examination. Dennis had taken the Fifth Amendment when he was called to testify in Ray's case, but Walsh argued that he was present when Kathy and Brenda testified about statements he allegedly made, and Walsh should be able to ask him whether their testimony was true or false.

Klein argued again that what was said at Ray's trial was irrelevant to this trial, and, furthermore, Dennis had taken the Fifth Amendment, and to make him answer questions about his role in that trial would violate his right not to incriminate himself.

ADA Walsh slammed his hand on the judge's desk. "If he's going to testify, he waives the Fifth Amendment. He can't agree to testify to some things and not others. And everything that goes to his credibility is relevant. He can't have it both ways."

Judge Mandelbaum said to Walsh, "You've got a bad habit of slamming things on the furniture."

"I'm sorry, your honor. I apologize."

"Alright," the judge said. "I need to think about this. And, as a matter of fact, we all need a break, and the jury could use a break. So, we'll resume Monday morning. I'll render a decision then."

Dennis was disappointed because he wanted to get his testimony over with, one way or the other. Now, he'd have to wait through the weekend, and he felt disconcerted because he hadn't quite followed the legal arguments. They were confusing, and he hated the uncertainty of not being able to figure out what questions could be asked of him and what was going to happen next. He followed the others back into the courtroom.

His father was waiting for them. "What did they say?" Dominic asked.

"Adjourned until Monday," Klein said. "She has to decide what questions the DA can ask."

Kathy was coming back from the ladies' room, walking fast toward them.

"You're not going to believe this," she said. "But I think I saw McConnell in the hallway. He saw me and went down a staircase."

"Are you sure it was him?" Dominic asked.

"Yeah. I'm pretty sure."

"Which staircase?"

"The one directly across."

"I thought he was missing," Dennis said.

"He is," Dominic said, "In fact, there's a warrant for his arrest."

"What the hell would he be doing here?" Dennis said.

Dominic was thinking the same thing. He was concerned, and called Detective Cruz. He told him what happened, and told him to come to the court and look at the video surveillance tapes to see if it was really McConnell.

Later that afternoon, Cruz called Dominic.

"It was him alright," Cruz said. "The video caught him coming in the building, going around to the courtrooms, and reading the calendars. I can't figure what he would be doing there."

"He was obsessed with Ray's trial; now he's obsessed with Dennis' trial," Dominic said. "He takes them personally, and blames them for his problems. He must be flipping out."

"Whatever it is, it's not good," Cruz said. "He knows there's a warrant on him. Why would he risk going into a court building?"

"If he was crazy enough to shoot people," Dominic said, "who knows what else he's crazy enough to do. Notify headquarters, and also the U.S. Marshals. They're supposed to be looking for him."

"Alright, I'll take care of it. Be careful," Cruz said.

Dominic hung up, then called Dennis. "Why don't you and Kathy stay here with us tonight?"

"How come?"

"I got a bad feeling," Dominic said. "And I'd be more comfortable with the two of you here."

"Maybe you're getting paranoid, Dad."

"Just do what I tell you," Dominic said.

Dominic hung up, checked the Glock automatic pistol holstered on his belt, made sure there was a bullet in the chamber, then went upstairs to his rifle closet, and unlocked it.

CHAPTER FORTY

On Monday morning, Judge Mandelbaum announced that questions about Dennis' role in Ray's trial would be allowed. This was major disappointment to the defense.

The jury was brought in. The judge greeted them, gave updates and instructions, and said to Klein, "Call your next witness."

"Call the defendant, Dennis Carbonaro," Klein said.

With every juror staring at him, Dennis felt his heart pounding as he took the witness stand and was sworn in.

Klein began his direct examination slowly, giving Dennis a chance to settle down. But Dennis could still feel his heart pounding. From the front spectator row, his father signaled to him to breath in and breath out for eight seconds each, something he had taught him as a way to slow down his heartbeat. Dennis tried that, and it helped.

Klein asked questions, not about Ray's trial, but about the depositions in the civil suit that followed. He went into this area rather than let Walsh bring it up later. It was standard trial practice to bring out bad evidence yourself and take the sting out of it before the other side could play it up.

"Do you remember statements from Ray's deposition being read to you in your deposition?"

"Yes," Dennis answered.

Klein then read from the deposition transcript where Ray said that Dennis had hidden Rolex watch in his mattress and that he, Ray, threw it off the Whitestone Bridge. "Do you remember that?"

"Yes."

ADA Walsh might have objected to this line of questioning on grounds that it was leading the witness, but he was glad that Klein was putting this subject on the record, so he didn't object.

"How did you feel when you learned what Ray had said?" Klein asked.

"I was stunned," Dennis said. "I couldn't believe my own brother would do this to me."

"In what way?"

"That he was switching places with me. He's the one who had hidden the watch in the mattress. I found it by accident, and then realized that Ray was guilty for the BMW robbery. To get rid of the watch, I threw it off the Whitestone Bridge."

"After you learned what Ray had said at the deposition," Klein said, "did that give you some concerns?"

"Yes. I knew that he was going to testify in the upcoming BMW robbery case, and I was worried that he might say the same thing he said in the deposition—that he would say that it was me who had the Rolex watch, not him. I thought he might try to shift the blame for the robbery from him to me."

"So, what did you do?"

"I went to see him, to ask him what he intended to say."

"Where did you go?"

"To our apartment in Ridgewood."

"Did you go there intending to kill him?" Klein asked.

"No. Of course not."

"Did you go there to fight with him?"

"No."

"You wanted to find out what he was going to say when he testified?"

"Yes."

"And what happened when you got there?"

Dennis was so anxious to tell his story that he talked too fast and his heart began pounding again.

"He accused me of telling Kathy Reynolds about the Rolex watch that was in his mattress."

"You mean the Rolex stolen in the robbery?"

"Yes."

"Then what happened?"

"He punched me in the face and knocked me to the floor."

"Okay. Take your time," Klein said, "What happened next?"

"I called him crazy, and he really lost it. He punched me again."

"Were you on the floor?"

"Yes. I think my head was under the kitchen sink. I tried to get up, but he kicked me in the head. I could see in his face that he was really going to kill me. So, I kicked him in the balls, but that only made him madder."

"You said you could see in his face that he was going to kill you, what do you mean by that?"

"His eyes were wild. He had a crazed look. Something you would see in a horror movie."

"Were you frightened."

"Yes. I was frightened."

"What happened then?"

"He hit me on both sides of my head, and I think I blanked out for a second. Then I felt him choking me. I was able to break the chokehold, but he punched me in the face again."

"Then what happened?"

"I rolled on my stomach to protect myself, but Ray was choking me from behind. As I tried to push myself up, I felt the hammer under the sink. I twisted myself around as best I could, and swung the hammer. It must have hit him, but he punched me at the same time, and I was knocked out."

"What happened next?"

"I woke up, and saw Ray lying on the floor."

"Was Ray moving?"

"No."

"Was he breathing?"

"I don't think so."

A deadly silence filled the courtroom. Even the judge was riveted.

Klein waited a moment before breaking the silence. "No further questions," he said. "Your witness," he said to Walsh.

Judge Mandelbaum said to Dennis, "I'm sure you could use a little break. Let's take a ten-minute recess."

The ten-minute recess turned into a half-an-hour. Dennis was glad to have finally testified to what had happened and he thought it went well. Klein, however, was worried, and reminded Dennis, "On cross, he he'll ask you what you told Kathy and Belinda about the robbery. That's going to be a problem. If you deny it, he could put them on the stand to contradict you.'

Klein stared at Dennis waiting for his response, and was surprised when Dennis said, "Why should I deny it?"

"Because you'll be getting yourself in a lot of trouble."

"Not as bad as being charged with murder."

"That's true," Klein said. "I can't tell you what to say. In fact, I don't know what to tell you to say."

Dennis didn't answer.

As they walked back to the courtroom, Dominic took Dennis' arm, and whispered, "Keep your answers to yes and no. Don't embellish."

"I'll try." Dennis said.

Dennis returned to the witness stand for his cross-examination.

"I remind you, you're still under oath," the judge said.

Dennis nodded.

ADA Walsh moved to the lectern, clearly relishing his chance to cross-examine Dennis, whom he blamed for his loss in Ray's robbery trial.

"Now, Mr. Carbonaro," he began, "You had several reasons to kill your brother. Isn't that so?"

"Objection," Klein stood. "Assumes facts not in evidence."

The judge pondered the objection for a moment. "Overruled. Proceed," she said.

"You can answer," Walsh said.

"What was the question again?" Dennis said.

The court reporter read the question back from the transcript. "You had several reasons to kill your brother. Isn't that so?"

"No," Dennis said.

"Well, weren't you angry at him for physically and sexually abusing your girlfriend, now your fiancée, Kathy Reynolds?"

The simple answer was yes, but Dennis had to say more. "Yes," he said, "but that didn't mean I wanted to kill him."

"Miss Reynolds told you that he had abused her. Right?"

"Yes."

"And shortly after she told you that he abused her, you went to this apartment and struck him with a hammer. Correct."

"I struck him with a hammer, but I didn't go there intending to fight with him," Dennis said. "He attacked me, and I acted in self-defense."

Walsh said, "I move to strike that answer as unresponsive. The question called for a simple yes or no."

"It was responsive to the implication in your question," the judge said. "It's admissible."

Walsh put down one yellow-legal pad and picked up another from the prosecution's table. It had a list of questions that he would ask in rapid-fire succession.

"Now, before you went to Ray's apartment, you were in the 9th police precinct waiting for your father. Is that correct?"

"Yes."

"And while your father was occupied investigating a crime, you left the precinct without telling him. Correct?"

"Yes."

"You didn't tell anyone. Isn't that true?"

"Yes."

"After you left the precinct without telling anyone, you drove to Ray's apartment. Correct?"

"Yes."

"And in the apartment, you had your encounter with Ray? Correct."

"Yes."

"And you hit him with the hammer?"

"After he attacked me, and was choking me."

"And he fell on the floor. Correct?"

"Yes."

"He was lying there. Correct?"

"Yes."

"Did you know whether he was alive or dead?"

"I wasn't sure. I checked his breathing and his pulse."

"But you didn't call an ambulance. Right?"

"That's right."

"You didn't call the police. Right?"

"Right."

"You left without telling anyone. Right?"

"Yes"

"You didn't attempt to render first aid? Isn't that true?"

"Yes."

"To your own brother you wouldn't give first aid."

"By then I was sure he was dead."

"You drove back to the 9th Precinct, which was full of police. And you didn't tell anyone there that you had struck Ray with a hammer. Right?"

"Yes."

"Your father was there, and you didn't tell him either. Correct?"

"Correct."

"And you pretended that you had been at the precinct all along. Isn't that true?"

Dennis hesitated.

Walsh raised his voice. "You pretended that you had been there all along?

"Yes."

Dennis slumped in his chair, realizing how bad this looked, and thinking that the jury was probably going to convict him.

Bye the way," Walsh said. "After your brother supposedly hit you, did you go to the hospital?"

"No."

"Did you go to the doctor?"

"No."

"Did you take any photographs of your alleged injuries?"

"No. I should have, but I was so shocked at the time, I wasn't thinking straight, and wasn't reporting the whole incident."

"And why weren't you reporting the whole incident, as you call it?"

"Mostly because I couldn't face telling my parents that I killed their son," Dennis said.

"Oh, so it had nothing to do with being charged with murder?"

"Of course, it did. But I could face that. I knew it was self-defense. I wanted to avoid telling my mother and father."

Walsh took another legal pad with more questions.

"At the precinct, you were told that your brother had been killed. Correct?"

"Yes."

"But you didn't tell anyone that you were the one who did it. Correct?"

"Yes."

"Now, you want the jury to believe your story that this was all self-defense. Is that right?"

"Yes."

"You want them to believe that your story of self-defense is truthful. Right?"

"Yes."

"Yet you weren't truthful with the police. Right?"

"Yes."

"You knew the police were going to conduct an investigation to find out what happened, but you didn't tell them what happened. Right?"

"Yes."

"In fact, the police subsequently arrested other people for Ray's murder. Isn't that true?"

"Yes."

"But you didn't tell anyone. And you let the charges go forward against the other people. Correct."

"Yes."

"And you want this jury to believe that you're a truthful and honest person, telling them the truth?"

Klein stood. "Objection. Argumentative."

"Sustained,' the judge said, "move on."

Dennis was glad to get away from that subject, but realized that his honesty had been impeached, and he again resigned himself to being found guilty.

Walsh picked up another legal pad with more questions. He moved in front of the jury box, because he wanted Dennis to have to look at the jury when he answered the next set of questions. He was going to ask about Ray's trial and Dennis' solicitation of perjury to get Ray acquitted.

"Now, you saw most of your brother Ray's trial for robbery. Correct?"

"Yes."

"And you know that a young woman, Belinda Ramos, testified in the trial?"

"Yes."

"And who is she?"

"She's a friend of my fiancée."

"Does she work as a waitress at McCoy's Bar and Grill?"

"Yes."

"Isn't it true that you told Miss Ramos that you committed the robbery that Ray was on trial for?"

Walsh waited for the answer, hoping Dennis would deny it.

Dennis didn't answer right away. He was making up his mind. He knew that if he denied it, Belinda could be called to contradict his testimony. He decided, like Kathy, that he was going to stick to the truth, come hell or highwater.

Walsh interrupted his thoughts. "Can you answer the question?"

"Yes." Dennis said.

"Yes, to what? You can answer the question, or, yes, you told her that you committed the robbery?"

Everyone in the courtroom seemed to be straining to hear the answer.

"Yes. I told her that I committed the robbery," Dennis said loudly and clearly.

Walsh hadn't expected him to admit that, and he was thrown off course for a moment. Then asked, "You did this because you wanted her to repeat it in court?"

"Yes," Dennis said.

"So, you wanted her to commit perjury?" Walsh asked.

"She wasn't committing perjury," Dennis said. "She repeated what I told her, and she believed it."

"But it was not the truth?"

"That's right."

"With or without her knowledge, you put her up to misleading the court. Correct?"

"Yes."

Walsh turned to face the jury and spoke directly to them. "So, you misled the court then," he said, "but you expect us to believe that you're not misleading them now. That you're suddenly telling the truth?"

Dennis nodded toward the jury. "Yes, because I am telling the truth. Why else would I admit these things? I made a mistake in Ray's trial, because I thought he was innocent. But now I know all the trouble I caused. And I would never play games with the truth again."

Flippantly, Walsh said, "How convenient."

Although it wasn't a question, Dennis took advantage and answered, "I'm telling the truth. My brother was going to kill me. It was like a nightmare. I had to protect myself. I didn't want to hurt him, but I didn't want to die on that kitchen floor."

The jurors were looking intently at him.

Walsh said, "You just happened to have a hammer in your hand and hit him directly in the temple."

"Finding the hammer was by chance. If he wasn't choking me, I never would have found it," Dennis said, sincerely.

Walsh sensed that he was losing this argument. He blurted out a question, "If this was all an accident, wouldn't it be fair to say that you would have called an ambulance to try to save him?"

"I didn't want my brother to die," Dennis said. "I loved him. He was my older brother. That's why I did what I did during his trial. I tried to help him, not kill him."

Walsh decided that it would be better to quit than to keep going down this road.

"No further questions."

The judge asked Klein, "Do you have any more witnesses?"

"No, your honor, the defense rests."

"Alright, in that case, we'll adjourn until tomorrow morning for closing arguments."

The judge thanked the jurors for being so patient, and told them not to discuss the case amongst themselves and to avoid any outside sources of information. "If something comes on television, change the channel, and, for heaven's sake, don't read any newspaper articles."

CHAPTER FORTY-ONE

For the closing arguments, Dominic sat next to Dennis at the defense table. Kathy sat in the first spectator row behind them. The case was still in the news, and the courtroom was filled with onlookers, press people, off-duty cops, and a dozen Carbonaro relatives. There weren't family members of the victim, on one side, and family members of the defendant, on the other; there was only one family for both sides.

Klein's closing argument went straight to the point. "Ladies and gentlemen of the jury, this is as straightforward a case of self-defense as you can get. The defendant has testified under oath that he was suddenly and viciously attacked by his brother, that he feared for his life, and that he protected himself by swinging a hammer, which he had a right to do under our laws of justification and under the law of nature.

"The prosecutor, Mr. Walsh, for whom I have greatest esteem, has tried to present a case of intentional murder, but there's no evidence that supports that or overcomes the defendant's account of what happened in the apartment.

"The prosecutor points to a supposed motive for Dennis to go to the apartment to kill his brother—that he was angry about Ray physically and sexually abusing Kathy Reynolds. But, when Dennis heard about the abuse, he didn't go looking for Ray, he told Kathy to go to the police and to get an order of protection, which was a sensible, non-violent response.

"To the contrary, it was Ray who had a motive for attacking Dennis. As Ms. Reynolds testified, she told Ray that Dennis had told her about the stolen Rolex watch, and, because of that, she was breaking off with him. Ray left her apartment in an ugly mood and went to the Ridgewood apartment. It just so happened that at about the same time, Dennis went to the apartment to ask Ray about his upcoming testimony. Ray, blaming Dennis for telling Kathy about the watch, attacked Dennis.

"It was Ray, not Dennis, who was acting in an aggressive, violent manner."

Klein took a drink from a water bottle, then continued.

"The prosecutor poses an alternative motive for Dennis to want to kill Ray—to prevent him from incriminating Dennis in his testimony at the upcoming robbery trial. Dennis admitted under oath that he went to the apartment to talk to Ray about his testimony, but not to kill him. Just think how implausible that is. You heard the testimony of Doctor Choudry about how muscular and strong Ray was. You heard about Ray's propensity for violence, about him assaulting someone in a bar with a beer bottle, and working as a bouncer in both a strip-club and an illegal after-hours joint. You don't hold jobs like that unless you're an aggressive person and a formidable fighter. And Ray was all of that.

"Ask yourselves, would Dennis, would anyone, go to the apartment to kill Ray without a gun or a knife? Would he rely on finding a hammer under the sink? It's too implausible.

"And you heard from Doctor Alawadi about the steroids and cocaine in Ray's system, and how these chemicals make people violent and aggressive. This is powerful evidence that supports Dennis' sworn testimony that Ray suddenly punched, kicked, and choked him.

"Ask yourselves, if you were in Dennis' position, with a hulking, crazed man attacking you, ready to kill you, wouldn't you defend yourself, wouldn't you have the right to defend yourself.

"The primary evidence in this case comes from the sworn testimony of Dennis Carbonaro. You heard and saw him, and I'm sure you evaluated his testimony. It was clear, honest, and direct. The prosecution may try to claim that you can't believe him because at a prior trial, the trial of his brother, he misled the court. The defendant admits that. He admits that he tried to save his brother, whom he is now accused of murdering, but, as he told you, that was a mistake that only caused trouble for him and others, a mistake he would never make again."

Klein moved to the front of the jury and leaned on the rail.

"Let's assume that you're concerned about his conduct during the prior trial, that he may have mislead the court or committed a crime. I submit to you that no matter what crime a person may have committed at an earlier time, they do not lose the right to justifiably defend themselves when they're being attacked and someone is trying to kill them. That's what Dennis did here. He defended himself."

Klein paused and gave the jurors a moment to ponder what he had said. Then he continued, "Now, ladies and gentlemen, the judge will instruct on the law of self-defense, and on the standard needed to convict someone of a crime. The judge will instruct you about the presumption of innocence. She will instruct you that the prosecution has the burden of proof and must prove a case beyond a reasonable doubt. In this case, the defense has presented proof of self-defense. The prosecution must disprove that defense by proof beyond a reasonable doubt. And the judge will instruct you that it is a high standard, and the reasons for having such a high standard.

"Ladies and gentlemen, after you consider all the evidence presented in this case and as you apply the law as the judge will instruct you, I'm confident that you'll do the right thing, find the defendant not guilty, and let him go back to his family and his future wife. Thank you."

When Klein finished his summation, Dennis whispered to his father, "He convinced me." Dominic thought that was funny, but he didn't have an inclination to smile.

Since Klein's summation was over so quickly, Judge Mandelbaum took only a ten-minute break and then had ADA Walsh proceed with his summation.

Walsh had assumed he would begin after lunch, and he was not quite ready. He had been formulating his speech while Klein was talking, and he had difficulty with it. This case presented an unusual situation. In the past murder cases that he had tried, Walsh had focused on the victim and victim's family, always feeling that he represented them in their quest for justice. But, in this case, the victim's family and the defendant's family were the same. Somehow, it seemed that he had the same sympathy for Dennis that he had for Ray, and he had enormous sympathy for the defendant's parents—one son killed, one son on trial for his death.

His closing argument seemed ambivalent. Although he recounted the evidence, he wasn't forceful, wasn't passionate. Maybe because he was prosecuting Dominic's son, his heart wasn't in it. Instead of drilling down and emphasizing each fact, he summarized.

"The defendant admitting striking his brother in the head with a hammer," he said. "He admitted failing to call for an ambulance. He admitted failing to inform the police, or even his father. He failed to tell them that he was the one who killed Ray. He pretended that he was in the precinct lounge to establish an alibi. And he allowed charges of murder to be brought against others when he knew he was the one who did it. All of these facts point to his guilt.

"He had, at least, two motives to kill his brother. We're not required to prove either in order to prove guilt, but we submit them to you, members of the jury, for your consideration. And we submit to you that the motives should be considered when you decide whether the defendant's actions were premeditated, intentional, or not.

"As for self-defense, if you find that the defendant went to the apartment to threaten or assault his brother, his claim of self-defense is irreparably damaged. You can't start a fight, then claim self-defense. The judge will instruct you that if you withdrew from the fight, you could claim self-defense, but the defendant never testified that he withdrew from the fight."

At this point, Klein objected, which was unusual during a summation, but he wanted to interrupt Walsh's argument. "The prosecutor is mischaracterizing the evidence. Dennis never testified that he started the fight, so withdrawing from the fight is not an issue. He testified that Ray started the fight."

"Overruled," the judge said. "This is argument. The jury will weigh the evidence for themselves."

Walsh went on recounting the prosecution's evidence, and finished by saying, "Ladies and gentlemen, this case has been proven to you beyond a reasonable doubt. There's no question who killed Ray Carbonaro. The defendant admitted it, and he had more than one motive to kill him. His claim of self-defense is full of holes. He wants you to believe that he found the hammer by accident under the sink. He wants you to believe that he was unconscious when Ray was hit in the temple with the hammer. And he wants you to believe that he's telling the truth now, when we know his past conduct of misleading the court and the jury in his brother's robbery case, which resulted in his brother being acquitted, a miscarriage of justice. Let's not have another miscarriage of justice here. The unlawful killing of a human being, requires justice. There's only one thing left for you to do. Impose justice, and find the defendant guilty."

Hearing the prosecutor's words, Dennis saw his defenses collapsing. His knees trembled slightly. His father noticed it.

"Buck up," Dominic said. "Not matter what, everything is going to be okay."

Dennis tried to smile and think of something to say, but couldn't. He turned to look back at Kathy. She nodded, understandingly.

The judge stood and announced, "We've made remarkable progress today. Two closing arguments in one day in a trial like this is an accomplishment. I'd like to congratulate everyone for their efforts. In fact, if I move with the same alacrity as our distinguished counsels, we may be able to finish with the jury instructions today."

After another short break, the judge did move with alacrity, and covered the legal principles that applied to the case in less than an hour. She explained the elements of murder, manslaughter, and criminally negligent homicide, and the differences between them. The most pertinent difference was that causing the death of someone by striking them with intent to kill is murder, but causing death by striking someone with the intent only to seriously injury them is manslaughter.

She explained that for criminally negligent homicide there was no need to prove the death was caused intentionally. It could have been caused by negligence through the use of a dangerous instrument, such as a hammer.

The jury could convict on one or all of the charges, or could acquit on all.

The judge covered the burden of proof, and gave the accepted version of proof beyond a reasonable doubt, saying: "Proof beyond a reasonable doubt is proof that leaves you firmly convinced of the defendant's guilt. There are very few things in this world that we know with absolute certainty, and in criminal cases the law does not require proof that overcomes every possible doubt. If, based on your consideration of the evidence, you are firmly convinced that the defendant is guilty of the crime charged, you must find him guilty. If, on the other hand, you think there is a real possibility that he is not guilty, you must give him the benefit of the doubt and find him not guilty. But keep in mind, it's not just any doubt, it must be a reasonable doubt."

With the instructions completed, the judge gave the case to the jury. She told the jury that they would be sequestered at a nearby hotel during their deliberations. They had been forewarned of this possibility, but the judge made a last-minute decision. She told them again not to discuss the case with anyone or watch or listen to media reports about the case.

"Those are your instructions. If, as a group or individually, you have questions or problems during your deliberations, give the court officer a note."

Waiting for the verdict was excruciating, but everyone pulled together and tried their best to stay optimistic. Klein said that Dennis' testimony was magnificent. "I don't know what the verdict will be, but he couldn't have done a better job."

After the second day of deliberations, everyone went to the Carbonaro house where Marie had a meal ready for them.

Dominic said, "This is an open and shut case of self-defense. The jury might be taking so long because they like staying in a fancy hotel and getting free meals."

"You're a cynic," Klein said.

"I am, but it's been known to happen."

"I can't believe anyone would do that," Kathy said.

Dominic smiled. "You're absolutely right. Don't pay any attention to me."

Dennis didn't talk much. He thought about going to prison. His mind raced from possibility to possibility. He decided that if he went to prison, he'd workout with weights every day to toughen up so that he could defend himself, in necessary. He also thought that he could use the law library, maybe take online courses, get prepared for law school and the bar exam. A surprising number of prisoners had done just that. Although, in his case, a murder conviction might preclude him from admission to the bar, but he could try. He also thought about more desperate possibilities. He imagined escaping, taking on a new identity, and leaving the country.

On the third day, late in the afternoon, everyone was expecting the jury to retire and be sequestered in the hotel for another night. But, at five to five, the jury sent out a note saying that they had reached a verdict.

Everyone, including a dozen Carbonaro relatives who had waited around, rushed into the courtroom. Kathy held Dennis' arm, and sat on one side of him at the defense table. Dominic sat on his other side.

"Bring in the jury," Judge Mandelbaum ordered, and the jurors ceremoniously filed in, slowly and silently. They looked to each other and sat down in unison.

Dennis didn't know whether that was a good sign or a bad sign. He looked at Klein, who shrugged his shoulders. He didn't know either.

"Forewoman, have you reached a verdict?" the judge asked.

"Yes, your honor, we have," she said, and handed the verdict sheet to the bailiff.

The judge looked at it, gave it back to the bailiff. "Very well, the defendant will stand."

Dennis stood with his father and Kathy holding his hands.

The bailiff asked the forewoman, who was standing in the jury box, "On count number one, murder in the second-degree, what is your verdict?"

"Not guilty," the forewoman said.

There was a collective gasp of relief from the spectators, but then a silence as they waited for the next count.

"On count number two, manslaughter in the first-degree, what is your verdict?"

"Not guilty."

Dominic and Kathy squeezed Dennis' hands harder. He felt relieved but knew there were two more serious charges.

"On count number three, criminally negligent homicide, what is your verdict?"

"Not guilty."

Some in the audience shouted "Yes!"

The judge banged her gavel for quiet, and the bailiff continued.

"On count number four, assault in the first-degree, what is your verdict?"

"Not guilty."

Smiles and hugs burst out at the defense table. The Carbonaro relatives came forward to congratulate Dennis, Dominic, and Kathy, hugging and kissing them.

The judge gaveled the room to order, and everyone went back to their seats.

She thanked the jurors for their service, dismissed the charges against Dennis, and discharged him. She didn't offer any apologies.

As relieved as Dennis felt, he also felt an overpowering sadness. The ordeal was over, but it had drained him and his family, and he hadn't forgotten that Ray was still dead. He saw a pained look on his father's face, and thought that he must also be thinking about Ray, and the tragedy of his lost life.

Dennis hugged his father again. "I'm sorry for everything, Dad. I hope, somehow, I can make it up to you." They both had tears in their eyes. Kathy saw that, and began crying, too.

As everyone surrounded Dennis, she decided to fix her makeup in the bathroom. As she walked through the hallway, she was surprised to see McConnell. He saw her, but looked down at his cell phone, ignoring her as she walked past him.

When she returned to the courtroom, she told Dennis, who told his father. Dominic reacted immediately, rushing quickly out of the courtroom. He wasn't armed, but was going to confront McConnell, ask him why he was coming to the trial. Dennis followed him, but McConnell was gone.

Dennis was relieved. He had had enough excitement for one day. "Let's go home, Dad."

At the Carbonaro house, Marie hugged everyone as they came in the house. Dominic had called her right away with the good news. Plenty of food was spread out on the dining room table. More relatives and friends than had been in the court arrived at the house.

Although Dennis was exhausted but did his best to join in the celebration. Everyone was talking to him, asking what he was going to do now, and making suggestions. He enjoyed it, but he really needed to think about what to do next. He watched Kathy serving the food, and he took her hand. "I need you for a moment," he said, leading her outside where they stood on the top of the stoop. "Well, now that I'm a free man, are you still going to marry me?"

"I would have married you, even if you weren't," she said. "We could have had one of the prison romances."

"And the conjugal visits would have been great." They both laughed, kissed, and went back inside.

While they were on the stoop, McConnell was parked down the block, watching them.

CHAPTER FORTY-TWO

M cConnell had been in hiding since the day he failed to show up at federal court and the bench warrant was issued. Leading up to his decision not to appear, he suffered every day, thinking about his circumstances. His suspension from the NYPD, and then his arrest by the F.B.I., had crushed him. The personal humiliation he felt had grown worse each day. It was like a giant knot tightening in his stomach, and no matter how hard he tried, he couldn't untie it. His head was filled with angry and spiteful thoughts, and he had made several angry outbursts such as the one he made at the lawyer Kilkenny's office. With increasing frequency, images from Iraq kept recurring to him, mostly of the firefights and his platoon buddies being killed or wounded.

He was infuriated that despite his service on the battlefield, he would be prosecuted and subjected to denigrating speeches, like the one that the pompous AUSA had made at his arraignment. He had fought for his country, had put his life on the line every day as a police officer, never took a dime, and now they were castigating him as a corrupt cop for doing his job. And this was all happening because of that liar, Dennis Carbonaro, and some dirtbag criminals who were making phony accusations against him.

He knew a lot about them, and kept his own records about their activities. He knew about Arturo and his criminal enterprises. He knew about his payoffs to politicians, and he wondered whether Dominic Carbonaro was on Arturo's payroll. After all, Ray Carbonaro had worked as a bouncer in Arturo's clubs, the Kit-Kat and the 444.

Although he was suspended, he continued investigating Arturo's organization, hoping to find something to discredit his accusers.

Over the years, he had worked in his own way to come up with good arrests. He always said, "You have to be out there, patrolling, looking around, talking to people. You have to have a line in the water if you want to catch a fish. A sharp detective could see things on the street, follow them up, and tumble onto criminal activity."

Once, while patrolling in a quiet residential neighborhood, he noticed closed-circuit-security cameras on the top of a locked gate to a driveway. He wondered why in such a quiet neighborhood. He kept an eye on the driveway, and then one day, saw a man at the gate, opening the lock. He approached the man, identified himself as a detective, and asked him what was in the back of the driveway. Coincidentally, the man had taken amphetamines, which could act like a truth serum. Without hesitation, the man told him that in the back was a garage where guns, stolen property, and drugs were stored.

"Show me," McConnell said, and the man led him into the garage and showed him pistols, rifles, packages of amphetamines, cocaine, and stolen property worth about a half-million dollars. McConnell obtained a search warrant, and made an outstanding arrest, which led to other arrests. He was given a commendation for it.

Now, ten-years later, he drove around Washington Heights in his black SUV Chevrolet Blazer, patrolling just as though he were still a working detective. When he had been suspended, he had to surrender his department-authorized firearms, but he had a collection of unlicensed guns. Over the years he had seized many guns from criminals, and sometimes kept them for himself. In a tool chest in the back of the car, he had an UZI submachine gun, and a .45 caliber Colt automatic pistol.

As he drove past the Kit-Kat club and 444 club, and along St. Nicholas Avenue, he spotted Arturo, Aldo, and Gino coming out of the Bodega Association headquarters. They walked north. He followed them for a block, then pulled over, and watched them with the binoculars that he had used in Iraq. As the three men were walking, they were laughing. He was sure that they were laughing at him, at what they had done to him, and something in his mind snapped. Through the binoculars, he saw them for a moment like the enemy Iraqi soldiers that he had fought and killed. The maxim in Iraq was: "Eliminate all threats before they eliminate you."

He drove a block past them, pulled the car over, jumped out, and, moving quickly, put a rag over the front license plate, and a piece of cardboard over the back plate. He popped open the back lift of the SUV, and from the tool chest, took out the UZI submachine gun and a thirty-round ammunition clip. He shoved the ammunition clip into the gun, got back in the driver's seat, made a U-turn, and drove on the wrong side of the street, so that he could pull up next to the three men. As he drew parallel to them, he stuck the UZI out the window, and began firing. He was surprised that Aldo had a gun and returned fire at him, but he gave another burst of gunfire, and Aldo went down.

Gino had run a few feet before he fell, and Arturo was on the ground. McConnell thought about getting out of the car and finishing them off, but, instead, fired another burst at each of them, and drove away.

Functioning as though in a trance, McConnell felt as he had when he completed a mission in Iraq, a strange kind of euphoria, glad that he had been victorious, glad that he had eliminated his enemies. He assumed they were dead, but if they weren't, he thought that they'd think twice about testifying against him.

Now, all he had to do was disappear for a while. He drove north on Broadway into the Bronx, stopped at his apartment in Riverdale, gathered his cash, packed clean clothes in a gym bag, turned off his cell phone and left it in a drawer. Out of a closet, he took two prepaid burner phones that he had previously purchased from a vending machine. They couldn't be traced to him and couldn't be used to track his movements. Then he drove north out of the city.

Upstate, he found a cheap motel, gave a phony name, and paid cash.

The next day, he bought the newspapers, and found an article about the shooting. He wasn't mentioned. There was an assumption that it was an organized-crime hit. However, he knew that wouldn't last. Sooner or later, they'd suspect him. He'd have to stay ahead of them.

He checked his car for bullet-holes from Aldo's gun. One had hit the driver's side mirror. The glass was broken, but the spent bullet must have fallen away somewhere on the road. Another one hit the front hubcap. He took the hubcap off, and found the spent bullet lodged inside of it. These were the only two. Aldo was not such a good shot, he thought. Only the bullet that hit the mirror was close. It was good news because he wouldn't have to dump the car. But he'd have to dump the UZI, so he checked out of the motel, and drove north to an area in the Catskill Mountains where he used to go deer hunting.

In the woods, he threw away the spent bullet and the hubcap. Then he wiped clean and disassembled the UZI, and, one piece at a time, threw the parts into different sections of a reservoir.

For two weeks, McConnell move from cheap motel to cheap motel, then, not seeing or hearing anything that he was a suspect, decided to go back to the city.

He stopped at his apartment, and approached the building cautiously, wondering if the NYPD or the feds had staked it out. The NYPD might suspect him of Arturo's shooting, and the feds could be looking for him on the bench warrant for the federal civil rights charges. Either could be waiting for him to come home, but he didn't spot anything suspicious. He went to the management office, and spoke to Charlie Townsend, the managing agent.

"How are you?" Townsend said.

"Fine, thanks," McConnell said. "Has anyone been around asking about me?'

"No. I don't think so," Townsend said. But he said it without looking McConnell in the eye.

McConnell had a way of intimidating people by staring them down and waiting for an answer. "Are you sure, maybe you missed them?"

Townsend averted his eyes again. "I could ask the maintenance men."

From Townsend's evasive manner, McConnell assumed that he wasn't being truthful. He figured that the investigators had talked to him, and asked him not to mention that they had been there.

"That's alright, thanks," McConnell said, while thinking that this meant he was a suspect after all.

On the day that he had failed to appear in federal court, he had gone to the court two hours early. He parked under the highway of the FDR drive at a spot between the Williamsburg and Brooklyn bridges. Then he walked over to City Hall Park, and sat on a bench from where he could see the federal court.

If the task force detectives were going to arrest him, this would be the most logical place to apprehend him. He knew they would be there early to set up a stakeout. So, he got there earlier to watch for them.

His thinking proved correct. At eight o'clock, ten detectives gathered in front of the building. Then they split up. Eight detectives took stations around the front, back, and sides of the building; two went inside. McConnell was sure that the two that went inside were Carbonaro and Cruz.

"That's it," McConnell said to himself. "They've made up my mind for me. I'm not walking into the lion's den. I'm not going to give them the pleasure of putting handcuffs on me. Carbonaro would enjoy that too much."

As he walked back to his car, he decided that, later, he'd call his lawyer, Kilkenny, and ask him to arrange for his surrender to the feds on the bench warrant, which would be to the U.S. Marshals, not Carbonaro or the NYPD task force.

But he changed his mind and didn't call Kilkenny, and didn't stop at his apartment, but drove straight upstate to find another cheap motel. On the way, he stopped at a liquor store and bought a bottle of Johnny Walker Black whiskey. I'm going to need it, he thought. A sense of doom overcoming him. Somehow, he had figured that he could get through this, but now he realized that he wouldn't. He had no money coming in. He had a few thousand bucks in the bank, but that wouldn't go far. I'm going to wind up sleeping in the streets like a bum, he thought. With his good credit, he had always been able to borrow money, but as soon as the federal bench warrant dropped on him, his credit would dry up. So, he went to an ATM in a bank lobby and withdrew the money he had left in the bank.

For another week, he grappled with what to do. He put off calling Kilkenny, and tried to figure a way out. He had a wild and extreme idea to go back to Iraq or somewhere, and sign up as a mercenary soldier. But, if he did that, he'd never see his kids again. He dismissed the idea for now.

The more he thought about his circumstances, the angrier he got. He had a list of people to blame, including the Carbonaro's, and especially Dennis Carbonaro. He'd started the chain of events that had led to his arrest. He hoped Dennis would get convicted of Ray's murder. That, at least, would be something that he could take credit for. He would be remembered as the one who stuck with the case and solved it. He should also get credit for proving the innocence of the three guys who had been falsely accused of the murder.

When Dennis' trial began, McConnell knew he shouldn't go near it, but he couldn't stay away. Even with the bench warrant hanging over his head, he had to be there. He drove to the Queen's courthouse, parked his car, and watched the entrance through his binoculars. He saw the Carbonaro's arrive.

Wearing sunglasses and a cap, he went into the building and up to the courtroom where the trial was being held. He read the calendar posted outside the courtroom, and smiled with satisfaction to see written, "People v. Dennis Carbonaro, Charge: Penal Law: 125:25, Murder, Second Degree."

He opened the courtroom door slightly to look in and see what was going on. He saw Kathy was on the witness stand, and almost went in to take a seat among the spectators, but he'd be risking arrest. Instead, he walked around the halls, coming back every so often to peek into the courtroom. He saw ADA Walsh standing in front of the jury, and Klein and Dennis sitting at the defendant's table.

When he was outside but near the courtroom, Kathy came out and walked past him. He wasn't sure whether she had recognized him. He quickly went down a staircase, and left the building as fast as he could without drawing too much attention to himself.

Despite the risks, he went back to the court every day, and, on the day of closing arguments, he peeked in and saw Klein giving his summation. Later, he saw Walsh giving his.

During the three days of jury deliberations, McConnell stayed around because he wanted to be there when the guilty verdict was rendered.

On the third day, TV news-station panel trucks surrounded the courthouse. McConnell assumed that they were there because a verdict had been reached. So, he went up to the courtroom. He wanted to peek in, but two court officers were guarding the door and not letting anyone else in while the verdict was being read.

McConnell stood off to the side and waited. Then he heard celebratory shouts, which could only mean that Dennis had been acquitted. Smiling and shaking hands, spectators came out of the courtroom. He edged into the crowd and closer to the courtroom. Through the open doorway, he saw Dominic and Dennis embracing, then Dennis and Kathy hugging. He left, and went back to his car.

The first thing he did was pound on the dashboard. He couldn't believe that they let that lying bastard off. His credit for solving Ray's murder had been stolen from him, another case of a slick, crafty lawyer bamboozling a jury. And he was sure that when he came to trial on those bullshit civil rights charges, some government lawyer would paint him as a racist, and they'd convict him for being a white cop oppressing poor immigrants and minorities.

To no one in particular, he shouted, "I can't stand this anymore. I'm not taking it anymore. It's got to end. I just can't stand it." People passing by heard him and quickly moved away.

When the Carbonaro's and their friends and relatives came out of the court, he saw them go to the parking lot, get in their cars, and drive away together in a caravan. He followed.

The caravan drove to the Van Wyck Expressway heading south toward Kennedy Airport. At the Belt Parkway, they turned west toward Brooklyn, got off at the Rockaway Parkway exit into Canarsie, and continued to the Carbonaro house where Marie greeted everyone at the door.

From a block away, McConnell watched with his binoculars. His thoughts were disjointed. One minute, he was seething with anger over Dennis' acquittal, the next, Ray's acquittal. He blamed Klein for the trials, and blamed Dominic for orchestrating everything, including the accusations against him by Arturo, Aldo, and Gino, which led to his bogus arrest by the F.B.I.

Then his mood changed, and he was overcome with remorse, not for the shooting, but for getting himself into this situation by being an aggressive cop. Nobody backs you up. He felt sick for what he had done to his family. How was he going to take care of them, put food on the table?

He drove closer to the house and double parked. Dennis and Kathy were outside on the stoop, talking and kissing.

Seeing this ignited something in McConnell. His hands began to shake, and his head felt as though it were boiling with hatred. Hatred for everything, everything around him, everything about his life.

He racked the slide of his .45 caliber automatic to make sure there was a round in the chamber, got out of the car, and walked toward the stoop with the gun at his side. Dennis and Kathy were preoccupied with each other, unaware of his approach.

He walked slowly toward them, mumbling over and over, "Forgive us our trespasses, as we forgive those that trespass against us."

Still unaware of him, Dennis and Kathy went into the house.

McConnell stopped at the bottom of the steps for a moment, then went up to the front door, and knocked.

No one answered. He knocked again, and stood with the gun in his hand. When the door opened, he raised the gun, opened his mouth wide, pressed the barrel of the gun against the roof of his mouth, and pulled the trigger.

Dennis saw McConnell's head explode. A mist of blood sprayed into the air, and McConnell was thrown backwards down the steps.

Inside the house, someone shouted, "What was that?"

Dominic recognized it as a gunshot, and ran to the door. He saw the body sprawled out at the bottom of the steps, and he saw Dennis staring in frozen disbelief. "I think it was McConnell."

People began to come outside, but Dominic told them to stay inside. Then, he went down the steps and saw that it was McConnell.

"Get a sheet to cover him," he told someone. "And call 911. No, I'll call."

But he didn't have to call. Neighbors who heard the shot or saw the body called the police. Within minutes several patrol cars and an ambulance arrived.

CHAPTER FORTY-THREE

The horror of what just happened shocked everyone. Most of the guests wanted to leave right away, but Dominic asked them to wait for the police.

While they waited, some began eating and drinking again.

Captain Corcoran, Lieutenant Duffy, and a dozen detectives arrived to conduct the investigation. Most of them knew McConnell, and were as shocked as everyone else. They began processing the crime scene, taking statements from the guests, and canvassing neighbors. They found two eyewitnesses from across the street who had seen what happened and saw McConnell shoot himself, confirming that his was a suicide, not a homicide.

Dennis was asked to come to the local precinct to be interviewed.

Dominic asked Captain Corcoran, "Does Dennis have to be interviewed today? He's been through a lot. Getting acquitted of murder, then witnessing the goddamn suicide."

"He seems remarkably calm," Corcoran said. "Let's ask him if he's up to it."

Dennis said that he wanted to get it over with, and agreed to go to the precinct.

Captain Corcoran and Dominic went with him and sat in on the interview. Because of the family connection to the NYPD, a detective from the district attorney's office, John Culpepper, conducted the interview.

After preliminary questions, Culpepper asked Dennis how close he was when the shot was fired. He asked him if he had tried to grab the gun.

Dominic became concerned that Culpepper might be implying that Dennis fired the gun. He stood up, "Why would you ask such a question? We have two eyewitnesses."

"I have to cover all possibilities," Culpepper said.

Dominic slammed his hand of the table. "That's enough. This interview is over," he said, and he and Dennis left the precinct and went home.

Back at the house, some guests had tried to restart the celebration, but there wasn't much enthusiasm for it, and as the night wore on, only a few people remained.

Dominic, Dennis, Kathy, Cruz and Marie's brother, Antony, were sitting at the basement bar, drinking wine and talking about what happened. Antony said that McConnell would burn in hell.

Dominic surprised them when he said, "Whatever happens in the afterlife, it's a real tragedy that his life on earth ended this way."

"I don't see how you can say that," Anthony said, "He came to your door and could have killed your son."

"Maybe he was going to, but he didn't," Dominic said. "I'm guessing that at the last minute his conscience or something stopped him. He couldn't do it."

Kathy had been terribly upset by the shooting, but was now calmer, glad that Dennis was alright, and she saw Dominic's point. "I'll bet he was brought up religious," she said, "and, I think, what they instill in you when you're young, stays with you until you die."

Cruz refilled the wine glasses. "Well, it didn't stop him from shooting Arturo and the other two."

"We don't know that for sure," Dominic said.

"I'd bet money on it," Cruz said. "And he wouldn't have any trouble shooting them. Religious or not, he was so obsessed with criminals that he'd execute them all himself."

"I guess so," Dominic said, "you knew him better than anyone else."

"That's true, and very sad to say. He was on the outs with his family. All he had was the job, and the job turned against him."

Dominic grabbed a pool cue. "That's enough cops and robbers for today. How about a game of pool?"

Dennis, leaning toward Kathy, said, "That's my dad's answer to everything. Just play a game of pool."

Dominic heard him, smiled broadly, and patted him one cheek. "Just because you're not guilty anymore, don't get smart with your father," he said, then kissed him on the other cheek.

After holding in his emotions for so long, Dennis was overcome by the realization that his ordeal was over. Not only for him, but also for his father and mother, and for Kathy. He began to choke up, and went out into the backyard so that no one would see the tears welling in his eyes.

When Arturo read about the suicide, he concluded that McConnell was the one who had shot him. Too bad he's dead," he said to Cartwright. "Now, I can't kill him myself."

"Maybe you could sue him," Cartwright said.

"That's not a bad idea. Somebody should pay for what happened to me. I could get that lawyer, Klein, to do it. He knows all about it, and all the players. The police department would have to pay."

Arturo called Klein, who said that he would be glad to take the case. "It may be difficult to establish liability, but the police department will want to avoid the bad publicity, and they may settle quickly"

"I don't want a small, quick settlement," Arturo said. "I'm entitled to get what I deserve for my injuries."

"We can try," Klein said.

With Dennis' case finally over, Dominic agreed to take a long vacation, and told Marie to pick someplace she wanted to go.

Dennis and Kathy set the date for their marriage for June after they completed their college semesters. Beyond that, Dennis set his sights on law school and thought that he'd work for Klein as an intern until he graduated and passed the bar. But a few weeks later, after a Sunday dinner, while Marie and Kathy cleared the dishes and prepared dessert and coffee, Dominic showed Dennis a copy of the lawsuit that Klein had filed against the police department on behalf of Arturo for being shot by McConnell.

Dennis looked at it then angrily threw it on the table. "I've changed my mind. I'm not working for him."

"Because of this lawsuit?" Dominic said.

"That's right."

"You could learn a lot from him," Dominic said, "follow in his footsteps."

"I don't want to follow in his footsteps. He's the one who took Ray's lawsuit against the police when he shouldn't have, and that's what got me arrested for murder. He pretends he's all about justice, but he's really only about the money."

"I don't see how suing the police department is justice," Kathy said. "McConnell's the one to blame."

"There's a lot of blame to go around," Dominic said. "There were a lot of causes of what McConnell did."

Dennis was not sure what his father meant by that. He wondered whether his father was blaming him for getting Ray off by the contrived testimony. That's what started the ball rolling, and was the primary cause of what followed.

But Dominic was thinking of something else. If he hadn't gone to see Arturo, and if he hadn't mentioned that McConnell was trying to frame Dennis, Arturo wouldn't have orchestrated the accusations against McConnell. Being arrested and humiliated caused McConnell to go insane, and his act of murder, so contrary to his self-image, led to his suicide.

"The whole thing is a tragedy," Dominic said. "McConnell was too inflexible for our system of justice. He took it personally when a criminal got off."

"I can't believe you still have such sympathy for him, after what he did to us," Dennis said.

"No sympathy. I'm just trying to understand him, and why it happened."

Dennis thought that it was all too complicated to understand. A thousand factors had contributed to why it happened. He knew that he shared some of the blame, actually, a lot of it, maybe all of it.

The others could see that he was troubled. Kathy sat next to him and put her arm around his shoulders. "Are you okay?"

Dennis thought to say out loud what he had been thinking. He thought to apologize to them, but a silence filled the room. They understood. There was no need to explain.

Dominic grabbed a pool cue. "How about a game of pool?"

Milton Keynes UK
Ingram Content Group UK Ltd.
UKHW040123170324
439511UK00004B/201